Praise for *The Library of Lost and Found*

"This is one of those lovely, heartwarming stories that restores your faith in human nature."
—B. A. Paris, *New York Times* bestselling author

"An introverted librarian opens a book into a fantasy world that also reveals secrets from her grandmother's past... [A] charming story."
—*Publishers Weekly*

"Phaedra Patrick has written a hymn to books and how they can bring love—even miracles—into your life."
—Antoine Laurain, author of *The Red Notebook*

"An affirmation of the power to reinvent our lives...*The Library of Lost and Found* is illustrative of its author's bona fides as an imaginative teller of character-driven stories. Be prepared for it to break, and then bless, your heart."
—*The Free Lance-Star*

"Phaedra Patrick's characters are vibrant, quirky, and real, and you'll be cheering for Martha as she discovers who she really is."
—Amy E. Reichert, author of *The Coincidence of Coconut Cake* and *The Optimist's Guide to Letting Go*

"A gem of a book. I loved it."
—Sarah Morgan, *USA TODAY* bestselling author

"All of Patrick's books give me the warm fuzzies and her latest is no different."
—*Charlotte Sun*

"I would recommend this novel to anyone who enjoys quirky characters and unexpected plot twists."
—*Missourian*

Also by Phaedra Patrick

The Curious Charms of Arthur Pepper
Rise and Shine, Benedict Stone

PHAEDRA PATRICK

The LIBRARY of LOST and FOUND

FROM THE LIBRARY OF:

_____

PARK
ROW
BOOKS

PARK™
ROW
BOOKS™

Recycling programs
for this product may
not exist in your area.

ISBN-13: 978-0-7783-0982-6

The Library of Lost and Found

First published in 2019. This edition published in 2020.

This edition published by arrangement with Harlequin Books S.A.

Park Row Books
22 Adelaide St. West, 41st Floor
Toronto, Ontario M5H 4E3, Canada
ParkRowBooks.com
BookClubbish.com

Printed in Italy by Grafica Veneta

For Mum, Dad, Mark and Oliver

The
LIBRARY
of LOST and
FOUND

1

Valentine's Day

As always, Martha Storm was primed for action. Chin jutted, teeth gritted, and a firm grip on the handle of her trusty shopping trolley. Her shoulders burned as she struggled to push it up the steep slope toward the library. The cobblestones underfoot were slippery, coated by the sea mist that wafted into Sandshift each evening.

She was well prepared for the evening's event. It was going to be perfect, even though she usually avoided Valentine's Day. Wasn't it a silly celebration? A gimmick, to persuade you to buy stuffed furry animals and chocolates at rip-off prices. Why, if someone ever sent her a card, she'd hand it back and explain to the giver they'd been brainwashed. However, a job worth doing was worth doing well.

Bottles chinked in her trolley, a stuffed black bin bag rustled in the breeze and a book fell off a pile, its pages fluttering like a moth caught in a spider's web.

She'd bought the supermarket's finest rosé wine, flute glasses and napkins printed with tiny red roses. Her alarm clock sounded at 5:30 a.m. that morning to allow her time to bake heart-shaped cookies, including gluten-free ones for any book lovers who had a wheat allergy. She'd brought along extra copies of the novel for the author to sign.

One of the best feelings in the world came when she received a smile of appreciation, or a few grateful words. When someone said, "Great job, Martha," and she felt like she was basking in sunshine. She'd go to most lengths to achieve that praise.

If anyone asked about her job, she had an explanation ready. "I'm a guardian of books," she said. "A volunteer at the library." She was an event organizer, tour guide, buyer, filer, job adviser, talking clock, housekeeper, walking encyclopedia, stationery provider, recommender of somewhere nice to eat lunch and a shoulder to cry on—all rolled into one.

And she loved each part, except for waking people up at closing time, and the strange things she found used as bookmarks (a nail file, a sexual health clinic appointment card and an old rasher of bacon).

As she rattled past a group of men, all wearing navy-and-yellow Sandshift United football scarves, Martha called out to them, "Don't forget about the library event tonight." But they laughed among themselves and walked on.

As she eventually directed the trolley toward the small, squat library building, Martha spied the bulky silhouette of a man huddled by the front door. "Hello there," she called out, twisting her wrist to glance at her watch. "You're fifty-four minutes early..."

The dark shape turned its head and seemed to look at her, before hurrying away and disappearing around the corner.

Martha trundled along the path. A poster flapped on the door and author Lucinda Lovell beamed out from a heavily filtered photo. The word *Canceled* was written across her face in thick black letters.

Martha's eyes widened in disbelief. Her stomach lurched,

as if someone had shoved her on an escalator. Using her hand as a visor, she peered into the building.

All was still, all was dark. No one was inside.

With trembling fingers, she reached out to touch the word that ruined all her planning and organizing efforts of the last couple of weeks. *Canceled.* The word that no one had bothered to tell her.

She swallowed hard and her organized brain ticked as she wondered who to call. The area library manager, Clive Folds, was taking his wife to the Lobster Pot bistro for a Valentine's dinner. He was the one who'd set up Lucinda's appearance, with her publisher. Pregnant library assistant, Suki McDonald, was cooking a cheese and onion pie for her boyfriend, Ben, to persuade him to give things another try between them.

Everything had been left for Martha to sort out.

Again.

"You live on your own, so you have more time," Clive had told her, when he'd asked her to take charge of the event preparations. "You don't have personal commitments."

Martha's chest tightened as she remembered his words, and she let her arms fall heavy to her sides. Turning back around, she took a deep breath and forced herself to straighten her back. *Never mind*, she thought. There must be a good reason for the cancelation, a serious illness, or perhaps a fatal road accident. Anyone who turned up would see the poster. "Better just set off home, and get on with my other stuff," she muttered.

Leaning over her trolley, Martha grabbed hold of its sides and heaved it around to face in the opposite direction. As she did, a clear plastic box slid out, crashing to the path. When she stooped to pick it up, the biscuits lay broken inside.

It was only then she noticed the brown paper parcel propped against the bottom of the door. It was rectangular and tied with a bow and a crisscross of string, probably left there by the shadowy figure. Her name was scrawled on the front. She stooped down to pick it up, then pressed her fingers along its edges. It felt like a book.

Martha placed it next to the box of broken biscuits in her trolley. *Really*, she tutted, the things readers tried to avoid paying their late return fees.

She wrenched back on the trolley as it threatened to pull her down the hill. The brown paper parcel juddered inside as she negotiated the cobbles. She passed sugared almond–hued houses, and the air smelled of salt and seaweed. Laughter and the strum of a Spanish guitar sounded from the Lobster Pot and she paused for a moment. Martha had never eaten there before. It was the type of place frequented by couples.

Through the window, she glimpsed Clive and his wife with their foreheads almost touching across the table. Candles lit up their faces with a flickering glow. His mind was obviously not on the library.

If she's not careful, Mrs. Fold's hair is going to set on fire, Martha thought, averting her eyes. *I hope there are fire extinguishers in the dining area.* She fumbled in her pocket for her Wonder Woman notepad and made a note to ask the bistro owner, Branda Taylor.

When Martha arrived home, to her old gray stone cottage, she parked the trolley outside. She had found it there, abandoned a couple of years ago, and she adopted it for her ongoing mission to be indispensable, a Number One neighbor.

Bundling her stuff out of the trolley and into the hallway, she stooped and arranged it in neat piles on the floor, then wound her way around the wine bottles. She found a small free space on the edge of her overcrowded dining table for the brown paper parcel.

A fortnight ago, on a rare visit, her sister, Lilian, had stuck her hands on her hips as she surveyed the dining room. "You really need to do something about this place, Martha," she'd said, her eyes narrowing. "Getting to your kitchen is like an obstacle course. Mum and Dad wouldn't recognize their own home."

Her sister was right. Betty and Thomas Storm liked the house to be spic and span, with everything in its place. But they had both died five years ago, and Martha had remained in the property. She found it therapeutic, after their passing, to try to be useful and fill the house with stuff that needed doing.

The brown velour sofa, where the three of them had watched quiz shows, one after another, night after night, was now covered in piles of things. Thomas liked the color control on the TV turned up, so presenters' and actors' faces glowed orange. Now it was covered by a tapestry that Martha had offered to repair for the local church.

"This is all essential work," she told Lilian, casting her hand through the air. She patiently explained that the shopping bags, plastic crates, mountains of stuff on the floor, stacked high on the table and against the wall, were jobs. "I'm helping people out. The boxes are full of Mum and Dad's stuff—"

"They look like the Berlin Wall."

"Let's sort through them together. We can decide what to keep, and what to let go."

Lilian ran her fingers through her expensively highlighted hair. "Honestly, I'm happy for you to do it, Martha. I've got two kids to sort out, and the builders are still working on the conservatory…"

Martha saw two deep creases between her sister's eyebrows that appeared when she was stressed. Their shape reminded her of antelope horns. A *mum brow*, her sister called it.

Lilian looked at her watch and shook her head. "Look, sorry, but I have to dash. I'll call you, okay?"

But the two sisters hadn't chatted since.

Now Martha wove her way around a crate full of crystal chandeliers she'd offered to clean for Branda, and the school trousers she'd promised to re-hem for her nephew, Will. The black bin bags were full of Nora's laundry, because her washing machine had broken down. She stepped over a papier-mâché dragon's head that needed a repair to his ear and cheek after last year's school Chinese New Year celebrations. Horatio Jones's fish and potted plants had lived with her for two weeks while he was on holiday.

Her oven door might sparkle and she could almost see her reflection in the bathroom sink, but most of her floor space was dedicated to these favors.

Laying everything out this way meant that Martha could survey, assess and select what to do next. She could mark the task status in her notepad with green ticks (completed), amber stars (in progress) and red dots (late). Busyness was next to cleanliness. Or was that godliness?

She also found that, increasingly, she couldn't leave her tasks alone. Her limbs were always tense, poised for action, like an athlete waiting for the pop of a starting pistol. And if she didn't do this stuff for others, what did she have in her life, otherwise?

Even though her arms and back ached from handling the trolley, she picked up a pair of Will's trousers. With no space left on the sofa, she sat in a wooden chair by the window, overlooking the bay.

Outside, the sea twinkled black and silver, and the moon shone almost full. Lowering her head towards the fabric, Martha tried to make sure the stitches were neat and uniform, approximately three millimeters each, because she wanted them to be perfect for her sister.

Stretching out an arm, she reached for a pair of scissors. Her wrist nudged the brown paper parcel and it hung precariously over the edge of the dining table. When she pushed it back with one finger, she spotted a small ink stamp on the back.

"Chamberlain's Pre-Loved and Antiquarian Books, Maltsborough."

"Hmm," she said aloud, not aware of this bookshop. And if the package contained a used book, why had it been left at the library?

Wondering what was inside, Martha set the parcel down on her lap. She untied the string bow and slowly peeled back the brown paper.

Inside, as expected, she found a book, but the cover and title page were both missing. Definitely not a library book, it reminded her of one of those hairless cats, recognizable but strange at the same time.

Its outer pages were battered and speckled, as if someone had flicked strong coffee at it. A torn page offered a glimpse of one underneath where black-and-white fish swam in swirls of sea. On top were a business card and a handwritten note.

Dear Ms. Storm,

Enclosed is a book that came into my possession recently. I cannot sell it due to its condition, but I thought it might be of interest to you, because of the message inside.

Best wishes,
Owen Chamberlain
Proprietor

With anticipation making her fingertips tingle, Martha turned the first few pages of the book slowly, smoothing them down with the flat of her hand, until she found the handwritten words, above an illustration of a mermaid.

June 1985
To my darling, Martha Storm
Be glorious, always.
Zelda
x

Martha heard a gasp and realized it had escaped from her own lips. "Zelda?" she whispered aloud, then clamped a hand to her mouth.

She hadn't spoken her nana's name for many years. And, as she said it now, she nervously half expected to see her father's eyes grow steely at its mention.

Zelda had been endlessly fun, the one who made things bearable at home. She wore turquoise clothes and tortoiseshell cat's-eye-shaped glasses. She was the one who protected Martha against the tensions that whirled within the Storm family.

Martha read the words again and her throat grew tight.

They're just not possible.

Feeling her fingers slacken, she could only watch as the book slipped out of her grip and fell to the floor with a thud, its yellowing pages splayed wide open.

2

The Little Book

As Martha picked the book up from the floor, she tried to focus, thinking if she'd seen it before. Zelda's name and her message somersaulted in her head. However, her brain seemed to be functioning on low power, unable to make sense of this strange discovery. A shiver ran down her spine and she placed the battered book back down on the table.

Her shoulders jerked in surprise when the cuckoo popped out of the clock on the wall and sang nine times. Turning and heading for the back door, Martha was keen to take in some fresh air.

Outside, a sharp gust of wind whipped her hair and she rescued strands from her slightly too-wide mouth. Her thick walnut curls had graying streaks that gave her hair a zebra-like appearance, and her eyes were so dark you might assume they were brown, not seaweed green.

Her paisley skirt and her supermarket-bought embroidered T-shirt gave little protection against the chilly night. Fancy clothes weren't much use when you lived on top of a windy cliff, and sensible shoes were a must. She was a big fan of a sparkly hair slide, though. A tiny bit of shininess nestled in her curls.

Walking to the end of the garden, Martha wrapped her arms across her chest. When she was younger, she used to sit on the cliff edge with her legs dangling, as the sea crashed and swirled below. She'd rest a writing pad on her knees and think of ways to describe the moon.

It looks like a bottle top, a platinum disk, a bullet hole in black velvet, a silver coin flipped into the sky...

She'd write a short story to share with Zelda.

"Yes," her nana would proclaim with zeal. "Love it. Clever girl."

But now, as Martha stared up at the sky, the moon was just the moon. The stars were only stars.

She'd lost the desire and ability to create stories, long ago, when Zelda died, taking Martha's hopes and dreams with her.

Martha tried not to think about the message in the book, but it gnawed inside her.

It was too late to ring Chamberlain's bookstore and she didn't like to disturb Lilian during her favorite TV program, *Hot Houses*. It was her sister's guilty pleasure, the equivalent of an hour in a spa away from her kids, Will and Rose. But she was the only person Martha had to speak to.

She nodded to herself, headed back inside the house and picked up the receiver.

As the phone rang, Martha imagined her sister with her feet curled up on her aubergine velvet sofa. She worked from home as a buyer for an online fashion store and would be wearing her usual outfit of white stretch jeans, mohair sweater and bronze pumps. Her hair was always blow dried into a shiny honey bob.

Her call was rewarded with a prolonged yawn. "It's Friday evening, Martha." Lilian's diamond rings chinked against the phone.

"I know. Sorry."

"You don't usually call at this time."

Martha swallowed as she glanced at the mysterious book. "Um, I know. I'm just hemming Will's trousers, but something strange has happened."

Lilian gave a disinterested *hmm*. "Can you drop them off for me as soon as you've finished? They're too short and he's going to school looking like a pirate. And did you reserve that new Cecelia Ahern for me?"

"Yes. I've put it to one side. About this strange thing—"

"I could do with a nice read, you know? Something relaxing. The kids are really sulky at the moment. And Paul is, well..." She trailed her words away. "You're lucky, not having anyone else to worry about."

"It might be nice to have someone," Martha mused, as she surveyed her bags and boxes and the dragon's head. "What were you going to say, about Paul?"

"Oh. Nothing," Lilian mumbled. "I thought you liked living on your own, that's all."

Martha chewed the side of her thumbnail and didn't reply.

Lilian and Paul had been married for twenty years. In the same year they walked down the aisle, Martha moved back into the family home to help their parents out. Only intending it to be for a short while, they grew more and more reliant on her. She'd ended up caring for them for fifteen years, until they died.

Sometimes, she still glimpsed her father in his armchair, his face set in a wax-like smile, as he requested his slippers, his supper, the TV channel switching over, his copy of *The Times*, a glass of milk (warm, not hot).

Her mother liked to crochet small patches, which she made

into scarves and bedspreads for a local residential home. Martha's later memories of her were inherently linked to Battenberg-like pink-and-yellow woolly squares.

Lilian helped out sporadically, when her other family commitments permitted, but her efforts amounted to bringing magazines, or reams of wool, around for Mum. She'd sit with Dad and read his beloved encyclopedias with him. She, Will and Rose might set up a family game of Monopoly, or watch *Mastermind* on TV.

The day-to-day domestics, the help with hair washing, the administering of painkillers, trips to the doctors, outings for coffee mornings to the church, cooking and cleaning fell to Martha.

"Now, why are you calling?" Lilian asked.

Martha reached out for the book. It looked smaller now, less significant. "There was a parcel waiting for me at the library tonight. It was propped against the door."

"My Cecelia Ahern?"

"No. It's an old book, of fairy stories, I think." Martha read the dedication again, her nerve endings buzzing. "Um, I think it belonged to Zelda."

"Zelda?"

"Our grandmother."

"I *know* who she is."

An awkward silence fell between them, so thick Martha felt like she could touch it. Images dropped into her head of sitting at the garden edge with Zelda, their heels kicking against the cliff. "Don't you ever wonder what happened to her?"

"We know. She died over thirty years ago."

"I've always felt that Mum and Dad didn't tell us the full story, about her death—"

"Bloody hell, Martha." Lilian's voice grew sharp. "We were

just kids. We didn't need a coronary report. You're far too old for fairy tales, anyway."

Martha's shoulders twitched at her sister's spiky reaction. *You're never too old for stories*, she thought. "I'll bring it to the library tomorrow," she said, her voice growing smaller. "If you're passing by, you can take a look. There's a dedication inside, but there's something odd about it."

Lilian didn't say anything.

Martha added, "It's the date—"

The phone receiver rattled. "I have to go now."

"But, the book—"

"Look," Lilian said, "just stick it on a shelf and forget about it. You've got loads of other stuff to do. I'll see you soon, okay?" And she hung up.

Martha stared at the phone receiver and listened to the hum of the dialing tone. Her sister sounded more stressed than ever and she hoped she wasn't overdoing things. She made a mental note to finish Will's trousers as soon as possible, to try to put a smile back on Lilian's face.

Snapping the battered book shut, she told herself that her sister was probably right. After all, she was the successful sibling, the one with the good job, luxury bungalow and two great kids. And Martha had pressing things to do, like feeding Horatio's fish and watering his plants. The school might want the dragon's head back soon.

She reached out for her Wonder Woman notepad and opened it up, and red dots of lateness seemed to glare at her like devil's eyes. She should select what to do next, complete the task and mark it off with a neat green tick. But her thoughts kept creeping back to the book. She couldn't stop her brain ticking with curiosity and disbelief.

Although her nana might have written the words and dated the dedication, there was something terribly wrong.

Because Zelda died in February 1982.

Three years *before* the message and date in the little book.

3

Beauty and the Beast

Betty, 1974

Betty had recently switched from buying best butter to margarine. She could feel the floorboards through the small hole in the sole of one of her beige court shoes, and her favorite navy polka-dot skirt was missing a button. She now snipped her own wavy bobbed hairstyle into shape.

It made sense, to her, that she should look for a part-time job. But her husband, Thomas, was a traditional man. He believed that he should be the breadwinner and that Betty should look after their home and two daughters, Martha and Lilian. It meant that money was often in short supply in the Storm household.

Thomas also preferred the girls to read educationally. He had recently acquired a set of twenty encyclopedias from a work colleague, and he liked the family to look through them together in the evening.

So Betty didn't tell him about the new book she'd bought. With its handsome forest-green cover and gold embossed lettering, she hadn't been able to resist the copy of *Beauty and the*

Beast. She had loved the story when her mother, Zelda, used to read it to her, and she was sure that Martha would love it, too. Sometimes, it really was easier to keep things to herself.

Thomas had returned home early from work that afternoon and was taking a nap in his chair in the dining room. His copy of *The Times* was spread out on the lap of the black suit trousers he wore for his accountancy job, and which he also wore outside work. The room smelled of the freesias he bought for her each Friday.

Betty studied his face to make sure he was definitely asleep. Straining to reach up on top of the kitchen cupboard, she slid the book from its hiding place and tucked the pink-and-white paper bag under her arm.

She trod softly around her husband, and as her skirt brushed his fingers, he gave a loud snort. Betty froze on the spot, her body stiff. She deftly moved the book behind her back and held her breath, waiting.

The cuckoo clock ticked and Thomas emitted a small snore. Betty held her pose a while longer before she crept out of the room and closed the kitchen door behind her.

"Are you okay, Mum?" Martha raised her head. She lay on the rug on her stomach, scribbling down a story in her notepad.

"Of course, darling," Betty said, with a smile. "Just trying not to wake your dad." She stood and gazed at her two daughters for a few moments. They made her heart swell, and she marveled at how different they looked from each other.

Lilian was asleep, curled up on the chair. At four years old, she hadn't yet outgrown her afternoon naps. Her fine blond hair shone like a halo in the afternoon sun and she had peach fuzz for skin.

Martha was the opposite. Her unruly hair never shone or lay flat, and Betty braided it into a fat plait to try to keep it under control. Four years older than Lilian, Martha loved to lose herself in reading and writing stories. Lilian was more pragmatic, like her father. She listened to fairy tales with a furrowed brow, announcing that Cinderella's glass slippers would break if she danced in them and that mice could not turn into horses.

Betty stooped down and ran her hand down Martha's plait, giving the end a playful tug. She slid the book out of its bag and presented it on the flats of her hands.

A smile spread across Martha's face. "Is it for me?" she asked.

Betty nodded once and pressed a finger to her mouth. "Shhh." She pointed toward the door, then made a pillow with her hands. She moved a cushion on the sofa and settled down, then beckoned for her daughter to join her.

Martha scrambled to her feet and nestled on the sofa, too. Betty took a few moments to relish the warmth of her hair, tucked under her chin. She ran her hand over the cover of the book and made a show of turning the front page. "Ready?" she asked and Martha nodded. The room fell still and Betty began to read.

Yet she found herself doing so in a hushed, hurried fashion. After every few lines, she flicked her eyes towards the dining room door and cocked her head, listening out for movement in the kitchen. Thomas usually napped for at least ninety minutes, but she wanted to be sure. Even though she tried to enjoy the story, she stumbled over the words.

Martha leaned her head against Betty's shoulder. She reached out to touch the words and pictures.

Betty had just uttered, "...and they all lived happily ever after," when the door handle creaked slowly down. Nimbly, she slipped the book under a cushion behind her and sat up to attention. The door seemed to take forever to open.

Thomas was a big man, six-feet-two and heavy-set, with

black slicked-back hair that shone like tar. Fourteen years older than Betty, and just four years younger than Zelda, he had the old-fashioned look of a fifties matinee movie idol. "Now, what are my girls up to?" he asked as he entered the room. "Anything good?"

Betty felt her cheeks flush as she thought about the book. She felt a little guilty now for buying it and hiding it from him. "We've been doing a bit of reading, haven't we, Martha?"

Martha nodded.

"Fantastic," Thomas said. Raising an eyebrow, he shifted his eyes across the room before they settled on the bookcase under the window. All twenty encyclopedias sat in a line, with no gaps. He stared at them for a while before he stepped forward and circled an arm around Betty's waist. He enveloped her into a hug, grinned and then flipped her backwards, as if they were doing a tango. Holding his face close to hers, he planted a kiss on her lips. "Have I told you how lovely you look today?"

Betty laughed, her heart fluttering at his gesture.

He pulled her upright and they smiled at each other for a moment. Then a slight frown fell upon his brow. He looked over her shoulder, reached down and took hold of the cushion on the sofa. "Oh, what's this then?" he asked, his voice full of surprise as he moved it to one side. "Is it a new book?"

As he picked it up and studied the cover, Betty swallowed. He must have had eagle eyes to spot it there. Now she had to explain herself and her mouth grew dry. "Yes," she said lightly. "I was going to tell you about it. It was on special offer in the bookstore, and the girls haven't had a new storybook for a long time. It's so beautiful and I…"

Thomas nodded. Still holding the book, he reached up and stroked her cheek. "That's so thoughtful of you, but they only got the encyclopedias recently. They're much better for them than this kind of nonsense. And we don't want to spoil them, do we? Money is tight, too." He lowered his voice. "Hmm, perhaps I could do you a favor, and take this back to the shop."

Betty felt she couldn't argue with his logic. When he explained things to her, about their finances, about why he didn't want her mother to buy silly toys for the girls, he always made sense. If she ever tried to put her own point forward about anything, he listened, but ultimately, he was older and knew what was best.

With a mixture of sadness, guilt and gratitude, she handed him the pink-and-white-striped bag with the receipt inside. "Thank you," she said quietly.

"Anything to help," he said with a peck to her cheek. He slipped the book into the bag and tucked it under his arm. "Now I'll let you get on with your reading. I think Martha might like the section on flowers in the encyclopedias."

"She's read it a few times already," Betty said quietly.

"Her favorite, obviously."

As Thomas moved away, back towards the door to the dining room, the doorbell rang.

Betty knew he didn't like her to open the front door to strangers, so she walked over to the window. Hitching the curtain to one side, she saw her mother's blond curls wrapped up in a silk scarf. Her long turquoise dress flapped in the breeze, and Betty could already smell her perfume, Estée Lauder's Youth Dew. "It's Mum," she said over her shoulder.

Thomas's spine stiffened. "What does *she* want?" he asked with a sniff.

Martha jumped up. "Nana." She rushed past him into the hallway and yanked open the front door.

Zelda entered the living room with her granddaughter's arms wrapped around her waist and with her cheek pressed firm to her bosom.

"I've written a new story, Nana," Martha said.

"Fabulous. I can't wait to hear it." Zelda gently peeled Martha away and looked around. "Well, hello, Thomas," she said, as if noticing him for the first time. "That bag you're holding is pretty. Are you embracing your feminine side?"

Thomas flashed a stiff smile. "Nice to see you, Zelda. This is just something I'm returning to the shop for Betty."

"That's so *very* thoughtful of you."

Betty wondered if anyone else could detect the disdain in Zelda's and Thomas's voices when they spoke to each other. Thomas's tone grew a little higher and quicker, and Zelda's was more nasal with a hint of a sneer. There was always tension between the two of them, but she did her best to ignore it.

Her mother had told her many times that Thomas was too stiff and set in his ways. Whereas Thomas thought Zelda was too flighty and didn't take things seriously enough.

"It's a copy of *Beauty and the Beast*," Martha said. "We got to read it before Dad takes it back. You'd have loved it."

"I'm sure I *would* have done," Zelda said. She glared in Thomas's direction. "Luckily, I've brought something else for you, my glorious girl." She reached into her large turquoise handbag and pulled out a flamingo-pink plastic mirror the size of a dinner plate. It had white plastic daisies around its frame.

Martha gasped. "It's beautiful. Thanks, Nana," she said as she took hold of it. "'Mirror, mirror on the wall…'"

"'Who's the fairest of them all?'" Zelda said. "You and Lilian are. You can use this to see how pretty you both are."

Betty watched as Thomas's eyes narrowed with disapproval.

"That's very kind of you, Zelda," he said. "But the children have got far too many things already. You should save your money for a rainy day."

"Where's the fun in that?" Zelda shrugged. She knelt down

on the floor. "Now, don't let me delay you, Thomas. No need to stay around on my behalf."

Thomas ran his tongue over his top teeth. He stared at Betty, trying to catch her eye, but she pretended not to notice and glanced away. Eventually he said, "I'll see you later," and closed the door behind him.

Zelda gave a pronounced sigh, exaggerating her relief that he'd gone. "Now, I want to hear this new story of yours, Martha. Will you tell it to me?"

Betty watched through the window as Thomas walked down the path and opened the gate.

Martha dropped down cross-legged to the floor. Her plait swung as she picked up her notepad and found the right page. She cleared her throat and began to read aloud...

The Bird Girl

Once upon a time there was a girl who lived with her mother, father and sister. Although they should be a happy family, the girl often felt sad but didn't know why. She sensed something strange in the air but didn't know what it was.

Each night, when she went to bed, the girl dreamed that she was a bird. She would fly high into the sky, where being clever and perfect all the time didn't matter.

One night, after a family tea where tension seemed to dance, unspoken, around the table again, the girl sat in her room, wringing her hands. She was fed up and she decided to try to glue feathers to her arms and legs, so she really could be like a bird. After taking a long time to carry out her task, she opened her bedroom window. But the ground looked too far down and she was afraid to jump.

In the morning, she peeled off the feathers and this made

her skin red and sore. To explain it, she told her parents that she'd got sunburned while playing outside. But they were too busy looking after her little sister to be interested.

On the next night, the girl took the feathers and did the same thing. But, again, she couldn't bring herself to leap out of the window.

And the pattern continued, night after night.

The girl would spend time with her family. She'd feel something wasn't right and then she'd apply her feathers.

One evening, as the girl clenched her fists, unable to bring herself to jump again, a blackbird stood on the window ledge. He tapped his yellow beak against the window, inviting the girl to open it.

The girl did so and crawled out to join him. The blackbird cocked his head and waited beside her for a long time, until she finally found the courage to step off.

On this first night, the girl tumbled to the ground and into a bush, where the branches and twigs scratched her face. The blackbird flew down and watched as she climbed out.

On the second night, the girl landed with such force that her knees buckled. But the blackbird stayed by her side until she could walk back to the house.

On the third night, the girl flew out over the garden gate, high into the sky, where she almost touched the stars. Then she landed at the edge of a beautiful lake.

Everything was quiet, still and beautiful, and the blackbird settled on her shoulder. But although she had flown, the girl felt sad. "I don't know what to do, little bird," she said. "For a long time, I've felt like flying away, but now I'm not so sure. Do you think I should stay at home, even though I feel like I don't belong there?"

The blackbird flew away and reappeared with a broken

piece of mirror which he held up. The girl looked at her reflection and saw that the feathers she applied each night had grown into her skin. While she was waiting for things to change at home, she had changed, too. She had grown more determined and independent and, looking at the little blackbird, she made up her mind.

Even though she didn't know if the world was ready for a bird girl, she stood on her tiptoes and flapped her arms. Then she and the blackbird flew away, never to return.

4

Library

Sandshift was once a thriving town, where the majority of folk relied on the fishing trade to make a living. But now it derived most of its revenue from day trippers who descended at the weekend, to look for fossils in the shale on the beach, or as a good spot for dog walking.

Before Martha headed to the library, she took her usual brisk twelve-minute walk down to the seafront. Her morning routine involved stretching her legs, getting some fresh air and contemplating all the things she wanted to accomplish that day. Then she could put a dash next to them in her notepad, her code for *to be completed today*.

Last night, after her call to Lilian, she was too tired to do any more sewing. She certainly didn't have the time or energy to look through the mysterious book again or read any of its stories. Before going to bed, she placed it in her handbag, ready to show it to Suki at work.

As she walked along the beach, Martha felt like she was wading through treacle. Her steps were trudging and her body was squeezed of life. As she pressed her hands against her tightening chest, a ball of anger flared inside at her own silly fatigue.

You need to be more efficient, or else you'll never get your jobs done.

She decided that working her arms like pistons would get her blood flowing. She pumped them as she marched across the sand and past a large cave with a dark teardrop-shaped opening. Pausing for a moment to admire the white lighthouse that stood like a lone birthday candle on the rocks jutting out to sea, she watched as an orange swimming capped–head bobbed in the gunmetal waves.

I hope that person has got a towel, she thought, looking around for it on the sand. *I hope they know about the riptide in the bay.*

A swift walk along the water's edge, sea foam fizzing around her shoes, brought her to a bronze mermaid statue, the town's main landmark.

The mermaid's tail was a crescent moon curl and her long hair straggled over her shoulders. She sat on a rock looking out to sea, forever waiting for fishermen to return in their boat, the *Pegasus*. The engraving on her plaque said,

DEDICATED TO THE SANDSHIFT SEVEN, CLAIMED BY THE SEA IN 1965.

A violent storm had sucked the *Pegasus* under. It created widows and orphans and it was as if a thick gray smog hung over the town ever since. There had only been one survivor that fateful night, a young man called Siegfried Frost, the eighth person on board the boat.

Even though the accident happened before she was born, the roots of Martha's hair still stood to attention when she read the names of the seven crew members. She knew them by heart, but still looked at them each day.

Using a tissue, she plucked a piece of chewing gum off the mermaid's tail, threw it in a bin and set off back up the hill, still punching her arms.

When Martha stepped inside the library, she closed her eyes and inhaled the earthy, almond scent of the books. If she could bottle the aroma, she'd wear it as a perfume, *L'eau de la Bibliothèque*.

She took the small battered book from her bag and gave that a sniff, too. It smelled musty and sweet with a hint of something else that she couldn't place, maybe amber or cinnamon.

The library was part run by the community since the local council made some drastic budget cuts. It was overseen by Clive Folds from his modern office in Maltsborough, where he was supposed to plan and ensure that two assistant librarians were always on duty. But since their colleague Judy went on long-term sick leave with a bad back, more responsibility had fallen on Suki's and Martha's shoulders.

Fortunately, Thomas and Betty had left Martha and Lilian a fair-sized chunk of money in their will. Martha had almost used up her amount and, more than anything, she wanted a permanent position at the library.

She'd helped out there for over four years, had a diploma in English literature, adored the books and wanted to help people. However, Clive had personally turned down three of her job applications. He displayed a penchant for younger, fresh-faced workers.

Martha now had a job application form in her desk drawer for her fourth attempt.

She had scanned through it many times already. With almost three weeks until the deadline, she hadn't yet made a start on it. Each time she looked at the headings for qualifications, experience and previous employment, her heart stung from Clive's rejections.

Working at the library made her feel more alive. She could picture crawling on all fours across the floor, with Zelda. They used to walk their fingers across the rainbow of book spines and stroke the covers. They whispered and shared stories.

When Zelda died, Martha found solace in the gray stone building with its flat roof and tall skinny windows that looked out over Sandshift Bay. She spent hours with her cheeks pressed to the cool glass, furiously wiping away her tears as she stared down at the golden curve of the beach.

She wedged herself in the corner of the fiction section, knees tucked up to her chin, reading books after school or at the weekend. And as the pages grew bumpy with her tears, they helped her to cope with her grief. She shuddered at James Herbert and Stephen King, read about misfit schoolgirls and ravenous rats, got lost in the lush worlds of Evelyn Waugh, and learned some of the mysteries of men from the steamier moments in Mills & Boon. The library had been her Narnia, and it still was.

Martha found Suki sitting behind the front desk with a pile of books stacked almost as high as her nose. She had worked here for less than five months, another of Clive's young appointees.

Even though she wore floaty paisley dresses down to her ankles, beaded sandals and a nose ring that looked more suited to a California music festival, Martha thought that Suki was good at her job. She was practical and nothing fazed her. Were they friends? She didn't know, unsure what you had to do to make that happen.

Now Suki peered out with red-rimmed eyes from under

her blunt blond fringe. The lilac dip-dyed ends of her hair were soggy with tears.

Instinctively, Martha flew into action mode, shoulders back, chin raised. She dug her hand into her pocket and pulled out a packet of tissues. Holding one out at arm's length, she waited until it tugged like a fish pulling on a line. There was a loud nose blow from behind the book pile.

"Is this about Ben again?" Martha asked gently. "Didn't he like the food you made for him?"

Suki's nostrils flared and she fanned a hand in front of her face. "He collected his stuff from the spare room and didn't even try my cheese and onion pie."

Martha had grown used to Suki's misuse and mispronunciation of her words and didn't correct her this time. She glanced at her burgeoning belly. "I bet they were delicious. Let me get you a nice cup of tea and a biscuit. I've brought a cushion for your back, and an article on breastfeeding. How long is it now until the baby arrives?"

"Six weeks. Ben's still hooking up with that girl he works with. He says he can't make up his mind between us. I'll have to give him a culmination."

"Do you mean an ultimatum?"

"Yeah, one of those. Me and the bump might have to get by without him."

"Are you sure you can't work things out?" Martha opened a drawer and slid her hand around inside. "You could take a minibreak together. Or, I'm sure I saved a magazine piece on couple counseling."

Suki wrung the tissue in her hands. "He just needs to make up his bloody mind. I still love him, though. You know what that's like, yeah? Even you must have been in love, once."

Martha retracted her hand. Her blood cooled at the words, *even you.*

There had been someone who loved her, a long time ago, before she moved back into her family home to care for her parents.

She and Joe used to dance in the sea at dusk, whatever the weather. They sat on a blanket on the floor of the teardrop-shaped cave and read aloud from books together. He scratched their initials onto the cave wall, and she painted her toenails petal-pink for him.

For five years, he'd been part of her life, helping to fill the gap that Zelda left behind. Martha had imagined marriage and their carpets scattered with brightly colored picture books. But then she'd made a huge decision and it made her dreams fall apart.

These days, Martha knew she wouldn't ever win a beauty contest, but when a reader sidled up to the desk, rubbed their chin and said, "I don't know the title of the book, but the cover is red, and I *think* there's a picture of a dog on the front," she had the answer.

"We're talking about you, not me," she said hurriedly. She made Suki a cup of tea and placed a heart-shaped biscuit on her saucer. She took a blue satin cushion from her shopping bag and plumped it up. Taking Zelda's book from her bag, she set it on the table.

"Urgh. Is that one of ours?" Suki dabbed her eyes. She positioned the cushion behind her back and bounced against it several times.

"No. I saw someone lurking outside the library last night. I think they left it for me."

"You came to work?" Suki frowned. "For the author event?"

Martha nodded.

"But Clive was supposed to tell everyone that Lucinda couldn't make it. Her publisher called him."

Martha quickly lowered her eyes. "He didn't tell me."

Suki's face fell. "Oh god, sorry, Martha. I didn't know. I was occupational with Ben and the baby."

"It's fine," Martha said, even though it wasn't. "It means that I found the book. It's from someone called Owen Chamberlain."

Suki sat more upright. "Oh yeah. Chamberlain's is the new bookshop behind Maltsborough lifeboat station. Well, it's new but sells old books." She picked the book up and leafed through it. "These illustrations are gorgeous."

"There's a message inside from my grandmother, Zelda. But she passed away three years before the date."

Suki frowned. "That's weird, like an Agatha Christie mystery or something."

"Or, perhaps a mistake. That's the more obvious conclusion."

"Are you going ring him?"

Martha hesitated. Recalling Lilian's disparaging words about the book made her palms itch. "My sister said to leave it alone."

"But the desiccation is to you, not her."

"It's dedication," Martha corrected her. She stared at the phone on the desk, and thoughts of Zelda crawling on the library floor came back to her again. Even now, she still missed her.

"I suppose I could call him," she said, finally. "To tie up loose ends with the situation."

"Definitely."

Martha slid the handwritten note out of the book, to read the phone number, but as she did, the library doors opened. A breeze lifted the note from her fingers. It swept into the air and down onto the floor like a feather.

"Yes," Lilian spoke loudly. "You do have to stay here."

Will and Rose appeared around the corner first. They both wore jeans and baggy hooded tops, and their droopy mouths said they'd prefer to be somewhere else.

Thirteen-year-old Will's spiky hair was platinum blond a contrast to the black of his thick eyebrows. Rose was three years younger. Her hair was the color of autumn leaves, a soft copper. It fell in spirals around her oval face.

Lilian nudged them forward and rubbed the corner of her eye. "Hey, how are you, Martha?" she said. "I've stopped by for my Ahern."

"I've got it here. And I've brought the old book I told you about."

Lilian raised her palm and briefly closed her eyes. "Okay, but I need to ask you for a favor. Do you mind looking after the kids? I've got an errand to run."

Will rolled his eyes. "Oh, sure. You're going to Chichetti's in Maltsborough, Mum. Your friend invited you to lunch."

Lilian fixed him with a stare and gave a stilted laugh. "Well, *yes*. Annie and I will eat, but we also have other things to do." She stepped closer to Martha and lowered her voice. "I want to talk to Annie about something. It's important. The kids will be no trouble. They'll just read books and things."

Martha had received a telling off from Clive when Will and Rose last hung out at the library. He accused her of mixing business and family life. "I'd love to help, but—"

"Great," Lilian said, with a sigh of relief. "Thanks so much. I'll be back by two. Or two thirty. Perhaps three… Now, I have to dash."

"But about the book—" Martha picked it up and proffered it to her sister.

Lilian froze, then tentatively took hold of it. She briefly flicked through the pages and her lips pursed into a thin line when she reached Zelda's message.

"Have you noticed the date?" Martha prompted.

Color seemed to seep from Lilian's cheeks. She cleared her throat. "Zelda probably wrote it down wrong, that's all."

"That seems a strange thing to do."

Lilian handed it back. She hitched her handbag up on her shoulder. "I don't know why you're getting obsessed with that crappy old thing, especially when you're surrounded by so many lovely books. Just chuck it away. It's probably full of germs."

Martha heard the irritation in her sister's voice and decided not to press things further. But although she smiled and said, "Well, okay then," she couldn't help wondering why Lilian was so dismissive of the intriguing little book.

Will took off his boots and stretched his legs out, creating a hurdle to the history section. "Any chance of a brew?" he asked Martha.

Rose sat cross-legged in front of the YA shelves. She stabbed at her phone screen with her index finger. "I'd love one, too. You make the best cups of tea." Her eyes shone as a neon-yellow trophy exploded.

"Of course," Martha said. "Would you like a biscuit, too? Freshly baked."

Will and Rose nodded in unison.

Branda was the next person who needed help, with her photocopying. Her real name was Brenda, but everyone switched the *e* to an *a* without her noticing because she only wore clothes she classed as a "dee-signer brand." Three years ago, her husband left her for a family friend, so Branda hit him where it hurt—in his wallet. Today she wore a crisp white shirt with hand-painted eagles on the shoulders, and a black leather skirt with bright yellow stitching. Her bluey-black hair was coiffed into a small crispy beehive.

"I'll do it," Martha said, wrestling the paper out of her arms. "You have a nice sit-down. Do you have extinguishers in the Lobster Pot? Your candles could be quite a fire hazard."

"I only use the best beeswax, Martha," Branda said. "Extinguishers would spoil the restaurant aesthetic. I stow them away in the kitchen."

After that, Martha showed a young man with multiple face piercings how to search for jobs online. She changed a plug on a computer that didn't fit the socket properly, even though she should report electronic stuff to Clive. She issued a new library card and replaced two lost ones. A man from the garden center asked where he could buy brown fur fabric, because the staff wanted to dress up as woodland creatures. He wanted to go as a ferret. Martha located a book in the sewing section on making costumes for children. "You can tape pieces of paper together and scale up the pattern in size," she said. "In fact, I'll do it for you…"

"You make everything so easy for people," Suki said as the man walked away with the book and a six-feet-tall piece of paper with a man-sized ferret outfit sketched on it.

"Thank you."

"Too easy… Have you called Chamberlain's yet?"

"I've not had the chance."

"You've got time now. Think about yourself, for once."

Martha felt a lump rise in her throat. It happened now and again, if anyone displayed unexpected thoughtfulness towards her. She tucked in her chin and swallowed the lump away, but she also felt a weird flutter in her stomach, as if she'd swallowed something that was still alive. A new bookshop and the opportunity to find out more about the old book were a real temptation. She wondered how Owen Chamberlain had traced her, and what he knew about the book and Zelda's message. "Well, okay," she said.

She dialed the number for Chamberlain's but didn't get a reply, so she rang a further three times in a row. "I don't know how Mr. Chamberlain expects to make a living, if he doesn't pick up the phone," she said. "Did you know that eight out of ten businesses fail in their first year of trading?"

"That's a lot. Go over to Maltsborough to see him," Suki suggested. "I think the shop closes at one thirty today and doesn't open again until Wednesday. I've got things covered here."

But Martha had duties to perform. The library didn't close for another fifty-three minutes. She looked over at her niece and nephew, still studying their phones. "I can't go. Someone might need me."

As the morning ticked by, Martha carried over *Skulduggery Pleasant*, *Divergent* and *Percy Jackson*, and placed the books on the table beside Will. He smiled but didn't pick them up.

Martha found *Little Women* and *Chocolat* for her niece. Although Rose muttered, "Thanks," Martha could tell that the books would remain unread. She kept the two of them topped up with cups of tea.

She also tried to call Owen Chamberlain a further two times but the phone still rang out.

Siegfried Frost shuffled into the library and, as usual, didn't say hello. The reclusive seventy-something always wore the same gray knitted hat, the same texture and color as his wiry hair that sprang from under it. His beard obscured his lips, so on the rare occasions he spoke, you couldn't see them. His brown mac almost reached the ankles of his frayed, turned-up jeans. He'd moved into the old Sandshift lighthouse after the *Pegasus* accident.

His fingers crept towards the battered book and he picked it up.

Martha shot out her hand to stop him. "That's not actually a library book."

Above his gray whiskers, Siegfried's eyes didn't blink. He twisted his upper body, moving the book away from her. Flicking through it, he paused to peer at an illustration of a blackbird.

Upside down, Martha read the title of the story, "The Bird Girl."

An image slipped into her head then vanished just as quickly, of her reading a story to her mum and Nana. It was one she hadn't thought of for a long time and her head felt a little floaty. She reached behind her for a chair, her hand hovering in the space above it.

"You look like you've seen a ghoul," Suki said.

Siegfried dropped the book back on the table and shuffled away.

Martha immediately picked it up again. The ground seemed wavy beneath her feet. "I think I know the story that Siegfried was looking at." She turned the pages and located it, her eyes scanning the words. She stared at its title. Gingerly, she lifted the book to her nose and inhaled, recognizing the smell as a hint of Youth Dew. "I have *got* to read this."

"Sure. I'll make you a coffee."

Martha sank into the chair and traced her finger down the words. She read the story twice, recognizing "The Bird Girl" as one she'd made up many years ago.

She turned the pages and other words and titles began to leap out at her. Stories told by Zelda to Martha, created by Martha for Betty. Stories the three women had shared together.

What on earth are they doing here?

"You look very pale." Suki returned and placed a steaming cup of coffee on the desk.

Martha nodded. She got to her feet and knocked her hip against the desktop. Coffee splashed onto the corner of Branda's photocopying. She took a tissue and dabbed it, her fingers feeling strangely big and clumsy. "I know the library doesn't close for twenty-three minutes, but I need to go," she said. She surveyed the room, making sure that everyone was able to cope without her.

"You're going home?"

"No. To Chamberlain's."

"Oh." Suki raised an eyebrow. "Good incision."

"It's decision. And sorry, I won't drink the coffee, though it does look very flavorsome. Apologies for the spillage." Martha reached down and picked up her bag. Her hands shook as she placed the book carefully inside it.

Stepping into the history section, she spoke as loudly as her small voice allowed. "Will and Rose, put your shoes back on. We're going over to Maltsborough."

5

Bookshop

As they walked to the bus stop, Martha glanced over both shoulders to make sure that Clive wasn't around to see her leaving work early. She asked Will and Rose if they'd prefer to go to the bookshop with her, or to meet their mother at the restaurant.

Will lowered his phone. "Chichetti's does an amazing chocolate fudge cake. Can we go and get a slice?"

"Mum sounded like she needed some time out," Rose said cautiously. "Like, *without* us."

Will shrugged and returned to his game.

"I'm sure your mum will be pleased to see us," Martha said, though she wasn't convinced. "But I must get to that bookstore before it closes."

"What time's that?" Rose asked.

"One thirty, I think."

"But it's almost one o'clock now…"

When the bus rumbled up five minutes later, they got on board. Will and Rose made their way to the back seat and positioned themselves as far away from each other as they could.

Martha sat down between them. She touched the sparkly slide in her hair and held on to her bag.

Her upper body did a strange dance as the bus turned and wound its way out of Sandshift and up onto Maltsborough Road. She raised her head to look down at the bay, where the sky was a shroud of mist hanging over the gray-blue sea. Siegfried's lighthouse gleamed in the hazy February daylight, and Martha willed the bus to get a move on.

Maltsborough was Sandshift's wealthier neighbor. It had a run of smart seafront bistros, a bank, a grand hotel with turrets, fish-and-chips shops galore, a museum and a state-of-the-art library that had a coffee shop, gift shop and large lights that looked like giant blue test tubes hanging from the ceiling. It attracted lots more funding than Sandshift and was where Clive sat in his office, hatching plans for budget cuts, synergy and synchronicity.

Chichetti's was a new Italian restaurant on the high street with floor-to-ceiling windows overlooking the promenade. It was the kind of place where eating pasta and being seen were of equal importance to diners.

Martha, Will and Rose stood in a line, on the pavement outside, looking in.

Martha spotted her sister's gold pumps near the window. She raised her hand to wave, but then paused with her hand midair. Lilian was leaned forward over the table with her face pointing down. Another woman, who Martha presumed must be Annie, had an arm wrapped around her shoulder.

Martha slowly lowered her hand but Will didn't seem to notice there might be something going on. He rapped loudly on the window and gave a double thumbs-up to his mum.

Annie shook Lilian's shoulder, and she sat up abruptly. She

knocked her glass of white wine with her wrist and it wobbled. A passing waiter reached out and steadied it.

Lilian blinked hard at Martha, Will and Rose. She got up so quickly her stool rocked, and she sped towards the smoked-glass front door.

"What are you doing here?" she asked breathlessly as she stepped outside. Her eyes were pink and glistening above her puffy cheeks. "It's only twenty past one."

Martha swallowed. "Are you okay?"

"I'm fine. Just a spot of, um, hay fever."

"I have a packet of tissues in my bag. They're extra soft and have aloe vera in them."

"I'm fine," Lilian said. "What's this about?"

"Sorry for bringing the kids early, but I want to get to that bookshop before it closes. Will and Rose don't want to join me. I think they want food instead—"

"I'm really hungry," Rose said.

"Me, too." Will nodded.

Lilian knitted her hand into her hair and didn't speak for a while. She took a deep breath and held it in her chest. "I suppose that's fine. We're just about to order dessert." Then her eyes grew harder. "I hope this isn't about that old book?"

Martha felt as if she was shrinking in size, like Alice in Wonderland after drinking from a potion bottle. "The shop doesn't open again until Wednesday," she said meekly.

"I told you to leave it alone."

"I just want to find out where it came from, that's all."

Lilian pressed her lips together. "It's your choice," she said finally. "I don't know why you're so interested in that stupid old thing, anyway. You could join us for a lovely dessert instead."

"Oh yeah, go on, Auntie Martha," Rose said.

"The chocolate fudge cake is really gooey." Will licked his lips.

Martha stared inside the restaurant, at a waiter who glided past carrying an enormous ice cream sundae. Her mouth began to water. "I, um…"

"And I need to ask you for another favor," Lilian added.

"Yes?" Martha said. She fumbled in her bag for her notepad and pen and flipped to her current task list. "What is it?"

"Will you look after the kids the weekend after next? I need to, um, work away."

"I bet it's at a posh spa," Will quipped.

Lilian fixed him with a brief stare, then found a smile for Martha. "I have a few things to sort out. Can we make it an overnighter?"

Martha wrote this down and thought about it. Now that they were getting older, Will and Rose hadn't slept at the house for a couple of years. Her parents' old bedroom was full of bags and boxes. "I'm happy to have them during the day, but there's not enough space for them to—"

"Great," Lilian interjected. "Thanks, Martha. Now, let's grab that dessert."

Martha's mind ticked between her two options. She was here now, but Chamberlain's closed in a few minutes. She placed her notepad in her handbag and fastened the zip. Lilian's eyes still looked tense, but it could be because of the pollen. "The restaurant looks lovely, but perhaps some other time…"

A veil seemed to slip across Lilian's features. She wrapped her arms around Will's and Rose's shoulders. "You seem to remember our grandmother as some kind of fairy godmother figure," she said sharply. "It really wasn't the case."

Martha's mouth fell open a little. "Zelda was wonderful. She was bright and fun, and always…"

Lilian shook her head. "Sometimes, Martha," she said as

she placed her hand against the restaurant door. "It's easy to remember things differently to how they actually were."

Martha could hear faint electronic tunes from the amusement arcades on the seafront, but the street where Chamberlain's Pre-Loved and Antiquarian Books was located was quiet, except for two seagulls cawing and flapping over a dropped bag of chips.

Suki said the bookshop was new, but the shade of the duck egg–blue paint coating the window frames and door, and the semicircle of silver lettering embossed on the large windowpane made it look a couple of centuries old.

Flustered after her uncomfortable discussion with Lilian, Martha struggled to regulate her breathing. Her chest felt tight again and she gave it a rub. There was something about the flicker in her sister's eyes that made her question her decision to come here.

Even though Lilian was the younger sister, she'd always taken the lead. When she first arrived home from the hospital, as a plum-faced newborn, she had assumed control. She would sleep and eat when she wanted, and the rest of the family had to fit their lives around her.

Thomas loved his new daughter. He cooed at her and puffed out his chest when he pushed Lilian in the pram, showing her off to friends and neighbors. He didn't allow any of the fun toys that Zelda bought inside her cot.

Martha could admit that, with her icy-blond hair and blue eyes, her sister was a beautiful child. However, her father's devoted attention to her made Martha feel like the ugly sister in comparison.

As she stood in front of the shop door, she lifted her chin. There were only a couple of minutes left until closing time and she had to follow her instincts. Twisting the brass knob, she opened the door.

A brass bell rang and she felt a little otherworldly as she inhaled the heady aroma of leather, cardboard and ink. Her eyes widened at the sight of the books lining the floor-to-ceiling shelves. There were hundreds, maybe thousands, some worn and some like new.

Her forehead crinkled a little with disapproval as she spotted a screwed-up tissue and a felt-tip pen without its lid on the desk. There was a small heap of sweet wrappers, several key rings and a plastic pug dog with a nodding head. Her own house might be *busy*, but this shop looked disorganized, in need of a good system.

A long wooden ladder, leaning against a bookshelf, stretched from the floor and rose upward as far as Martha could see. There was a pair of legs, with feet facing her, clad in monogrammed red slippers. The toes wriggled as if their owner was listening to music that nobody else could hear. The ladder rungs creaked and bowed as the legs climbed down.

The red slipper–wearer was tall with a circular face. His sandy hair was pushed back off his forehead and streaked white around the temples. A red silk scarf framed his open-neck black shirt and his gray suit fitted loosely over his large rounded chest. He wore four colorful pin badges. One featured an illustration of a book, and another said, "Booksellers—great between the sheets." Martha noticed that his hand was large enough to hold several books in its span and that he had a smear of ink on his cheek.

Martha tapped her own face. "You have a smudge."

"Oh." The man put down his books and lifted his scarf. He used it to rub his face. "I keep finding bruises in strange places, but it's ink from the books and newspapers. There," he said triumphantly. "Is that better?"

Martha stared at his cheek, which was now denim blue. "You may need a mirror."

"I don't think I have one."

Taking the battered book from her bag, Martha searched for a spare space on the countertop. "I think you might have left this for me?"

"Ah, you must be Martha?" Owen smiled and held out his hand.

Martha hesitated. Although she liked to help library-goers, physical contact was something she tried to forgo. Helping her parents out of their chairs was as close as she'd got to others for a long time. She reached out and lightly shook his hand, then quickly let it go. "May I ask where the book came from, and how you found me?"

Owen picked it up, handling it as if it was an injured baby bird. "A fellow bookseller sent it to me for repair. But it's in such a bad state and would be too expensive to reconstruct. When I told him the price, he told me not to bother. I paid him a tenner for it because I could sell some of the illustrations. But then I got The Guilt."

"Guilt?"

"I can't bring myself to disassemble books, even if they're beyond rescue. I always end up keeping them. But then I can't sell them, either." He dropped his voice to a whisper. "Though, over the years I bet my wives would have liked me to."

Martha blinked, wondering just how many times he'd been married. He did have an air of Henry VIII about him.

"When I flicked through this one," Owen continued, "I spotted your name in the dedication and knew it from leaflets about the library. There aren't any other Martha Storms in the telephone directory, so it had to be you."

"Were you huddled by the library door yesterday evening?" Martha asked with a frown.

"Yes, that sounds like me."

"I called out to you, but you vanished."

"Really? I didn't hear anything. I was on my way to the footie match with my son—he was waiting in the car. There was an author event on or something, so I left the book by the door."

"The event was canceled. It was written on the poster."

"Oh." Owen scratched his head. "I don't think I was wearing my glasses."

Martha noted that his sentences were as higgledy-piggledy as his bookshop. He started to speak then looked distracted, as if he had to physically search for his next words. "Where did your contact get the book from?" she asked.

Owen scratched his head, leaving his hair stuck up on top. "I'd really have to ask him or check my notes. I do write these things down…sometimes…"

Martha waited for him to look around but he didn't do anything.

"You look a little disappointed, or puzzled," he said.

She twisted her fingers around her wrist, wondering if she should tell him the reason for the book's importance. "The dedication inside is from my grandmother, Zelda," she said. "But the date she's written is three years *after* she died. The stories in the book are also…well, personal."

Owen cocked his head to one side. "I'm not sure what you mean?"

"Um," Martha said, scolding herself for mentioning the last bit.

"You can tell me anything." Owen held up three fingers of his right hand. "I'm a bookseller and we have a code of secrecy."

"Really?"

"Well, no." He grinned. "I just wanted to assure you."

Martha stared at him, wondering if he was a little crazy or not. But with what she had to say, he might think the same thing about her. After Lilian's negative reaction to the book, she just wanted someone to listen to her and take this strange situation seriously.

"I used to write stories, when I was younger," she admitted. "I only shared them with my family, Zelda mainly. And now I've found them here, printed in this book. They're alongside other ones she and my mum told me."

Owen rocked back and fro on his heels for a while. He worked his mouth. "I've certainly not heard that one before."

Martha wasn't sure if he was mocking her or not. She wished that the ground would swallow her up, or that a bookshelf would fall over and squash her flat.

Owen picked up the book and leafed through it again. "Publishers usually print the title of the book on each page, but it's missing here. It looks like the book might be self-published, so it will be more difficult to trace...not impossible, though." He tapped the side of his nose. "I'll get back in touch with Dexter, my contact. I'll see if he remembers where it came from. He *knows* people."

He sounds like the James Bond of the secondhand book world, connected to a secret underground network, Martha thought.

"I'll make a note of some of these story titles." Owen picked up a pen and took hold of a scrap of paper. "Or perhaps I can keep this for a while?"

Martha clicked her tongue. She didn't want to let the book out of her sight.

"I'll take good care of it."

"Hmm, well, okay then. But I'd like it back as soon as possible."

"I promise to call you on Monday."

Martha took her purse from her bag. "How much do I owe you, for the book, and your research?"

"Now put that away, I don't want any money." He raised a palm. "Just buy me a coffee sometime."

Martha took out a ten-pound note and waved it. "Please take this remuneration."

He shook his head. "Tell you what. I'm just about to close the shop, and there's a nice café called Love, Peace and Coffee just around the corner. It's perfect for sitting in the window, reading and eating cake. Why don't we grab a table and you can tell me more about these intriguing family stories of yours?"

Martha felt her cheeks reddening. She hadn't been invited out for a coffee by anyone for a long time. Plus, something her father used to say, when she was younger, popped into her head. "Watch your cake portions, Martha. You'll always be beautiful to me, but you're the type to put on weight easily."

She paused for what felt like an age, thinking of a reason to give Owen for not joining him. Eventually, she said, "Sorry, but I don't eat cake."

"Oh." He squinted. "Perhaps just a coffee, then?"

Martha started to back up, across the shop towards the door. "Not today, thank you. If you find out anything about the book, do let me know." She fumbled behind her and opened the door. "I'd be most obliged.'"

"I'll need your phone number." Owen reached out with one hand, as if trying to catch her coat. "Or I can call the library…"

Martha stood with one foot inside the shop and the other on the pavement outside. She imagined Clive's smug face if he took a personal call for her. He'd enjoy berating her.

She stepped back inside the shop, took a piece of paper from her notepad and quickly wrote down her home number.

Owen made a great show of folding it neatly and placing it in his jacket pocket. "Fantastic," he said. "I'll be in touch."

6

The Reading Group

On Monday afternoon, when Martha pushed her trolley towards the library, it felt like it contained bricks rather than bottles of cordial, biscuits, Horatio's fish food, some of his potted plants and copies of her new book-rating spreadsheet. She wanted to turn it back around, to wheel it home, but she'd offered to host the fortnightly reading group session. Suki was attending a maternity appointment.

Martha had spent the previous day filled with worry and regret, that she'd left the book with Owen to research. Her eyes kept searching out her phone, to see if he might have found something earlier than expected and left her a message. However, no one called.

The illustrations and stories in her head were like a film that wouldn't stop. It was as if the book held hypnotic powers over her. Memories were beginning to trickle back, of her stories and the atmosphere in the Storm household that influenced her to write them.

Trying to sleep last night had been hopeless. She tossed and turned and, when she was awake, her concentration flitted away from the tasks she'd assigned herself. Will's trousers remained unfinished and she'd tripped over a box of Branda's chandeliers. The Chinese dragon's eyes seemed to follow her around the room.

She usually hoped that all the reading group members would turn up, but today she wished that no one would. Feeling frazzled, she just wanted to go home and wait for Owen's call.

Branda was already waiting outside the library. She waved a violet-taloned hand. *"Enchanté.* What book are we reviewing today?"

Martha stifled a sigh. The group were supposed to have read Lucinda Lovell's latest, in preparation for the Valentine's Day event that didn't happen. *"Distant Desire,"* she said as she unlocked the door. She pushed her trolley into the corridor and walked with Branda into the main room.

"Oh. I didn't read it. Not *noir* enough for my liking," Branda said.

Covering a yawn with her hand, Martha took her Wonder Woman notepad from her pocket. She examined the green ticks and amber stars, but her weary eyes made them look fuzzy. Not able to concentrate properly, she put her pad away and began to rearrange chairs around the table. She took out copies of her new spreadsheet, ready to hand out to the group.

Branda smoothed down her orange skirt with a graffiti design on the front and didn't help. "We should read a thriller next," she said. "A dark Scandi one."

When a dragging noise sounded from the hallway, Martha paused in mid-spreadsheet distribution. Nora entered, pulling two overstuffed black bin bags.

She had been single for a few years, since her husband died in a car accident, and was now on the lookout for Husband Number Two. Even though she was almost as wide as she was tall, and dressed in jewel-colored velour tracksuits, Nora wasn't short of male attention on the numerous dating sites she'd started to frequent. However, she expected her suitors to look like the bare-chested men on the covers of the racy novels she devoured, so was always disappointed when she met them in person.

"I honestly do not know where all the washing machine engineers have vanished to," she huffed as she deposited her bags in the middle of the floor. "Can I leave these with you, Martha, love? Just another bit of laundry, to add to the stuff you're doing for me."

Martha had already laundered numerous loads for Nora and received little thanks in return. She pressed the tip of her tongue against the back of her teeth, trying to form the word *no*. But she couldn't let it out of her mouth. Like a smoker trying to quit who finds their fingers reaching for a cigarette, she found a weary smile. "Of course," she said.

"Cheers, my dear."

Horatio was next to arrive. He wore his captain's hat and a navy suit with gold buttons. He ran a small aquarium from his garage, charging £2 for adults and £1 for children to enter the gloomy space during the summer season. His wife often accused him of loving his fish more than her, and he was slow to deny it. Setting his hat down on the table, he ran a finger over his white brush of a mustache. "Did you bring my fish food back for me?"

Martha nodded and handed over two shopping bags. "And some of your potted plants, too. Don't forget that you still need to collect your fish."

"That's grand." Horatio reached into his pocket, took out a two-pound coin and pressed it into her palm. He curled her hand around it and patted. "Treat yourself to something nice."

Martha unfurled her fingers. It had cost her several times that amount for the extra fish food she'd bought, but it seemed churlish to mention it. "Thanks," she said. "That's very kind of you."

Siegfried entered the room and sat down. He took off his gray hat and held it on his lap with both hands. He didn't say hello to anyone but muttered something about Clive being late and to start without him.

Martha waited for the group to settle down, take off their coats, shuffle in their chairs and take things from their pockets and bags. Clearing her throat, she picked up Lucinda's book. "Let's make a start," she said, trying to inject brightness into her voice to mask her exhaustion. The quicker she could get the session going, the sooner she could get home to check for messages on her answering machine. "We've all been reading *Distant Desire*, so who wants to kick-start our conversation? You'll find new sheets in front of you, to help organize your thoughts."

Branda unzipped her handbag and took out a pair of over-sized round sunglasses. She set them on top of her bluey-black hair. "I hoped to see Lucinda at the event. She's awfully filtered in her photo and I wanted a closer look, you know, to see if she's had anything *done* to her face."

"Oh yes." Nora circled a finger around her own forehead and mimed an injection. "It was a shame she had to cancel."

"I've been reading a book about a prison officer," Horatio said. "Very insightful. One of the inmates was a murderer but cared for a goldfish in the prison."

Martha was surprised to find that her usual patience was evading her. The group members often got sidetracked with their conversations and she could handle it, but today it needled her. "That's lovely about the fish," she said, shortly. "Now, let's get back to *Distant Desire*. I have some discussion questions…"

Horatio, Branda and Nora didn't look remotely interested.

Siegfried played with a piece of loose wool on his hat and Martha felt her neck flushing from frustration. "Or, perhaps you'd like to read a passage from the book, Branda?"

Branda used her hand as a shield and whispered into Nora's ear. Nora gasped in reply.

Martha stared at the two women and wondered if she had actually turned invisible. If she pulled a silly face, or did a waltz, would anyone even notice?

She stood for a few moments and looked down at *Distant Desire*, but instead she pictured Zelda's book and the blackbird illustration. She shook her head and the image vanished. The sound of Branda and Nora talking persisted as a loud buzz. "Siegfried," she tried. "Perhaps you'd like to read for us?"

Siegfried's eyes shifted to the right, as if checking that the front doors were still open.

Horatio held up his palms. "I didn't read the book," he said. "Too busy cleaning out the aquarium."

Martha's felt her temples begin to throb. She wrapped her fingers tightly around Lucinda's book. When anyone in the group wanted her to do things, she did them. It would be nice if they returned her favors, occasionally.

She didn't want to read aloud, not having done it since Will and Rose were small. Being a focus of any attention made her cheeks go blotchy. "Anyone?" she asked again, to blank faces.

Trying to fight off feelings of resentment, she opened the book. She ran her finger down the page but her eyes were sore and wouldn't focus properly. She hastily selected a paragraph, any passage, to win back their attention, and began to read. "'She reared up in front of him,'" she started.

Nora and Branda stopped talking.

Martha took a breath. At last, this seemed to be working. Everyone was looking at her. "'She reared up in front of him. Her breath was heavy, like a cheetah who'd run across a semi-

THE LIBRARY OF LOST AND FOUND 61

arid desert. She was tall, and her red silk dress clung to her
body, emphasizing the swell of her'...um..."

Her eyes widened as she read the next words to herself, and
then out loud. She didn't recall them being this passionate.
"'Of her,' um, 'large, heaving...' Apologies, that part doesn't
seem very, um, suitable..." She coughed and tried to find another section to read instead.

Branda tittered. Nora followed suit with hiccupping giggles. Siegfried flicked his eyes toward the sci-fi shelves and
Horatio grinned. "Carry on," he said.

Martha's cheeks began to burn. If she touched them with
a wet finger they might hiss. A pain traveled up her wind-
pipe and stuck in her throat like a swallowed sweet. *Stop it*,
she wanted to say. *Stop laughing at me.*

The library doors opened and she was glad of the interrup-
tion, until she saw Clive strolling inside. He folded his arms
and leaned casually with one shoulder against a wall. He wore
a brown baggy suit that was too big for him, and his lemon-
yellow shirt puckered across his chest. He had a surprisingly
small head for his body, and orange freckles pocked his bald
head so it resembled a quail's egg. Watching intently, he smiled
at the group. "It looks like we're all having fun." He smirked.
"Are you okay, Martha? Your face is rather colorful."

She looked away from him. "Yes, of course."

The laughter in the room bounced around in her head. She
quickly reached out for a biscuit and took a bite. She munched
and the crumbles swelled in her mouth. The more she tried
to swallow, the more she struggled. She glanced around for a
glass of water but she'd forgotten to set them out.

The other group members looked at her as she gasped for
air. "You should have a drink," Branda said, without moving.

Siegfried stood up.

Martha raised her hand, telling him she was okay. She speed-walked into the small, dark kitchen. Spinning on the tap, she filled a glass with water and gulped it down. With her head hanging over the sink, she pinched the top of her nose and took deep breaths. The chattering and laughter in the library carried on as she stood alone.

After a few moments, she sensed that someone else had joined her and she turned to see Clive. He loomed in the doorway, standing there like her father used to do, making his presence felt. "Do you need anything?" he asked silkily.

"No, thank you. I'm fine now." Martha cleared her throat.

"Good. I wanted to speak to you alone, anyway," he said.

"Is it about Lucinda?"

Clive scratched his neck. "No. What about her?"

"I didn't know she'd canceled. I brought a trolley full of things. I spent a lot of time—"

"Of course, you knew," he snapped. "I told everyone."

Martha shrank like a salted slug. "Not me."

"You probably forgot or didn't pick up my message." He waved his hand dismissively. "Anyway, I heard that you requested an application form for the full-time position."

"Um, yes."

"Yes, indeed," Clive said. He folded his arms. "I've had a lot of interest in the role. Several young people with good experience, in fact."

Martha felt her insides sliding. "That must be very encouraging for you."

"Yes. I just didn't want you to be, um…disappointed."

Martha thought of the application form in her desk drawer. She hadn't even completed one word and Clive was already priming her for rejection. She opened her mouth to tell him how much she wanted the job, what she could bring to it, and how she was probably just as qualified as anyone else, but his lips were set in a fine line.

As he obstructed her way out of the kitchen, Martha had a flash of memory. Her father embraced her mother, tipped her back and kissed her, then held up a book. Martha and her mother had read it together, but she never saw it again after that day. *Beauty and the Beast.*

She hadn't thought of it for a long time and, for some reason, the memory unnerved her. The picture stuck there, like it had been pasted in her brain.

Glancing around, the kitchen walls seemed to contract, closing in on her. Her head began to feel light and she took a tentative step forward, indicating that she wanted to leave. "Sorry, I need to..."

But Clive remained there, solid and imposing. Although he was just a man, he seemed like a brick wall.

Martha bent her head, and her heart pounded. She desperately wanted to get out of this confined space. Screwing her eyes shut, she stepped forward. The door was out of reach, behind Clive's back, but she headed for it, anyway.

She felt her arm brush against the sleeve of his jacket and heard his feet move to one side.

When she finally lifted her head, she was back in the main room of the library. After the gloominess of the kitchen, she raised a hand against the glare of the fluorescent lights.

"Will you read another passage from the book for us?" Horatio winked at her.

"Can I get the washing back from you tomorrow, Martha, love?" Nora asked.

"Apply for the job, if you think you have a chance," Clive said behind her.

Martha looked back and saw his freckled scalp and blubbery lips, shining under the ceiling light. She turned and focused on Horatio's gold buttons, lipstick on Branda's front tooth and Nora's silver fillings as she laughed.

"Do you have any gluten-free biscuits?" Branda asked.

"It will be good practice for you," Clive said.

"Can you be a love and drop the laundry off for me?" Nora said. "My back is playing up."

"No," Martha said very quietly. Partly to the group, and partly to the image of her father in her head, as he held out his hand for *Beauty and the Beast*. She clenched her fists but the chattering and laughter droned on.

"There's not long until the deadline," Clive said.

"The lid is missing off this fish food. Come and take a look," Horatio grumbled.

"We should read a Scandi thriller next, Martha." Branda tapped her nails on the table. "Much more exciting than this one."

"I usually use fabric softener," Nora mused. "Can you be a love and pop some in your machine? My towels were a bit scratchy."

Martha felt a rumbling, volcano-like, deep within her. A pain stabbed her chest and she pressed her hands against it, pushing it away. Something very strange was happening to her body and she couldn't control it. Fear flickered in her eyes as she wondered what it was.

"I always wash at forty degrees," Nora said. "I suspect you set your machine at thirty, Martha, love."

"I think the Scandinavians write better thrillers," Branda said. "Don't you agree?"

The noise in the room seemed to escalate, reaching a cre-scendo in Martha's head. She raised her hands, holding them flat against her ears, yet she couldn't block out the racket that hissed and hurt her brain.

And the next thing she heard took her completely by surprise. It overwhelmed and startled her.

It was Martha's own voice, very loud and very clear.

"No," she said. "No. No. NO."

7

Crabs

The minutes following Martha's outburst whizzed past in a haze. The members of the reading group stared at her, but she couldn't absorb their expressions. The word *no* ricocheted in her head.

She whispered a quick, "Sorry," and tugged her coat from the back of a chair. She stuffed her notepad into its pocket.

As she moved quickly, her knee cracked as she stumbled over one of Nora's bags of laundry. Wobbling for a moment, she managed not to fall, and she padded her hands against the walls of the corridor to make her way to the front doors. After forcing them open, she surged outside, blinking against the brightness of the daylight.

Martha stood for a moment, shielding her eyes and not knowing what to do, or where to go. The cool February breeze kissed her fiery cheeks. She clumsily pulled on her coat, pushing an arm down a sleeve with such force that the lining ripped.

"Martha." A man's voice growled from behind her.

Startled, she turned to see Siegfried, hunched in his long

coat. When he reached out, his fingers skimmed against her wrist. Martha inched away.

He took a small step towards her and her own shuffles graduated to small steps backwards, then became bigger strides. All she could picture were laughing faces, mocking her.

She moved with pace, a small jog, along the street and past the cemetery. She'd left her handbag behind and felt her sparkly hair slide slip out. She saw it fall, then shine on the pavement before she moved on.

Her head reverberated and she couldn't think about anything clearly. As she crossed the road, a lorry sounded its horn. Everything around her sounded louder, the wheels on a bus roared on the tarmac, and she winced when a seagull cawed overhead. A car was suddenly upon her, the driver flashing his lights and shaking his fist as she leaped out of the way.

Silly, silly woman, she scolded herself. *What on earth will people think of you?*

I've left Nora's washing behind. How will I get it clean now?

Clive Folds will never give me a job.

I've not explained how to use the book-rating spreadsheet.

Shame prevented her from returning. She thrust her head down and speed-walked on, her shoulders feeling too light without her bag.

Fine drops of rain prickled her face before they turned to fat drops and she swiped them away with her fingers. A bus pulled up alongside her and the driver opened the doors. Martha hesitated, not knowing where it was heading. She pushed her hand into her pocket and felt loose change.

"Are you gettin' on board or not, darlin'?" the driver called out to her.

Martha stood motionless as people moved towards her on the pavement. A woman wearing a see-through plastic mac chased after her King Charles spaniel, and kids laughed and shoved each other as they made their way home from school. She wondered if Will and Rose were among them and, not wanting them to see her like this, she darted on board.

"Where to, darlin'?" the driver asked.

"Maltsborough, please."

"Single ticket?"

"Um, yes."

The doors shushed shut and the bus set off.

Hanging her head, she made her way to the back and slumped down onto the seat she'd shared with Will and Rose the previous day. The windows were steamed up and some-one had drawn a heart with their finger in the condensation.

A hot tear trickled down her cheek and she brushed it away, angry at her own behavior. Resilience was something she'd perfected over the years, as she catered to her parents' needs.

Towards the end of his life, her dad had shrunk in size but was still almost six feet tall. It took all her strength to help him upstairs to bed. She'd formed a hard shell to deal with the monotony of making breakfast, watching the morning news on TV, listening to the same radio shows each day, making coffee and fresh biscuits. She, her mum and dad all watched the lunchtime news together, accompanied by ham sandwiches (made by her, of course). A few quiz shows followed before Thomas and Betty took a long nap while Martha dusted and tidied around. Then she cooked dinner, usually something traditional like beef and potatoes, or a steak-and-kidney pie. This was followed by a spot of encyclopedia reading, and more news and quiz shows. She ran them a bath, helping them both into the water, one after the other, before assisting them to clean their teeth and get into bed. When she turned off the lights, there wasn't much point doing anything for herself, so she retired for the night at the same time.

She hadn't actually noticed when her parents' needs surpassed her own, like Japanese knotweed overtaking a garden. She just focused on being helpful, a dutiful daughter.

It was clear to her now, though, that she'd given up her own chance of happiness to facilitate theirs.

She took her notepad out of her pocket and stared at the green ticks, amber stars and red dots. They were a constant reminder that her only worth was in helping others.

The bus came to a halt in Maltsborough and everyone but Martha got off. She stayed on board and waited, wanting to get even farther away from Sandshift. The driver poked his head out and called down the aisle. "This is the last stop, darlin'. Hop off."

Reluctantly, she stepped off and found herself on the promenade.

Even though Maltsborough was shutting down for the day, it hummed with noise and activity. Some shop owners were already locking their doors and pulling down metal shutters over the windows. A line of traffic curved along the high street, car lights illuminating the rain that fired down. In an hour's time, all that would be open in the town were the bars and restaurants, and the amusement arcades.

Rain bounced off pavements and made people yelp, jump and run with their coats held over their heads.

Martha stooped over. Moving quickly along the seafront, she passed a group of teenagers who were bunched together, spearing chips with plastic forks.

The rain grew heavier, slinking its way down the back of her neck and soaking through the toes of her shoes. Unsure of where to go, she ducked under a shiny yellow canopy and found herself standing inside an arcade.

As children, she and Lilian weren't allowed to play on the amusements. Thomas said it was gambling, and that "No one benefits except for the arcade owners." Martha used to gaze longingly at the bright flashing lights and plastic horses jerking along their racetrack as he tugged her past them. Sometimes Zelda gave her and Lilian a sneaky penny or two to spend, but it was under strict instruction that they didn't tell their father.

Martha could usually tell when Zelda had defied Thomas, because there'd be a sticky silence around the table at teatime. Every scrape of cutlery, each bite of food would be amplified. Betty tried to overcompensate for Zelda's misdemeanors by fussing around Thomas.

Martha and Lilian had learned to be on their best behavior when this happened. They tried to be nice and good for their father, until his stormy mood blew over.

Now Martha stood and watched the rain pouncing down, and she edged farther inside the arcade. She found herself standing next to an electronic game machine where large plastic crustaceans crept out from under jagged red rocks. They chanted, "We are the bad crabs." For fifty pence, you could take up a big mallet and bash them.

"We are the bad crabs," the voice repeated and Martha's fingers twitched. There was an unusual stirring inside her stomach, of wanting to do something for herself, for once. A touch of rebellion. She had already made a fool of herself in front of people she knew.

Does it really matter if I do it again, in front of ones I don't know?

Tensing her jaw, she delved into her pocket for a fifty-pence piece and held it over the slot. A high-pitched electronic voice said, "We're ready to begin!" and Martha defiantly pushed her coin in.

Taking hold of the mallet attached to a chain, she poised, ready. Even though she still felt exhausted, she found the energy to swipe the mallet through the air. Missing the first crab, her shoulder jolted as it connected with the plastic rocks. But then she thought about the members of the reading group and managed to bring it crashing down on the head of the second crab and then the third. She hit the fourth and the fifth and kept on hammering as the crabs said "Ouch," and "Yow."

Adrenaline coursed through her veins and, with each bash, an urge to laugh rose inside her. She was so focused on the bright plastic and flashing lights that her shame and embarrassment of running away from the library evaporated.

When the game ended, she frantically felt in her pocket for more coins, eager to feel the rush of whatever-it-was again. It had been a long time since she felt so invigorated. She fed more money into the machine, then swiped and bashed until her right shoulder felt like it was on fire.

Her eyes glinted as red numbers rolled, reaching the high score, then shooting fifty points above it. This was *glorious*. A strange sensation enveloped her body but she couldn't pin down what it was.

She stared down at the last fifty-pence piece in her hand. One last go. As she pushed in her coin, across the room she saw a man holding on to the hand of a toddler. The girl clung onto a soft Minion toy and her eyes were wide open. The man pointed in Martha's direction and she saw he was talking to a police officer. The officer started to walk and there was no doubt he was headed in her direction.

"Madam," he said when he reached her. He had hairy hands like a werewolf and his eyebrows almost met in the middle. He had the weary stoop of someone who'd been dealing with minor seaside offences all day. "I'm afraid I'm going to have to ask you to leave the premises. A father has complained that you're scaring his little girl."

With her cheeks afire, Martha traipsed away from the arcade. She examined the timetable on the bus stop and there was a forty-seven-minute wait until the next one. She also re-membered that the ticket she'd bought was a single, and she'd just used up all her cash. She was stuck in Maltsborough, un-sure how she was going to get home.

The rain had subsided a little and was now more of a sprin-kle, so she decided to go for a walk, to stretch her legs and allow her adrenaline to subside. The bright lights of the bars on the promenade shone in her eyes, so she stepped inland, behind the lifeboat station.

The street was in shadows, with the lights in the upstairs windows above the shops giving the pavement a golden glow. It was easy to imagine this part of town in the earlier days, with smugglers creeping along the skinny alleys between the houses, to cart their bounty to awaiting boats.

She weaved her way around puddles, until she found her-self outside Chamberlain's. The door wore a Closed sign and, inside, the shop was pitch dark.

She peered in the window, at the display, at a vintage edi-tion of *The Hobbit*, old train magazines and a full series of *Famous Fives* piled haphazardly. The sight of Anne and Timmy on the covers made her heart flip. They were her favorite characters, though Zelda said they were too middle-class and that she preferred the tomboy, George.

The corner of the window featured an eclectic array of leaflets—a one-eyed black cat found near the sports center, a fairground in Benton Bay and an advert for Monkey Puz-zle Books. She reached out and touched its logo, a tree with books as its leaves.

Moving towards the doorway, Martha mused if Owen lived above the shop, or if he had a house elsewhere. Her fingers curled in her pocket as she fought the urge to knock on the door. The sign confirmed that the shop didn't open again until

Wednesday. But Owen *had* said that he'd call her. At home, the red light might be flashing on her answer machine.

After the disastrous reading group session and being asked to leave the arcade, Martha wondered if she had anything to lose. In fact, the thought of doing something out of character again gave her a small buzz. And she wanted Zelda's book back.

She knocked on the glass, not giving herself the chance to talk herself out of it. Her pulse raced as she waited for a response.

A few moments later a light went on in the back room. A large, dark shape moved through the doorway and towards the door. A face appeared at the glass and Martha raised her hand in a short wave.

"Martha." She heard her name, muffled, from inside the shop. The door rattled and opened. Owen stood with bare feet. His suit was crumpled and he munched on a slice of toast. "You're soaked wet through."

She nodded meekly, noticing that the sleeves of her coat shone wet in the dark.

"When I left you the message, I didn't expect you to come over," he said. "Come inside."

Martha heard her shoes squelch as she stepped into the shop. So he *had* rung her. Wondering if he'd found anything made the skin on her forearms tingle.

"I'll put the kettle on…" He glanced at the small puddles on his floor. "And my slippers, too." He closed the door behind her and locked it.

She followed him around the counter and into a storeroom. It was full of boxes, but not positioned neatly, as in her dining room. These ones were all different sizes, stored at angles. Some were ripped with books poking out and some were still taped up.

"Sit down." Owen gestured to a high wooden stool and she

hitched herself up onto it. He tapped the switch on the side of a kettle and an orange light glowed. "I thought you might be interested in my message."

Martha wasn't sure how to tell him that she didn't know what it was. But then he might think her showing up on his doorstep at night was very strange. So instead she said, "Yes. Very much."

Owen peered into a cup, then shook in instant coffee from a jar. He poured in hot water, then added a glug of milk and a spoonful of sugar, without asking how she took it. "Here," he said. "This should warm you up."

Martha wrapped her hands around the cup and waited for it to cool down. Owen leaned casually against a stack of boxes that was taller than him. "Better?" he asked. "Do you want a slice of toast?"

She shook her head and a raindrop trickled down her forehead. "No, thank you. About your message…" she hinted.

"It's a gorgeous title, isn't it?" Owen said.

"Yes, it's lovely."

"Very evocative."

"Yes. Um, what was it again?"

Owen shrugged. "*Blue Skies and Stormy Seas.* Dexter had to do a fair bit of searching around to find it. He left me a message this afternoon and I called you straightaway."

"I was hosting a reading group, at the library."

"And you got my message and came over?" he said with a smile.

"Something like that."

"Dexter thinks the book was definitely self-published. He's going to see if he can find out where it was printed and the date."

"And did he find out the author's name?" Martha asked casually, as she blew into her coffee.

"It's by E. Y. Sanderson," Owen said. "Dexter doesn't think he's written anything else."

Martha's fingers twitched. Her cup shook and coffee ran, hot, over the back of her hand. It dribbled along her wrist and down her sleeve.

"Whoops." Owen ripped off a piece of kitchen toweling and handed it to her. "Are you okay?"

She nodded.

"You kind of threw coffee at yourself."

Martha dabbed at her wrist. "I think the author is a *she*," she said quietly.

Instinctively, she knew deep inside that there could only be one possibility for the book's authorship.

"Excuse me?"

"E. Y. Sanderson is a lady," she told him. "Ezmerelda Yvette Sanderson. It's my nana's full name."

Owen insisted on driving Martha back home. She sat in his car stiffly, aware that her wet coat would dampen the seat. The foot well of his old Ford Focus was full of stuff—screwed-up carrier bags, paper bags and car park receipts. "Sorry about the mess," he said as he batted an empty sandwich packet off the dashboard.

Still feeling dizzy from the revelation that Zelda had written the book, Martha sank down in her seat.

"It's so cool that your grandmother was the author," Owen said as they turned the corner, onto the coastal road back to Sandshift. "But didn't you say they were *your* stories?"

Martha nodded. It was too confusing to think about this now. She wondered why she'd never seen a copy of the book before, if Zelda had written it. With too many questions swirling around in her head, she just wanted to get home. She managed to answer Owen's comments and questions with a range of *hmm*s and nods, until they neared the library.

Martha pulled up the collar on her coat, in an attempt to go incognito in case anyone was around. "Please drop me here," she said, when they reached the end of her road.

"Are you sure this is close enough to where you live?"

"Yes," Martha said, momentarily distracted by the sight of her shopping trolley parked back outside the house. She wondered if Siegfried had returned it. "It's a narrow road to get the car down. I'll walk from here."

"I'll call you about the book as soon as Dexter gets back in touch."

"I don't know how to thank you."

Owen shrugged. "Coffee and cake is always good."

Martha got out of the car and gave him a small wave. As she took her keys out of her pocket, she caught sight of something small and glinting in the trolley. She picked out her hair slide and held it between her thumb and forefinger for a moment. It shone under a streetlamp and she fastened it back into her hair.

When she opened her front door, the dragon's head gave her a stiff smile, and she gave it one in return.

The cuckoo clock ticked and Martha stood in the middle of the room. It had gone past nine o'clock, her father's supper time, and it still felt strange that he was no longer here. There was no smell of burnt toast, the way he liked it.

Martha patted the dragon on its head and swung an invisible mallet through the air. She tossed her notepad onto the dining table, too tired to take a look at which tasks she'd failed to accomplish.

As she slumped in the wooden chair and looked out the window at the glistening sea, she leaned over and pressed the button on the answer machine. Then she closed her eyes and let the sound of Owen's warm tones wash over her. She liked the way he said *Blue Skies and Stormy Seas*, like he was reading a bedtime story.

She thought about the strange sensation that had engulfed her in the arcade, as she bashed the crabs. She'd been unable to identify it before, but now she could.

Freedom. She imagined it might be what freedom felt like.

8

Chinese Dragon

"Martha. *Martha.*"

A voice shouted from outside and the doorbell rang, but Martha wasn't sure if the sounds were in her dream or not.

She'd slept fitfully through the night, dreaming of the Sandshift sea, and its inky waves. A fishing boat rocked, in trouble, and she stood rooted to a spot on the sands. She frantically waved her arms but there was no one around to see or hear her. As she waded into the water, it sloshed around her ankles, then her knees and thighs. The boat bobbed and vanished. Martha tried to shout, but the water lapped at her chest and then chin. She felt the sea bed beneath her toes and then it was gone. Twisting in the water, she was far from shore. The waves chilled her bones and pulled her under. No one could save her. She thrashed until she gave up and let herself sink slowly down.

It was a recurring dream that she'd had since she was a child. Sometimes it might be months until it invaded her sleep, and she thought it might have gone, but then she'd close her eyes and find herself battling the ferocity of the waves again.

"*Martha.*"

The call of her name brought her back to the safety of her own room. She opened one eye and then the other. Relief washed over her when she realized she was in her bed.

With a shiver and her nightie clinging to her chest from sweat, she noticed she'd kicked all the covers off the bed. She scooped them up and gathered them around her. Her arms were sore and stiff from handling the hammer, and she groaned as she pulled on her dressing gown. As her previous day's actions began to speckle back into her memory, she didn't want to see or speak to anyone.

The doorbell rang again and she slid wearily off the mattress. She pushed her feet into her slippers and trod downstairs. Grudgingly opening the front door, she blinked against the daylight.

"Congrats, you did it!" Suki thrust a small bunch of freesias at her chest. She wore a long purple tie-dyed dress and glittery sandals more suited to the Mediterranean. The back of her hands were henna-painted with intricate flowers.

Martha took hold of the freesias and stared at them, remembering how a vase full always sat on the dining room table. As soon as her dad died, she bought roses instead. "I did what, exactly?" she asked.

"You said *no*. It's a spectacular phenomenon–on, or whatever the word is."

"Thank you, but not really." Martha fiddled with her dressing gown belt as she recalled her behavior. "I need to apologize to everyone. I overreacted and need to explain that..."

However, Suki crossed her legs and bounced up and down. She pushed Martha's handbag into her arms. "You left this behind at the library yesterday. Sorry, but I need the loo," she winced. "The baby is kicking my bladder."

Martha glanced behind her, at her job-laden floor. Nora's bin bags looked like giant boulders and the Chinese dragon's head grinned at her with its wonky white teeth. She didn't want Suki to see all her stuff. "Um, I—"

But she had already pushed past and vanished up the stairs.

Martha set the freesias in some water. She moved a few of Horatio's potted plants off the dining table and set the vase down. Staring around the room, she wondered what she could do to quickly tidy up the place, but she'd need a small bulldozer to make any impression in the next few minutes.

"I'm not sure why making an idiot of myself is cause for celebration," she said, when Suki returned. "I'm sorry for..."

However, Suki stood with her mouth hung open. She didn't look around at the boxes and bags. Instead she focused on one thing. "Is that a Chinese dragon?" she asked.

Martha gave a small shrug, remembering Lilian's disbelieving stare when she first encountered the colorful beast. "It's only the head, and it's child-sized. I said I'd fix his ear and cheek for the school..." She trailed her words away, her offer suddenly sounding ridiculous. As she surveyed her other tasks, she couldn't even recall volunteering to do some of them, though her notepad would tell her otherwise.

"It's awesome." Suki dropped awkwardly to her knees while holding her bump. Placing her hand in the dragon's mouth, she tested the sharpness of its teeth with her fingers and ran her palm over its shiny red tongue. "Why do you need to say sorry to people?"

"For whatever you heard. For being rude."

"You stood up for yourself. I feel quite proud of you."

Martha wondered how anyone could feel this way about her. She pulled out her wooden chair and sat down with a thump. "How do you even know all this?"

"Horatio told me. He said he liked your traumatic reading."

Martha hoped she meant *dramatic* reading. She held her head in her hands and couldn't think what to say. Everything seemed to be failing. Her quest to be reliable and indispens-able was falling apart. "I made such an idiot of myself in front of Clive, and I really want the job at the library. Sorry."

"You shouldn't keep saying that. You don't owe anything to anyone. Don't come back to the library until you're ready. Clive can help out, for once." Suki gave an impromptu guf-faw of laughter. "It's so like you, to tackle a dragon's head."

Martha opened her mouth to protest, then realized she couldn't do it. Suki was right.

She surveyed the dragon's head, and the absurdity of having this monstrous beast in her dining room made a small ner-vous laugh rise. "I don't know anything about papier-mâché."

Suki heaved herself upright. "Well, I do. I love crafty stuff. I've always wanted to try papier-mâché but didn't have a proj-ect. I'll help you, if you like? It will keep my mind off Ben."

Martha stared at her. *She* was the one who helped people out. Suki was the first person in a long time to offer her any assistance.

She had an overwhelming feeling of wanting to throw a hug but wasn't sure if it would be welcome, or if she even re-membered how to do it correctly. She tensed her arms to stop herself. "I'd really appreciate that," she said.

"Now, what did Owen Chamberlain say about your book?"

Pleased by her interest, Martha explained how she had vis-ited the shop, and that Owen received the book to repair from one of his contacts.

"I called there again last night, after the reading group ses-sion," she said. "He found out the book's title is *Blue Skies and Stormy Seas*, and it was written by E. Y. Sanderson. That's my nana's full name. What's really strange is that the stories are ones she told me when I was a child, and ones I made up to share with her. She must have written them down and printed them in the book." She shook her head, thinking how un-likely this sounded.

She waited for Suki to tell her she was being ridiculous, as Lilian might, but instead the young library assistant folded her arms. "Well, it sounds like you're determined to find out more," she said.

Martha considered this for a moment. She thought about how Lilian always told her what to do, and how she obeyed without question. Just as she always did what her father wanted. Doing things for others no longer gave her the rush of satis-faction she looked for.

Instead she found herself wanting to explore the unusual feeling of freedom that she'd experienced in the arcade. She couldn't remember the last time her nerves jingled with an-ticipation, and she decided that she quite liked it. "Owen is going to try and find out the name of the printer and date of the book, to see if it ties in with the date of Zelda's dedica-tion. Of course, that's highly unlikely—"

"But what if it does?"

Martha flicked her hair. "It won't do. I mean, it's not pos-sible. Zelda died three years before that date, so it can't be right. Owen's info will just clarify that."

"And then what, *Miss Marple*?"

"I prefer *Lisbeth Salander*." Martha shifted in her chair. "I suppose everything will go back to normal." Images flashed in her head of saying no to the reading group, and the orange plastic crabs, and Owen and his red monogrammed slippers, and she wasn't sure what *normal* was any longer.

"And what if you find out otherwise?"

Martha shrugged.

"Well, what would *Lisbeth* do?"

Martha mused upon this. *The Girl with the Dragon Tattoo* wouldn't sit on her backside and do nothing. She wouldn't let

Lilian dictate what she did. She wouldn't offer to wash chandeliers or water potted plants. "She'd take matters into her own hands," she said. "She'd move things along."

"Sounds like a good idea."

Martha nodded. She considered her next move. Although it was Tuesday and she knew Chamberlain's wasn't open, a call to say thank you for the ride home wasn't unreasonable. And she could ask if there had been any advancement in Dexter's research.

"I'll get dressed and have something to eat," she said. "Then I'll make my move."

Martha took a long, hot bath, then made beans on toast and coffee. She moved a couple of boxes from her dining room floor and placed them against her wall.

She was pleased that she'd answered the door to Suki. It had been good to have another person in the house, other than Lilian.

After the cuckoo sang three times in the afternoon, she positioned herself in the wooden chair, straightened her skirt and picked up the phone.

When Owen didn't pick up and she heard his answerphone message, she felt a plunge of disappointment; however, she didn't hang up. She inhaled, closed her eyes and then spoke. "Hello, Mr. Chamberlain. I wanted to thank you for your kindness last night, for driving me home. And I also wanted to…"

As she thought of what to say next, someone answered. "Hello," a voice said. "Who is this?"

Martha frowned, sure she'd dialed the number correctly. "It's Martha Storm, from the library."

"Oh, sorry. I couldn't get to the phone in time. Dad's out… This is Greg."

"Greg?"

"Owen's son."

Now he said this, it made sense to Martha. He spoke in a similar way to Owen, searching around for his words. His voice was a little deeper and slower.

"Well, I'm sorry for disturbing you," she said, surprised at how disappointed she felt not reaching Owen. "Please tell your father I rang, and—"

"Dad told me about you," Greg chipped in. "I've not seen him so animated for a long time. You're phoning about the date and photo, right?"

Martha's right eyebrow twitched upwards. "Um, I don't know anything about those."

"Oh, right. Didn't you get Dad's email?"

"I'm not at work today to access a computer." She ran a hand through her hair. "What's the photo of?"

"I'm not sure. It's part of a newspaper clipping, I think. Dexter emailed Dad and he forwarded it on to you."

Martha bit her lip, wondering how she could get to see it. The library closed on Tuesdays and she didn't want to wait until the next day. Perhaps she could let herself into the building without bumping into anyone who'd witnessed her embarrassing outburst.

"Um, is that okay?" Greg asked.

"Yes. It's fine," Martha said, her eyes flicking towards her pantry, where she kept a set of emergency keys. "I'm sure I can figure something out."

9

Sandcastles

Betty, 1976

Betty smoothed down her new orange silk dress and admired her matching pumps. The dress was a little too tight, and the cut wasn't one she'd have chosen for herself. The shoes were also slightly wide for her feet. But how wonderful it was for Thomas to treat her, for her thirtieth birthday.

The new hairbrush and hand cream that Martha and Lilian bought her lay on the bedcover, and the girls were now downstairs preparing her breakfast.

Thomas stood on the other side of the bed, waiting for Betty's reaction. "They do fit, don't they?" he asked.

Betty didn't answer at first. She didn't want to admit she needed a larger size dress, as that might spoil his efforts. If she lost a little weight, the dress would fit perfectly. If she concentrated when she was walking, the shoes wouldn't slip off. "Yes, of course," she said with a smile. "They're so lovely. Thank you."

"Fantastic," Thomas said. "You look beautiful."

As she reached down to pick up the ripped wrapping paper,

Betty couldn't help wondering how much the dress and shoes cost. Whenever she wanted to meet a friend for coffee, or buy a new jar of face cream, she had to ask Thomas for money. Most of the time he gave it to her freely, but sometimes he questioned her, reminding her that it didn't grow on trees.

She crumpled the paper into a ball and held it. The one thing she wanted above anything else, was the one thing she didn't have. A job. Then she could earn money and buy things, for her and the girls. She'd be free of the embarrassment of asking Thomas for it.

When she gave a little sigh, he detected it. "Is there anything wrong?"

"No. I was just thinking that I'd like to contribute, financially, to the household. The dress and shoes are so lovely, but I need some practical clothes to wear, too. The girls are growing out of their things…" She sought out her husband's eyes. "I'm thinking of looking for work."

Thomas nodded, an understanding smile on his face. "You know, that's one of the things I love about you, Betty. You're always so considerate, thinking of others. But you do such a great job at home. You should enjoy your time with the girls, while they're young. Let me take care of all the boring adult stuff. I loved that my mum stayed at home. She didn't work and the whole family really benefited from it. Besides…" he hesitated.

"Yes?"

"Well…" His pause went on for too long. "You're not getting any younger, and you don't really have any experience."

Betty could admit this was true. She was only nineteen, fresh out of secretarial college, when Martha appeared. She suspected the skills she'd learned there would be out-of-date in today's workplace. She hadn't had a chance to put any of them into practice. "I could learn on the job," she said. "And it would be nice to meet new people and have a few adult conversations during the day."

Thomas gave a roar of laughter. "Yes, you can't really call conversations with your mother *adult*, can you? All I'm saying is, there's no rush. Lilian is only six. Why not wait until she starts secondary school?"

Betty gave a wry smile as she fingered the ball of wrapping paper. As usual, he made sense. "It was just a thought."

"And a very practical one." He kissed her on the forehead. "Now, I thought that the girls and I could take you to the beach, for a picnic lunch. I can't think of a nicer place to spend your birthday afternoon."

Betty's smile froze on her lips. "Oh. I said I'd take them to the funfair in town, with Mum. I thought you'd be in work today."

"I took the day off especially, as a surprise," Thomas said. "I'm sure your mother will understand."

Betty stopped herself from sucking in through her teeth. "I've already arranged to meet her there. We were going to get hot dogs and candy floss."

Thomas pursed his lips. "Really? You want the girls to eat that stuff? Those types of places aren't clean. And then, there's the people…"

"What do you mean?"

"The awful types who run those places." He sniffed. "I'm sure Martha and Lilian would prefer a lovely family picnic instead."

Betty closed her eyes, feeling pulled in two between Thomas and her mother. "It *is* my birthday," she whispered, to see if he might reconsider.

"Of course it is." Thomas walked over and planted a kiss in her hair. "So, it's totally your choice, birthday girl. I *know* you'll make the right one."

★ ★ ★

Martha folded her arms and huffed when Betty told her that they weren't going to the fair. Lilian let out an indignant, "No." She stomped around for a while and threw a doll on her bed.

Betty gritted her teeth while she made the sandwiches and sausage rolls. She picked up the phone and called her mother.

"Your husband thinks he's in charge," Zelda said, when Betty explained Thomas had taken time off work for a picnic. "The girls want to go to the fair."

"It's a beautiful day, and they'll love sandwiches down on the—"

"It's *your* day," Zelda interrupted. "*You* should decide."

Betty felt her temples begin to throb. "It's fine, Mum. I don't mind."

"I wanted to take them for candy floss."

"They can have an ice cream instead."

"Okay then. I'll get them a cone each with syrup and sprinkles. And a chocolate flake."

Betty screwed an eye shut as a sharp pain pierced her forehead. "Um, I think Thomas wants the picnic to be for just the four of us."

"Oh, just ignore him for once." Zelda sighed. "I'm sure he won't mind if I tag along, too."

It had been a long, hot summer. Dogs panted into rock pools and lollies melted on their sticks as soon as their wrappers came off. Betty and Thomas carried the wicker picnic basket between them, holding a handle each. Betty's head pounded as she spread out a tartan blanket on the sand and she wished she'd taken a paracetamol. She wriggled to get comfortable in her new dress.

Martha and Lilian discovered a broken purple bucket and

spade and they started to play with them before their dad could tell them the toys were *dirty*.

Thomas sat in a deck chair with his ankles crossed. He wore his suit and work shoes even though the sun beat down, making sticky fingers out of his black hair.

Zelda appeared beside the mermaid statue and waved.

Thomas sat up taller and his eyes narrowed. "Is that bloody *Zelda*?"

"Um," Betty glanced over. She hadn't been able to find the words to tell him that her mother was coming along and she felt her shoulders shrink. "Oh yes, it is."

"Did you invite her?"

Betty's mouth grew dry as Thomas's eyes bored into her. She jumped to her feet and waved both arms, an attempt to tell her mother not to buy any sweet stuff. They should eat the sandwiches first. But it was too late. Zelda vanished behind the ice cream van. "She kind of invited herself," Betty said.

Zelda reappeared a few minutes later. Her long turquoise dress billowed in the breeze as she carried back five cones, each with two chocolate flakes and multicolored sugar sprinkles on top.

Martha and Lilian ran towards their nana and excitedly prized their cones from her fingers. They ran their tongues around the ice cream, catching the dribbles.

Thomas glowered, his face scarlet and shiny. He sniffed and looked away when Zelda offered him a cone. She shrugged and ate his, as well as her own.

After they finished the cones, Betty unpacked the sandwiches. They were met with little enthusiasm. "I'm too full," Martha groaned, and Thomas gave Betty a knowing nod.

Lilian sat by Thomas's feet with her cheek pressed against his trouser leg. She only took two bites of her sandwich, then traced her fingers lazily in the sand. Thomas reached out and ran his hand softly over the top of her hair.

Martha shoveled sand into the cracked bucket. She patted it down, then upturned the bucket. "Ta-da," she said as she slid it off to reveal her creation. A corner of a turret slipped away, the sand too dry to take hold. "It's Rapunzel's castle, Mum."

"It's beautiful, darling," Betty smiled.

Thomas lowered his paper. He leaned over and examined it. "Now, that's not very good, is it? It's falling down." He lifted his leg and brought down the heel of his shoe, grinding the castle flat. "Try building another one."

Martha stared at the ruins and then at her father. Her nostrils flared. She snatched up her sandwich and took a huge bite, staring at him and chewing with her mouth open.

Betty pushed her tongue against her teeth. *Don't say anything*, she willed. *Just leave it.* She walked her fingers along the sand to take hold of Martha's hand, but felt it snatch away.

"I passed by the funfair," Zelda said as she bit into a sausage roll. "It looks ah-mazing. With a capital A."

Thomas turned the page of his newspaper noisily.

"Yes, but, let's stay here," Betty said. "It's so lovely, all sitting together in the sunshine."

Zelda gave a small "Hmm," then tossed her head. She picked up her bag and rooted around inside it. "I've brought your birthday present," she exclaimed. "I almost forgot to give it to you."

Martha and Lilian stopped what they were doing and shuffled forward on their knees. Zelda handed Betty a small silver package.

Betty took hold of it and squeezed. Thomas lowered his paper and peered over the top.

"Go on. Open it. The suspense is killing me." Zelda laughed.

Betty slowly peeled off the tape and opened the paper. There was something small, red and satiny nestled inside. It seemed to have thin strings and see-through bits. Martha frowned at it, trying to make out what it was. When Lilian reached out with one finger to touch it, Betty quickly folded the paper up again. "That's, um, lovely. Thanks, Mum."

"Hold it up," Zelda said. "You've not seen it properly. It's all in one piece. When I saw it, I had to buy it for you. And no doubt, Thomas will benefit, too." She gave an exaggerated cough and a speck of sausage roll pastry flew from her mouth, flecking Thomas's trousers.

He looked down at it in disgust and held up his paper to cover his eyes.

Betty felt her cheeks burning. Why couldn't her mother buy her bath salts or a nice scarf, something pretty that she couldn't afford herself? She knew Thomas would hate the gift, especially as her mum had presented it in front of the girls.

She often felt like there was an electrical storm around him, and she could sense it crackling now, between him and Zelda. She wondered if her mother could feel it, too, but Zelda always seemed oblivious to the impact of her actions or words on others.

"Thank you," Betty said again, and she shoved the red silky gift to the bottom of her handbag.

A little later, Betty watched as Zelda and Martha knelt down, their heads dipped into a huge hole, digging with their hands. The tightness of her dress prevented her from joining in.

"We're going to find Australia soon," Zelda shouted out. "Or hell. I think I can see the tips of the devil's trident down here."

Thomas glared in her direction but focused his attention

on Betty instead. "Please do something about your mother. She's always filling Martha's head with nonsense."

"They're only playing, Thomas."

"But it influences Martha to write those silly stories of hers."

Betty counted to five silently in her head. "I'll see if they want to do something else. We could maybe go and look inside the cave."

Thomas nodded. "That's a good idea. And I think I'll have a sleep, after that delicious lunch. What a shame there's so much of it left over."

Betty stood up and picked up her new shoes. She walked over to tell Zelda, who gave Thomas a sideways glance. "Tell me we're not being sent away because of His Royal Highness?" She sighed.

"No, of course not. We can shelter from the sun for a while. Martha's shoulders are looking a bit fiery. Put some sun cream on," she said, but Martha stood up and began to run towards the teardrop-shaped hollow.

The sand on the floor of the cave was cool and the walls were clammy. Zelda and Martha took it in turns to yodel, their voices booming around inside. At the back of the cave there was a gap in the rocks, a vertical, person-sized slit.

"Can we go through there?" Martha pointed.

"Let's just sit down, and keep our clothes nice and clean," Betty said. She had been through the gap once with a local boy, Daniel McLean. She still remembered his fingers, warm through the thinness of her cotton shirt. They'd held hands in the darkness and kissed, her first time. Reaching up, she pressed her fingers to her lips and held them there. Daniel was the opposite to Thomas. He was sensitive, caring and her own age. She still missed him.

"We can try to squeeze through." Zelda took off her headscarf and sunglasses, then stuffed them into her pocket. "I'm ready for action if you are."

Martha tugged on Betty's hand. "Come on, Mum."

Thoughts of Daniel disappeared as Betty looked out at her husband in his deck chair. From the way his hands had fallen to his sides, she could tell he was asleep. His newspaper had dropped to the ground and Lilian played by his feet. "It's okay, you go ahead," she said. "I'll stay here."

"What for?" In the dimness of the cave, Zelda's eyes squinted. "So Thomas can keep an eye on you?"

"Oh, don't be silly, Mum," Betty said, moving her hand away from Martha's. "I think he's asleep, and I need to watch Lilian."

Zelda climbed up the rocks with bare feet. There was a flash of turquoise as her skirt disappeared through the gap, then her hand reappeared in a playful claw. "Grrr."

Martha followed her. She giggled and grabbed hold of her fingers. "Bye, Mum," she said as she vanished, too.

Betty idled around, walking in small circles, tracing her toes over shells and shingle. After a couple of minutes, she heard a big splash and then another. Raising herself up onto her tiptoes, she called out, "What's going on back there?" She listened out for a reply, but all she could hear was splashing and laughter. She stepped up onto a rock and poked her head into the gap, her eyes adjusting to the gloominess. "Helloooo."

Her mother and daughter sat in a pool of shallow water. Their skirts swirled as Martha hit the water with her palms and Zelda flicked back.

Betty smiled but then felt it slip. Her mother and daughter were so close to each other. She'd noticed that if Zelda was around, Martha ran to her first, if she skinned her knee or wanted to share a book. She also saw that Thomas and Lilian had formed a two-person mutual fan club.

Betty was the odd one out.

She shivered as a drop of water fell onto her shoulder from the roof of the cave. *What a silly thought*, she told herself. *It must be the heat.*

"Tell me a story," Zelda asked Martha. "I want one about jewels, or a mermaid."

"You tell *me* one," Martha flipped her wrist, splashing her nana's chest.

"No, you tell me." Zelda used both hands to push the sea in her granddaughter's direction.

Martha's laughter ricocheted and they both stood up, their dresses clinging, soaking, to their thighs.

Betty cupped her hand to her mouth. "Don't get too wet in there," she called, but they were only interested in each other. She didn't usually feel jealous, but as she watched her mother and daughter, it crept over her now like winter frost across a window.

She glanced outside at the beach, watching as Lilian stood up and skipped towards the cave. "Daddy's fast asleep," she said when she arrived. "What shall we do now, Mummy?"

Betty took her hand. "What do you want to do, darling?"

"The fair. Let's go to the funfair."

Betty shook her head. "Sorry," she started. "Daddy says we can't go there."

"But he's asleep."

Betty chewed her lip as she pondered this. Thomas had only been asleep for a few minutes. He'd complained about being tired after a busy week at work. She had enough time to take the girls, and her mother, for a quick visit. If he woke up, she would say they'd been for a walk.

"Pleeeease, Mummy."

Betty scratched her neck. Then Martha and Zelda's laughter echoed around inside the cave, and the envious feeling crawled over her again.

This could be a chance for the four of them to spend time together on her birthday, her original plan. She could escape the constant tension between her mum and husband.

If she swore them to secrecy, she could keep everyone happy.

And with that thought, Betty made a decision.

She angled her face towards the slit in the rocks again and shouted. "Okay, let's go to the funfair. You can tell your story on the way, Martha, and dry off your clothes."

She listened as the laughter stopped. "Dad said we can't go," Martha hollered back.

"Oh, that's okay," Betty called out, nonchalantly. "I'm sure he won't mind."

Again, she had to wait for the reply.

"Okay," Martha said. "We'll come back out."

Betty took Lilian's hand, and Zelda held Martha's. They walked out of the cave and across the sand, toward the mermaid statue, and Martha told her story.

The Fisherman and the Mermaid

Each day at sunrise, a lonely mermaid watched as a handsome fisherman loaded lobster pots into his boat. Even though she loved the sea, and the fish, and her friends, the mermaid wished that she could be with the fisherman instead. He looked strong and caring, and his life on shore seemed idyllic.

One day, a silvery sea lion appeared on a rock beside her, as she combed her hair. In his flipper was a large cone-shaped shell. "If you blow into this shell," he said, "it will allow you to grow legs so you can go ashore. You can meet your fisherman. However, you won't ever be able to return to the sea."

For six days and six nights, the mermaid swam up and down the shore. She watched the fisherman carry out his empty lobster pots to the boat, and watched as he brought them back again, with orange claws poking through.

On the seventh day, the mermaid decided that she'd had enough of the sea and she yearned for something different. She wanted to be with the fisherman. So, she took hold of the shell and blew into it. Then she closed her eyes and everything fell dark.

She woke on the sand, with the sun shining into her eyes, and she felt strange because her tail no longer flicked. In its place were two feet with pretty toes. And the fisherman stood, tall, above her. He held out his hand to help her to stand up, and it was difficult because she'd never done it before.

He led her to his hut on the beach, where he read stories to her, about the sea, until she felt stronger. However, whenever he asked where she came from, she made up a story. She didn't tell him that she once lived in the sea.

Soon, the fisherman and the mermaid fell in love and they had a baby together. But when their little girl was born, she had a fish's scaly tail.

"I can't understand it." The fisherman scratched his head.

"Me neither," the mermaid lied and cried. "What can we do?"

The mermaid and the fisherman talked for many nights until they reached a decision. They would set the baby free in the sea. They were very sad but the baby was unhappy in the hut and her eyes lit up when she saw the waves.

As soon as the fisherman and the mermaid lowered her into the water, a smile fell on the baby's lips and she swam away.

"She'll visit us each day, don't worry," the mermaid told the fisherman, as she held his hand tightly.

But they never saw their daughter again. And, although the mermaid loved her husband with all her heart, she wished that she hadn't met him, because she had been happy as she was.

10

Photograph

Martha picked up the key from the hook in her pantry and stared at it. It had hung there for two years, unused, on a piece of tatty pink ribbon. Clive had asked her to look after it in case the burglar alarm sounded out of hours at the library.

"Everyone else has a family," Clive had said, with a condescending smile. "If you get a call in the middle of the night, it doesn't matter as much, does it?"

Martha slipped the key into her coat pocket. She flipped on her hood and left the house.

She'd missed out on her walk down to the mermaid statue that morning, and she didn't go there now.

Horatio was sweeping out his aquarium, and she saw Branda struggling to open the door to the Lobster Pot, because her arms were laden with designer label shopping bags. Martha thrust her head down, pretending not to see them, and carried on.

Her limbs weren't stiff when she walked, and she didn't need to pump her arms. She walked swiftly and with purpose, directly to the library.

She glanced around furtively before she opened the doors

and then locked them behind her. Leaving the light turned off, she made her way into the main room.

The building was deliciously quiet and the books stood in lines like silent soldiers. The daylight outside was dimming, so the room was in semidarkness. Long shadows cut across the carpet and walls and Martha trod quietly across the carpet. Her book-rating spreadsheets still lay on the table, along with two copies of *Distant Desire*.

Usually, Martha would tidy things up, but today she sat down at the desk and switched on the library computer. It was an old thing, constructed from white plastic that had turned a creamy yellow over the years. It clunked and whirred, as if there was a small man sitting inside it firing up cogs and flicking switches. Finally, the library logo appeared and she typed in her password.

There were a few emails from Clive and she ignored those. She only had eyes for the one from Owen. She paused, her fingers hovering over the keys, before she clicked on it.

Hi Martha

Dexter called this morning. He found that your book was published in 1985, so the dedication to you looks like its dated correctly. We also managed to trace the company who printed it, to Scandinavia!

Dexter said there was an old newspaper clipping in the book. He gave it to his wife because she likes vintage stuff. I asked him to copy it and I've attached it here, so you can see if it means anything to you.

See you soon for coffee?
Owen

Martha scratched her head. Scandinavia? How could her stories have reached all that way? And if her nana had written the message in 1985, then it meant her parents *had* lied about her death. She circled a hand over her stomach, rubbing away a feeling of unease.

Clicking on the attachment in the email, she watched as the screen spooled before the image opened. It was on its side, so she turned her head to the left to see it properly. It was grainy, a small article about a funfair, and Martha immediately recognized the three people in its accompanying photo.

She and Lilian sat on a wall, either side of Zelda. Behind them, Martha could make out a sign for the Hall of Mirrors. Her nana grinned and there was a black spot under her top lip. Martha moved her face closer to the screen, wondering what it was. As she stared at it, a memory emerged and developed in her mind.

At the fair, Zelda had eaten a toffee apple and there was a crunching sound. When she pulled it away from her lips, a molar stuck out of the red shiny sugar, leaving in its place a bloody gap. Zelda plucked it out and held it up, and the three of them marveled at the size of its root.

Martha didn't remember having a photograph taken, though. And she thought that her mother had been there, too.

She touched her nana's cheek and then focused on the image of herself. An impromptu sob rose inside her, brought on by this younger portrait. She'd never thought of herself as being pretty before but, in this image, she most certainly was.

Her hair frizzed out of its plait. She was smiling and looked carefree.

Martha reached up and touched her existing dry curls.

As she closed the image, she wondered how the clipping came to be inserted into the little battered book.

Rubbing her chin, she was about to close Owen's email when she spotted an addition to his message.

PS: I've also tracked down another copy of your book! Rita at Monkey Puzzle has a pristine version. I'll see what she can tell us about it ☺.

Martha swallowed. She spun to one side and then the other in the swivel chair. Another copy? She was sure there must only be one. This pristine version would have its cover and title page intact. She ran her hand across her neck, feeling an overwhelming urge to see and touch this other copy of the book.

She wondered how long Owen had gone out for, and when he'd next be in touch. Perhaps he'd contacted Rita already.

Standing up, Martha paced the library, up and around the few aisles. She pressed book spines back into neat lines and straightened any that had fallen over. She gathered her rating spreadsheets together and stared out of the window at the setting sun. It cast a lemony glow on the rippling waves.

"It's my book and my stories," she whispered to herself, her shoulders wriggling with frustration. She was having to rely on Owen taking things further, to find out more. But if Rita knew anything about *Blue Skies and Stormy Seas*, Martha wanted to hear it firsthand. She didn't want to wait.

She turned and stared back at the computer.

Although she was grateful for Owen's help, she wanted more control in this search for the truth. She walked over to the desk and sat down again.

Her computer session had expired, so she retyped her password and clicked on the internet logo. She typed "Monkey Puzzle Books" into Google and there was only one listing in the UK. She reached up and ran her finger over the digits of the phone number. "Hello, Rita," she said aloud.

First, she fired off a quick email to Owen, to thank him for the image and info about the Scandinavian printer, and to pass on her gratitude to the mysterious Dexter.

Then, in the graying light, she picked up the phone. She had decided to make her own call.

As the dialing tone rang, she neatened up a pile of college class leaflets on the desk. The library doors rattled and Martha froze, almost dropping the receiver.

"Damn, it's shut," she heard a woman say.

Sliding her eyes, Martha waited for her to leave. There was muttering, another shake of the doors and then footsteps moving away.

Finally, from the other end of the phone, there was a crackle and a friendly voice. "Hay-lo. Monkey Puzzle Books. Rita speaking."

Martha cleared her throat. She opened her mouth but no words came out.

Deep breaths, she thought to herself. *Just say something. Anything.*

Closing her eyes, she pictured the task written in her notepad with a giant green tick next to it. "My name is Martha Storm," she said. "I'm calling about a book called *Blue Skies and Stormy Seas.* I believe that you own a copy."

"Ah, Owen Chamberlain left me a message about that today. Don't you just love that enchanting little book? When I think about it, I can almost feel the sea spray on my face and hear birds singing. It's wonderful." Rita spoke breathlessly. She sounded like she could find wonder in everything, even men digging a hole in the road or a letter landing on her doormat. Martha imagined her as bespectacled and big-boned. She probably waved her arms around a lot and wore chunky, bright jewelry.

"My grandmother wrote it, though my copy is falling apart. Owen said that yours is in good condition," she said.

"It is, and you must be so proud of your grammy. You must come and see my copy sometime. I'm on the high street in Benton Bay. If you live near Owen, it's around eighty miles from you. He's a real sweetheart, isn't he?" She gave a booming laugh.

"Um, yes, he is... I wondered where your copy came from?"

"Ha, it found me in a most unusual way," Rita said.

The hairs on her Martha's arms rose to attention. "It *found* you?"

"Ah, yes. Shall I tell you all about it? It's most wonderful." Rita didn't wait for a reply before she shared her recount, telling it like a story.

"One day, a small crowd gathered in the village square, not far from my bookshop. I was out on my lunch break when I heard a woman's voice. It was loud and clear above the chattering of the crowd. Wonderful. Street performers in the Bay are always worth a watch, so I squeezed my way to the front and I saw two women. One was in a wheelchair and she read aloud from a book. She had the most expressive voice and everyone around me listened in, captivated. I remember her story was one about a mermaid and a fisherman."

Martha shifted in her chair. "Please go on."

"Afterwards, the strangest thing happened," Rita said. "The lady reading the book closed it and placed it on the ground. Everyone clapped and cheered, but the two women didn't stay and listen to the applause, or to collect any money. They both moved on quickly, away from the crowd.

"A few people around me stayed and eyed up that little book, lying there on the ground, but they eventually edged away. I'm a real nosey parker, though, and wanted to take a closer peek.

"It had a burgundy cover. Just wonderful. I couldn't resist reaching down and picking it up. I was going to hand it back to the ladies but I couldn't see them anywhere. It started to rain, so I tucked it under my coat. When I got back to the shop and pulled it out, I found a note attached to the back cover."

"A note?"

"Ah, yes. I still have it. Let me find it for you, so I get the words exactly right."

Martha waited and listened to shuffling from the other side of the phone. A shiver of anticipation ran down her spine.

"Here it is," Rita said, when she returned to the call. "The note said, 'Read me. I'm yours.'"

Martha frowned, not able to understand why anyone would read and then discard a book in this way. It was most illogical. Books were for keeping and admiring, reading and treasuring. If the two ladies didn't want their book any longer, why hadn't they given it to charity, or to a secondhand bookstore? Also, it meant this copy of *Blue Skies and Stormy Seas* belonged to someone else, before Rita. Another owner in the chain. She fell silent and pressed her fingers lightly against her neck. "That's most unusual. Is there anything else you can tell me about the two ladies?"

Rita made a clucking sound with her tongue. "Hmm, let me think," she said. "The woman in the wheelchair was a funny old thing. She was dressed head-to-toe in turquoise and wore these big old sunglasses. The other woman seemed to be looking after her. I think her name is Gina."

Martha felt the back of her neck prickle. She reached behind her and gave it a scratch. Looking up, she noticed that the library was now in complete darkness. All she could make out were silhouettes of the shelves. The backs of her hands glowed silver from the computer screen. "Did you ever see them again?" she asked.

"Once or twice. They're from the old vicarage."

"In your village?"

"Ah, yes. In Benton Bay."

Martha closed her eyes and saw turquoise. She imagined sunlight bouncing off cat's-eye sunglasses.

Could the woman in the wheelchair possibly be my nana?

Or is that a ridiculous thought?

Also, how long ago had this happened? The book, with its speckles and yellowing pages, was over thirty years old.

She gulped and tried keep her voice steady. "You've been so helpful, Rita. Thank you for your time. I have one last question."

"Ask away."

"Do you remember when this happened?"

"When?" Rita asked with a chortle. "You make it sound like a historical event. The book came to me just before Christmas. Three months ago, if that."

11

Taxi

Martha looked out of her sitting room window at the wisps of clouds hanging like cobwebs in the powder-blue sky. Pockets of white tulips had sprung around her garden gate and everything looked fresher. She could see streaks of cobalt woven among the grays of the sea, although there were still icy crackles on her metal watering can. As she paced around her dining room, the boxes surrounding her felt like gravestones hemming her in.

She'd spent the previous night ruminating, telling herself that the woman from the vicarage couldn't possibly be her nana. Yet she wanted to be sure. At the very least she could find out how the woman who read aloud from the book came to have a copy. And why she wanted to give it away.

She wiped away a speck of dust from the windowpane as she contemplated, then ruled out, contacting Lilian. She didn't want to be told by her sister that she was being ridiculous and should leave things alone. Dropping her hand to her side, she gave a sigh.

Is it so wrong to do my own thing, for once?

She walked into the kitchen and opened the cutlery drawer

to get a spoon for her breakfast cereal. At the front, there was a stack of business cards that her mum used to save. They were fastened together by a green rubber band. Martha noticed that the top one was for a taxi service.

She pulled it out and stared at it as she munched her muesli. She turned it over and mused as she sipped her coffee.

The thought of knocking on the door of the old vicarage and asking two strangers what they knew about the little battered book made her stomach cramp.

The final months she'd spent caring for her parents had been a broken record of routine, and acting with immediacy wasn't her style. However, after her conversation with Rita and the events of the last few days, Martha's skin tingled as if she was plugged into an electric socket. She knew she was ready to make a move, to take a step out of her comfort zone.

She had to do something.

She picked up the card again and, before she could tell herself not to, she phoned for a taxi.

Her stomach jittered as she waited for it to arrive. She busied herself by washing her breakfast pots and moving things around on the dining table. She tried not to think about the journey she was about to undertake.

When a car horn beeped outside, she touched her hair slide to check its positioning. She called out, "Just a minute," even though she knew the driver wouldn't be able to hear.

Locking the front door behind her, she then slid into the back seat of the taxi. "Please take me to the old vicarage in Benton Bay," she said.

An hour and a half later, Martha stood outside a pretty redbrick building. It had a pointed roof, immaculate lawns and a path that wound up to a scarlet-painted front door. It had a brass fox-shaped knocker and an oversized letterbox. Ivy sprang around the frame and a hanging basket was overgrown with pansies and big primroses. The property looked homey, like the owners loved and looked after it.

She stood with her hands behind her back, staring at the house. Her feet felt glued to the spot and a voice in her head told her to turn around and go home.

"I *can't* do it," she told it. "I have *got* to do this."

Her pulse raced as the door began to slowly open. As a lady appeared on the doorstep, to put out some empty milk bottles, Martha stepped quickly to the side. Obscuring herself behind a tall privet hedge and peeping through a gap in the leaves, she wasn't quite ready to make her next move.

The lady had dove-white long hair, tied into a high bun, and Martha wasn't sure if her crease-free beige trouser suit looked more like a carer's outfit or a safari one. She was probably in her early seventies, too young to be Zelda.

So, could this be Gina?

The woman went back inside and Martha exhaled. Her heart was thump-thumping too wildly, making her feel faint, so she decided to pace down the country lane for a while, to allow herself time to calm down.

As she walked, delaying what she'd come here to do allowed her more time to mull things over. Her breath grew shallow as she considered possibilities and argued with them in her own head.

If my grandmother is here, what shall I say to her?

But, of course she won't be here, she's dead.

But that's what your parents told you. The message in the book tells you otherwise…

You need to find out what happened.

The wind whistled through her skirt and her neck felt full of knots. Was she just being ridiculous? How could it possibly be true that Zelda was here, after being gone for more than thirty years? Her own gullibility made her want to gag.

She also pondered if her own father was capable of conjuring up such a lie, about Zelda being dead, and she recalled a happening from her past.

In her first year at secondary school, she had written a story in English class and her teacher, Mr. Brady, insisted she read it aloud.

Martha had slipped down in her chair with her arms folded tightly, squirming with both embarrassment and pride. She only just managed to squeeze out her words.

After the lesson, Mr. Brady said he was going to enter her story into an interschool competition. "Each school can make one entry and I'm going to submit yours. There'll be a ceremony in Maltsborough for the nominees, and I think you have a good chance of winning a prize."

Martha skipped home and told her parents. "Please, can we keep that evening free?" she begged.

Her mum immediately scooped Martha into her arms and congratulated her, but her dad pursed his lips. "How many entries will there be?" he asked.

Martha felt her excitement sliding. "They're from schools all around the North of England. But Mr. Brady chose mine to represent our school."

"That's brilliant. Well done," her mum said.

Her dad gave a tight smile. "The odds are against her," he said to Betty. "And, it's rewarding Martha for making up her stories. She's stopped reading the encyclopedias."

"We've had them for ages, Dad. I know everything in them," Martha chimed in.

"Oh, really?" Thomas gave a short laugh. "Short stories

aren't very useful when you apply for a job as a secretary, or accountant, are they?"

"There are other jobs, too," Betty interjected. "Creative ones…"

Thomas stared at her. "I'm not sure what *you'd* know about that."

"Now, that's not fair. I want to find work."

"Can I go or not?" Martha pleaded, desperate to win the competition and prove her father wrong.

"No. We have other plans that evening," he said.

Martha never found out what those plans were, if there were ever any at all. The prize ceremony came and went, and the Storm family remained at home. Martha won second prize and received her certificate in a plain brown envelope from Mr. Brady, after class, rather than on stage. When she showed it to her dad and asked again, why she couldn't have collected it in person, he shook his head.

"You shouldn't have questioned me," he said. "That's why I didn't go ahead with my existing plans or take you to the ceremony. You ruined it for yourself. Plus, you didn't even get first prize."

For weeks, Martha cursed herself for not keeping her mouth shut. But as she grew older, she began to suspect there'd never been another event that night, and that her father had lied. And she found that he told more untruths, over the years, big and small.

So if there was even the remotest chance that Zelda was still alive, she *had* to find out.

Eventually, buoyed on by murmuring conversations with herself, Martha walked up to the garden gate. She tightened her fingers around the handle, pressed down and pushed it open.

Her surroundings seemed to fall eerily quiet, without birdsong or the rustling of wind in the trees. Her footsteps on the paving stones sounded extra loud as she headed towards the front door. Her heartbeat raced in her ears.

She raised her hand, rapped three times with the fox knocker, then waited. She readied herself with a friendly smile.

Seconds then minutes passed, and the door remained closed. No one came to answer it.

Gradually, her jaw ached from smiling.

She *knew* there was someone in there.

Martha tried again but there was no reply, so she did a small sidestep to glance through the front window. It allowed her to see right through to the back of the house, to the kitchen. She saw that the back door was open. A figure moved across it and Martha felt her neck muscles strain.

Perhaps they can't hear me.

Or, perhaps they're pretending not to hear me.

She swept her hand around under the ivy surrounding the door, looking for a doorbell, but couldn't find one.

A fence ran along each side of the house, tall slats of wood painted pale green, and she pressed an eye against a button of daylight. She watched as a small black Scottie dog scampered across the back lawn. White sheets billowed on a washing line, alongside a turquoise duvet cover and a long skirt the same shade.

Zelda's color.

Martha knocked on the door one last time with three loud raps, using her knuckles this time. When she drew them away, they were red and the skin had broken. She blew on them and waited.

This time she heard footsteps and a lock rattling.

Her stomach tightened.

The door opened and the woman who might be Zelda's carer stood in front of her.

Her eyes were a startling sea-glass blue, contrasting with her white hair. Under her beige trouser suit, she wore a white top that could either be a blouse or a work shirt. Her coral-orange toenails peeped out from her khaki sandals and a watch hung upside down, pinned to her chest. "Yes?" she asked with the apprehension of someone who answered the door to too many cold callers.

For a moment Martha felt as if she didn't inhabit her own body. Her feet were planted firmly on the ground but her head felt floaty, far away. She was aware that she might be staring. "Are you Gina?" she asked.

The woman's forehead wrinkled. "Yes," she said, her voice tinged with suspicion.

Any words Martha had lined up suddenly stuck in her throat. This was all so difficult to explain and she wasn't sure where to start. She was here, probably chasing a ghost. The first word that came out of her mouth was her customary, "Sorry."

The next thing she said sounded obtuse, even to her. So she couldn't imagine how it might sound to this woman. "I'm looking for Ezmerelda. Zelda Sanderson."

The woman clamped her teeth together so her cheeks twitched. "Who is asking?" She had a slight Nordic accent and pronounced each of her words clearly.

And with her throat terribly tight, and tears threatening to spring to her eyes, Martha uttered the words she'd never imagined she'd get to say again.

"I'm her granddaughter. I'm Martha Storm."

12

Wheelchair

Gina stood motionless for a while. Her eyes narrowed as she studied Martha. "I think you may have the wrong address," she said. She raised her hand and started to close the door.

But Martha heard a warble in her voice, a hint of a lie. After all the things she'd discovered to do with the little book, she couldn't let this go. She quickly angled her head to the side, to peer through the diminishing gap. "I don't think so. A book led me here. *Blue Skies and Stormy Seas*, by E. Y. Sanderson."

Gina's fingers tightened around the door and her knuckles whitened. She hesitated for a few moments before she pulled the door back open. Retracting her hand, she fingered the timepiece on her jacket.

Martha didn't want any yearning to show in her face, to give away how important this was to her. She had to stop the questions of what had happened to Zelda, all those years ago, from rampaging in her head once and for all. She concentrated on keeping her face as expression-free as possible, though she was sure her eyes shone with hopefulness.

Finally, Gina glanced back over her shoulder, towards the kitchen. "You had better come inside."

Martha stepped into the hallway. She cast her eyes around, at the floral wallpaper and the cream, green and brick-red Victorian tiles on the floor. Photos lined the walls in a multitude of different frames but her eyes flitted over them, not able to settle on the scenes and people they featured. The smell of cake warmed the air, making it feel like a family home, the opposite to her own house.

The black Scottie dog scampered towards her, his claws skittering on the hallway floor. She bent down to ruffle him under the chin and saw his name tag in the shape of a silver bone. Percy.

"Stay here, please," Gina said crisply, as if she was a doctor's receptionist and Martha was a patient who'd turned up very late for her appointment. She walked to the kitchen and closed the door behind her.

Martha stood for a moment, wondering what she should do. It seemed impolite to look around the hallway, for clues of her grandmother, so she crouched and continued to admire Percy. He was delighted by the attention but her hands shook as she stroked his head.

As Percy flipped over with his legs raised in the air, Martha could hear the murmur of voices and the scratch of her nails on the dog's stomach. She felt almost motion-sick, her head swaying, as she waited, and waited.

Every inch of her body felt alert. The roots of her hair were on end and she could hear every noise. She detected two voices in the kitchen and a strange sound of something moving around in there.

Time ticked by too slowly before the kitchen door finally opened again. Gina ventured out of the room first and, through her legs, Martha caught a glimpse of a wheel. She saw a few inches of turquoise blanket.

Gina stood to the side and a woman in a wheelchair

rolled forward. Martha saw her hands, then her shoulders and headscarf.

Everything seemed to fall into slow motion.

Martha lifted her head and stopped stroking Percy. He butted her hand, eager for more petting. She stood up, leaving him staring up at her. Her knees felt like they weren't her own.

She tried to find a smile but felt her face begin to crumble. Her chin shook with disappointment.

She was standing in a hallway with two people she didn't know.

A sob wracked in her chest and she fought against it. Then a tear spilled down her cheek and she angrily tore at it with her fist. She'd made a big stupid mistake. Her nana had died a long time ago and she was here, making a fool of herself.

The woman in the wheelchair was a stranger.

She wasn't Zelda.

In one last desperate attempt, Martha frantically searched in her head, for images of her nana that she could associate with the person sitting in front of her, but she couldn't find anything.

Her nana had tanned long legs and cartwheeled on the beach. However, this woman's ankles, peeking out under the blanket, were gnarled with blue veins. Zelda's blond curls used to escape from her headscarf but this woman covered every hair on her head. Martha's grandmother had skin that crinkled with laughter around her eyes, yet the stranger's face had deep folds like creases in a velvet curtain.

Martha berated herself. Just because she believed in fairy stories when she was small didn't mean they came true. One of her knees buckled and she had to focus on remaining upright.

In a brief flashback, she remembered her nana hoisting her skirt above her knees to show off her new cork-wedged sandals but going too far and giving a couple of workmen a flash of her knickers. She saw her with hairpins poking out between her lips like strange teeth as she set her hair in rollers.

The word *sorry* bubbled on her lips, but she couldn't let it out in case a blub followed it. And she knew she wouldn't be able to stop crying—at her own stupid belief and at how pathetic she was. Traveling all this way had been a huge mistake.

She watched the woman's eyes shifting over her, examining her from top to toe, taking in every detail. She lingered on Martha's hairstyle, her clothes, the shape of her body, the size of her hands, before finally settling on her shoes.

She's wondering who the hell I am.

The woman rubbed her nose, her eyebrows knitted. A sudden blast of laughter burst from her lips. She threw her head back and then forward again. "Ha ha."

Martha didn't know what to do, or what was going on.

The woman laughed for a while and then her smile gradually subsided. It was replaced with a searching squint of her eyes. Then she opened her mouth to speak. "Bloody hell. Is it really you, Martha?"

Time froze as Martha's senses homed in on her words. The hairs on the back of her neck pricked to attention.

It was a voice that she knew.

And had loved.

Martha forced herself to look harder at the woman sitting in front of her. She was small and hunched, with her body half obscured by her blanket. She had a missing tooth, on the top row and to the left, and Martha remembered the toffee apple incident at the fair.

The missing molar was the key for her to begin to unlock the rest of the woman's features. Perhaps she did recognize her kind blue eyes.

"Z-Zelda?"

"That's my name. Don't wear it out," the old woman said, still grinning.

Martha reeled to the side and pressed her hand to the wall.

Her memory of the younger version of Zelda and the woman in front of her slowly started to align. It was like watching a person swimming underwater. First you could see only their shape and colors, and it was only when they broke the surface that you could see them clearly.

And now she knew in her bones that her nana was sitting here before her.

"You're a bloody grown-up lady," Zelda said, her eyes glistening. Her hands clutched the blanket on her knees. "In my head, you're a teenager." Then her smile faltered. It slipped away, replaced by one of bewilderment. "You even have stripes in your hair."

Martha took a step forward. She cleared her throat. "Zelda Sanderson?" she asked formally, her eyes still questioning. She couldn't believe that the woman who helped to raise her, who shared stories with her, who she believed to be dead, was here. "Nana?"

As she said that word, it sounded beautiful but bizarre, too, because she was middle-aged and the woman in front of her was an old lady. Martha had laid her to rest in her mind many times. She'd said goodbye. Forever.

"Is it *really* you?" She gasped.

Zelda gave a slight nod. She wiped a tear away with a crooked finger. Then she held out her hand.

Martha looked over at Gina, not quite sure why she was seeking some kind of permission from the lady who answered the door. Gina semiclosed her eyes and turned her head away.

Hesitantly, Martha stepped forward and reached out. When she took hold of her nana's fingers they felt like brittle twigs. She held them lightly, not wanting to squeeze any tighter in case they snapped. "I thought you were gone. Mum and Dad told me you died—so how can you be here?"

Zelda lowered her eyes and stared at her lap. "I'm so sorry…" She pulled her hand away and fumbled up her sleeve for a handkerchief.

Martha's temples pulsated. "But why would they tell me that? What happened?"

"I *never* thought I'd see you again…" Zelda shook her head.

"Where have you been?" Martha let her hands fall. "My parents lied to me… Do you know they died?"

Zelda gave the slightest nod. "Yes. A few years ago. I know about them."

"So, why didn't you—?"

"Stop now," Gina snapped. Her features were frosty as she moved to the center of the hallway. Martha had to step backwards to give her some space. "Ezmerelda needs to take things easy."

The tendons in Martha's neck strained. She balled her hand into a fist. "It's been over thirty years. I *need* to know—"

"It's best if you leave now," Gina said.

Martha glared at her. "But we need to talk."

"The doctor has told Ezmerelda to rest up, with no excitement."

Zelda reached out and tugged on Gina's jacket. "Please. Martha is here and this is all so…bloody weird and amazing."

Gina's eyes remained hard.

"I feel as fit as a flea, honestly. I've already promised not to cartwheel for a while."

"I don't want to cause any trouble," Martha pleaded. "I found a dedication in a book but the date was wrong, and I managed to trace it to here. I didn't expect to find that Zelda is still alive."

Gina lifted her chin. Her voice softened a little. "I know

you have lots of things to discuss, but it is something to arrange for another time. This is a big shock for everyone."

Even though Martha felt her cheeks burn with frustration, she pursed her lips. "Yes. Yes, it is," she agreed, finally.

"We can meet properly, soon." Zelda said. "After I've rested."

"You need to lie down," Gina said.

"I will do. I promise." Zelda turned her attention to Martha. "There's a funfair in town, not far from here."

"You will *not* be going there." Gina folded her arms.

Zelda widened her eyes. "Hold your horses, Gina. I was about to say there's a small café at the fair. They do milkshakes and you can watch the rides."

"I am not stopping you from seeing your granddaughter. I am trying to *protect* you."

Martha stepped forward, wondering why this white-haired lady had such a big say in her nana's life. "Surely, it's up to Zelda."

Gina cast her a withering stare.

Zelda wheeled forward an inch. "I'm not trying to escape." She sighed. "I won't be going on the roller coaster. After the godawful doom and gloom of hospital it will be good to get out. I'd like to be around people enjoying themselves, who don't have ailments and injuries. What's wrong with going to the café?"

Gina moved her arms out of their fold. "Okay," she said, eventually. "I will give it some thought."

"Can I have your phone number, Martha?" Zelda said.

Martha took her Wonder Woman notepad from her pocket. She wrote down her address and phone number. After tearing out the sheet of paper, she handed it to her nana. "Call me anytime," she said. "I'll be waiting. I still live in Mum and Dad's old house."

Zelda nodded. She tucked the paper into her pocket and raised her hand in a fragile wave. "Thanks for finding me."

Martha's feet felt rooted. She didn't want to leave, but Gina had raised herself to full height. She stood stiffly, her body rigid.

Not knowing whether to kiss her nana on the cheek or not, Martha decided against it. When Gina followed her to the door, it felt like she was being escorted off the premises.

"She is an old lady," Gina hissed as she took hold of the doorknob. "I do not know why you've turned up after all this time, but it is my job to look after Ezmerelda. I will not let anything or anyone get in the way. I want to make sure you are clear about that."

Martha swallowed, taken aback by her forceful tone. "Yes."

"Good. Goodbye."

Martha crooked her head to the side briefly and mouthed, "Goodbye," to her nana. Then she stepped over the threshold and back onto the path. She didn't hear if Zelda said goodbye or not, and she was glad that she hadn't. Saying farewell to her all those years ago had been hard enough, without doing it again.

The door shut and Martha walked toward the gate. Her knees had jelly for joints and her fingers were numb as she opened it. Her hands shook as she pushed them into her pockets, but as she raised her face to the wind, the daylight seemed much brighter.

Taking a deep breath to steady herself, she closed the gate and looked down the country lane one way and then the other, wondering where to go. For someone so focused on planning, she'd overlooked something very big. She'd not given any thought to how she was going to get home.

13

Monkey Puzzle

Martha walked down the country lane for more than a mile before she spotted a wooden sign that told her the town center was a farther mile away. She was aware of putting one foot in front of the other but found herself unable to take in her surroundings. It was as if she was gliding in a dream. Her heart pounded so strongly it felt it might burst out of her chest.

My nana is alive.

As she passed by hedgerows and fences, she half expected a man to leap out holding a microphone and wearing a manic grin, to tell her that she'd been pranked for one of those shouty Saturday night TV shows. "Surprise. You thought you'd found your nana, but it was all a big joke. Bad luck."

Adrenaline flooded her body and she wanted to break into a run, to feel the wind whooshing through her hair.

She wanted to scribble down all the questions that were piling up in her head, down in her notepad. She'd mark them with an amber star, because they were all in motion but none of them resolved. Her discovery of *Blue Skies and Stormy Seas* was rewriting her family history as she knew it.

She also knew that among the highs of happiness of discovering Zelda, secrets and lies were lurking.

She passed by a church and her stomach hardened as she remembered her dad telling her she couldn't go to her nana's funeral. "It's not an experience for young people," he'd said. "You can find your own way to let her go."

"I want to say goodbye properly," Martha had insisted.

"Your mother and I will attend. Not you."

"Your dad has made up his mind," her mother had repeated, over and over, as Martha pleaded to go.

"I don't want to go to a funeral, anyway," Lilian had said when Martha tried to get her on her side. "People crying and sniffling and wearing black. No, thank you."

Martha had walked around the cemetery for weeks after Zelda died. She'd read every single gravestone but couldn't find anything with her nana's name on it. She scoured through the remembrance book in the church, and there was nothing there, either. She wondered if her grandmother had originated from somewhere other than Sandshift, so the funeral might have been held elsewhere. It was a puzzle she couldn't solve.

However, now she knew the reason she hadn't been able to find anything to do with Zelda's death.

Because it hadn't happened.

The revelation made her feel both ecstatic and sick at the same time.

And with these thoughts tangling in her head, Martha didn't even notice that she had walked the rest of the distance and arrived in the village.

Benton Bay was the type of place that spelled out its name in flowers on a grass verge, and it still had a red telephone box on a corner.

Still in a daze, Martha meandered past a baker's shop, newsagent, chemist and butcher's shop. When she looked in the window, at the strings of sausages, she pictured Zelda chasing her across the lawn, holding on to raw sausages and shouting, "I've got giant fingers."

She half smiled at the memory and continued along the street, not really noticing the shops and people surrounding her. But then something made her halt in her tracks. A wooden sign, hanging on chains above a door, featured a tree and book logo.

Martha stood beneath it and looked up. "Monkey Puzzle Books," she said aloud. Her senses lit up as she admired the shop's cream-painted mullions and the colorful array of children's books and soft toys on display in the window. She reached out to touch the glass.

She paused on the pavement for a while, thinking of how Rita's words had led her to the vicarage and to Zelda, and about the pristine version of *Blue Skies and Stormy Seas*. She *had* to go inside.

Pushing open the door, she saw a woman standing behind the counter, wearing a green-and-blue woolen shawl and a chunky gemstone necklace. Her skin was black and glowing, and her shiny, curly hair sprang down either side of her orange-framed glasses.

Martha instinctively knew this was Rita.

"Hello, my lovely," the lady said as she patted a sleepy dachshund dog who lay in a basket on the counter. "Can I help you?"

Martha glanced around the gorgeous shop. There were tables with small blackboards on easels that announced Benton Bay Bestsellers and Seaside Stories. The children's area had low plastic yellow chairs and beanbags. A man who wore a purple bobble hat and wellies stood reading books in the New Fiction section.

"Um, hello. I'm Martha Storm," she said shakily as she approached the counter. "We spoke on the phone about my grandmother's book and—"

Without warning, Rita launched forward, as if diving over the counter. She reached out her fleshy arms and her pat on Martha's back was more like a thump. "How marvelous that you're here. You should have told me you were coming."

"I only decided this morning..."

"Fantastic, and Owen should be back any minute now."

Martha swallowed hard. "Um, Owen?"

"Oh." Rita pulled away, her hands still holding onto Martha's shoulders. She cocked an eyebrow. "Haven't you traveled here together?"

"No. I came alone."

Rita peered over the top of her glasses. "Ah, well, it doesn't matter how you got here, or who you came with. It's wonderful you stopped by." She grinned. "I expect you'll want to take a peek at my copy of *Blue Skies and Stormy Seas.*"

Martha nodded.

"Follow me through to the back room, my lovely."

Martha's stomach flipped a little with guilt as she followed Rita behind the counter and through a beaded curtain. Perhaps she should have told Owen that she'd made contact with Rita, after everything he'd helped her out with.

I hope he doesn't think I'm ungrateful.

The office in the back of the bookshop was neat and tidy. There was an old oak rolltop writing desk, and shelves full of books covering each wall. As she peered closer, Martha was pleased to note they were all in alphabetical order by the surname of the author, just as she was used to in the fiction section of the Sandshift library.

The books seemed to assure her that she'd done the right thing, searching for Zelda, and her shoulders relaxed a little.

"Take a seat," Rita said and pulled on the back of an old wooden chair with six wheels and a cracked red leather seat.

Martha's nerves were still on edge and static crackled through her skirt as she sat down. "It's like Aladdin's cave in here."

"So it is." Rita laughed. "I can't imagine my life without books. I grew up with my three sisters and we always read together, under the covers and at the breakfast table. We had to share a bedroom, all four of us crammed in. Reading allowed us to escape, to imagine that our bunk beds were tree houses or flying carpets. Each Sunday, we read under the monkey puzzle tree in the park, and I named my shop after it. We loved books more than we loved boys. Which probably explains why I'm still single." She laughed throatily and ran her fingers across one row of books and then the next one down. Peering at the titles, she slid a handsome burgundy-and-gold book off the shelf and presented it to Martha. "Here it is. Isn't it a thing of beauty?"

Martha's head felt floaty as she reached out to take it. The book looked regal in all its finery. She settled it on her lap, where it felt reassuringly heavy. She touched her nana's name and read it out loud. "E. Y. Sanderson."

"Your grammy?"

Martha nodded. "I traveled here to follow your lead, about the ladies who read aloud in the village square. The old woman you described, in the wheelchair, turned out to be my nana, Zelda."

"Oh, how marvelous is that?" Rita clamped a hand to her chest. "You must be ecstatic, my lovely. And does she still have the most wonderfully clear reading voice?"

Martha wasn't sure. Zelda had looked rather frail and tired in her chair. She couldn't imagine her reading aloud to a crowd of people, but she nodded, anyway. She leafed through the book, her eyes falling once more on the illustration of the blackbird.

"You stay and look at it for as long as you like." Rita nodded. "I'll return to my shop in case I have any customers. And my Bertie is a little bit poorly today, poor old boy."

Martha nodded. She touched the blackbird's beak and wondered who drew him.

The more she looked at this intact version of the book, the more she remembered bowing her head down over her notepads as her characters came to life. She'd listened to the princesses, mermaids and birds in her head and wrote down their words.

But what she found most incredible was how Zelda had remembered these fairy tales, many of them Martha's stories, and captured them within the yellowing pages of the small book.

Why are they here?

She also recalled how her stories used to flow so easily, until Zelda's passing stopped them like a dam.

"I have so many things to ask her," she said to the blackbird. "It's hard to know where to start. It's been so long."

Martha felt warm and content in the back of the shop, surrounded by books, and time slipped away. She could hear Rita making enthusiastic phone calls in the shop and, through the beaded curtain, she saw her arms waving, just as she imagined they would do. Martha read *Blue Skies and Stormy Seas*, cover to cover, relishing holding and reading this proper, intact version.

When she next looked at her watch, she saw that almost an hour and a half had passed by. The bell above the shop door rang and when Martha heard Owen's voice, she sat up straighter in the chair. It was warm and rich and made her toes twitch in an interesting way. She found that the glow she usually only experienced from people's gratitude began to trickle over her body. For a few moments she closed her eyes, savoring the sensation.

With some reluctance, she put the book down and stood up. Pushing her way through the beaded curtain, she reentered the shop.

"Martha, I didn't know you were here." Owen's wide smile slipped into a small frown. "Did you tell me you were coming and I forgot?"

Rita finished her phone call and placed the receiver down. "I thought the two of you had traveled here together," she said. "But Martha said she came alone."

Owen looked from Rita to Martha. "I could have driven you here."

The tips of Martha's ears felt a bit hot, another strange feeling that she attributed to shame, for not telling Owen that she was coming here. "It wasn't a planned journey, more of a spur-of-the-moment thing."

Owen cocked his head on one side. "You got my email, then? I said that *I'd* contact Rita."

"I couldn't wait." She glanced away. "I booked a taxi. Sorry, I should have told you."

"But a taxi must have cost you a fortune…how are you getting home?"

Rita laughed at him. Her orange glasses slipped down her nose. "She's only just arrived. Give the lady some time."

Owen fiddled with the badges on his lapel. "Um, sorry."

"It's okay. I came here to try and find Zelda. It turns out that she's alive and lives close by."

"Really?" Owen pressed his hand to his chin. "That's absolutely incredible. I was going to offer to take Rita out this afternoon for a slice of cake and a coffee. Your news definitely calls for a celebration—we must all go together."

"Oh." Rita's smile faded. "I'm so sorry, Owen, but I can't

make it, my lovely. I'm taking Bertie to the vet and want to get the old boy looked at, as soon as possible. I'm afraid it will just be the two of you."

Owen walked with Martha to a café called the Potted Shrimp, though it served coffee and cake rather than seafood. Orange nets on the walls bulged with plastic crabs and the menus were shaped like seashells. The plastic covers on the tables were printed with waves and fish.

Martha shifted in her seat, not entirely comfortable about being here with him. If she ever went to cafés, it had been to take her parents out for a bowl of soup, to escape the monotony at home. As she perused the menu, she wasn't sure how an Americano differed to a macchiato. When the waitress sidled over, she said, "Just a normal coffee for me, please."

Owen clicked his tongue as he tried to decide. He unfastened a button on his jacket and swept his hand through his hair, making a small tuft on top. "I'll have the same, and a slice of date and walnut cake," he said. "Hmm, but then there's the sticky toffee pudding, and the carrot cake sounds good, too."

Martha preferred it when people knew their own minds, weighed things up and made decisions. It was something she'd had to do for her parents. It was something she did when she had to break things off with Joe.

She peered at Owen over her menu, silently urging him to choose quickly. "Sometimes there's no right decision. Just the one you make at the time," she said.

"No, it's okay." Owen grinned at the waitress. "I'll stick with my first choice, date and walnut. The cake is famous here. You should try it, Martha."

As she placed a hand on her stomach, Martha smiled politely. Feeling its fleshiness, she remembered her father's words about getting chubby. It was funny how she could still hear him in her head, even now. "Not for me, thanks."

When their coffees arrived, Owen stirred his and leaned forward in his chair. "It is so amazing that you've managed to trace Zelda."

Martha slowly angled her body away from him, as tactfully as she could, to create more space between them. "I know, though I don't think her carer, Gina, is too enamored about it. And I've had to take a day away from my other jobs to travel here."

"I thought you worked at the library—do you have another job, too?"

"Not really. I help people out with their things."

"That's kind of you. I suppose if it's Gina's job to look after your gran, she might feel protective over her."

Martha sipped her coffee. "That would be understandable but she seems rather overzealous. And everything feels very strange, too. Zelda and I are different people to who we were, all those years ago. I was only fifteen when she died. Or, um, didn't die."

"You're still the same people, underneath," Owen offered.

Although he was trying to be kind, his statement rather oversimplified things, Martha thought.

She had once been a shiny-eyed teenager, and Zelda a vivacious blonde. Now they were both mature women who hadn't seen each other for more than three decades. She had no idea if they were still the same people, or not.

"Rita's personal copy of *Blue Skies and Stormy Seas* is wonderful," she said. "I need to find out how Zelda came to publish the fairy stories."

"You'll be able to ask her, face-to-face." Owen tore open three sugar sachets and tipped them into his coffee, one after the other. "It's a shame we have to grow up, isn't it? When you're a kid, you never question if a man can really turn into a frog, or if a girl can be the size of a thimble."

"I think my sister, Lilian, always did," Martha said with a tight smile. "I used to love writing stories, when I was younger…" She trailed off her words, not sure that she wanted to share more information than this with him.

"And do you still write?"

"I grew out of it," she said quickly.

"Maybe it will come back to you one day. I bet you like to read, though?"

"Anything and everything, if I get time."

If I don't feel guilty not doing other things, she thought.

Her heart still pulsated at cheesy vampire romances and teen dystopian adventures. She was partial to a good biography, particularly by ageing but still glamorous film stars, though never ones by reality TV stars or footballers. Her back chilled when she turned the pages of thrillers with spiky orange capital letters and she brushed away tears after reading misery memoirs. She couldn't understand library-goers who turned their noses up at commercial books, announcing that they only enjoyed literary reads. To her, authors should write what they wanted and readers had their pick of thousands of books to enjoy.

She thought about the stack of unread books piled high on her dining table that she'd neglected, to focus on her jobs for other people instead. Whenever she lifted one to read, a voice in her head (her own) told her to put it back.

"You've got other things to do, Martha."

"You should always make time for books," Owen said. "Do you have a favorite?"

Martha knew her answer straight away. "It's got to be *Alice in Wonderland*. I like Alice's practicality and how she takes everything in her stride. She meets these odd creatures in magical situations and it never fazes her."

"So, you're a bit like Alice, then?" Owen dug a fork into his cake.

Martha gave a small, embarrassed laugh. "What, sensible and orderly?"

"I mean that you're inventive and curious, and make sense of strange things…"

Martha dipped her head, surprised he had seen her in this way. She supposed it was a compliment of sorts, and it made her feel a little shinier. "Thank you," she muttered and fiddled with her hair slide. "And what book do you like best?"

Owen thought for a while as he finished his cake. "That's like choosing a favorite child or pet. But I do enjoy a good *Jack Reacher*. It's because he's the opposite to me. He's tough and I'm not—I bet he's got rock-hard abs." He pointed at his stomach with both forefingers. "But my belly can double as a book rest."

"I bet he can't repair books the way you can."

"That's true." Owen laughed. "I don't think he owns monogrammed slippers."

"I've only read a couple of the books. Does Reacher have many wives, too?" Martha asked, then wished she hadn't.

Owen gave her a bemused smile. "I don't have any wives at the moment… I have a few of the books, though. I can lend you one."

Martha gave a small laugh. "I work in a library."

"Aha. So you do."

They finished their drinks and Owen insisted on paying, even though Martha shot out her hand and tried to grab the bill. "I really should pay for the coffees, to thank you for your help," she said.

But Owen had already taken ten pounds from his wallet.

"You can pay the next time," he said. "When you've finished your coffee, I'll drive you home."

As she took the last sip of her drink, Martha didn't argue with him. She rather liked his words, *the next time.*

If she dwelled on them too much, she'd manage to persuade herself they were terrifying. So instead she focused on seeing them for exactly what they were, friendly and something she should welcome.

14

Postcard

Over the next couple of days that followed, nothing could spoil Martha's mood. Since she'd reconnected with Zelda, she felt lighter, reenergized, her fatigue lifted. When she headed down to Sandshift Bay for her morning circular walk, she no longer punched her arms to motivate herself. Her limbs moved fluidly, without effort.

When she read the names on the mermaid statue, they still tugged at her heart but she found a positive in that Siegfried had survived. As she looked across at the lighthouse, she wondered how he coped with losing his fellow crew members from the *Pegasus*. She knew from experience how events from your past could shape your future.

Martha also started to work her way through her tasks with renewed interest and vigor. She squirted washing-up liquid into a bath full of warm water and dipped Branda's chandeliers into it. She lightly worked on each individual crystal with an old toothbrush. They now sparkled and looked like new. Will's trousers were hemmed, pressed and bagged. She planned to start working her way through the Berlin Wall of boxes. If Lilian didn't have time to help her, then Martha would do

it, anyway. It would keep her busy while she waited for Gina
or Zelda to get in touch.

Each time Martha completed a task, she moved its plastic
box or bag to the side of the dining room. When she gave
the job a big green tick in her notepad, her cheeks shone with
pride.

There was now a definite path from her front door to
her kitchen, rather than a maze. She could walk through the
house without feeling like she was a horse competing in the
Grand National.

She tried not to think about the date in the book, or what
happened in the Storm family to make her nana disappear,
because she was sure she'd find everything out, the next time
she saw Zelda.

Owen's advice also rang in her head. He had put into words
what she already knew—that she should make more time
to read. So she made sure she stopped working on her tasks
at 7:00 p.m. sharp. She made a cup of tea and curled up in
the wooden chair by the window overlooking the bay. She
wrapped a blanket around her legs and read a *Jack Reacher*. And
although she enjoyed his ruggedness, toughness and solution
for every problem, she decided that she actually preferred a
kinder, gentler sort of hero.

When Martha returned to work at the library, her stomach
jumped with nerves as she opened the doors. She had already
conjured up a picture of Branda, Nora and Horatio gossip-
ing about her. She imagined Clive's face would be smug and
knowing. Her legs shook as she walked up to the desk.

However, when she peered cautiously around, everything
seemed okay. The library exuded calm and the books surrounding her gave her the same warm welcome they always

did. When she took her job application form out of the drawer, it didn't look as scary as she thought it might.

"Just complete it and apply," Suki said as she rubbed her bump. "Time is ticking away."

"I know. It's just so important that I want to get it right. I've applied three times for a role here already, and been turned down," Martha explained. "Statistically, I'm not likely to get it."

"Why not? Satan-istically, you do a great job."

Martha considered this. *Because there's always someone younger and brighter than me*, she thought. *Because I've not written anything expressive for years.*

The interview would be with Clive and he'd have penned a black mark against her name, after their encounter in the kitchen. "I'm determined to give it a go. I just need more time, to think about what to write."

"Just say how much you love books and helping people," Suki said with a shrug. "No one does it better."

Martha gave her a grateful smile and again felt like throwing a quick hug. Instead she picked up a stack of books from the returned pile. She examined the codes and numbers on their spines and carried them back to their shelves. She recommended a couple of feel-good novels to a lady who wore a yellow silk scarf with sunflowers on it, and she rearranged the thriller display.

She had just bent down to slide a book about tractors back into place in the transport section when Siegfried appeared in the same aisle. Not acknowledging her presence, he pulled his gray hat down and headed to the romance books at the end. After scanning the shelves methodically from top to bottom, he slid out four paperbacks, then carried them over to a table in the corner. He opened the first one and began to make notes on a piece of paper.

Martha stared after him, wanting to thank him for returning her trolley and hair slide after her outburst. But he arched
his arm in front of him, like a schoolboy in class preventing
anyone from copying his work.

"Siegfried's got a pile of love stories," Suki whispered when
Martha returned to the desk. "Is it true he was on board that
fishing boat, that cat's-eyed?"

"Capsized? I believe so."

"Perhaps that's why he doesn't speak much."

"I think you might be right. He—" Before Martha could
give her thoughts, Nora appeared.

She wore a pair of emerald-green leggings and a matching
velour hoodie with *Juicy* written on the back in silver lettering. She approached the desk with trepidation, as if she was
teasing a tiger with a piece of grass.

"Um, Martha, love," she said, unable to meet her eyes. "I
wondered if you've done my washing and ironing yet? And
you left two bags of it behind in the library when you went,
um, berserk."

Martha pictured Nora's laundry folded neatly into the bin
bags at home. She'd washed but not ironed it and felt strangely
unflustered by its lateness. And she didn't feel like apologizing
or offering to do the additional washing she'd run away from.

Not wanting to help was an alien feeling to her and she was
finding it intriguing, something she wanted to experiment
with further. "I'm afraid that I'm not taking on any more
jobs for people until I've cleared my current consignment.
I'll bring back the laundry I've already done for you, when
I'm ready. If you desperately need it before then, you can call
around to collect it."

Nora stepped back. Her eyes widened a little. She suddenly
affected a stoop and rubbed her spine. "Oh no, it's okay. Re-

turn it for me when you can. It's my bad back, you see, Martha, love. Besides, I think I've found a washing machine engineer. I'm seeing him on Sunday."

"Tradespeople don't usually work at the weekend," Martha warned.

"He was on a dating site and we're meeting in a wine bar. I've not mentioned my machine yet, but I'm hoping we can come to a mutually beneficial arrangement." She glanced across the library to the fiction section. "Is Siegfried single? Is he good with machinery?"

Suki rolled her eyes.

After this, Martha showed a young couple, who both wore ripped jeans and biker's jackets, how to use the photocopier to print posters for a local gig. As they argued over the enlarging facility, how many copies they needed and which way round to place their original copy, she left them to their own devices.

A man wearing a khaki parka coat with sky-blue fur around the hood wanted to hire all the available *Die Hard* movies. Instead of finding them for him, Martha directed him to the DVD section. She told a woman who wore a fleecy red-and-yellow jester hat, complete with bells, to return the books she'd browsed through back to the shelves, rather than leave them on the table.

Branda was the next to arrive. She took a batch of Lobster Pot menus out of her purple handbag. Glancing at her watch, which had two black panthers as the hands, she asked, "Will you laminate these for me, Martha? I've gone a little darker on the restaurant branding. Moodier. More Scandi *noir*."

Normally Martha would say yes and get straight onto it, but today she thought before she spoke. "Leave them on the desk. I'll do my best, if I get time."

Out of the corner of her eye, she saw Suki nodding at her, proudly.

★ ★ ★

When Martha arrived home, she made herself a cup of tea and, while waiting for it to cool, she pushed a couple more of the plastic crates to the side of her dining room. After she placed the dragon's head on top of them, the pile looked like a strange totem pole.

When she sat down in her wooden chair, she now had space to stretch out her legs. She straightened them out, one at a time, and rotated her ankles without kicking against bags or boxes. It felt so good.

It was only when she'd finished her drink and conducted a small dance along the freed-up pathway that she saw the postcard on her doormat. It poked out from under leaflets for home cleaning services and pizza delivery.

After picking it up, she first admired the illustration of a black Scottie dog on the front, then turned it over. On the back there was a first-class stamp and her name and address. The handwriting was in small capitals, neat and robot-like.

SUNDAY, NOON, FUNFAIR ENTRANCE, BENTON BAY

NO EXCITEMENT
NO SUGAR
NO ALCOHOL
NO BETTING
NO HEAVY CONVERSATION
NO LATE RETURN

FROM GINA

15

Fairground

When Martha arrived, ten minutes early, at the entrance of the fairground, she positioned herself next to a six-feet-tall fiberglass ice cream, which had a face and a big tongue. Although she craned her neck to peer to her left and right, she couldn't see her nana's wheelchair or Gina's white hair.

There was a flutter in her stomach and her heart thumped, as if she was on a first date. She wandered around in small circles on the pavement and rummaged through her handbag, to pass the time until they arrived.

More than anything, she wanted to find out how and why her nana was still alive, but as each minute ticked by, her hopes subsided. Her steps grew slower and her shoulders drooped. She looked at the postcard, to check the date and time.

Where is Zelda?

It was 12:16 p.m. when she eventually saw her nana and Gina approaching with Percy trotting alongside them. Even though her excitement was dampened by the sight of the stern carer, she still felt like skipping to her nana's side, as she did when she was young. She wanted to wrap her arms around her, to assure herself that she was really here.

She strode over to greet the two women and spotted that Gina's lips were set in a hard, thin line. Martha felt a flare of anger in her stomach at why this woman was being so hostile towards her. Shouldn't she be more pleased that the woman she cared for was reunited with her long-lost granddaughter? Martha repeated the last line on the postcard to herself—*no late return*. Gina made her nana sound like a library book.

"Shall we agree ninety minutes maximum?" Gina said. She wore a beige trench coat with boot-cut jeans and gray loafers. She looked softer today, with her snowy hair in loose waves. Zelda was in her wheelchair, with a turquoise blanket tucked over her legs and a silk scarf wrapped around her head.

"That's not very long." Martha frowned. How could they possibly fit years of conversation into such a short time?

"It is enough, for a first outing."

"I am here, you know." Zelda raised a hand. "I can speak for myself."

Gina looked at her. "Ninety minutes only, today. And please be sensible, Ezmerelda. Hook the Duck or the penny arcades are fine, but I do not want you to dislocate your shoulder on anything like the coconut shies."

Martha curled her fingers to stop herself from intervening. She spoke through her teeth. "Is there anything *I* should know about health matters?"

"No," Zelda spoke up. "I've got a bad dose of old age, that's all. It's bloody awful. No cure."

Martha tried not to laugh and she felt the tension between the three of them ease a little. "We'll just grab a coffee, or a bite to eat in the café. An ice cream sundae will be as adventurous as we get," she told Gina.

Her nana's carer twitched a wry smile. "And that just shows how little you know Ezmerelda," she said.

★ ★ ★

"She's just trying to look after me, in her own way," Zelda said, her lips ventriloquist-still as she waved goodbye to Gina.

"She's very, um, firm."

"It's just her way."

The two women headed through the entrance arch and into the main body of the fairground. Martha remembered them as magical places: the flashing lights, the blast of music and the laughter. But now she saw danger and neglect. Thick black cables running across the floor might trip you up. She noticed the chipped paint on the Waltzer cars as they spun around their circular track and she found the smell of fried onions sickly. Everything seemed louder and brasher.

Her neck felt stiff as she thought of how many years had passed between her and Zelda. If you loved someone so much in the past, would the future only disappoint? Could the years melt away so easily, or would they be like a wall of ice?

"The café looks nice," she said as they moved towards it, though it didn't look very pleasant at all. Two flat wooden clowns held up a menu board on which everything was served with chips. "I don't think I've ever had chips and cheese before."

"Are you even hungry?" Zelda stopped her wheelchair abruptly.

"Well, not really."

"Good." Zelda took hold of her wheels and pushed forward with her hands, skillfully spinning in the opposite direction. "Follow me."

"Where to?"

"I want to see the rides."

Martha sped after her. Her brow furrowed. "But, we need to chat—"

"We can do it later."

Martha glanced at her watch. Ten minutes had already gone by. She opened her mouth to insist they talk now, but Zelda sat upright in her chair. "Candy floss," she said with a sniff. "Let's get some."

"Gina said you're not allowed sugar."

"I won't tell her if you don't."

Martha's jaw clenched. "I have her list."

"I'm eighty-nine, Martha," Zelda huffed. "I have few pleasures left in life. What's the worst that could happen if I eat candy floss?"

"I don't know." Martha sighed. "Diabetes? Tooth decay? Obesity?"

"Been there. Done that. Well, maybe not obesity." Zelda wheeled towards the candy floss stand.

Martha dug her hand in her hair, frustrated that her nana preferred to eat pink fluffy stuff rather than discuss the last three decades.

"It's my treat," Zelda shouted over her shoulder.

Martha caught her up. "I'll get it." She pulled the purse from her bag. "Then let's find somewhere quiet."

Zelda reached up and slapped a ten-pound note on the counter. "A candy floss each, for me and my overcautious granddaughter. Extra-large ones, please."

Their flosses quivered in the breeze as they carried them. Martha examined the mound of pink sugar, not having eaten it since she was a teen. She wondered if she'd hear her father's voice when she tasted it. Closing her eyes, she listened, but all she could hear was the hum of rock music thrumming from the Waltzer. She slowly leaned her head to one side and took a small mouthful. The sugary strands dissolved deliciously on her tongue.

"Throw it away," her dad said, somewhere from the base of her skull. *"It will rot your teeth. It's not healthy."*

Martha tried to ignore him, but the candy floss grew sweeter and more cloying. It seemed to expand in her mouth. Not able to enjoy it any longer, she dropped it into a bin.

"We should go on at least one ride," Zelda said, staring at the dodgem cars.

Martha coughed. "We can't go on those. You might—"

"What? Fracture my hip? I did that when I fell over a rake in the garden. If I break something else, it should be doing something fun. I'm the adult, remember?"

Martha stared at her. "We both are."

"Oh yes." Zelda grinned. "I forgot."

Martha didn't recall her nana being this strong-willed. In fact, she could only recall a sense of her personality rather than definite traits. She was beginning to realize that it was impossible to remember everything about a person from the past. You formed your own idealized picture of them, rather than an accurate one. The Zelda she'd held in her head for decades was a superhero, an ally, her best friend. Yet here, now, she was a frail old lady in a wheelchair, and a stubborn one at that. "Let's go back to the café with the wooden clowns," she pleaded. "There's so much we need to catch up on. I need to know what happened." She felt her throat tightening with emotion as she spoke. "Why did you leave? Why did my parents tell me you were dead?"

Zelda reached up with both hands and took hold of Martha's coat. Her eyes shone with longing. "*Please* let's look at the rides for a while. When I look out of my window at home, I see green fields and buttercups and blue sky, and it's beautiful. But sometimes I want a different view, to watch people and things going on. Elderly people don't just want to look at photos of the past, or of a nice bloody view. I want to see bright lights, and hear music, and see young people having fun. I want to *remember* doing it myself."

Martha looked down at her nana's knotted hands. She swallowed away a lump in her throat. "I know, but I *lost* you..."

Zelda let go. She pushed her wheels a little forward and then back again. "People only see my chair, or a woman who looks like a bloody walnut. In my head, I'm still a young woman. My body just lets things down."

Martha bit her bottom lip. When she was younger, she'd had her fair share of wolf whistles, and men had admired her face and figure. She found love with Joe. But when she started to look after her parents, she seemed to fade out of sight. She was no longer Martha in her own right, but Thomas and Betty's caring daughter. Her pretty, colorful exterior faded like a magazine left in the sun. "I still see you in a skirt with a crazy cat print. I see you squeezing into caves and digging in the sand to find Australia," she said.

"You do?" Zelda's eyes grew glassy.

Martha nodded. She worked her tongue around her teeth. If she did something that her nana wanted to do, it might make her more willing to talk. "Now, where do you want to go?" she asked.

"This way." Zelda wheeled forward, expertly avoiding people's feet. "Beep, beep. Dalek coming through," she called out.

They reached the carousel where wooden white ponies wore shiny red saddles and black leather reins. Their carved golden manes and tails seemed to flow in the wind as they bobbed up and down on twisted poles to the sound of organ music. Zelda halted her chair at the metal barrier. "Isn't it the most glorious thing you've ever seen?"

Martha nodded. Despite her nana's exaggeration, it really was magnificent.

"I can't see the horses properly. Help me out." Zelda wrestled off her blanket. She folded it roughly, then pushed herself up out of the wheelchair. Martha grabbed her arm and helped her to her feet. The ride slowed to a halt and laughter filled the air as people filed past on their way off. "Do you want to go on?" Zelda asked.

Martha laughed at the absurdity of her question. "It's for kids, not us."

"It's for anyone." Zelda looked around. "I don't see a sign to say adults aren't allowed."

"It's a long time since I went on a carousel."

"They're easy. All you have to do is sit down."

The last time she'd been on one, Martha shared a horse with Joe. She sat up front with him behind her. They'd got lost in the music and sounds as he nuzzled the back of her neck. When they got off, a woman told them off for making out in front of her kids.

If Martha concentrated, she could still feel his breath on the back of her neck and the warmth of his arms around her waist. Thinking about him made her feel a bit drunk. "Gina said no rides," she muttered.

"She would say that." Zelda raised her hand and beckoned over one of the fairground workers. "Can you help me onto a horse?"

"Sure can." The man's biceps were almost the same width as Zelda's waist. He was dressed all in black and his goatee beard looked like it was painted on. He wrapped his arm around her and shouted, "Hoopla," as he helped to hoist her up.

"Now, Daisy," the man said into the horse's ear. "You look after this young lady." He took money from Zelda and patted the horse's rear end. "Do you want a leg up, too?" he asked Martha.

"No thank you, very much." She tried to hold her skirt down as she clambered into the saddle.

"Giddyup," Zelda shouted and shook her reins.

Martha cheeks glowed with embarrassment. She looked

around her but no one else seemed to notice, or care, that two mature ladies were about to ride on the carousel.

The circular platform started to rotate and Martha's horse rose and fell. His name was embossed on his collar. Dobbin. "Well then, Dobbin," she whispered. "Zelda really wants to do this. Then I'll ask my questions."

"Yahoo," Zelda shouted and lassoed her hand in the air as the ride grew faster. And Martha couldn't help smiling.

Round and round they went and Martha couldn't remember the last time she'd had so much fun. When she got off her legs shook.

"What do you recommend next?" Zelda asked the goatee-bearded man.

"The Tornado is pretty crazy." He grinned. "Though I think you could handle it."

"No." Martha shook her head. "No. No. NO."

The Tornado was a red-and-blue metal construction that looked like handwriting in the sky. It was thirty feet high with two loops in the rail. Passengers were secured in by harnesses that slid down over their heads, so their legs could dangle freely.

"We're not going on there." Martha gulped. Nausea swept over her when she saw the carriages turn upside down and heard the people scream. "Let's go somewhere else. Somewhere more—"

"Sensible?" Zelda interjected. "Where you can question the life out of me?"

Martha hitched her handbag farther up her shoulder. "You must have things to ask me, too. Don't you want to tell me about what happened, all those years ago?"

Zelda readjusted her headscarf, taking a long time. She didn't speak.

Martha waited as the Tornado carriages shot past her, the screeches assaulting her ears. She raised her voice above the noise. "I want to know why you left Sandshift."

Zelda twisted her head. She raised her hands to her ears. "Sorry. I can't hear you."

Martha closed her eyes, took a deep breath and held it in her lungs. She waited until the carriages rattled and swerved away. She moved closer to her nana and bent over so her mouth was near her ear. "Don't you want to know about Thomas and Betty? About me and Lilian, and how we all coped without you? We *loved* you, Nana…"

Zelda patted her headscarf. She took hold of her wheels and spun them, almost running over Martha's foot as she rolled away. "It's much too noisy to talk here," she said. "Let's find another ride."

Martha grimaced as she watched the back of her chair. Gritting her teeth, she strode after her. Peppering her nana with questions wasn't working and she needed something to make her more amenable. After discounting the Waltzer and the fun house, her eyes settled on the ghost train. "Would you like to go on that?" she pointed.

Zelda gave a small, satisfied smile. "Okay. That looks ah-mazing."

A giant skull's eyes glowed tomato red and its jaw opened and closed, baring broken teeth. Kazoo-like noises and the screeches of passengers sounded when the wooden doors swung open. The carriages featured vampire heads, grinning and baring bloodied fangs.

Zelda parked up her chair again and hoisted herself out of it. They stood behind three men who wore white vest tops. "Do you want to go on before us, ladies?" one of them asked. He had a red devil tattoo on his left shoulder.

"That's okay. You go—" Martha started to say.

"That's very kind, gentlemen." Zelda beamed and squeezed past them, to the front of the queue.

When they sat down in their carriage, Martha tugged at the strap to make sure they were fastened in securely.

The ride started off reassuringly slow. The carriage rattled along the track towards two swing doors. Then they were plunged into darkness. A neon-yellow tunnel rotated and their carriage seemed to rise sideways up the wall. Disorientated, Martha shut her eyes until they jerked around a corner.

Three skeletons rode bicycles around a gravestone, and a man lurched forward in his electric chair before the power supply dial on his chair revved up to full power. With a crackle, he slumped back, his head lolling to the side. Martha tightened her grip on the bar as the carriage veered tightly around a sharp bend and out into the daylight. The people in the carriage in front screamed and dipped out of sight. Martha and Zelda's own carriage slowed, allowing a glimpse of the oncoming drop.

"Brace yourself," Zelda shouted.

Martha did as she was told. "Argh." The plunge made her teeth chatter and she nipped the end of her tongue. Zelda's laugh bellowed, and Martha found that she was laughing uncontrollably, too, even though she didn't want to.

Their carriage rose up and they reached the top of another dip. A gust of air came at them, causing Martha to screw her eyes shut. When she opened them, Zelda had her arms raised, her hands snatching in the air. "My scarf," she cried out.

Martha turned her head to watch as the scarf hung in the air for a moment before it blew away on another blast of air. It looked like an exotic bird flying over the heads of the people below. "We can look for it when we get off," she said.

As she turned to reassure her nana, their carriage thumped into a set of double wooden doors with a Keep Out sign. Entering the darkness, Martha blinked hard, questioning what she had just seen.

Zelda no longer had her blond princess curls.

In their place were a few wispy gray strands, and nothing else.

Their carriage shunted past a giant spider with moving mandibles and flashing green eyes, and something tickly trailed across their faces, but all Martha could picture in her mind was her nana's smooth head.

When the ride finished, she was glad to scramble out. She felt like she was still moving, her legs unsteady, as she offered Zelda her hand.

"Shall we go on again?" Zelda asked.

"Don't you want to look for your scarf?"

Zelda ran her hand over her head. She gave it a rub at the back. "Someone has probably found and kept it. Let's not waste any time. We don't have much of it left."

Martha looked at her watch. "We have twenty minutes before Gina arrives."

Zelda fixed her eyes somewhere in the distance and she touched her head again. She stared for a while, unblinking, before she cleared her throat. "That's not what I meant," she said.

16

Read Me

They moved away from the ghost train and found a quiet spot behind the café. "Don't tell Gina about the candy floss," Zelda said.

"I won't do that." Martha swallowed, lost for words as the music faded away. There were no longer any lights and bustle to distract them.

"You may have noticed I have a shop dummy–look going on," Zelda said.

Martha nodded. Her tongue was dry and she tried to focus on her nana's eyes instead of her head.

"It's okay." Zelda sighed. "It's quite obvious. You're not being rude by looking. I can't stand wearing wigs, they're so scratchy. I thought you might have guessed about…" She ran her hand down the back of her skull.

"No. I just thought you liked scarves." Martha let her gaze follow Zelda's fingers. She saw a scarlet scar that ran up the back of her neck to the top of her head. Hearing a gasp, she realized it came from her own lips. "Is that why you were in the hospital?"

"That was for a minor op. The scar's from an operation I had for a brain tumor," Zelda said plainly. "They got rid of most of it, but my hair didn't grow back properly. Two disasters for the price of one, eh? It looked a lot worse with the staples. Like I had a bloody small ladder running up my head."

Martha couldn't absorb her words. She wanted to sink down and sit on the ground with her head in her hands, but she told herself to be calm, for Zelda's sake. "They got rid of most of it?" she repeated.

"There was a bit they couldn't quite get to, like when there's some yogurt left in the pot and you can't reach it with your spoon."

Martha squeezed her eyes shut. She wanted to shout out that this was so bloody unfair. She'd rediscovered this amazing woman, and she had been going through *this*. And without her family around her, too. "It's not really the same, is it?" she blurted. "I mean, are you okay?"

"I can't complain. At my age, something is going to get me, sooner or later."

Martha held her hand to her mouth. "How can you be so bloody blasé about this?"

Zelda didn't speak for a while. She seemed to diminish in size and suddenly looked really old. She fixed her gaze on the wooden clown menu and her fingers tightened on the arms of her chair. "Because the alternative is howling my heart out," she said fiercely. "Getting angry would be a waste of my precious time. I'm here and you're here. We've just been on the ghost train together, and who'd have thought that would ever happen?" She took a deep breath, as if steeling herself for her next words. "I never thought I'd see you again, before I..."

Words jammed in Martha's throat. It hurt when she swallowed. "Before you, what?"

Zelda let out her breath in a whistle. "They tell me different things, those bloody doctors. I never know who's right and who's wrong, and they all just look like kids. I don't have a crystal ball, but it's unlikely I'll see Christmas."

Martha's stomach plunged, as if she'd stepped into an elevator shaft. "You have less than ten months?"

"More like four."

Martha swayed and struggled to remain upright. Her future flashed through her head. She'd already pictured that Zelda would be a big part of it. She choked back tears and focused on the roof of the Waltzer. Someone had thrown a red high-heeled shoe up there, and a broken umbrella. A chill crept over her and she tried not to breathe in case she let out a cry. The top of her nose stung as she fought back her tears.

The two women stayed silent for a while.

Zelda slowly released her grip on the chair. "What will be, will be," she said, her eyes shining with tears.

"But we have so much to talk about. I need to know what—"

Zelda held up her hand. "I only want to look forward and not back."

Martha pushed her striped hair back off her forehead. "How can we do that? My parents lied to me about your death. You've been missing from my life for years. We need to discuss it all."

Zelda shook her head fiercely. "Do we have to, Martha? Can't we pretend that it didn't happen? Can't we just have some fun together?"

"*Blue Skies and Stormy Seas* brought me to you. Why did you write it? You put a message inside a copy, so you must have meant to give it to me..." Martha reached out and gently took hold of her nana's shoulder.

"Gina warned me you'd have a lot of questions." Zelda rubbed her nose.

"I think that's an understatement."

Without warning, Zelda jerked back. She grabbed hold of her wheels and maneuvered her chair. She rolled past the café and into the main body of the fairground again. "We should go to the entrance, to wait for Gina," she said over her shoulder.

"We haven't finished talking," Martha called helplessly after her.

"We have, for today. And there's something I want to do."

Martha helped to push Zelda towards the entrance gate. She still had so many questions turning over in her mind as they neared the fiberglass ice cream cone. Keeping hold of her emotions was like trapping a whirlwind in her chest. She didn't know when she'd see Zelda again, to ask her these things.

"Pass me my bag, please," Zelda said when they reached the entrance.

In a haze, Martha reached down and pulled it out from under her chair. She thought that Zelda might want a drink of water, or to take a tablet. However, her nana took out a copy of *Blue Skies and Stormy Seas*. It had a burgundy cover and gold lettering, a pristine copy like the one at Monkey Puzzle Books. Surprised to see it, Martha let out a puff of breath.

Zelda opened the book. She waited until a group of people approached. Then, hesitating like a conductor before they waved a baton at the orchestra, she cleared her throat. "Ahem. 'The Puppet Maker,'" she read aloud. Her voice was as loud and clear as Rita said it was.

Martha's limbs grew rigid as a young couple paused to listen. "What are you doing?" she hissed.

Zelda batted her hand and raised her voice a notch. "'A

puppet maker and his wife had been married for many years but couldn't have the children they longed for…'"

The young couple pushed their pram a bit closer. The three white-vested men from the ghost train stopped to listen. As Zelda read more of the story, a small crowd gathered around her. Two teenage girls laughed behind their hands. The young couple crouched down so their lips were level with their toddler daughter's ears. The tattooed men shrugged at each other.

Martha felt like her feet were set in tarmac. She wanted to walk away, to distance herself from this strange situation. But she had to wait until her grandmother finished the story, one Martha made up when she was a girl. She listened with a mix of dread and intrigue.

As Zelda read on, Martha couldn't enjoy her words. Her chest hurt and she raised herself on her tiptoes, looking for Gina. The recital was over in a few minutes but it felt like much longer.

"The end," Zelda announced as she finished the story.

When she closed the book, Martha exhaled with relief.

A few seconds of silence passed, before one person clapped, and then another. The man with the red devil tattoo whooped and his friend whistled. Zelda gave a small bow. She fumbled in her bag and took out a pen and pad of sticky yellow notes. After writing down a few words, she stuck a note to the front of the book. "Put it flat on the ground," she told Martha.

"The book?"

"Yes."

"Why?"

"There's no time to explain. I can see Gina coming."

Martha did what her nana asked. She placed the book on the pavement and stood up too quickly. With her heart leaping around, she took hold of the back of the wheelchair.

The tattooed man peered down at the book and picked it up.

And, as she began to push her grandmother away, Martha caught a glimpse of the words written on the yellow sticky note.

"Read me. I'm yours."

17

Puppets

Betty, 1978

Two years ago, on Betty's birthday, she, Zelda, Martha and Lilian enjoyed a fantastic, too-brief, forty minutes at the funfair, sharing laughs and toffee apples. And when they crept back across the sand, all hand in hand, they shared secret smiles as they waited for Thomas to wake up.

The girls did as they promised and didn't mention the trip to their dad. Betty thought everything was fine, until Thomas bought a copy of the *Maltsborough Times*. "There's a very interesting story about the fair in here, Betty," he said with a smile.

She knew from the singsong of his voice that something wasn't right. His smile was too wide and fixed. "Why don't you tell me about it?" she replied, feeling her cheeks beginning to glow.

Thomas placed the paper down on the table and tapped it with his finger. "I'll leave this here. You can take a look at it yourself. Then you might understand how disappointed and hurt I am by your actions. Have you forgotten how much I helped you, when we first met? My family warned me about marrying in haste and I wanted to prove them wrong. But, well…" He looked down and shook his head. "You've let me down, and you've let yourself down, too."

Betty waited until he'd left the room. Her hand shook as she pulled the newspaper towards her. There was a photo of Zelda, Martha and Lilian, sitting on a wall outside the hall of mirrors. Her mother gave a gap-toothed grin. The date was displayed on a wooden board behind them.

Knitting a hand into her hair, Betty hissed. "Bloody hell, Mum."

Why the hell had she let a photographer take a snap? It must have been when Betty went to retrieve her purse after leaving it at the toffee apple stall. "The trip was supposed to be our secret."

She glanced up nervously at the closed door. Behind it, Thomas would be waiting for her explanation. She'd have to take full responsibility for the visit to the fair, or perhaps she could say that Zelda insisted.

Now she had to face the consequences of her actions. It might result in a day or two of stony silence, or a cut to her household budget.

Still, it was only what she deserved, she supposed. If Thomas acted a little too controlling sometimes, then she shouldn't be surprised.

After what happened before they married, she only had herself to blame.

Betty thought she saw Daniel today. He was down on the beach, standing next to the mermaid statue. His hair was mussed up from the wind and his cheeks red from the cold. She took a few steps down the slope towards him, his name on her lips. But she stopped herself from calling him, knowing it was no use. He wouldn't see her or might not want to know her. After all this time, she should let things be.

Then the man turned and laughed, and she saw it wasn't him.

Pressing her hands to the knot of dismay in her stomach, Betty twisted on her heels and walked back towards the town.

When she passed a group of young women heading down to the beach, she couldn't help but feel envious. They wore the new long floral skirts and blouses with big collars. She still sported the dress and shoes Thomas bought for her birthday, two years ago.

The women were only a little younger than she was. No doubt they were going to chat and have fun, and she was married with daughters aged twelve and eight. She felt so much older. Ducking her head down, Betty looked at her watch. She said she'd be home within half an hour and picked up pace.

Ever since the day Thomas saw the photo in the newspaper, he questioned where she was, who she was with and how long she'd be. He did it pleasantly, always with a smile, but she was under no doubt that he no longer trusted her.

When Betty arrived back home, she found Martha lying on her stomach on the rug in the front room. She moved her legs back and fro as if kicking through water. Her books and pens lay scattered all over the floor as she wrote in her notepad.

"Oh, Martha." Betty sighed. "Look at this mess. I want everything to be perfect for when your father gets home."

"It's not mess, it's work."

"Whatever it is, it needs tidying up."

Martha swung her plait off her shoulder. "Dad's not even here. He's gone for a walk with Lilian. Why do we always have to run around after him? It's like he's the king of the castle or something."

Betty saw the fiery spark in her eyes. Her adolescent hormones had kicked in recently, bringing bouts of sullenness and uncooperativeness. However, when Martha was with Zelda, she was like a small girl again, sweet and smiley. She often heard her own mother's words when Martha spoke. "Now, come on. Be nice…" she prompted.

"I *know* that Dad doesn't like Nana."

"You're being silly. Of course he does."

Martha rolled her eyes. "She hasn't been over to the house for weeks. Whenever she buys us something, we're not allowed to have it."

"Some of your grandma's presents are…inappropriate."

"They're always fun. And *you're* not."

Betty held her breath. She smoothed down the front of her dress, not in the mood for a battle of wills. "If you're so fed up here, you should have gone for a walk, too."

"I wasn't invited, and it's so obvious that Dad prefers little *Miss Perfect* to me."

Betty set her shopping bags down on the floor. She knew that Thomas gave more attention to Lilian, but she wasn't going to admit it to Martha.

"Your dad and Lilian have similar interests, that's all." She walked over and reached out for Martha's plait, but her daughter ducked her head out of the way. Betty withdrew her fingers. "Now, let's get this stuff tidied up. Instead of writing your stories, let's make a list together, of all the things we need to do before your dad gets home. Then we can tick them off when we've done them."

Martha still glowered. "Lilian never gets told off, and she can do whatever she likes. She gets away with *everything*."

Betty's neck muscles grew stringy, at Martha for being so challenging, and also because she spoke the truth. "Don't talk about your father in that way."

"Why do we always have to do what he says? It's not fair."

"Your dad works hard for us, and I have to put this shopping away." Betty turned and headed for the kitchen.

"Stand up for yourself, Mum." Martha got up and followed her. "You said you wanted to find a job…"

"It's probably too late for that," Betty said as she tugged a jar of pickled onions out of her bag. She found herself repeating the words that Thomas had drummed into her. "I've not worked before. I don't have any experience."

Her fingers slipped on the jar and she could only watch as it fell from her hand, crashing to the floor. Vinegar blasted out, splashing her legs and seeping across the linoleum. "Damn it," she said under her breath. She picked up a cloth and saw that Martha had moved away, towards the front door.

"I'm going out," she said.

"Where to? Will you give me a hand to clean up this mess?"

Martha shook her head. "I'm going to see Nana. She's the only one who listens to me around here. Dad treats us like puppets and you can't see it."

"He's a good man…"

Martha shook her head. She opened the door, stormed outside and slammed it behind her.

Betty stared at the onions on the floor. They seemed to look up at her like eyeballs, and she felt her own eyes prick with tears.

Martha was right with a lot of what she said. But it was all too late to turn the clock back.

She threw down a cloth and stamped on it. She mopped the floor, then marched into the front room. To the sound of the ticking cuckoo clock, she dropped to her knees. Pulling Martha's books towards her, she tried to make a pile. After scooping them together, she hid them behind the sofa, ready to tidy them away properly later on. A pen lay across Martha's notepad. Her latest story lay freshly written.

Betty put the pad on her knee. A tear plopped onto the page and she wiped it away with the side of her hand. Then she read on.

The Puppet Maker

A puppet maker and his wife had been married for many years but couldn't have the children they longed for. This made them very sad and each night, the wife cried and pulled at her own hair. "I love you but I want us to have a family," she said. "I want to give you two daughters."

One night, as the puppet maker's wife slept, a bolt of lightning struck down a tree in the garden. The puppet maker decided he would carve the wood.

He shut himself away in his workshop and created the two largest puppets he'd ever made, in the shape of two girls. He attached strings to them and made crisscrosses of wood so he could manipulate their limbs. He added wool for their hair and painted their faces so they looked almost real. When he had finished, they were perfect.

When his wife saw the puppets, she cried tears of joy. "These are the daughters I've always longed for," she said.

The puppets joined them at the dining table for each meal, and each night the puppet maker and his wife put them to bed. They talked to them and cared for them, and the puppet maker's wife almost forgot they weren't real.

One night another storm came. This time, the lightning struck the house and the puppet maker screwed his eyes shut. "I wish the puppets could be proper girls," he said.

In the morning, when he and his wife went to the bedroom, two real girls lay in the beds. They peeped at them from over the covers.

"My daughters," the puppet maker's wife cried out and scooped them into her arms. "I shall call you Mary and Lola."

At breakfast, Mary didn't like the breakfast cereal and asked for fruit instead. Lola asked to wear a different color of skirt. The puppet maker's wife was so happy that she didn't care. However, the puppet maker wasn't happy. He thought the girls were rude to question what he gave them.

The four of them shared some lovely times as a family, going for picnics and paddling in the sea. However, the girls didn't need the puppet maker to operate them any longer. They acted how they wanted to.

One night, Mary and Lola didn't go to bed when the puppet maker told them to. Their disobedience was increasing and it made him feel angry. So, when they had fallen asleep, he fastened strings around their wrists.

"Let them go," his wife pleaded. "They are real children, not puppets."

"They must learn to do things my way."

"I don't agree."

The next night, while his wife slept, the puppet maker fastened strings to her wrists, too.

When she woke in the morning, she shook her wrists with dismay. "Fetch me some scissors," she whispered to her daughters. "I will set you both free."

"And you must join us," Mary and Lola said.

But their mother shook her head. "I love your father, so I must stay here. It would break his heart if I freed myself, too."

Mary and Lola pleaded with their father to let the three of them go, but he wouldn't listen. So that night, whilst he slept, they asked their mother to cut their strings.

Lola left and never returned, but Mary stayed behind

with her mother. *"If you won't leave then I must stay, too,"* she said.

"No. You must go," her mother begged.

But Mary refused.

And the puppet maker's wife knew that even though Mary was free from her strings, staying at home was like being tied to her crisscross of wood, forever.

18

Boxes

Martha tried to keep busy, to keep her mind off Zelda until she next got in touch, but her nana had a way of invading her thoughts. She pictured the scar on her head and her gap-toothed smile as she laughed on the ghost train. She saw the two of them standing behind the café, as Zelda revealed her time was ticking away.

When she went into the library, she found herself almost blubbing during the children's storytelling hour. She took out a couple of Nicholas Sparks tearjerkers on loan.

With each conversation Martha had, and with each discovery she made, she felt like she was staring into a child's kaleidoscope. With each tiny twist, the picture moved and formed a different one.

She should be happy, ecstatic even, that her nana was alive. However, the reality came with a black cloud above it that wouldn't drift away.

I've found something so precious, but I might not have it for long.

She kept thinking about organizing her mum and dad's funerals.

Thomas died first, on a cold wintery morning. Martha

made his breakfast and shouted him to come downstairs. When he didn't arrive, she found her mum sitting on the edge of the bed. "I can't wake him, Martha…"

Martha hoped that his passing might bring about a renaissance for her mother, a chance of freedom without the constraints Thomas set for their lives. However, Betty was lost. Her life and routine had been built around him. Everything she did catered for his likes and dislikes, his wants and needs.

Betty had fallen outside, just seven months later, and broken her hip. The doctor said her bones were brittle, from years of dieting. Martha visited her in the hospital twice a day, but her mother didn't have the will to get better.

It was Martha who visited the undertakers and booked the cars and flowers. She sent out notes to neighbors and organized a buffet in a local pub after the service. Lilian contributed financial support rather than emotional. The two sisters' worlds, so different, became even more so.

Martha wouldn't say their parents' lives were wasted, but they were severely restricted.

I want to support Zelda's last months, to allow her to be free.

With these thoughts about her parents and Zelda ringing in her head, Martha decided it was time to finally tackle the Berlin Wall of boxes.

She counted them and reached fifty-three. There was an array of different sizes—cat food boxes, washing powder, plain ones from the post office, and she wondered how she had gathered so many together.

She remembered crying as she folded in her mum's clothes and placed in perfume bottles and ornaments. There were things she should just throw in the bin but couldn't bring herself to do so. Half-used jars of hand cream and her mother's scent on handkerchiefs conjured up too many memories. So she had placed things in the boxes and closed up the flaps.

Out of sight, out of mind.

Thinking of Zelda's words about letting go of the past, she stood on her wooden chair and slid a box off the top of the giant wall.

Opening it up, she found it contained random items, such as an old camera, an Egyptian cat statue, a Russian doll and a few photo frames without prints in them. Although she remembered some of the things, none held any real sentimental value. She repackaged them and marked the box with an *X* to indicate its contents should go to the charity shop.

Another box was packed full of her mum's books, the spines all facing upward in a line. Martha ran her finger along them—fashion, astrology, family sagas, feel-good novels. She placed the collection on her To Keep pile, to browse through properly another time. Perhaps she could pass them on to Owen. She liked the idea of other readers getting pleasure from them.

Her fingers lingered on the box before moving it to the side of the room, realizing that her brain had conjured up a reason to contact him again.

With each box she relocated from the Berlin Wall to the charity pile, Martha felt a little lighter, as if she'd been carrying a heavy backpack that she'd just shrugged off. She found the task in her notepad and proudly changed the red dot of lateness to an amber star.

One box contained the rug she used to lie on when she was a girl. As she unfurled it and laid it on the floor, dust motes danced in the air and she ran her hand through them, marveling as they sparkled. She leaned down to straighten the tassels on the rug and then got down on the floor. Lying down on her belly, she grinned as she kicked her legs back and to for a while, with her chin resting in her hands.

The only things missing from the scene were her writing pad and pencil.

★ ★ ★

Martha had just wrapped her arms around a fifth box, edging it off the top of its pile, when the phone rang. She peered over the cardboard, down to see her own feet, and stepped off the chair. Dumping the box on top of the dining table, she batted a stripe of dust from the arm of her long-sleeved T-shirt and picked up the phone. "Hello?"

"Good morning," Gina replied.

"Oh," Martha said, not expecting her voice. "How are you?"

"Fine. Thank you for asking." Gina's words were clipped, as if she was making the call against her will. "I would like to ask you a question, about the fairground."

"Yes, of course." Martha wondered if she was about to be berated for breaking the *no sugar* rule, or perhaps the *no excitement* one. She had definitely bent the *no heavy conversation* one. She swallowed hard, as she wondered if her nana had reported her for asking too many questions.

To distract herself from the uncertain feeling in the pit of her stomach, she lifted one of the flaps on a box and spied a pair of binoculars. She remembered her father taking them to the beach and pointing them at Betty rather than out to sea.

"Did Ezmerelda do a Read and Run?" Gina asked. "She left with a copy of *Blue Skies and Stormy Seas* in her bag, but when I unpacked her things it was not there."

Martha frowned to herself. "I'm not sure what you mean. What's a Read and Run?"

"They are something Zelda decided she wanted to do, after her operation. She goes somewhere, takes a copy of her book and reads it aloud in a public place. Then she leaves it for someone else to discover."

Martha cleared her throat. She didn't want to implicate her grandmother but felt she didn't have a choice. "Zelda read aloud from the book and placed it on the ground. It happened so quickly, I didn't know what was going on."

"I knew it," Gina said with a weary sigh. "I wish she would stop them."

"Why does she do it?" Martha asked. To her, it seemed bizarre that her nana would want to share the stories.

Gina fell silent before she spoke. "Ezmerelda says she wants to bring those stories to people, as many as possible, in the time she has left. I assume she has told you about her situation?"

Martha closed her eyes. "Yes."

Gina tutted. "She thinks that she is still eighteen years old. You are lucky she did not make you go on any rides."

With a spike of guilt in her stomach, Martha felt she ought to admit the truth. "We, might have, um…"

However, Gina interrupted her. "Please wait a moment. Ezmerelda is here now and wants to ask you something. Goodbye." And with that, the phone rattled as she passed it on.

"Martha," Zelda said, her voice lively. "Are you okay? I've rested up."

Martha's eyes crinkled at the sound of her voice. "I'm so pleased you've called. I was worried you might be tired out. after the fair. I know I asked a lot of questions…"

"Yes, you did," Zelda said. "I'm not really surprised. Look, I know it's short notice, but are you free for dinner? There's a few friends coming over."

Martha found herself grinning. She'd prefer to see her grandmother alone, without having to deal with Gina's trickiness. And she wasn't sure how she was going to get to Benton Bay again, but she wasn't going to turn down this opportunity to see her nana. "This evening?"

"Yep."

"I'd love to."

"Fantastic." Zelda waited a while before she lowered her

voice to a whisper. "I told Gina we went for coffee at the fair. No rides. It helped to keep her sweet after my Read and Run."

"I don't think you were supposed to do that, either."

"Tsk. Gina used to do them with me, until she got all careful. Anyway, be here for seven o'clock. Bring tiramisu—and, oh, fetch a friend."

Martha stared at her phone. There was one person above anyone else that she should take to meet Zelda.

However, the last time she spoke to Lilian she told her to leave the book alone.

Yet it had opened up this whole new other world. Martha wanted to tell her sister that she had found Zelda, that their nana was still alive. But how would she take it? Even Martha couldn't quite believe it had happened.

When Lilian answered the call, she sounded tired again. "Hi, Martha. Don't tell me. You've *finally* finished Will's trousers?" she said.

"Actually, yes," Martha said. "I'll drop them around for you."

"And you haven't forgotten that you're looking after the kids on Saturday?"

"No. I'll try to clear a space in the house."

"Hmm, I bet that's easier said than done."

"Yes, but I've made a start. I've unpacked five of Mum and Dad's boxes this morning. Do you want to take a look through any of their stuff?"

"I don't think so. It's been so long, and I have lots of photos and memories. I don't want to get all misty-eyed about the past. Not at the moment, anyway."

"Well, okay." Martha fell quiet for a while, trying to work out how to approach the subject of their nana.

"Great. Well, it was good to speak to—" Lilian started.

Realizing she was about to hang up, Martha raised her voice. "Wait. Don't go. I need to ask you something."

"What?"

"Can you join me for dinner this evening?"

"Really? At the house? Can you even find your dining table? What's the occasion?"

"I've been invited somewhere and I'd like you to join me."

Lilian hesitated. "I think this is the first time you've ever invited me to do something social."

"Sorry."

"I think I'm free. Where is it?"

Martha wound the telephone wire around her wrist in a bracelet and then back again. She tried to rehearse words in her head but they jumped around. She knew that saying this wouldn't be easy, and she just had to go for it. "I know you said to leave the old book alone, but I couldn't do it. I found the date of the dedication was correct. Nana published the book and did sign it, in 1985."

Even though Lilian was over a mile away, Martha felt the air chill between them.

"What does *that* have to do with dinner?"

"I'll try to explain," she said with a swallow. "Owen Chamberlain, at the bookstore, traced another copy to Monkey Puzzle Books in Benton Bay. The owner, Rita, found it in a very odd way. Two ladies did a reading in the street and left it behind."

"I don't understand why you're telling me this."

Martha took a deep breath. She screwed her eyes shut, preparing herself to tell the next part of the story. "I found out that one of the ladies was Zelda, Lilian. Our nana is still alive."

She paused, thinking that she might hear a gasp or a *"What?"* from Lilian, but the only sound that came from the other side of the phone was the clunk of her sister's rings against the receiver.

"Um, did you hear what I said?" Martha asked after an unbearably long few moments.

"Well, yes," Lilian snapped. "And it's absolutely ridiculous. Zelda died years ago. We both know that."

"We *thought* we knew." Martha waited a while longer. The quietness was strange, like they had both entered a large church and were trying not to make a sound. When her sister didn't speak, she began to babble. "I met up with her, Lilian."

"You did *what?*"

"I was going to tell you about it, before I went to Benton Bay, but I had to go, there and then. It all seemed so surreal. But she was there, Lilian. I found her. I didn't recognize her at first. I mean, it's been so long—"

"It *can't* be her."

"She has the missing tooth. Do you remember the toffee apple at the fair? I went to her house, then we met at the fairground in Benton Bay. It's definitely her."

"I told you to leave all this alone." Lilian's voice was strained, like she was trying to squeeze on board a packed train.

"I know. I'm sorry. Please don't be mad at me."

"I don't know if I'm angrier with you, or at her."

Martha frowned. "Why would you be angry with Nana? Our parents told us she'd died. Why on earth would they do that?" Her voice pinged up a notch. "I looked after them for fifteen years and they never said a thing. They must have known all that time. Do you know what's gone on?"

Martha heard scratching, perhaps Lilian's fingernails against her chin, or in her hair. She waited until her sister's words flooded out.

"Look, I've just looked at my diary, and I *am* doing something tonight. Paul mentioned his friend might call round. I hope he doesn't expect me to cook anything, because it's not fully confirmed yet. I don't even know who she is. I mean, I expect it's a *her*. He seems to associate with women freely these days…"

Martha tried to decipher what Lilian was talking about and why. There seemed to be a huge disconnect in their conversation. "So, you can't make it tonight?" she confirmed.

"No. And I don't think that *you* should go, either."

She sounds like Dad when he told Mum not to do something, Martha thought.

"Some things are better left in the past, Martha," Lilian said. "Zelda wasn't a reliable person. It's very strange to hear she's alive, after all this time, but it's unlikely she's still got all her marbles intact. She could tell you anything, and you wouldn't know if it was the truth or not."

"She's told me very little. That's why we should both go to dinner. You can meet her. We can ask her things and try to find out what's gone on."

"I'm very sorry, Martha," Lilian said shortly. "I don't think I want to know. It's been such a long time and, well, I want to spend time with Paul. Things are rather tricky between us at the moment…"

"You didn't tell me that."

"Some things are easier to keep to yourself. You don't want everyone to know."

Martha felt her stomach dip. "But I'm your sister."

"I know." There was a noticeable pause before Lilian spoke again. "Look, just be careful with Zelda. Some things aren't what they seem."

A strange realization began to creep over Martha. Perhaps it was sisterly instinct. "Did you know about any of this?" she asked. "Did you know that Nana might be still alive?"

The question heralded Lilian's longest silence yet. The

cuckoo popped out of the clock and sang twelve times as Martha waited for her response.

"I didn't know that Zelda was still alive," Lilian said finally. "But I *did* know that she didn't die in 1982."

Lilian's last words made Martha's stomach turn over. Her hand shook and she tightened her grip on the receiver. She longed to question what her sister knew, but she could tell from her clipped tone their conversation was over. Martha offered to tell her how the dinner party went, and Lilian replied with a muted, "Okay."

Martha decided to try and blank her sister's words from her mind. She would find out soon enough, for herself, that evening. She couldn't imagine how and why Lilian might know something like that and not tell her.

She concentrated on moving and looking inside more of the boxes, picking up speed as she removed them from the stack. She rummaged through the contents quickly, and she soon grew sweaty with her face turning red.

She was going to the dinner party, whether Lilian liked it or not.

19

Balloon Head

In the early afternoon, Martha had just finished drinking a cup of tea when the doorbell rang. She felt a little spaced out because, after her conversation with Lilian, all she had managed to eat for lunch was a slice of toast. Wiping her hands on a pot towel, she opened the door.

Suki stood there, her arms weighed down with shopping bags. Her bump poked through her open coat, and her nose was pink from the wind. "I thought we could take a look at that dragon," she said, raising her bags by an inch.

Martha instantly reached out and tugged them off her. "You should not be carrying those in your condition. The ligaments in your back can relax during pregnancy, making you more susceptible to injury."

"It's not like I'm weight lifting." Suki shrugged. She stepped inside and slipped off her coat. She circled a hand over her stomach. "This baby is heavier."

Martha couldn't prevent herself from flying into organizer mode. "Sit down and I'll make you a drink," she said. "The sofa is the most comfortable seat, not the wooden chair. I'll move some boxes. Do you have enough cushions for your back? I'll get you a coffee. Is caffeine okay when you're pregnant?"

Suki held up her hands in surrender. "I'm here to try out papier-mâché, not for butler service. I'm not very thirsty." She held onto her belly as she maneuvered herself down onto the floor. After reaching up and taking the dragon's head from the crates, she set it down on her lap. "Things are looking tidier in here," she said. "Have you had a sort out?"

Martha nodded, then narrowed her eyes. "Are you sure you're okay?"

"Yes."

"Well, okay. I decided that I couldn't wait any longer for my sister to help me look through the boxes, so I made a start."

"Good for you. It looks much better." Suki pulled her bag towards her and took out a large plastic bowl. She sprinkled gray powder into it and poured in water from a bottle. Taking a wooden stick, she gave it a stir. "This is how you make the papier-mâché. Stick your hand in. It feels like clay."

Martha knelt down beside her and rolled up her sleeves. She reached into the bowl. The mixture felt rather pleasing, cool and soothing to her fingertips. A sense of calmness washed over her as she pressed the mixture, feeling it squish and move.

Suki tilted and examined the dragon's face. "I think I'll glue a small piece of card over the hole in his cheek, then apply the papier-mâché over the top of it." She took a scoop of the mixture and began to spread it out under the dragon's eye using her forefinger. "I remember doing this at school."

"Me, too. We glued strips of newspaper to a balloon, then popped it and turned it into a head."

"Yes. And stuck wool on for hair."

They grinned at each other, at finding a common experience.

Suki took a moment to reposition her dress over her bump

with the heels of her palms. "Do you have any children, Martha?"

Martha fell quiet. It was a question that made her want to retract her head like a tortoise. She stretched out her neck and gave her throat a brief stroke.

As a younger woman, she'd always imagined her life with children in it. She'd never pictured an alternative.

There's still time, she used to tell herself when she reached thirty-seven, then thirty-nine and forty-one. But as she got older, so did her parents. As their health got worse, their dependence grew greater.

When she turned forty-two, Martha started to have a recurring dream that temporarily replaced her one about drowning. In it, she daubed on scarlet lipstick, went to a bar and sat on a high stool, sipping a margarita. A man would stroll in, usually looking a lot like Joe, and join her. After a few drinks, they'd slip away to his place for a night of torrid passion.

But then she'd wake up. She'd hear Thomas coughing or Betty flushing the toilet and she'd come back down to earth with a thud.

As she got out of bed to help them, her cheeks would be fiery with shame. However, she'd also feel a kernel of longing, because a huge part of her wanted to try out the dream for size, in real life. She was more likely to have a child through a one-night stand than by meeting and starting a relationship with someone.

She hadn't heard her biological clock ticking, as such. It was more a landslide sensation as her hopes slipped away.

When a doctor informed her that she was entering an early menopause, Martha finally laid her hopes for a family to rest. She dedicated herself fully to looking after her parents. Her dreams of seducing a stranger subsided, and the one about struggling in the sea returned.

"No. I never married," she told Suki, hearing the regret in her own voice. "Though I almost did, once..."

Suki nodded empathetically. She dabbed and patted the dragon's ear. "Ben and I nearly did, too, before it all went wrong. I could see our future together so clearly, like it was a photo, but not filtered and posted on Instagram yet. Now I wonder why I was so blind. I think he was always too repugnant to commit, but I chose not to see it."

Martha wasn't sure if she meant *reluctant* instead, or if she had used the correct word.

"What's your story, Martha? What happened to you?" Suki asked.

Martha hadn't talked about Joe since they split up. His was another name that her dad didn't like mentioned in the house.

In her mind, though, she could still see her ex-fiancé's ruffled mousy hair, the goofy grin that belied his fierce intelligence. She felt his hand in hers, and it still surprised her to wake up and find that she wasn't in her twenties and he wasn't beside her.

"You'll probably spend our wedding morning darning socks for someone else," he used to tease.

He was the opposite to her, a calm, chilled man who let worries and stresses flow over him like a trickling brook. And she was the one who scurried, made lists and was forever busy. He encouraged her to be the person she wanted to be.

As she traced her fingers over the papier-mâché, smoothing out the lumps and bumps, she found herself wanting to tell Suki more about Joe. It was suddenly important that this young woman knew her as someone other than Martha, volunteer librarian, laundry-doer and dragon head–rescuer.

She wanted to say his name out loud, to remind herself that he had existed, once.

"We lived together in a small cottage, just over a mile from here," she said. "It had the tiniest rooms and was always cold, whatever the season, so we had to wear lots of layers to keep warm. But it was ours and we loved it. We were happy with the simple things in life—paddling in the sea, eating fish and chips on a bench in the drizzle, or an evening at home watching TV wrapped in a blanket.

"We'd been together for four years when we booked a church for our wedding. We didn't want a posh ceremony, or anything fancy for our reception. We were happy with pie and peas and pickled red cabbage, served in the church hall." Martha felt her eyes shine as she talked, but the sparkle faded when she thought about the next part of her story.

"Then my dad got sick. He'd always been pretty active, but he slowed right down and had difficulty walking. He went for tests and was diagnosed with rheumatoid arthritis. It meant he couldn't work."

Suki shook her head, her lips tight. "Oh, I'm so sorry..."

"He'd never liked the idea of my mother having a job. So there wasn't any money coming in to the house. Joe and I helped them out financially, all we could, but we were saving for our wedding. Joe always felt like he'd done something wrong because Dad wouldn't speak to him properly, but it was just his way.

"Anyway, while Dad was going through his tests, Joe was offered a job in New York. He was a journalist and a friend asked him to work on a new newspaper out there. It was an amazing opportunity, for both of us. I was working in a bookshop at the time, and I was ready to try something new."

Martha swallowed as a wave of regret swept over her. She had to take a minute before she carried on. Spotting a small gash under the dragon's chin, she pointed it out to Suki.

"I couldn't leave my parents behind, though. Dad was depressed after his diagnosis and Mum was wearing herself out, looking after him. She wanted to find work, but he wouldn't listen. So I suggested that Joe should fly out to America first. He'd find us a place to live and get settled in. We'd postpone the wedding, so he could concentrate on his new job. I'd join him as soon as I could. It'd give Dad longer to see if he felt better, and Mum could secretly look for work. It all sounded so, um..." She struggled to find a word.

"Feasi-bubble?"

"Yes, feasible. But Dad didn't improve. His condition worsened and some days he was in a lot of pain. Mum found it hard to cope with him, so I ended up staying longer."

She looked down as she remembered her mum gripping her wrists, her neck all sinewy. "Please don't leave me alone here, Martha," Betty had pleaded. "Not while he's like this. Promise me. You can go to Joe when things get better."

And Martha made her promise.

"But, you did join Joe eventually?" Suki looked at Martha expectantly.

Martha wiped her hands on a piece of tissue. "I flew out to see him for a few days, and he showed me all these amazing sights, the Statue of Liberty and the Empire State Building. It was like we'd never been apart. But I could see things had already started to change. He talked about our future, but I was worried about my parents. They needed me more than Joe did..."

"Couldn't your sister have helped out?" Suki brushed at a smudge of papier-mâché that had dried and whitened on her cheek.

"Lilian had just got married and Joe waited for me, for over a year. But we only saw each other that once in New York. His job made it difficult for him to come home. Eventually, we both realized that I wasn't going to join him, and we put things on hold."

She gave a small sniff. Her words started to stick in her throat. "After a few months, Joe met someone else and she fell pregnant straight away. He married her instead of me."

She took a small ball of papier-mâché and squashed it between her thumb and forefinger, briefly imagining how her life could have been so different. If only she hadn't tried to be the perfect daughter. If only she had been braver. She'd have had the foundations in place for a different life, but she let them crumble.

"Well." Suki sat back on her heels. She gave an indignant sigh. "It just shows that Joe wasn't the right person for you."

A lump swelled in Martha's throat. Her eyes filled with tears, blurring her vision. "I know that he *was* the right person. I just had to make a choice. I did my best to please everyone." She gritted her teeth to try to stop the flood of emotion that was threatening to overtake her.

Don't have an outburst and show yourself up again, she told herself.

"You always try to please everyone else, rather than yourself," Suki said.

Martha pressed the dragon's chin too hard, her finger pushing through the fresh mush. She stared at the hole, then blindly around the room. "Sorry, I've damaged your repair." She attempted to stand up.

Suki placed her hand on her arm, the weight of it pulling her back down. "Don't worry about that. I'm so sorry, Martha."

"They were my family and I couldn't let them down. It's too late for change now." Martha slumped back down onto the floor.

"Don't be so daft. My mum must be around your age and she's just bought a posh little apartment in Marbella-ella, or however you say it. Her new fella is only five years older than me. You're only as old as you feel."

"But I feel bloody ancient."

"Well, you don't look it," Suki said, before she took a second glance. "Well, perhaps you could do with a freshen-up. Just like this dragon. I'll redo his chin, then he's finished."

"What happens then?"

"We'll leave him to dry, for a day or so. Then he needs a light sandpapering and a rubdown of his rough bits. I've brought some paint, and we can resurrect him to his former glory."

Martha flicked a smile. "I wish someone could do that for me. I'm going to my nana's for dinner this evening."

Suki looked her over from head to toe. "Well," she said. "I have no other plans for the day, and I have my makeup bag with me. We could give something a try, if you like?"

20

High Heels

Martha had always been wary of hairdressers. The giant posters of glossy-maned twentysomethings displayed in salon windows usually bore no resemblance to the bored women who sat inside, holding cups of tea and sporting silver foil in their hair.

On one occasion, not long after her parents died, she plucked up the courage to venture into a Maltsborough salon. She took along a photo she'd trimmed out of a magazine. Gingerly presenting it to a pretty girl with jumbo caramel curls, Martha admitted that she'd not had a professional haircut for some years.

The girl made all the right noises, then took up her own personal challenge, to produce a hairstyle as little like the one in the photo as possible.

Martha left the salon with a haircut resembling poodle ears, her curls tight and crispy.

Since then, she'd managed her own hairdressing agenda, consisting of a once-a-year snip at her dead ends, and a conditioning treatment if it came free with a magazine. So it was with extreme trepidation that she allowed Suki to hover around her head with a pair of scissors.

"We'll just do a little trim," Suki said. The bells on her ankle bracelet jingled as she circled Martha, peering into her hair as if she was looking for eggs in a large bird's nest. "I'll tidy up your hair, then we can try out some eyeshadow."

Martha nodded meekly. She tried not to grip the seat of the wooden chair as snippets of hair began to fall onto her lap, a strange mix of dark and light.

"It's just a haircut." Suki paused for a moment. "You're acting like you're in a rocket, bracketed for take off."

"Sorry," Martha said, thinking that's exactly how she felt.

The feeling of another person standing so close to her was unsettling. With her eyes screwed shut, she could hear the swish of Suki's dress as she combed and snipped. She smelled of patchouli and toast.

When Suki touched her hair, Martha felt like ants were teeming through her roots and she wasn't sure if it was delicious, or if she wanted it to end very quickly.

She concentrated on sitting still until Suki announced, "Done."

Martha opened one eye and peered up, then left and right. Alarmingly, she couldn't see any hair in her peripheral vision.

"Do you want a mirror?"

Martha didn't detect any concern in Suki's voice. She didn't have an oh-my-god-what-have-I-done tone. In fact, she sounded rather upbeat. "I'm not too sure."

"Okay. Well, I'll do your makeup next, then you can take a look." Suki took her cosmetic bag out of her handbag. It was purple and shiny, the size of a house brick, and looked just as heavy. "Can you sit still for longer?"

Martha nodded.

She used to wear a little mascara and a favorite dusky-pink Elizabeth Arden lipstick that Joe said he liked, and which gave her lips a natural color. But that was over twenty years ago, when her face didn't look like it needed a good iron after waking up in the morning.

She never bothered to apply makeup these days. It was supposed to enhance what you already had, but what if you didn't have anything in the first place?

The experience of Suki tending to her face was both intimidating and strangely relaxing—a brush to the cheeks, a finger blend to her eyes, the sensation of her eyelashes briefly lifting upward with the mascara brush.

"You've got good skin," Suki said.

Martha, not used to receiving compliments, wondered if this was a secret code for, *You have crow's feet and broken veins, but surprisingly no spots.* When Suki said she was going to give her a smoky eye, she thought of a finger ring of charcoal she had once given herself after overcooking some sausages.

She'd lost the ability to process a compliment. If someone said anything nice to her, by the time she'd mused over the conundrum of what it really meant and how to reply, the moment had passed.

After a further few minutes of dabbing, brushing and painting, Suki announced, "Ta-da. Take a look."

Martha pressed her lips together and they felt sticky, like she'd eaten honey. Her eyelashes felt a little crusty. "I'm not sure if that's advisable."

Suki pressed a small round mirror into her hand, anyway. She folded her arms and stood back.

Martha inhaled and held her breath, preparing herself for disappointment, or even horror. Her rib cage felt corset-tight as she slowly lifted the mirror, wondering what awful apparition might look back at her. She turned her face to the side and then the other, to view her reflection. The person looking back at her didn't look like Martha Storm.

"What do you think?" Suki asked.

Martha moved the mirror backward and then forward again. She tilted it and pouted to see her lip color more clearly. The peachy color on her cheeks made it look like she'd just got back from her brisk morning walk. Her eyelids shimmered with a soft olive and gold, and a fine flick of brown liner gave her eyes a feline quality.

Embarrassingly, she found herself brimming with tears. Deep lines appeared between her eyebrows as she tried to stop them.

I look more like the woman Joe fell in love with.

"I presume you're weepy because you like it, not because it's gross," Suki said. "The mascara is waterproof, so don't worry about that."

Martha blinked quickly to test out this claim. She peered into the mirror to check for smears or smudges and was most impressed that there weren't any. "You've made me look like an antiques show presenter," she said. "Thank you."

Suki frowned. "Um, is that good?"

"Of course." Martha pressed a hand to her hair, which was shorter but more full and curlier. "I look like me, only much, much better."

"You look lovely. And it wasn't hard to do. Next time I'll talk you through it."

"Next time?" Martha repeated, finding it difficult to tear her gaze away from the person in the mirror who looked like her more glamorous, prettier twin.

"Only if you want to."

"Yes." Martha nodded furiously, her curls bouncing. "Very much so."

Suki took a handful of products and stuffed them back into her cosmetics bag. "Have you ever thought about tracking Joe down?"

Martha tried to process the question. "No, why would I? He got married. To someone other than me."

"Yes, but that was ages ago. He might be divorced now. You should look him up."

"Oh no," Martha said. Looking to her past meant thinking about her parents, of her nana vanishing and everything around that. She didn't want to look back, only forward, as Zelda had prompted. "He moved on. He found a new life, without me in it. I was surplus to his requirements."

"Don't rule it out," Suki said. "Sometimes putting things to rest from your past can be catholic."

"Do you mean cathartic?"

"Probably." Suki was about to say something else when her mobile phone pinged with a text. She took it out of her jacket pocket. "Hmm." She grimaced as she read the message.

Martha ran a finger over her scratchy eyelashes and thought about Zelda's instruction to bring someone to dinner. She wasn't sure if Suki classed herself as a friend yet, or if she still belonged in the acquaintance category. But they had shared a unique experience together, with the dragon's head and her makeover. Although Suki was young and might have other offers on the table, it might help to distract her from thinking about Ben. "You said that you're not busy..." she started. "Perhaps you'd like to join me at my nana's house for dinner?"

"Oh." Suki wrinkled her nose. "Sorry, but I've just had a text from Ben. He wants to pick up some stuff and chat. I'll have to stay in, though I'd much prefer to go out with you." She stuffed her cosmetic bag back into her handbag. "It's probably time to give him my culmination."

Martha wished she could do something to help, but no longer wanted to suggest counseling or working things out. "Ben's an idiot," she blurted. "For letting you go."

Suki froze, with her hand in her bag, before she straightened her back. "Yes, he is. Thank you, Martha."

"Zelda told me to bring a guest, but it's not essential to my attendance."

Suki thought for a while. She zipped up her handbag and slung it on her shoulder. "You could invite Owen instead," she said.

Martha shook her head rapidly. Her new hairstyle felt swishy. "I can't do *that*."

"Why not?"

"He's probably busy. He's had several wives…"

"Is he one of those polygon people?"

"No. He didn't have them all at once, and he doesn't have one at the moment."

"Good. I'll call and ask him then, if you like?"

Martha shook her head again, even more profusely. "Oh no. I wouldn't want to intrude."

"Maybe he'll want to meet Zelda. I'd make it sound very consensual."

Martha hoped she meant *casual*. She didn't speak.

Suki raised an eyebrow. "Okay," she said, with an exaggerated shrug. "It's your choice."

Martha was about to say *no* a further time when she caught sight of her reflection in the window. Would she say no to Joe, if she could relive her time again? Or would she take a chance?

She knew the answer.

She also didn't want Gina and Zelda to think that she didn't have any proper friends, even if she didn't have. She owed Owen a thank-you for his research, and an apology for going to Monkey Puzzle Books without him. She looked at Suki and saw the disappointment etched on her face. After everything she'd done for her today, Martha wanted to please her.

"Well, perhaps you could ask him," she said, instantly regretting it. "Though I'm sure he'll be otherwise occupied."

Suki broke into a smile. She picked up her phone and shook it in the air. "I'll take this into the kitchen, before you change your mind," she said. "You stay here." Then she vanished out of the room.

Martha sat on her hands in case they started to shake. She wondered what the heck she'd just agreed to. Of course, Owen wouldn't want to join her, but it would make Suki happy to call him.

She hummed a little tune to herself as she waited, wondering where to buy tiramisu. She'd have to find one with good quality ingredients and which looked authentically Italian. A supermarket one probably wouldn't pass muster.

There was also the matter of her clothes. Now she had new hair and a new face, did her old clothes match?

When Suki reemerged from the kitchen, she wore a triumphant smile.

Martha found her own insides leaping around.

"Owen says he'll join you. He'll drive over and pick you up at five thirty," Suki said. "So now, before Ben arrives and stresses me out, I've got a bit of time. Shall we see if there's anything nice in your wardrobe for you to wear?"

"Okay." Martha clicked her tongue. "Though it'll probably be a fruitless search."

Martha kept pressing a finger to her lips, the pink balm proving irresistibly touchable. She and Suki stood together in Martha's bedroom. Out of all the rooms in the house, this was the one she kept in a minimalistic fashion. There were only her bed, a wardrobe, and a dressing table that she never used.

"Stop touching your mouth," Suki said. "Keep the balm tube so you can reapply it. And I'll leave some of the other makeup, too, for you to try out." She opened the wardrobe door and began to work through Martha's collection of long-sleeved T-shirts. Every so often she paused, tilted her head and then carried on, sliding the coat hangers along the rail.

She explained to Martha that there was such a thing as naff embroidery and lovely embroidery, but it was tricky to distinguish between the two. "A lot depends on the position and the motif. Roses are good but a boo-ket of flowers can be bad," she said as she pulled out a gray top, then put it back again.

"I think you mean bouquet, and I don't really understand."

"It's kind of an instinct thing. Anyway, you should find your own style and stick with it. If you like embroidered daisies on beige jersey, you should *own* that look. I always wear long dresses because I have dumpy legs."

Martha found it difficult to imagine that Suki had any legs at all under her long layers.

"I kind of go for boho-cheek, but a classic look will work best for you," Suki added.

Now that she was using Lilian-esque-type words, Martha decided not to say anything else. She let Suki do her job.

Martha had kept a few pieces of Betty's clothes in her wardrobe, and Suki located a fine-knit emerald-green sweater and a black pencil skirt. She teamed these with a pair of Betty's beige heels.

Martha felt that the color of the sweater was a little bright, too botanical, and the color of the heels reminded her of a dog's skin, underneath its fur, but she told herself to trust Suki's judgment.

She changed into the clothes in the bathroom. They were tighter than anything she'd worn before and she pulled at the sweater to loosen it. She was concerned it smelled a bit musty, so gave it a spritz of lily-of-the-valley air freshener.

"Leave it alone," Suki said. "It smells okay and you look great. Take a look in the long mirror."

Martha didn't want to do that. She knew she looked different because she felt different. Although she was comfortable with the amendments to her hair and makeup, extending change to her entire body might be a step too far. "No, it's okay. I trust you." She held her arms out to the side and waddled out of the bathroom.

"Try not to walk like a peregrine."

"Do you mean a penguin?"

"Whatever." Suki shook her head and held out a coat. It was one of Betty's, beige wool with a tie belt. "This will look good."

Martha took the coat from Suki and pulled it on, catching a brief whiff of her mother's perfume. It reminded her of the flowers her father bought each Friday.

A myriad of emotions washed over her for a moment—sadness, nostalgia, love and regret—but she didn't want to allow them to envelop her. She was actually having fun. Not in a running-along-the-sands-with-a-beach-ball type, but a grown-up version. She had to try to banish any doubts or concerns from creeping in.

"I have to go," Suki said, glancing at her watch. "You'll be okay?"

Martha gave a firm nod. "I have no choice." She tied the belt on her coat more tightly. Then she tried not to stumble as she made her way downstairs in the high-heeled shoes. "Please don't pick up your craft bags. I'll bring them to the library," she said as she opened the front door.

"Okay." Suki stepped outside. "Let me know when you want to paint the dragon's head. Or feel free to have a go yourself." She tugged her coat across her bump, the edges failing to meet in the middle.

"I will. Oh, and Suki," Martha called out after her as she walked away. "Thank you for a most enlightening afternoon."

"Ha," Suki said, glancing back over her shoulder. "You shall go to the ball, Ms. Storm."

21

Cake

Even though it was six minutes before the agreed time, Martha waited on the doorstep for Owen to arrive and pick her up.

She trotted to one side of the step and then the other, testing out the stability of her heeled shoes and the likelihood of twisting her ankle. A probability of around 35 percent, she reckoned.

She bent one knee forward and then the other, trying out the tightness of her skirt. It made her feel like her legs were bandaged together, and she didn't feel like Martha Storm, Volunteer Librarian any longer. The skirt gave her more of a Martha Storm, Wonder Woman feeling.

When Owen arrived, precisely on time, she was pleased to note, he got out of his car and opened the door for her. Martha hobbled over and just about managed to eke her legs high enough to climb into the seat.

"Will you be warm enough with bare legs?" he asked.

How lovely of him to show concern, she thought. Though she also felt a small jolt of disappointment that he hadn't commented on her drastic change of appearance.

She herself had spotted that he was wearing a salmon-colored scarf that, strangely, both complemented and contrasted with his red shirt. He'd added a badge to his lapel collection, this one proclaiming Bookaholics Anonymous. He had also cleaned the inside of his car. The foot well was empty and she could smell violets.

Without waiting for her reply, Owen bent down to fiddle with his car radio. "Sorry, but I've been trying to locate some music for us that isn't heavy metal or electronic dance… I may have failed."

They set off and drove up and along Maltsborough Road to the sound of AC/DC played on volume level two and a half.

"I'm so intrigued to meet Zelda and chat about her book," Owen said as they headed inland. "I have so many questions, about how *Blue Skies and Stormy Seas* came to be in print."

Martha wanted to find out the same thing, too. And this was good, she told herself, that his enthusiasm was firmly focused on her nana. Because, with her newly pinkened lips and appealing hair, the last thing she wanted was for him to think she'd invited him on some kind of date. "Getting answers from her is proving quite a challenge," she warned.

They stopped off to buy tiramisu from a delicatessen on the way, and a bottle of merlot. Martha peered down at the dessert as it rested on her lap, and it looked both assuredly fresh and authentically Italian. If she ate cake, then she was sure it would taste delicious.

She was pleased to find that her and Owen's conversation wasn't stilted at all, as they resumed their discussion about books. This time they talked about ones from their childhoods. Martha chose Enid Blyton's *The Magic Faraway Tree* because she loved the idea that creatures lived in a tree, in an everyday forest. Owen preferred *Treasure Island*. "It offers true escapism, buccaneers and buried gold," he said. "What more could a boy want from a book?"

★ ★ ★

When they reached the old vicarage, Martha's back felt a little damp with nerves, but she knocked firmly on the door. She remembered that her arrival hadn't achieved much enthusiasm from Gina the last time she was here.

However, Gina answered the door with a warm smile. She wore a blush-pink sweater and long cream skirt. Her long white hair was swept into a loose bun. She gave Martha a small kiss to her cheek.

Martha returned it, unsure whether to go for a double one that seemed to pass as a standard greeting these days. She stuck with the one. "I'd like to introduce you to Owen Chamberlain, a bookseller," she said. "He passed *Blue Skies and Stormy Seas* on to me. And this is Gina. She's Zelda's, um…" She didn't complete her sentence, unsure how Gina preferred to be addressed.

"Thank you for bringing the tiramisu," Gina chipped in quickly. "This looks lovely, Martha."

The sound of wheels trundling on wooden floor sounded in the hallway and Zelda appeared at Gina's side. She wore a turquoise paisley silk headscarf and a dress with a similar pattern. "Hello," she said and offered Owen her hand. "I'm Ezmerelda Sanderson, Martha's nana."

Owen shook it and smiled. "But surely you aren't old enough."

"You smoothie." Zelda batted her hand at him coyly. "Good choice of guest," she whispered to Martha as the four of them moved towards the dining room together. Owen and Gina went first, and Zelda and Martha followed. "And *you* look beautiful tonight. Absolutely glorious."

Under her beachy-peachy powdered cheeks, Martha blushed.

★ ★ ★

Everyone took their seats around the table, a tight squeeze in the cozy room, and Gina poured out glasses of blush prosecco. There were ten people in total, eight women and two men. Martha and Zelda sat next to each other and Gina guided Owen to the opposite end of the table, positioning him next to a young woman who wore a white silk lily in her hair and vivid orange lipstick.

At the other side of the room, Martha noticed a mantelpiece dotted with knickknacks, a white ceramic cat, swirly gold candlesticks and photos in an eclectic array of frames. From where she sat, she could see the shapes of people smiling in the photos, but couldn't make out their faces. She wondered if Zelda had any of the Storm family on display.

Martha waited until Gina filled her glass before she glanced briefly in Owen's direction.

"Is he your boyfriend?" Zelda asked.

Martha's cheeks flooded with color and she quickly sipped her drink. "Don't be silly. He's just a friend."

"I'd snap him up." Zelda nudged her arm. "He's hot."

"Zelda," Martha hissed, spluttering into her glass. The bubbles tickled her nose. She tried to focus her eyes anywhere other than on Owen. "I'm not a teenager."

"*Tsk*. When did you start calling me Zelda? I prefer Nana or Grandma."

The spread of food on the table looked delicious, baby new potatoes in minted butter, steaming carrots and green beans, a juicy nut roast and slices of beef. There was a huge bowl full of various breads, freshly made and served with salt and peppercorn butter.

As she sat stiffly in her chair, Martha found it difficult to relax in this strange setting. She looked around the room and everyone seemed to be chatting away, comfortable with each other. They were poised and knew how to act, and she didn't. She felt like she was on show, an oddity. Zelda's long-lost granddaughter who'd been allowed out of her overstuffed house.

She also knew that no one else was making her feel this way. She was doing it to herself. Her nana had just introduced her as "Martha. A book lover, like us."

"We like to eat Southern style," Zelda interrupted Martha's wandering thoughts as she handed her a bowl of coleslaw.

"Southern?" Martha thought of the UK. London and Brighton, perhaps even Kent.

"Gina and I lived in North Carolina for nearly thirty years, in a cute little town near Raleigh. We only moved back here, after my tumor op, for healthcare reasons. Sharing food was a huge thing out there, with friends and family. Can you hear my American twang?"

Martha nodded, having spotted that her nana's accent was no longer purely from Yorkshire.

She also noticed how Zelda said *"thirty years"* as if it was a blink of an eye, the turn of a page. But it hadn't been for Martha. It had been a long slog. There had been some rewards, knowing that her parents were comfortable and able to stay in their own home, but that couldn't compensate for the isolation and loneliness she'd endured. The nagging knowledge that she was missing out on life.

And all that time, Zelda had been cooking and feeding other people too much slaw. Shouldn't she have been in Sandshift, helping to look after Betty? Her own daughter?

Martha's throat tightened at her own selfishness. She didn't know why Zelda had gone, or how Lilian knew she hadn't died. She darted her eyes away from her nana.

"It gets a bit boring on my own, so I invite people over," Zelda said. "Pass me the wine and I'll pour you another one."

"I've got plenty left, thank you." Martha placed her hand on top of her glass, but Zelda tapped it away. She tipped the bottle until the fizzy pink liquid was just a millimeter or two from the rim. Martha had to sip it straight away so it didn't spill over. After her jumble of thoughts, she was glad of the warm rush it gave her.

Zelda turned her head and took up a conversation with a man to her left. He wore a tweed jacket and had wiry brown-blond hair and a slim mustache that moved as he talked. She introduced him, briefly, to Martha as "Harry, from the next village."

In turn, Martha found herself talking about her library work, to a lady who had a cut-glass accent and a distracting mole under her eye. Martha felt oddly proud when the lady laughed out loud at her story about the ferret-costumed man.

Eventually, when Harry excused himself from the table, Martha chatted with Zelda again. Her grandmother's cheeks were rosier now, her eyes a little pink.

"I think Harry likes you," Zelda confided, too loudly.

"Me?" Martha tried not to glance at the jolly fellow when he returned to his seat.

"I've told him you've got your eye on someone else. But Harry doesn't mind a bit of competition."

"Ha." Martha laughed nervously. Knowing it was pointless to scold her grandmother, she reached out for her glass and drained all her wine. The warm feeling it gave her helped her to feel less paranoid.

"Harry works at Sandshift football ground, arranging events and entertainment. He may come in handy for our plan of action."

Martha didn't know which word worried her most. *"Plan"* or *"action."* "What exactly is that?"

Zelda stared at her, as if she should know. "You witnessed my Read and Run?"

"Gina explained what it was."

"Well, I want my next one to be for as many people as possible. And I want you to join me."

"Thanks. I'm happy to come along and watch."

"Oh no." Zelda shook her head resolutely. "I want it to be a team effort. Me and you."

"You want to read a story from *Blue Skies and Stormy Seas*? At the football ground?"

"Yes. The crowd will love it."

Martha didn't have any experience of football matches but she very much doubted it. She ran a finger cautiously around the top of her glass. "With me?"

"Well, I don't want to do it on my own."

"Can't Gina help you?"

As Zelda glanced over at her carer, her eyes grew dimmer. "Gina's a good woman, but she wants me to put my feet up. She doesn't understand I want to spend time living it up, not sitting it out," Zelda said. "Plus, we won't charge a fee."

Martha pursed her lips. "I don't think I can do it. The stories in the book bring back a lot of memories. They're not all pleasant…"

"That's a good reason *to* do it."

Martha wondered if she was missing something. "I don't really see how."

Zelda squeezed her hand. "We can create new memories, together. You can write new stories."

This was all too much for Martha to take in. She had come here hoping to solve a myriad of family mysteries, about why Zelda vanished, what Lilian knew, and about how and why the book came to be in existence. But now, her nana was trying to sign her up as entertainment for a local football match.

"I can't write any longer," she protested. "Those stories were stupid, old-fashioned ones I made up when I was a child."

"Excuse me." Zelda removed her hand and folded her arms. "Those stories are ah-mazing."

"Well." Martha bristled. "I can't tell them any longer. They vanished from my head when you disappeared from my life."

"But I'm back now. Can't you just pick up where you left off?"

"I'm sorry, I can't."

The two women stared at each other and then looked in opposite directions.

"Well," Zelda said with a sniff. She rooted around up her sleeve for a tissue and patted it against her eyes. She flicked her head and her voice shook. "That's a *real* shame."

"I'll come with you, to the football ground. I just don't want to—"

Zelda cleared her throat. "It's one of my dying wishes," she said. "For us to do it together."

Martha's mouth dropped open. She took hold of Zelda's elbow. "Please don't say *that*."

"Well, it is." Zelda's voice wobbled. "That and being able to celebrate one last Christmas. Is it really too much to ask?"

Martha felt her chest ache with guilt. "No. It isn't too much," she muttered.

"Thank you," Zelda said with a tremble of her lip. "You're a good girl, Martha Storm."

When Martha felt a hand on her shoulder, she turned to find Owen smiling down at her. He placed a further glass of wine next to her plate. "This is a very nice chardonnay. Drink as much as you like. I'm sticking to the orange juice tonight for our drive home." He moved his head a few inches back and frown lines appeared across his forehead. "Have you cut your hair? It looks very stylish. The green sweater suits you, too."

Martha felt a giggle rise from deep inside her chest. It felt too girlish, not her. "Thank you," she said. A small hiccup escaped from her lips and then another. She placed a hand to her mouth to stop them and, as her shoulders twitched, she spotted Harry firing a grin in her direction.

The food was delicious, so different from the usual things Martha popped into the microwave or spooned onto toast. The wine loosened her words and made her feel less overawed at being surrounded by people.

When she eventually got to talk to Zelda again, she couldn't leave things alone. "Did you ever think of us?" she waved her glass around a little. "While you were in America?"

Zelda cocked her head to one side. "Of course I did. I might have been far away, but I thought about you. And Betty, too..."

"And Lilian?"

"Yes."

Martha rubbed her chin. "I spoke to my sister earlier. She said she knew you didn't die in 1982. She told me to be careful."

Zelda's expression didn't alter. Her face was still. "Well, I don't know why."

"I hoped you could tell me."

Zelda gave an exaggerated shrug of her shoulders. "Not really," she said. She helped herself to more wine.

A piece of potato seemed to swell in Martha's mouth. She chewed and swallowed it. "You've not told me yet why you left. Where did you go to?"

Zelda gave a small laugh but it sounded forced. "I didn't have much choice. It was probably for the best."

"I don't understand," Martha persevered. "How could you

not have a choice about leaving? And why would Mum tell me that you died?" She noticed that Zelda spoke to her, at times, like she was still thirteen years old.

Zelda toyed with a green bean on her plate with her fork. She scratched under her headscarf with a crooked finger. "I didn't know that Betty was going to tell you that. It wasn't part of the plan…"

Martha frowned at her. "A plan?" She let her knife fall to her plate with a clatter. "What do you mean?" She examined Zelda's face, but her nana averted her eyes.

"I, um…"

A clinking noise broke through their conversation. Gina drummed her fingernails against a wineglass. The ringing sound made everyone around the table stop talking.

"Just a few words, as we share our delicious food together," Gina said. "Whether Ezmerelda and I have known you for a short while, or for a long time, it is a real pleasure that you could join us tonight. We truly value your glorious support and friendship."

A round of applause and glass chinking went on around the table, followed by the lily-haired girl giving a small yelp.

"Now, eat what you want, drink what you can, and enjoy the moment." Gina raised her glass and everyone followed suit.

Martha lifted and gulped her own wine, managing to drink half a glassful at once. She waited for everyone to start eating again before she turned back to Zelda. "What plan?" she repeated.

But Zelda gave her head a shake. She held a finger to her lips. "Not now, Martha. You heard what Gina said. Enjoy the moment."

When the tiramisu and other desserts were passed around, Martha shook her head politely. She fended them all off with,

"Not for me," and "I've eaten far too much already," and "Yes, it does look delicious, but so many calories!"

She smiled and watched as everyone else plunged their spoons and forks into cream, sponge and cheesecake. She drank another glass of wine. It made her armpits feel hot and she plucked at the long sleeves of her sweater.

Sensing movement in the chair beside her, she turned to find that Harry had taken the place of the lady with the mole.

"I notice that ye haven't had any cake and thought ye'd like a slice of my fruit loaf," he said in a soft Scottish accent. "I soak the fruit in whisky, and only use the best ingredients. It's a recipe that's been handed down over generations in my family. Can I tempt ye with a slice?"

His eyes were a soft gray color, and his moving mustache was mesmeric. To refuse him would be like kicking a puppy, but Martha couldn't eat any of his cake. Her father's words would make it stick in her throat.

"It's lighter than yer usual fruitcake," Harry continued, eyeing it with pride. "But it has all the taste. Would ye like to give it a try?"

Martha liked how he didn't cut into it and force a slice onto her plate. He waited while she considered his offer. About to refuse, she caught a whiff of its aroma, rich and with a warm, spicy smell. Her mouth started to water and she could almost taste it on the tip of her tongue.

"You're getting a little chubby," her dad said in her head.

"Oh, shut up," she mumbled to him. "Leave me alone."

Harry's mustache dropped a little. "Sorry?"

"Oh." She blushed. "I wasn't talking to you. Just someone, um, never mind…"

Perhaps a small bite would be good, to sweeten her mouth after the meal, and to help soak up the wine. She closed her eyes and thought of the sweetness of the funfair candy floss on her tongue, before she threw it away. She ran her tongue around the inside of her mouth, imagining the sugary fibers dissolving.

Giving the smallest nod of her head, she wasn't sure if she was agreeing to a slice or not.

Harry beamed as he took up a knife and delicately cut a piece. He slipped it onto her plate. "I hope ye enjoy it. Ye can tell me later. And you and Zelda let me know about the football ground when ye're ready. I'll see what I can do."

Martha waited until Harry moved on to serving the next person before she picked up her cake fork. She dug it in, slicing off the smallest corner. Before her dad could speak again, she stabbed it and raised it to her lips. She pressed the cake against them for a moment, inhaling the aroma of juicy cherries and sultanas. After popping it into her mouth, she closed her eyes and chewed.

Her dad's voice tried to come through, but it sounded quieter, just a murmur.

So she took another forkful, then another. And with each chew his words vanished.

When she looked down at the few remaining crumbs on her plate, it was such strange sight that she laughed. Catching Owen's eye, he glanced across at her plate and his eyes appeared a little hurt. He stood up and made his way back over to her. "You told me that you don't eat cake," he said. "That's right, isn't it?"

"I usually don't—"

"It's a special cake," Harry cut in from the other side of the table. "It's made with love."

And Martha thought she saw the two men give each other a slight glare.

★ ★ ★

By the end of the evening, Martha was full of potatoes, fruitcake and too many glasses of wine. Her stomach pressed against the waistband of her pencil skirt and when she stood up, the room started to rotate. She tried to focus on the photographs on the mantelpiece and the bowls on the table, but she felt like she was on the fairground carousel again.

"Whoops," she said to herself, unable to remember when she had last drunk this much alcohol. Probably when Joe told her he was marrying someone else.

She wasn't sure if the hazy feeling was divine or too peculiar to enjoy. Moving away from her chair, she walked towards Owen. On the way, she glanced at a photograph on the wall of Zelda. She looked to be in her sixties and stood in front of a powder-blue clapboard house. Gina stood alongside her and she held up a basket of freshly cut flowers. They both looked happy and serene. Zelda didn't wear the exasperated expression on her face that she wore around Thomas.

She was happier away from us. Away from me, Martha thought.

She felt her ankle buckle a little and Owen reached out and took hold of her elbow. His fingers felt strong and safe. "Careful." He laughed.

"I'm absolutely fine," Martha said stiffly. She tore her eyes away from the photo. "These shoes are just causing a hindrance to my mobility."

"You can kick them off in the car. We should get going in a few minutes... I have an early meeting tomorrow."

"Spoilsport," she said, then thought how it was a word she didn't usually use.

"Why don't you go and freshen up, then we'll head off."

Martha concentrated on putting one foot in front of the other as she searched for the bathroom. She opened a couple of doors, a storage cupboard and a small sitting room, before deciding that she really needed to sit down. Behind a third door, she found a small bedroom with a single bed. It was covered with a pretty patchwork quilt and the pillow looked fluffy and inviting. It reminded her of her childhood bedroom and suddenly she wanted to be young again, to shut herself away from the adult world. Surely Owen wouldn't mind if she had a little rest.

The mattress squeaked beneath her, and one of her shoes fell off as she curled up her legs. Slowly, she felt herself tipping over to the side until her cheek pressed against the cloud-like pillow. Closing her eyes, she smiled to herself and everything seemed to fade into the distance.

Maybe she had time for just a small nap.

She wasn't sure how long she'd been there when she saw silhouettes standing in the doorway. She heard whispering and could detect who the voices belonged to.

Owen. "Maybe it's better to leave her here tonight."

Gina. "You do not want her to be ill in your car."

Zelda. "Let her nap. We could drop her home tomorrow."

Harry. "Oh. Is she asleep? I have another slice of fruitcake waiting."

Martha decided to wave an arm, to show how absolutely fine she was. Her eyes followed her fingers as they swept through the air. She stopped to gaze at the full moon, which shone through the window. Blinking at its beauty, she thought that she'd like to wrap her arms around it and give it a hug. She tried to sit up, but her cheek felt like it was glued to the pillow.

"Look at the moon, at how big it looks, everyone," she said, thinking that her voice sounded a little slurred. It couldn't be the wine because she'd only drunk three, um, four, perhaps five, glasses full. "It looks like a button that's fallen off a gi-ant's waistcoat, or a white chocolate drop…"

A shape moved across the room and she felt a hand slip into hers. "It's a silver sequin on black velvet," Zelda said. "It's a round of Edam cheese, cut in half. If you look closely, you can see mice lining up to take a nibble."

Martha felt tears welling in her eyes and she wasn't sure if they were happy, sad or wine-induced. "It's a giant eye looking down on us, or the head of a flashlight," she said. "It's a silvery porthole in the sky…"

Words danced in her head, appearing as if from nowhere, and they were nothing to do with her tasks. They were all to do with what she saw and felt. And she liked it. In fact, she liked it a lot. Squeezing Zelda's hand, she asked woozily, "Does anyone have a pen? I'd like to write some of this down."

22

Marriage Certificate

Martha's head pounded. She felt like she'd been in a jet plane looping the loop, rather than a journey back to Sandshift in Gina's old Volvo. Every bump in the road, each corner on the way, made her stomach roll. If she looked in a mirror, she was sure her face would be peppermint green.

She stood on the pavement outside her cottage, her ankles wobbly in Betty's shoes. The color of her sweater was too bright in the daylight and she hated knowing that she'd slept in it. Clasping a hand to her mouth, she waited to see if she was going to be sick.

How on earth can people do this for fun?

"You certainly hammered the wine last night," Zelda said with laughter in her voice. She and Gina stood either side of her. "Are you okay?"

"Uh-huh," Martha said, unsure.

"Make sure you drink plenty of water." Gina placed a hand on her arm. "Take some paracetamol."

Martha gave a watery smile, heartened by Gina's unexpected concern. She steadied herself by leaning against her shopping trolley. Her hand shook as she attempted to slide her key into the lock.

When she saw her red key fob it reminded her of a toy in the library. It was also red and shaped like a TV. You turned white knobs that made gray pencil-like lines appear on the screen, to create a picture. An Etch A Sketch. Kids spent hours twiddling and designing houses, animals and people. When you wanted to draw something new, you shook the screen and the image dissolved, sometimes leaving a few traces of lines behind. That's what Martha felt like now. Last night she'd had the beginnings of a picture, of what might have happened to Zelda all those years ago, but now she'd shaken and part wiped it out with her wine consumption.

She opened her front door. Her eyes were sticky and her mouth dry. She longed to peel off the tight skirt, yank off her shoes and crawl into bed. But Gina and Zelda had driven a fair way to escort her home. She felt she had no other choice but to invite them inside. To be a good host. "Thank you for a lovely evening," she croaked. "Would you like a coffee?"

Zelda leaned on Gina and looked up at the house. Her eyes swept over the windows, at the chunky gray stone and the curtains that probably hadn't been replaced since she last visited. "It looks smaller than I remember," she said. "Like a goblin's house."

Gina wrapped her hand around her back, to support her. "We will come in for coffee some other time, Martha. You look like you need rest. I will use your bathroom, then we will set off home. We can stop off for a drink on the way back."

Martha nodded gratefully. She directed Gina up the stairs and stayed with Zelda outside. Her grandmother was quiet, contemplative, as she peered up and down the street.

"It doesn't look like anything has changed around here," Zelda said. "Yet everything has. I can still see you running around outside with no shoes on, the soles of your feet black with dirt. We sat on this doorstep and read books together. I can picture the sun shining in your hair."

Martha felt her chin quiver. She wished the two of them were together back then, instead of now. "Come inside," she said.

Zelda shook her head. "I'm not ready for that yet." She stared into the distance, to where the street connected with the slope down to the beach. "There are a lot of memories in that house…"

"A lot of them are happy ones."

"Yes, I know that." Zelda flickered a small smile. "But some aren't."

Martha didn't want to allow any of those ones to flood into her head. It already ached enough. "Let's only think about the good times," she said quickly.

"Agreed. Let's create nice new ones."

Suddenly, Martha didn't want Zelda to go. She wanted to wrap her arms around her shoulders and nestle her head into the nape of her neck, like she did as a child. She wanted to smell only Youth Dew. "Will you visit me another time?" she asked. "You could stay over, if you wanted to…"

As Zelda opened her mouth to answer, Gina stepped outside. She wore a bemused expression. "You have a lot of intriguing things in your house, Martha. It is a most interesting way to live."

Martha glanced through the open door, at the bags and boxes in her dining room. They were stacked neatly, though the pathway she'd created to the kitchen didn't look quite as encouraging as it did before.

"This Saturday?" Zelda nodded. "I can visit and stay with you, then. That's okay, isn't it, Gina?"

Gina raised an eyebrow. "There is not much space. I am not sure we will fit in."

Zelda frowned. "I meant that *I'd* come and stay."

"Oh. I thought that..." Gina's shoulders twitched and she lowered her eyes. "Well, I suppose I could bring you."

"That's sorted, then," Zelda said. She didn't seem to notice that Gina's face had fallen. She turned towards the car, opened the door and climbed in. "I'll see you on Saturday, Martha."

"Yes," Martha said, wondering how she could possibly create room in the house by then. "I work at the library in the morning, so make it after 1:30 p.m."

Gina managed a half smile and got into the car, too. She turned on the engine and wound the window down. "I forgot to give you this." She posted a square, silver-foiled parcel through the gap. "Harry sent you some more cake. He said something about a football match. Do you know what he means, Ezmerelda?"

"No." Zelda wore a straight face. "I know nothing about that."

Martha waved them off and closed the door. She placed the cake on her kitchen worktop and traipsed up the stairs.

There wasn't anywhere for Zelda to sleep. And Will and Rose were supposed to be stopping over, too.

Martha felt much too ill to solve this problem now.

As if you don't have enough to do, she scolded herself.

When her head stopped throbbing, when she'd slept and taken some pills, when she was wearing her own clothes again, and when she had wiped away the mascara that was probably halfway down her cheeks, then she would try to ready herself for action again.

As she opened her bathroom cabinet and took out a box of paracetamols, Martha caught sight of the back of her hand.

She wondered why the words *Full Moon* and *Giant's Waist-coat Button* were scrawled across it, in her own handwriting.

After a few hours of sleep, Martha still wasn't quite in fully functioning mode, but at least her head had stopped clanging. She no longer felt sick and she forced herself to make a cheese sandwich and a cup of tea. Feeling semirevived after eating, she made her way back upstairs, where she stood with her hands on her hips and surveyed the master bedroom.

Martha slept in the smaller of the two bedrooms, the one she and Lilian used to share. Their parents used the one at the back of the house. It was double the size and overlooked the bay. It still contained their bed, which was like an island in a sea of Martha's favors.

There was a worn Victorian chaise longue that she'd offered to reupholster for a neighbor. It hadn't gone well, the teal velvet puckering and studs protruding. While she had been working on it, the neighbor bought a new one instead.

There was a mass of red velvet curtains that she'd shortened for Vivian Slater (now deceased) and a bag stuffed full of Hawaiian garlands that she'd offered to store for Branda's annual Hawaiian evening at the Lobster Pot.

She'd bought a few boxes full of fancy dress clothes from a flea market, sure they'd come in handy for plays at the local school. When she told the headmistress, she had patted Martha on the back of the hand and said, "That's a great idea, but we don't have a lot of storage space here. Perhaps you can keep hold of them for us…" That was three years ago.

Bin bags and other boxes lined the floor in here, too, all neatly labeled. All contained her parents' things, or stuff that didn't have a home, or jobs she'd taken on and hadn't given back.

Feeling daunted by the size of the task facing her, Martha

wrapped her arms across her chest. She wondered if Gina had glanced inside the room when she used the bathroom. Her cheeks flushed as she imagined what her nana's carer might describe her as. A hoarder? A bit strange? Can't let go of the past?

Could any of those be true?

Martha wondered how she could have let things get so bad. The house was a mess and it had to change.

She had to change.

As she tried to swallow away a chunk of paracetamol that had lodged itself in her throat, she realized she had less than three days to sort things out.

Before Zelda, Will and Rose came to stay.

Thank goodness for Betty's enormous collection of local business cards. Martha found one for a Man with a Van, Leslie Ross. He claimed to move anything and everything quickly. Without any work on for the rest of that week, Leslie offered to be with her within an hour.

Martha warned him to watch out, because the street was narrow. "Look out for the house with the shopping trolley parked outside," she said.

After dressing in her usual clothes, she took a further, preventive, paracetamol, and drank four glasses of water. She pulled on her yellow rubber gloves and, with her chest out and chin jutted, she launched into Operation Clear Out.

With a handful of fluorescent yellow cardboard stars (also from Betty's collection), she stuck one to everything she wanted to keep. Anything that had to go got a green star. Pink stars were reserved for the items that she wanted to return to their rightful owner.

If there was anything that Martha didn't need, no longer wanted or didn't remember, she tugged it out of the master bedroom and onto the landing. Finding no point in battling to carry items downstairs, she gave the smaller ones a firm shove off the top stair. She grinned as she watched them tumble, slide and crash to the bottom.

A small broken chest of drawers sledged down, and she threw a painting of a bowl of fruit like a Frisbee. She pretended to be a footballer as she gave a small plastic box full of Betty's old crochet patterns a firm kick. Then she trod downstairs and took great delight in slapping the pile with a bunch of green stars.

Leslie turned up and nodded all the time Martha explained what she wanted to achieve. He was a wiry man with rusty hair and he wore oversized navy dungarees. His movements were small and fidgety, like a bird on the lookout for bread crumbs. He didn't remove his white earphones as he talked.

"So, Ms. Storm," he repeated after her, his words as twitchy as his actions, "anything with a green star is going—the yellow- and pink-starred stuff is staying? I like to ask because some people tell me to move stuff and then they want it back, and sometimes I've finished my job and then people decide there's other stuff they want moving. Right?" He readjusted his left earplug.

"Yes." Martha nodded, in case he couldn't hear her.

"Good. Got it." He jerked his thumb at the pile at the bottom of the stairs. "You been having a good old clear out? A spring clean some people call it, even if it's not technically spring. Well, I'm not exactly sure if February is classed as spring or winter, it's one of those in-between months, isn't it? Some people might say it's one, and others, the other."

She nodded again.

"Good. People in this country just buy loads of stuff, don't we? You go on holiday and you only take a few things with you in your suitcase, and it does you just fine for a week or more. All good, you don't need anything else, don't even miss

it. Then, when you get home, you buy clothes, you buy furniture, you buy ornaments, you buy food, you buy paintings,
you buy this and you buy that, and you end up with a house
full of stuff. Is that what happened to you?"

"Something like that." Martha smiled wryly.

"You can live without it all, Ms. Storm. Most people can,"
Leslie said. "You'll see."

Leslie set to work immediately, moving the stuff from the
bottom of the stairs into his van, to dispose of. He worked
methodically, totally focused on the job.

The chaise longue proved tricky to get through the bedroom door and, even though Martha didn't really want to
keep it, she agreed to let it remain in the room. It didn't look
too bad after she'd vacuumed away the dust and covered her
untidy reupholstering with a blanket off her own bed.

Under a pile of her dad's black suits, she discovered an old
radio. After plugging it in, she fiddled with the knobs and
found a station that played rock music. She turned the volume up from two and a half to five (not loud enough to give
her another headache) and spent the rest of the afternoon and
evening blitzing her parents' old bedroom.

As she carried on with her mission, she imagined that she
might feel sad, nostalgic or melancholic, but instead she found
herself singing. With each item that Leslie removed, Martha's
shoulders felt lighter, as if she was casting off the person she
didn't want to be any longer.

She decided to reposition the chaise longue under the window, to allow more space to walk around the bed. Its wheels
squeaked as she tugged it. She moved the bed by a few inches,
too, and spotted a white envelope on the floor, in the space it
had vacated. About to toss it onto her rubbish pile, she opened

it first. There was a piece of paper inside and she read the words printed across the top.

"Marriage Certificate."

It belonged to her parents and, as Martha looked at it more closely, she thought of how they never mentioned their wedding. She could only recall them celebrating their anniversary once. They'd held a party in the dining room but she'd been too sick to attend. She'd stayed in bed, with her head under the covers and a bucket at the side of the bed. And the next day, her parents told her that Zelda had died.

In the dining room, there was a wedding photograph of her dad in a black suit and her mum in a white shiny dress with a nipped-in waist, but Martha didn't ever recall them reminiscing about their big day. She wasn't even sure where they'd gone for their honeymoon. Where did you go in the UK, if you already lived at the seaside?

After reading the certificate, she now knew they married in Sandshift church in February 1966.

Glancing around, she tried to find somewhere safe to put it, so it didn't get thrown away. However, her senses urged her to take another look.

Betty was nineteen years old and Thomas was thirty-three when they married.

February 1966 was only four months before Martha was born.

So, Betty must have been pregnant when she walked down the aisle.

Martha felt as if a small light flashed on in her head. Her parents had to get married for appearances' sake.

She'd always felt removed from Lilian but couldn't fathom out why, other than they liked different things. It was a feeling, rather than definite knowledge. Now, though, she had found a reason.

She was the daughter her parents didn't plan for.

They *had* planned for Lilian.

Her father wouldn't have liked an unborn child shaping his life.

Martha placed the certificate on the windowsill and told herself to forget it, that it didn't mean anything. She had to focus on clearing up.

But all the same, she couldn't stop her mind from flitting back, to the date printed on the certificate.

23

Midnight Mission

Martha carried on with her clearing-out session into the evening, and over the next two days. Slowly, the house started to look more like a home, rather than a scrapyard. It would be impossible to sort out absolutely everything in such a short time, but the changes she and Leslie made were immense.

The day before Zelda, Will and Rose descended, Martha washed four loads full of bed sheets and blankets. While the washing machine whirred, she introduced Leslie to the mountain of stuff in the shed. He cheerfully removed the old tools, piles of tiles, a rusty lawn mower and an old swivel chair, freeing the space up.

At teatime, he packed up his white van for the final time. "All good, Ms. Storm?" he asked before he left. "Do you feel better already? Most people feel a sense of relief when all their stuff has gone, but some get in a right old panic, kind of a what-have-I-done sensation, but that's totally natural. It's like a barn in there now, isn't it? Nice and spacious, big enough to have a dance in, if you like that kind of thing. Well, maybe not ballroom dancing, but room for a bit of a shuffle." He waited for her reply, with both of his thumbs stuck up.

"Don't worry about your stuff, either, about where it's going. I give some of it away to low-income families who can't afford much furniture. It helps them out. Then I'm happy and you're happy knowing you're doing some good. Most people like to know that."

Not quite sure if Leslie asked a question among all his words, Martha gave him a thumbs-up back. "Yes. All is good," she said.

Martha took a break for something to eat and she enjoyed beans on toast, sitting at her dining table. Horatio's fish swam in their bowl, and she wondered if they enjoyed their new view without the skyscrapers of boxes and books around them. She certainly did.

Her shoulders ached and her back was stiff, but she felt like a mountaineer on the verge of conquering Mount Everest, ready to stick a yellow flag on the summit.

Before she returned to complete her tidying up, she unwrapped Harry's generous slice of fruitcake. As she relished each mouthful, she pictured his twinkling eyes and mustache, and it made the cake taste even better than it did before. She wondered if her nana really did plan to do a Read and Run at the football ground. She hoped it was the wine talking, rather than Zelda.

After clearing her pots away, Martha used her shopping trolley to transport the remains of the Berlin Wall of boxes out into the newly vacant shed. She moved with determination and with her teeth set, ignoring the burning sensation that fired across the back of her shoulders.

The dragon's head took up a new position in the corner of her sitting room, ready for the next stage of his restoration.

This only left the tasks she'd taken on for others remaining. The items she'd marked with a pink star.

She found herself wanting to hold on to the fancy dress

clothes, just in case, but Branda's chandeliers and garlands, Will's trousers, Nora's laundry, the rest of Horatio's plants and lots of other things had to go.

Martha batted her hands together and stuck them on her hips. A strong yearning to complete her mission before Zelda, Will and Rose arrived gave her a firm push onward.

It was time to load up her trusty shopping trolley again.

At six minutes past 11:00 p.m., Martha left her home. The stuff inside her trolley was stacked as high as her chin and a trickle of perspiration wound its way down her back as she pushed it up the slope. She'd also packed a pad, pen and envelopes. She intended to write notes for people, to explain why their completed jobs had turned up, as if by magic, in their gardens, porches and sheds. She'd packed towels around Horatio's fishbowl so it didn't slide around.

She passed the pastel-colored terraced houses as she made her way to the Lobster Pot. In the front porch of the bistro, she stacked the boxes of chandeliers, one on top of the other, then placed the garlands on top. Inside, she could see Branda in silhouette standing on a chair and fastening a set of antlers to the wall. Martha decided not to disturb her and, under the orange glow of a streetlamp, she wrote her a note.

As she placed it under a pebble to weigh it down, doubt began to simmer inside her.

Will returning all these things take away my purpose?

If I'm not offering to help people out, what will I do instead?

Staring at the note, she considered whether to stuff it back into her pocket.

But then she gave her shoulders a shake. She now had an exciting story to share, about how a battered little book of fairy stories found its way to her, and the adventures it brought

with it. If anyone found that less interesting than Martha offering to do their laundry, that was their problem.

Encouraging herself to press on, Martha left the boxes and
note in place and pushed her trolley onward.

She visited Horatio's aquarium next. The converted garage
glowed a luminous green around the door, like a strange lab
in a sci-fi movie. There was nowhere to leave his fish, so she
held the bowl and knocked on the door. A few moments later,
it slid up and over.

"Martha, ahoy," Horatio said. "You've brought the girls
for me." He took the bowl from her and held it up, admiring his fish.

"I've had them for a while. You do want them back?"

"Yes. I wanted to spruce this place up first and get their new
tank in place. That's important, isn't it? Home sweet home.
And they look so well. Thanks for looking after them." He
set them down on the ground. "I don't have anything to give
you. This old place doesn't make much, but thanks for making them happy."

Martha carried on up the hill and past the library. In the
dark, the building appeared as just a black block but it still
radiated an aura of warmth for her. She pushed her trolley
around its perimeter and smiled as she recalled Owen crouch-
ing by the front doors.

She also pictured holding her nana's hand when, years ago,
they both carried bags full of library books away, eager to read
them together.

She tried to hold on to that feeling as she carried on her
journey, heading towards Lilian's house.

On the other side of the Sandshift football ground lay sub-
urbs of sprawling bungalows. They had neatly manicured
lawns and the air constantly hissed from the sprinkler systems.

On Lilian's gateposts, stone Dobermans sat to attention. A

tall wrought iron gate, decorated with gold roses and thorny stems, looked like it had been designed to make visitors feel unwelcome.

Lilian liked to share that the gardener who'd landscaped her garden once scored a silver-gilt at the Chelsea Flower Show. A statue of a Buddha sat cross-legged in the middle of her lawn with tiny holes in his head so water cascaded down his face into a small circular pond, full of ceramic water lilies. *Minimal-tranquil-chic* was how she described it.

All the lights in Lilian's house were turned off and Martha's nose twitched at the lingering smell of home-cooked cottage pie. She imagined her sister, Paul and the kids sitting around the table together. A family meal.

She gave a small sigh of regret, that it could have been her, living in a large suburban bungalow with her husband and children. However, there was no point dwelling on the past when she had a job to do.

She steered her trolley towards a privet bush and pushed it into the greenery to stop it from rolling away. After lifting out the bags containing Will's trousers, she opened the gate.

Martha padded along the gravel path as quietly as she could and headed around to the back of the bungalow. Lilian used her wood store as a locker and instructed anyone delivering goods to place the items inside it, so she didn't have to speak to them.

Martha folded over the top of the two shopping bags, so woodlice couldn't invade the trousers. An owl hooted as she placed them neatly on the top of the logs. She took out her pad, to leave a note for her sister.

She had just pressed her pen against the paper, when yellow light flooded the back garden. Blinking against it, she saw a figure looming up to the glass in the back door. Martha froze, wondering if it was Paul. As keys jangled in the lock, she gritted her teeth.

"Martha, is that you?" Lilian stepped out of her conservatory door and into the garden. She was barefoot and curled her toes up, away from the chill of the concrete paving flags. A dark dressing gown swamped her petite frame and she clamped her hand to her neck. Her usually mirror-shiny hair was mussy. "I thought you were a bloody burglar or something."

"You startled me, too. I've brought Will's trousers for you."

Lilian looked at her watch. "But it's midnight."

"That's why I didn't knock. Um, I've been having a clear out, to make room for Will and Rose staying over..."

"That's a big job."

"It's been going well." Even though her sister's shoulders were hunched and her eyes weary, Martha wanted to tell her about Zelda, too. "Do you mind if I introduce them to Nana?"

"I hope you're not telling me that *she's* going to be there?"

"I kind of invited her to stay at the same time."

The two sisters stared at each other.

Martha opened her mouth to speak but Lilian raised a hand to cut her off. She paused, then cast her eyes down. Slowly, her face fell. Letting out a sob, it rang around the garden.

"Oh no. What's wrong? Is this about Zelda?" Martha stepped forward. "Do you want a tissue? They have aloe vera in them, and—"

"No." Lilian wiped her nose with the back of her hand. She stood for a few moments, her toes still curled upward. "Please, will you come inside with me?"

Martha gazed over at her trolley, hidden in the bush. She still had lots of deliveries to make, but for the first time ever, her sister seemed to need her. "Of course," she said, her fingers flexing for her notepad.

"It's Paul," Lilian said between sniffs as they sat in the almost-completed conservatory with the lights turned off. The air smelled of fresh paint and Jo Malone Pomegranate Noir candles. "I think he's about to start an affair..."

"Oh." Martha leaned forward and the cream leather sofa squeaked. "No. That can't be right."

"He's working with a new girl, Annabel. She has huge boobs. Her eyebrows are like slugs, but Paul's smitten. He keeps talking about her. He says he doesn't fancy her, but I found emails between the two of them. They were flirting, and he's working away tonight. I don't know if he's with her, or not."

"But he loves you."

"I thought so, too." Lilian sighed. "He said that I'm cold towards him."

"But you're so perfect together," Martha said. "Like Romeo and Juliet, or Heathcliff and Cathy."

"Didn't their stories end in tragedy?"

"Hmm." Martha nodded meekly.

"Will and Rose are asleep," Lilian added. "They're excited about staying over at your place. They don't know there's anything wrong."

"You've got to talk to him. You're beautiful and he can't possible prefer someone with slug eyebrows."

Lilian gave a short laugh. "Thanks, Martha. I'll do my best. I've invited Paul to the hotel with me, when I work away."

"Do Will and Rose know that?"

"No. We've never been away without them. I think they might guess something wasn't right."

"My lips are sealed."

A car drove past, briefly illuminating their faces.

"So, you had dinner with Zelda?" Lilian toyed with the belt on her dressing gown. She turned her face so Martha couldn't see her features, in the darkness. "What happened?"

"I drank too much. I fell asleep after the dinner."

"I meant, with our grandma?"

"I think I know what you mean," Martha admitted. "I can't stop thinking about what you said. That she didn't die in 1982, and you knew that."

Lilian didn't speak for a while. "I shouldn't have said it."

"But you did. What happened?"

"What did *she* tell you?"

"Nothing." Martha gave an exasperated sigh. "Why do I feel that everyone knows something that I don't? Zelda had a brain tumor, and her health isn't good. She's an old lady and doesn't have much time left." She leaned forward with her elbows on her knees. "Don't you want to see her, Lilian? Perhaps she'll talk if you're there, too."

Lilian shifted in her chair. "About what?"

"About what went on in our family. Mum and Dad told us that she'd died, but she didn't. And you know something about that…"

"It was just something that Mum said, years ago. That's all. I didn't think too much about it at the time. Until you told me that Nana was still alive."

Martha thought how her sister's words sounded vague. She had sounded so certain the other day. "You told me to be careful…" she prompted.

Lilian leaned her head back and looked up at her large wooden ceiling fan. "You're digging up the past, Martha, when it's probably best to let it remain buried. I know you and Nana were close, but things must have happened in our family that we don't know about."

"I spent every day with Mum and Dad for years," Martha said. "How could I not know things? They told us a huge lie. Why would they do that?"

"I don't know." Lilian shook her head. "But they did, and

there must be a reason for it. Don't you remember how Nana and Dad didn't get on? She constantly wound him up."

"They weren't best friends, but they didn't hate each other," Martha started. Or had she forgotten things? Was she too busy writing her stories, trying to interpret the atmosphere in the Storm household, without actually seeing what was going on? "If you know something, Lilian, please tell me."

Lilian remained with her face in the shadows. "I don't know a thing about it," she said. "But I do know that I don't want our nana spending any time with Will and Rose."

24

Invitation

Betty, 1982

Asking people over for tea was something that didn't happen often in the Storm household. Thomas constantly made it clear that Zelda wasn't welcome in the house, and Betty's friends had dwindled so she didn't go out as much. Thomas didn't socialize, preferring to spend time at home. So Betty was surprised to find that he'd invited his parents around for tea, without asking her first.

Eleanor and Dylan Storm lived in a posh penthouse apartment in Cornwall, with a sea view. They sent Martha and Lilian checks for their birthdays and Christmas, and caught the train once a year for the long journey up to Sandshift for one of Dylan's golf tournaments.

Thomas, Betty and the girls usually met them in their hotel restaurant for a stilted Sunday lunch, where Eleanor would order a glass of champagne and barely touch her salmon. She wore small round felt hats pinned to the side of her head, and matching tweed jacket-and-skirt sets. Thomas insisted that

Betty, Martha and Lilian wear their best clothes when they went along.

Whenever Thomas talked about his mother, he made her sound perfect. She was a brilliant, loving woman who made the best cakes ever. She was a great seamstress and always kept a beautiful home. Betty noticed that Eleanor let her husband enter the room before her and agreed with everything he said, smiling beatifically at his comments.

To her, she was a reminder of how Thomas wanted her to be.

The day before Betty and Thomas's wedding, Eleanor took Betty to one side for a chat. "You're getting married so *terribly* quickly, I feel I hardly know you." Her eyes flitted, examining her from head to toe. "I want the *best* for my son and I want your assurance you only have his best interests at heart."

Betty thought that Eleanor's words sounded a little like a threat. "Yes. Of course. I'll do my best."

"Well." Eleanor sniffed. "Only time will tell if that's good enough."

When Betty walked down the aisle, Eleanor sat in the front row, her eyes pinned to her son. She didn't smile and wore a dark gray dress more suited to a funeral.

Throughout the ceremony and reception, Betty swore she could feel her new mother-in-law's animosity towards her.

Dylan Storm was friendlier. He was an older version of Thomas, but with granite-gray hair and jowls that wobbled. When he talked, he stood with his hands behind his back. The two men talked about the changing world of accountancy, the bible and cricket. Nothing that Betty could relate to.

"Your parents don't usually come over to the house," Betty said. "Is there a special occasion?"

Thomas tutted and shook his head. "Have you forgotten what special month and year this is?"

Betty frowned and could only think of one possibility. "Um, it's our sixteenth wedding anniversary."

"Well, of course it is."

"Lovely," Betty said, trying not to frown. They never marked their anniversary and didn't buy cards for each other. Sixteen years wasn't a traditional celebration.

"Mum and Dad haven't seen the girls for months. And I've invited Trevor, too," Thomas said.

"Your brother?"

"And his new fiancée. Teresa is training to be a lawyer."

"Ah." Betty nodded. She knew there was a brotherly rivalry between Thomas and Trevor, and she wondered if her husband was trying to prove some kind of point.

She also felt a sense of dread creeping over her, as she imagined spending an evening with Thomas's family. She'd have to do everything, from cooking to being a charming host. "That's a lot of people to fit around our dining table. Can't we go to a restaurant instead?"

Thomas laughed. "We're not made of money. I'm sure we can accommodate eight people."

Betty imagined the family and sports talk. "Surely there will be nine of us?" she said.

"Nine?"

"Well, we'll have to invite Mum, too."

"Zelda?" Thomas said as if her name had a nasty taste. "That's not a good idea."

"Why not? If we're celebrating our wedding anniversary, she should be there."

"Hmm. I'm worried about the girls. Martha's getting really disobedient. I think we can blame your mother for that."

"It's more likely to be her hormones."

Thomas's lips grew thin. "There's no need for such talk, Betty."

She stared at him and tried not to sigh. He was squeamish about any changes the girls were going through—periods, buying bras and teenage behavior. He liked to pretend such things didn't happen.

However, he was right about one thing. Betty had also noticed that Martha was increasingly tricky to handle. Sometimes it felt like she was slipping away and that Betty was losing her.

If Martha announced she was going to a friend's house to do her homework, Betty knew that she was really sneaking off to see her nana. She'd spotted the two of them in the library together and found Martha's stash of library books and handwritten stories hidden under her bed. Zelda hadn't called around to the house for almost two months and she had taken to calling Thomas "the Lord of the Manor."

The last time Betty bumped into her mum, she had a sparkle in her eye as she gushed about someone called George.

Betty was glad that her mum might have found someone special, after all this time. However, it added to the gulf of separation she felt, as her mother and elder daughter drifted further away from her. But, because of Thomas and his ways, she couldn't do anything about it.

She smoothed down her dress and rearranged her Friday freesias in a vase. "So, is it okay for me to ask Mum? It will look very odd if we don't invite her."

"My parents won't notice if she's not there. They only met her once, at our wedding."

"It won't look very good to Martha and Lilian, though. Or to my mother."

Thomas thought for a while then gave her a sideways look

that she hadn't seen him use before. "My boss, Anthony, mentioned your mother to me the other week," he said.

"He did?"

"He bumped into her recently and hadn't realized she was my mother-in-law. They went to school together and he had a bit of a thing for her back then." He screwed up his nose. "Goodness knows why. Since he's separated from his wife, he's gone all nostalgic."

"I think Mum is pretty enamored with her new boyfriend, George," Betty said.

Thomas folded his arms. "I'm thinking, perhaps I should invite Anthony to our anniversary tea, too. He's going to retire soon and his job will be available, so it's a good opportunity to make an impression. And it will even things up. If he and Zelda came, that would make ten guests, a nice round number."

Even though the idea of hosting Thomas's mum, dad, brother, brother's fiancée and boss filled her with dread, Betty's spirits lifted a little. The tea would offer her the chance to pull Zelda back into the family fold a little. Perhaps Eleanor and Dylan might be charmed by her. "Should I ask Mum if she's free that evening?" she asked hopefully.

Thomas looked as if he'd swallowed a wasp and was trying to spit it out. "I'll give it some thought," he said.

Betty walked down to the beach that afternoon. In early February, the sand was flecked with snow. The flakes drifted in the air and she remembered how she and Daniel used to stick out their tongues to catch them. It was impossible not to laugh when they did it. She poked her tongue out now and she giggled to herself before her smile faded away.

She stood in front of the mermaid statue, read the list of

the lost men and trailed her fingers over their names. Some had been so young, only her age. It was difficult to believe that the accident was over sixteen years ago now. Time had passed so quickly. Glancing at her watch, she saw that time had gone quicker than she anticipated. She brushed away the snow that had settled on the plaque, then set off to the baker's shop. Thomas wouldn't be happy if she returned late from buying the bread.

Unusually, Betty found Martha and Thomas in the sitting room together. Thomas flicked through his newspaper and Martha lay on the floor scribbling in her notepad. Betty was pleased that she couldn't detect any atmosphere. Everything felt, well, normal, and it was a welcome relief.

"I've been thinking," Thomas said, as Betty showed him the bread she'd bought. "We'll invite your mother over for the tea. I spoke to Anthony just now and he's definitely a bit misty-eyed over her. You'll have to warn Zelda, firmly, beforehand. I don't want any drama. No weird stories or mentions of her new boyfriend. And can she wear something other than a bloody turquoise nightie?"

From her spot on the carpet, Martha lifted her head. "What's this for?"

"It's for our anniversary tea, darling," Betty said. "Your dad's boss will be joining us. It turns out that he went to school with your nana."

"That sounds ace," Martha said.

And Thomas and Betty shared a small, rare, smile.

"Why should I do what the Lord of the Manor wants?" Zelda asked when Betty phoned her. "I'm guessing this is all for *his* benefit, and no one else's. Does he want to show off or something?"

"It's for both of us," Betty pleaded, even if there was truth in her mother's words. "I know he has certain ways, but it's our wedding anniversary, Mum. I know you'll want to see Martha and Lilian. Anthony is looking forward to seeing you again, too. Please come."

"I'm not sure. George and I may have plans."

Betty closed her eyes. She dug a hand into her hair and massaged her scalp. "Can't you can rethink them? It's been too long since we saw you."

"And whose fault is that? Not mine."

"Please don't make things difficult for me, Mum."

"But he's controlling you."

"It's not like that, honestly. Thomas looks after me and the girls and, well, if we have to do things his way, maybe it's worth it."

Zelda fell silent for a while. "When those girls get older, you'll be left on your own with him. He's the type who can't cope alone."

"He's not as bad as you make out. Thomas and Lilian get on. It's just Martha…"

"And me, too. He hates me."

"No, he doesn't."

"Humph. Well, I've noticed Martha is changing. She doesn't write as many stories as she used to."

"She's a teenage girl, Mum…"

"She's picking it up from you, Betty. The way you are. How can she grow into a confident young woman when she sees you kowtowing to Thomas? You're always making your lists of things to do, to keep him happy. She'll end up like you."

Betty felt a tidal wave of upset rising inside her. She tried to put a stop to it before it broke to the surface. "Don't say that, Mum. Martha's nothing like me. She'll leave home and meet someone. She can be something I'm not." Her last words rose upward. She needed to believe that her daughters would make different decisions to her own. "All you have to do is come around for tea. Be friendly with Anthony and civil with Thomas's parents. It will help to fix things between us all."

"I'm not the one who's broken them."

"Please, Mum. Just show up on time and behave. Is that really too much to ask?"

"Hmm." Zelda hesitated. "I'll try my best. Do you remember that story Martha told us, about a tiger and a unicorn?"

Betty smoothed a hand over her hair, relieved that things were agreed. "Not really. She shares them with you more than me."

"I'll tell it to you now," Zelda said. "I think it's relevant."

The Tiger and the Unicorn

A girl lived in a house at the edge of a forest. She had two best friends, a tiger and a unicorn. The tiger was fierce and strong. Though other people found him scary, he made the girl feel safe and protected.

Her other friend was a unicorn. She was magical and fun. They rode through the forest together with the wind in the girl's hair. The unicorn was mischievous and liked to play pranks.

The girl loved them both but found it exhausting, to keep her friends separate all the time. She thought how wonderful it would be if the three of them could learn how to be content together.

However, the tiger sniffed when she suggested this. "I am

a beast. I have my own ways. If I eat the unicorn, I cannot be held responsible because it's in my nature to do it."

The unicorn shook her mane and whinnied. "The tiger is no fun," she told the girl. "I'll be bored in his company. He always tries to be in charge, and we won't be able to do what we want."

The girl was torn, because she loved them both. She didn't want to offend either of her friends so she continued to spend time with them individually. However, when she was with the tiger she acted in one way, changing to suit him. And when she was with the unicorn, she acted in a different way.

Soon she began to feel that her personality was being split in two, and she just wanted to be herself.

One day, as she walked through the forest, she met a third creature, a bear. He lay on the ground and lazily scratched behind his ear. "You look troubled," he said to the girl. "What's wrong?"

The girl sighed and told him her problem, that she had two friends and they were making her choose between them. "Real friends wouldn't do that," he said. "They might be different, they might not mix, but they would never make you choose."

The girl nodded. The bear was right, so the next day she spoke to the unicorn, and then the tiger. She told them the same thing. "We must find a way to all get along, so I can be myself. Or else we'll have to go our separate ways."

The unicorn tried her best. She tried to be friendly to the tiger and was there when the girl wanted to play. But the tiger could not change. He sulked and wanted the girl to himself.

One day, the tiger ate the unicorn up whole. As he sat

smacking his lips, the girl broke down in tears and asked him why he couldn't respect her wishes. "Because I couldn't help it," he said. "Because I am a tiger."

25

House

On Saturday, Rose and Will wandered into the library without their mother. They stood in front of the desk, both wearing bewildered expressions. "Mum made us walk here on our own," Will said to Martha. "She said she didn't want to see anyone, and we had to pack our own bags."

Martha wondered if the *anyone* she wanted to avoid was Zelda.

"She's in a weird mood," Rose added. "She said you were lurking in our back garden at night."

As she stored their overnight bags under the desk, Martha's neck grew a little hot.

"I was merely returning Will's trousers. Next time, I'll teach the pair of you how to sew, so you can do it yourselves," she teased. "Then I won't have to visit your house at midnight."

Rose and Will stared at her.

"I can't do sewing," Will said.

"I'm scared of needles. And pins." Rose narrowed her eyes. "Are you wearing makeup?"

"A little bit…"

"It looks nice. Your lips are all pinky."

"What are we doing this afternoon?" Will asked.

Martha wasn't sure what to tell them. Lilian had forbidden her from introducing the kids to their great-grandmother, but she didn't have a choice. "A, um, family friend is joining us," she said. "We might all have a nice, quiet afternoon, down at the beach."

While Will and Rose squabbled over which letter the *Harry Potter and the Philosopher's Stone* DVD should be filed under, *H* or *P*, Martha took the job application form out of the drawer. She read through it again, refreshing her memory of the headings and what she had to complete.

"Are you *finally* going to fill that in?" Suki peered over her shoulder. "There's only a few days left."

Martha nodded. She wrote down her name and address then set down her pen. She wanted to share her story of what the library, and doing things for others, meant to her, but her discussion with Lilian made it difficult to concentrate.

"Just think of your Cumulus Vitae," Suki prompted.

"Cumulus is a type of cloud," Martha replied. "It's a Curriculum Vitae, and I don't have one."

"Right." Suki laughed. "I usually write notes down first. Then I copy them into the form. I make sure my passion shimmies through."

Martha agreed this was a most proactive approach. She mused for a while, then took up a blank piece of paper. She picked up her pen again and waited to see if her words would start to flow.

The library started to fill with parents and children. Most of the Saturday morning crowd were usually well behaved, but some rolling about on the floor always took place, mostly by children and occasionally some adults, too. Martha smiled with encouragement as Will stepped in to separate two young boys who were hitting each other over the head with the beanbags.

Three mothers brought a rug, which they spread on the floor, and proceeded to lay out a picnic of carrot sticks, hummus, sausage rolls and crisps in the fiction section.

"Can they do that in here?" Rose asked Martha. "It is allowed?"

"It's never happened before," Martha said. "Please ask them to move to the edge. And tell them not to leave any rubbish behind."

Rose shrugged and meandered over to the group. She pointed towards the other side of the room and the mothers nodded and gathered their things together.

Later in the morning, Clive strolled through the door. He carried a coffee in a large cardboard cup, from a posh coffee shop in Maltsborough. He sipped at it rhythmically with loud slurps. "Everything under control, Martha?" he asked, raising an eyebrow at her.

It was the first time she'd encountered him since she fled from the reading group. She was determined not to show any weakness and sat up a little taller in her chair. "Yes. All is fine," she smiled. "I'm taking a look at my application form. It's all looking very, very positive."

She watched Clive's Adam's apple dip as he swallowed his coffee. "Fantastic," he said flatly. "I, um, look forward to reading it."

After the library closed, Martha walked back to her house with Will and Rose. She made cheese sandwiches for their lunches, served with crisps and big mugs of tea. Then she explained that an old friend was going to be joining them that afternoon. "Her name is Zelda and I think you'll like her."

Rose gave a small wrinkle of her nose. "But me and Will thought we'd go for a mess around on the beach."

Martha looked out of the window. The sun shone on the waves, making them sparkle. Perhaps it might be better if her niece and nephew were out of the way when Zelda arrived. "That's fine. The two of you can go there now, if you like," she said. "I'll wait in for my, um, friend. Be back here in forty-five minutes."

"Okay." Will nodded, then paused with his hand in his pocket. "There is Wi-Fi down there, isn't there?"

Twenty minutes after Will and Rose headed out, Gina knocked on the door. She carried Zelda's turquoise suitcases into the cottage, a large one and an extra large. After that, she headed back to the car, then hoisted a fold-up wheelchair inside, too.

Zelda stood in the hallway, a little unsteady. She traced a finger along the floral wallpaper and held it there, as if propping herself up.

"Are you okay?" Martha asked.

Zelda nodded and looked around. "It feels so strange being back here. Like it's not quite real."

Martha understood what she meant. She felt the same way, too. "I've set up the main bedroom for you. Would you like to take a look?"

"That's Betty's room, isn't it?"

Martha bit the inside of her cheek. She'd not considered how her nana might feel, staying in her own daughter's room. "You can take my bed instead, if you like? My niece and nephew, Will and Rose, are staying over, too. They'll sleep on inflatable mattresses on the floor downstairs."

"I'll look and decide later, thank you." Zelda walked into the dining room, as if she was barefoot and treading on tacks.

She pulled out the wooden chair and sat down, looking out of the window at the bay. The daylight highlighted the creases on her cheeks and the fine hairs around her mouth. "Do Will and Rose know who I am?"

Martha shook her head. "I thought you should meet Lilian first, so I've told the kids that you're a friend, for now. Please don't say anything otherwise."

"I'll try my best."

Gina remained in the hallway and Martha headed back to speak to her.

"Ezmerelda's been quiet for most of the journey here," Gina said in a hushed tone. "If you can believe that."

Martha glanced over at her grandmother. She didn't seem her usual vivacious self. She was still looking out of the window, her expression contemplative. "Perhaps we should take her cases upstairs and give her a few moments alone."

She and Gina each carried a suitcase upstairs and set them down next to the bed in her parents' old bedroom. It was now clean and aired, and Martha had made the bed with fresh white linen. She'd left the window open and a breeze lifted the curtains and let them fall again.

"Your house looks very different to how it appeared the other day," Gina said.

Her approval suddenly felt really important to Martha. Gina was Zelda's carer, her guardian. "I've tidied up the best I can. I'm afraid I let things slide after my parents died," she said. The waxwork-like figures of Thomas and Betty in their final days flashed in her mind but she wouldn't let them stay. "I'm going to look at decorating next, but the amount of choice is so confusing."

"I went out to look at printed wallpapers a couple of weeks ago, and there were hundreds of patterns to choose from,"

THE LIBRARY OF LOST AND FOUND 241

Gina agreed. "It was most difficult. I ended up walking away, empty-handed."

The two women smiled at each other, glad they'd found something in common other than Zelda.

"I'll help Zelda all I can," Martha said. "It means a lot to me for her to stay here."

Gina gave a short nod. She seemed to measure up her next words. "It's special for her, too. Though I am concerned that being here will stir up memories."

"We could head down to the beach this afternoon, rather than stay around the house. My niece and nephew are down there, so we can say hello."

Gina gave a short laugh. "I think you'll find that Ezmerelda has other plans for you."

"Plans?" Martha's throat tightened.

"She said something about a football match. She watches them on the TV."

"Oh."

"I hoped she would relax more over the coming months and take things easier." Gina adjusted her handbag on her shoulder. "I suppose that is not her style. She will stay with you overnight and then I will drive back to collect her at 5:00 p.m. tomorrow. Do you still have the postcard with my rules written on the back?"

Martha nodded. "I love the illustration of the Scottie dog."

"I like to draw sometimes," Gina said. "Please try to adhere to as many of the rules as possible. I know you'll take care of her, and you have my number if you should need it."

After they made their way downstairs, Gina walked over to Zelda and bent her head. She said something, then planted a kiss on her lips. Even though she whispered, Martha overheard her.

"I will miss you."

"I doubt it." Zelda grinned up at her. "I'll be okay, though. See you soon."

Martha felt a prickle of embarrassment, like she had intruded on a private moment. There was a chemistry between Zelda and Gina that she hadn't noticed before, and Zelda's melancholy seemed to evaporate like a puddle on a hot day.

"Don't do anything adventurous," Gina said as she moved away.

"I promise I won't," Zelda said before she winked at Martha.

26

Football

"Let me get this right," Martha said as she counted on her fingertips. "You want to do a Read and Run, at Sandshift football ground, this afternoon? And you want me to accompany you?"

"Yes." Zelda nodded firmly.

"But I have the kids to look after..."

"They can join us. They'll *love* it."

Martha's heart thumped wildly. What on earth would Lilian think if she knew Will and Rose were accompanying their great-grandmother to a football match?"

"You look a little woozy," Zelda said. "Have you been drinking again?"

"No, I haven't," Martha said sharply. "I told you, I don't want to do this."

"I know, but it's my dy—"

"Yes, I know. Your dying wish. Why can't you have a normal one, like going to Disneyland, or lunch at the Ritz?"

Zelda's eyelids flickered. "We don't have to do it." She paused with a sniff. "I'm sure Harry will understand, if you tell him."

"Um, Harry?"

"I've arranged it with him."

Martha held her head in her hands. "And does Gina know about this?"

Zelda cast her eyes down.

"I thought not," Martha said and let out a long sigh.

The chant, "Sandshift United, rah rah rah. Sandshift United, rah rah rah," rung gladiatorial-like through the air as Martha, Zelda, Will and Rose approached the football ground.

Martha felt a bead of sweat form on her forehead and she brushed it away. She'd made an effort with her outfit today and wore Betty's green sweater and beige wool coat again. It made her underarms hot and prickly as she pushed Zelda's chair up the steep slope.

"I can do it. Let go of the handles," Zelda kept shouting.

But Martha sustained a firm grip. It gave her a focus, so she didn't panic about her nana's plan for another Read and Run. She'd heard of knees knocking but didn't think it actually happened. However, her knees were reverberating as they reached and entered the small reception area.

Harry was waiting for them, and Martha worried that the palm of her hand might feel clammy when he gave it a shake. "Martha," he said and kissed her on the cheek, too. "Ye're looking well. I'm glad ye ladies could make it." He grinned.

Will and Rose smiled hello and started to circle the room, looking at the photographs on the wall of the Sandshift United teams over the years. Martha had introduced Zelda to them as "An old friend of the family," and they hadn't asked any questions.

"We're raring to go," Zelda said. "Just try stopping us."

Martha smiled nervously from under her stripy hair.

"I've arranged for ye to go on the football pitch before the match. One of the lads from the accounts department wants to be a stand-up comedian, so he's having a go first. Then ye're on."

"So..." Martha's voice shook as she spoke. "We just walk out on the pitch, and Zelda reads aloud?"

Harry nodded. "She'll have a microphone, so the crowd can hear her."

"How many people are there?"

"Usually around two thousand."

"Two?" Martha pressed a hand to her neck.

"Sometimes three, for a big match. For a wee football team they attract a lot of supporters."

Zelda shoulders shrank. She fingered the blanket on her lap. "My throat is a little croaky," she said, glancing away. "I hope I'll be okay."

Martha fixed her with a glare. "Yes, you *will*," she said.

The accounts-person-come-comedian stood in the center of the pitch. From the tunnel, Martha couldn't hear his words properly. She could see him gesturing with his hands, waving them around and standing with them on his hips. The rhythm of his patter stopped for a while as he waited for a response to his last joke. Martha listened out for laughter but there was only a mild titter.

Her stomach churned as he finished his set and shuffled past her, his back hunched. "I think I'll stick with invoicing," he said.

Will and Rose had opted for a tour of the grounds, offered by one of Harry's workmates, and Zelda and Harry were deep in conversation a few meters away. Zelda had a copy of *Blue Skies and Stormy Seas* set on her lap.

As she waited for their turn, Martha found that her feet wouldn't stay still. With a life of their own they shuffled and danced on the spot. She kept checking her watch and a sense of dread flooded over her as the seconds ticked away.

Giggles filled the corridor and a team of cheerleaders appeared around the corner. Slumping against the nearest wall, they chewed gum and stared at each other's phones. They all wore the same white satin shorts, heavily penciled-in eyebrows and hair in bunches.

One of them stared in her direction, slowly running her eyes over Martha's curly hair, her coat and then shoes. "Is she going to sing?" she whispered loudly to her friend. "Not exactly Beyoncé, is she?"

"More like Susan Boyle."

Martha looked for the exit but the girls had blocked the corridor, obscuring her view of Zelda. She stood on her tiptoes and her breathing quickened. Harry squeezed through the plethora of pom-poms toward her. "Don't be nervous. Ye'll be fine," he said, patting her arm. "It's a shame about Zelda's sore throat, but I'll tell ye what to do."

Martha's entire body stiffened. "Me?" she exclaimed.

Harry shrugged a shoulder. "She said that ye'll be doing the reading."

Martha shook her head wildly. "No. Definitely not. Please wait a minute…" She excused her way through the cheerleaders to where her nana sat, smiling sheepishly in her chair.

"What is this about?" Martha gestured with her hands. "Harry says you're not doing your reading. You claimed it was your dying wish."

Zelda looked up through her sparse eyelashes. "It is. I want to share the stories from the book." She glanced towards the pitch.

Martha narrowed her eyes. "Harry said you have a sore throat."

"I do." Zelda licked her top lip. "And there's more people than I thought, out there."

"You should have thought about that before you set this up." Martha lowered her voice to a hiss.

"Three minutes, ladies," Harry said as he joined them. "Time to get into position."

Martha rubbed her forehead. "I cannot do this on my own," she said.

"Please, Martha," Zelda said. "'The Tiger and the Unicorn' is an important story to me."

"Then you do it."

"I can't. Not today. I'm sorry." Zelda took hold of her hand and stroked the back of it. "To other people, our book might be just a few battered old pages, words and pictures. But when we read the stories, we remember how we felt when we told them. It may sound crazy, but the more people who hear them, the less I connect them to our family history. Do you understand what I mean?"

Martha clenched her teeth. She looked out at all the people in the crowd. and the blood running through her veins felt cold. She gave the slightest nod. "I think so…but…"

Zelda pursed her lips. "Please do this, and I promise I'll tell you the story behind the book."

Martha met her nana's eyes and blinked. "What? Everything? You'll tell me how and why it came to be?"

"Yes," Zelda said. "Absolutely everything."

Martha's heart thumped so loudly she was sure the microphone would pick it up. Her chest was tight and she could hardly breathe. As she walked out onto the pitch, the turf felt bouncy beneath her feet, and she concentrated on taking one step forward and then another, as she followed the cheerleaders. She blinked as she left the dark of the tunnel behind and squinted against the hazy white sky and emerald-green grass. She held one hand up against the weak sun as the noise of the crowd singing crackled in her ears.

Harry walked at the side of her. He turned this way and that, waving with both hands as if he was washing windows. Martha kept her own hands pressed to her sides. She could feel vomit rising in her throat and she swallowed it away.

Don't be sick. Don't be sick, she chanted to herself.

She reached under her coat and plucked at her sweater as she and Harry neared a microphone stand. As she swayed a little, he reached out a steadying hand. "Are ye okay?"

Martha glanced over to the side of the pitch, to where her nana sat in her wheelchair. With every nerve in her body, she sensed Zelda willing her to do this. Martha stood stiffly, her body trembling, before she gave a short nod. "I'm fine," she squeaked.

The football team stood in a line with their hands behind their backs. One yawned and there were a few sets of glazed eyes.

"Ye just take hold of the microphone. I'll switch it on. Good luck and enjoy yerself." Harry smiled at her.

Martha gave a rictus grin back. She took a few deep breaths and blew out through pursed lips. She glanced back at her nana one last time before she stuck out her chin and reached for the microphone. Her fingers fumbled and it slipped through them, as if it was coated in butter. Electronic feedback screeched around the arena and ripples of laughter rang around the ground. Martha scrunched up her shoulders against the noise.

"Get her off. Get her off. Get her off," a chant started. It gathered momentum until it echoed and surrounded her. "Get her OFF."

"Ignore them. They even sing that to their own team," Harry said beside her. He bent down, picked up the microphone and repositioned it. "Ye go for it. And I have some cake for ye and Zelda afterwards. A new fruity recipe."

Martha nodded. She touched the microphone lightly and cleared her throat a couple of times. "Um, hello," she croaked.

"Get her off. Get her off," the crowd sang in reply.

"Speak up. Ye're talking to two thousand people," Harry said and he moved away.

Martha massaged the back of her neck and felt her bottom lip wobble. She was on the verge of bursting into tears. *Useless.* That's how she felt. As useless as Clive Folds insinuated she was, as useless as her father often made her feel. Panic took hold of her legs, making them bow and wobble. She shuffled closer to the microphone stand but her feet were leaden. She stood still for a long time, wishing the football team would forget she was there and start the match without her. Then she could slink away and flee from the ground.

She peeked around again at Zelda, and her nana leaned forward in her wheelchair, giving her a double thumbs-up. "I love you, Martha," she shouted, cupping her hands to her mouth. "You are *glorious.*"

Martha looked away quickly as tears sprang to her eyes. Glorious was something she was when she was with Joe, before she looked after her parents. Glorious was something she was when she wrote her stories.

Not now.

She looked around at the hundreds of multicolored speckles of faces surrounding her and she struggled for air. Her fingers spasmed and she reached up, nervously pushing her glittery slide higher and tighter in her hair.

This matters to Zelda, she told herself. *Would you prefer to be here, or stuck at home washing chandeliers and hemming trousers?*

She imagined if her mother was here, Betty would encourage her, too. She'd want her to do something that wasn't dictated by Thomas.

She finally summoned the strength to speak. "Good afternoon," she said, and she was surprised at how loud and clear her voice sounded, amplified through the mike.

The cheerleaders stopped talking. They still chewed gum but they looked at her rather than at each other.

As Martha waited, the roar of the crowd died down.

She raised her copy of *Blue Skies and Stormy Seas* and her fingers scrabbled to find "The Tiger and the Unicorn." She waited a few beats to see if the words "Get her off" rose again, but all she heard was a bout of good-natured singing.

"I'm Martha Storm, from Sandshift library," she said. "My grandmother, Zelda, would like me to tell you a story I wrote when I was a young girl, because it's important to our family history." She paused again, wondering how shaky her words sounded to the audience. She tried to picture the football supporters as rows of cabbages, or minus their clothes. Harry stood a few meters away and she averted her eyes, so her mind didn't picture him naked, too.

After the blast of an air horn, she began to read.

Her first few words tumbled out and she stuttered a little, but she found her flow. She concentrated on the page, on the white paper and the dark gray words. Her surroundings faded away and she became only aware of the book and her own voice.

Stories could always take her elsewhere and she allowed this one to do it now.

She imagined herself in her teens, her feet kicking against the cliff at the end of the garden, and of Zelda twirling on the grass in a flowing dress. She saw herself crawling on the library floor, and Zelda making a claw of her hand as Martha described the tiger threatening the unicorn.

A feeling of peacefulness filtered over her, warming her skin like spring sunshine through a window. Her heartbeat slowed and she began to feel stronger, as if the words were somehow soaking into and strengthening her bones.

As she read, she felt she was giving this story a new life of its own. It was no longer a reflection of her childhood and whatever happened within the Storm family. It was just a story, to be shared and enjoyed.

When she finished it, she felt almost sad to reach the end and she closed the book. She took a moment before she said, "Thank you for listening, everybody."

Her hip knocked against the microphone stand and a small screech pierced the air.

Zelda had already stuck a yellow note to the back cover that said, "Read me. I'm yours." Martha's hand shook as she placed the book on the turf and stepped away.

Harry led with a round of applause, clapping his hands together flamboyantly. The cheerleaders raised their pom-poms and shook them in the air. One of the footballers reached up and surreptitiously wiped his eye with his finger.

As Martha walked off the pitch, her heart began to race again, but this time it wasn't from fear. If she had to put a name to it, then she might call it pride in herself, that she had been able to read to all those people and share the story for her nana.

A small round of applause sounded around the ground, growing louder. Glancing back, Martha watched a football player pick up the book and open it.

Zelda sat, waiting. "You did it," she said, her eyes swimming with tears. "You were bloody glorious."

Martha nodded. For once, she actually felt it.

"You were ah-mazing."

"Thank you." Martha closed her eyes and took a moment to listen to the crowd and the cheerleaders chanting. She let the feeling wash over her and enjoyed the tingly sensation it triggered in her fingers and toes. She grinned and, when she opened her eyes again, Zelda was still nodding her approval.

"Shall we go?" Zelda said. "Harry has some cake waiting for us."

Martha took hold of the back of her nana's chair and began to turn her around. "Cake would be lovely," she said firmly. "But first of all, you owe me *your* own story. About the book..."

27

Kite

After leaving the football ground, Martha, Zelda, Will and
Rose made their way down to the beach. Zelda promised to
share her story about the book but wanted to do it somewhere
more private than the football ground. Also, Martha wanted
to take a walk, to slow down her racing heart.

As they headed down the slope, she worried that Zelda's
wheelchair might pick up speed, like a racing car in the Grand
Prix. So she kept a firm grip on the back, tugging and digging her heels in, just as she did when handling her overloaded
shopping trolley.

Will and Rose, rather embarrassed that their aunt had read
a book in the middle of a football pitch, ran off ahead.

Martha and Zelda stopped when they reached the mermaid
statue. Martha took deep gulps of the sea air to try to stop her
limbs from jerking with adrenaline. "Now tell me about *Blue
Skies and Stormy Seas*," she said softly.

Zelda nodded. "I will do, but I want to look at the plaque
first." Her lips moved as she read the names of the fishermen
to herself. "It only seems like yesterday when the *Pegasus* went
down," she said. "I remember it well."

"Were you there?"

"I found out the morning after it happened. I was walking on the beach and could hear seagulls cawing. But when I got closer, I realized it was the sound of people crying. There was a lifeboat out at sea and I remember thinking it looked too orange against the gray waves. Two boats circled, round and round, like they were spiraling down a plughole." She made a twist with her finger.

Martha pressed her lips together, imagining the scene. "Did you know any of the men on board?"

Zelda took her time to speak. "I knew Siegfried Frost a little, and I think he survived. Another was Daniel McLean. He was just twenty years old, the poor lad. Your mum knew him, too."

"Siegfried still lives in Sandshift." Martha looked over towards the lighthouse. She tried and failed to picture the gray-bearded recluse as a young man. "He must only have been around Mum's age when it happened."

"So young," Zelda agreed. "Your mum wasn't much older when she got married."

"I know. I found the marriage certificate when I was cleaning the house. I didn't know Mum was pregnant with me when she walked down the aisle."

Zelda fell quiet. "How do you know about that?"

"Just from the dates. I wonder if Dad resented me, because he felt forced to get married…"

"Hmm." Zelda pursed her lips and looked out to sea. "They were different times, and your father was a complex man."

They stayed there for a few minutes. The wind lifted Martha's hair around her face while Zelda's headscarf made a fluttering sound. Sea spit speckled their cheeks.

"The book," Martha said. "You said you'd tell me."

Zelda turned her wheelchair away from the statue and faced

the sea. "When I left Sandshift, I wanted to get away from England. Gina's parents invited me to stay with them in Finland."

"You've known her for that long?"

Zelda nodded. "Her whole family was good to me. They welcomed me as one of them. I was terribly homesick for a while. I missed England and I left Betty behind." She rubbed her nose. "Gina put up with my gloomy moods, though.

"She's always said that writing is good therapy and thought I should keep my mind busy. So one day, she bought me a scrapbook and suggested I stick things in it. I'd kept some of the stories you'd written for me and I pasted them in.

"As soon as I'd done it, other ones started to flood back. There were ones I made up for you. There were stories I used to tell your mum, and ones she shared with me. I wrote them down. Not exactly, of course. Just whatever I could remember.

"Gina can draw well, though she won't admit it. One day when I was feeling low, she sat beside me and drew a blackbird. Then she pasted it next to one of your stories, 'The Bird Girl.' And over the next few weeks and months, she drew other things, too, a mermaid, puppets and a nightingale. We worked on completing the scrapbook together." Zelda paused and repositioned her blanket farther up her legs.

"Gina knew a local printer and when the scrapbook was finished she asked him to reproduce it, as a real book. She commissioned fifty copies for my birthday and it was such a glorious surprise. She turned the past into something beautiful for me, so I could face the future. She's an ah-mazing woman.

"We gave copies to friends and Gina's family, before we moved to America. I even came home, to give you your own copy..."

"Home?" Martha questioned. "You returned to Sandshift?"

Zelda took a deep breath and didn't let it go. Her lips

worked as if she was sifting through what she should and shouldn't say. "It was 1985 when I called back at the cottage. It was during the day and I made a big mistake. Betty was at home but so was Thomas."

Martha squinted against the daylight, an uneasy feeling swirling in her stomach. "And this was *after* my parents told me you were dead?"

Zelda gave a curt nod. "It was three years later. I wrote a message in a copy of *Blue Skies and Stormy Seas* and brought it for you. I knocked on the door, longing to see Betty, you and Lilian. But Thomas answered instead." She lowered her eyes and shook her head. "I tried to apologize to him."

"What did you need to do that for? Was it his fault that you left?"

Zelda placed a hand to her mouth. Her shoulders started to shake. "I begged to see you and Lilian... I said sorry, because I thought that's what Thomas would want to hear..."

Martha reached out and stroked her back. "What happened to the book you brought for me? Why doesn't it have a cover?"

"Your father tore it off when he threw it back at me. It hit me in the chest and fell onto the floor. I picked it back up and tried to offer it again but Betty, my own daughter, ordered me to leave." Zelda tried to blink away her tears, but they spilled down her cheeks. "She said that things were settled, without me. My coming home would mess things up for the family, she said. Everyone thought I was dead, and they wanted to keep it that way. I had to leave...again."

"But why did you go in the first place?"

Zelda shook her head slowly. Her fingers kneaded her blanket.

"What happened, Nana?" Martha asked softly.

Zelda gave the smallest smile as she reached out for Martha's hand. "It was the evening of your parents' anniversary party," she said. "I was invited, and I…" She stopped talking abruptly as footsteps pounded on the sand. Will and Rose ran towards them, whooping with their arms raised. Martha tore her eyes away from her nana.

A brightly colored kite bobbed in the sky. As her niece and nephew drew closer, Martha could see it was shaped like a parrot, made of red, green and yellow polythene, vivid against the milky sky.

"Look what we found on the beach," Rose panted as her feet came to a standstill.

Will's eyes were still trained in the air. "It has a thread attached but doesn't have a handle."

Zelda wiped her face with her fingers. "Can I have a turn?"

Will gave her a grin. "Maybe later. Can we run out towards the lighthouse, Auntie Martha?"

Martha glanced over at the craggy rocks. A gray figure stood at the end of them, looking out to sea. "Yes, but don't be long. I'm hungry."

She watched them run away and turned back to Zelda. "Do you remember when you could get so excited by a piece of colored polythene?"

"Remember it? I still do."

"You were invited to the party," Martha prompted, returning to their conversation. "What happened?"

Zelda pulled her blanket up farther up over her body. "You know what? I'm ever so hungry, too, Martha. Do you fancy going to the chip shop? I've not been to the one in the bay for ages."

"I asked you a question," Martha said firmly.

"I know you did."

"Well?"

Zelda spun the wheels on her chair. "Let's go," she said. "I really can't think straight without food."

28

Paint

Martha treated Zelda, Will and Rose to a portion of fish, chips and mushy peas each. The sky was darkening to indigo as they carried them over to a bench halfway up the cliff that overlooked the bay. It was more sheltered here, without as much wind.

Martha made sure her hair slide was secure before she opened up her carton. She was ravenous after the Read and Run at the football ground and their visit to the beach.

Zelda leaned back in her chair. She scratched around under her headscarf, unfastened and then removed it. After folding it into a small square, she put in into her pocket.

"Why haven't you got any hair?" Rose asked as she squeezed out a sachet of ketchup.

"I'm kick-starting a trend," Zelda said. "It's a strong look for us octogenarians. What do you think?"

Rose widened her eyes, then laughed. "I prefer you with the scarf."

"Why do you have a scar on the back of your head?" Will asked.

Zelda didn't miss a beat. "It's from a nasty crocodile attack. I wrestled it and won."

Will and Rose shared a shoulder shrug before they carried on eating.

Martha loved the ceremony of eating fish and chips outside, especially when it was cold. She liked to add too much vinegar so it pooled in the bottom of the carton in a brown puddle.

The four of them huddled in a line, their shoulders hunched and noses pink. They used both hands to hold their chip cartons, to keep them warm.

"What do you fancy doing, when we get back to the house?" Martha asked when they'd finished eating.

"I can show you how my phone works," Will offered.

"Can we play with the dragon's head?" Rose asked.

Martha thought of the beast, with his face part gray from the papier-mâché repair. "You can't really play with him because he belongs to the school. He's also waiting to be sandpapered and painted."

"We could do that," Will suggested. "I like painting."

"Me, too," Rose said.

Martha pictured her grandmother, niece and nephew sitting on the dining room floor, circled around the dragon's head, like it was a substitute campfire. It was a strange but rather wonderful idea.

"Okay," she said. "Let's give it a try."

When they got back to the house, Will's phone rang and he darted into the kitchen to take the call. "Okay, Mum. Yes, we're having a good time. Yes, we've eaten. No, I probably haven't drunk enough water."

Martha followed him. "Please don't mention the football ground or Zelda," she whispered. "I'll tell her about them."

Will gave a shrug. He closed the door behind him and his voice turned to a hum.

Martha maneuvered the dragon's head onto the floor and shook the tubes of paint out of Suki's shopping bag.

Rose crouched down beside her. She rearranged the tubes so the colors ran from light to dark.

"I'll just pop upstairs and unpack my things," Zelda said. She stood up from the wooden chair. "I'll pick a bedroom."

"Use mine if you like," Martha said.

After a few minutes, Will reappeared. He sloped into the dining room and slumped down on his inflatable mattress. Resting his chin on his knees, he played with the laces in his shoes. "Mum wants to speak to you," he said to his sister. "The phone's on the dining table."

Rose got to her feet and it was her turn to shut herself away.

Martha looked at Will's glum face. "Do you want a cup of tea? Do you need an extra pillow on your mattress?"

Will shook his head. He undid his laces and took his shoes off. He straightened them up side by side. "Nah. It's okay."

Martha studied him for a while before she lowered herself down, sitting beside him.

"I don't want a biscuit," he said automatically.

"Do you want to talk about anything?"

Will moved his head in a half shake, half nod.

Martha waited.

Finally, he worked his tongue around inside his mouth. "Mum and Dad aren't getting along at the moment."

"Oh." Martha thought about putting on a cheery face, of thumping his arm and telling him to keep his chin up. But she fought against the urge, not saying or doing anything.

"She likes everything to be perfect." Will sighed. "I can't leave socks on the floor or eat food in front of the TV. If she says I've got to be home at nine o'clock, god forbid if I'm even a minute late. Now she's asked me to make a note of everything we do this weekend, so she knows what's gone on. It's going too far. It's so crappy, trying to please her all the time."

Martha gave his arm a brief rub. She knew what it was like, trying to please a demanding parent. "Your mum likes to be organized," she tried to explain. "She's just trying to show an interest in you."

"It's more than that," Will said. "She's obsessed. It's like she thinks that someone is going to show up with a clipboard and give her marks out of ten for everything she does... everything we do."

"Your granddad liked everything done in a certain way, too. Perhaps it's rubbed off on your mum."

Will leaned back on the mattress and it squeaked beneath his elbows. He glanced around the room. "Gran wasn't that old when she died, was she? My mate at school has grandparents in their nineties."

"Zelda is almost ninety, too." Martha stopped talking, not wanting to let it slip to Will that she was his great-grandmother. "Your gran was only in her midsixties. I don't think she knew how to live without your granddad."

"What? She died of a broken heart?"

Martha mused on this. "Something like that."

Will folded his arms. "I remember them sitting around the dining table. Granddad gave us chocolate when Mum wasn't looking, and his hair was really black, like a vampire's. He liked flowers, didn't he? There was always a vase on the table."

"Yes, freesias. He bought them for your gran each week."

Will nodded. "Gran looked after us. She wore nice colors, like an exotic bird. Though she was always nervy."

"What do you mean?"

"Well, you know those horror films where there's a woman on her own in a spooky house, and she's walking along a dark corridor to investigate a strange noise in the kitchen? Like no one would ever do in real life. Well, Gran was like that, like she always expected something to jump out at her." He looked down. "I kind of miss them both."

Even though her parents had shaped her life, Martha also missed them. "Me, too," she said. She hesitated before she draped her arm around his shoulder, not sure if a thirteen-year-old boy would appreciate a hug.

Will pressed himself against her for a couple of seconds before he moved quickly away. "Cheers," he muttered.

Rose and Zelda entered the room again at the same time. Zelda lifted her nose and sniffed the air. "Is everything okay? Have I missed something?"

Will and Martha shared a brief smile.

"Nothing," Martha said. "We were just about to get started on the dragon's head. Choose which paintbrush you want to use."

The next two hours were ones that Martha knew she'd remember and relish for a long while. Time with her nana, niece and nephew might be short and she was determined to enjoy it.

After Martha gave the dragon a light sandpapering, Rose mixed the paint. She stuck her tongue out from the corner of her mouth as she concentrated on stopping it from oozing off the plate.

Zelda instructed her how to mix the colors. "For the dragon's fleshy tones, you can use white with a dab of red and yellow. Never add black to darken a color, or you deaden the shade."

"How do you even know that?" Rose marveled.

"My friend Gina is nifty with a paintbrush."

Will insisted his job was to hold the dragon's head up, so Zelda didn't have to lean down too far to paint his face.

Martha thrived on taking charge of instructions. "That

red is a little too bright, tone it down a little... Watch your sleeve doesn't dangle in the paint, Rose... Would anyone like a nice cup of tea?"

Will talked about Spotify on his phone, and Martha agreed he could play some music.

They painted the dragon to the sound of Katy Perry and Beyoncé.

"He looks friendly," Rose said, sitting back on her heels to admire their work. "I think he might live in the cave on Sandshift beach."

"Dragon's don't live on the beach," Will snorted. "They wouldn't be able to breathe fire because the sea would put it out."

"Of course they do," Zelda said. She pressed a fine paint-brush against the dragon's eye, adding a dot of white light to his pupil. "Haven't you ever heard of the Sandshift Dragon?"

"No." Will rolled his eyes, but then he leaned in a little. "What about it?"

"Tell us," Rose said.

Zelda made her hands into claws. "His body is iridescent like a dragonfly's and his scales look like rows of crescent moons. When you stare into his eyes, they look like they are full of fire. He isn't a red-and-yellow dragon, like this one. The Sandshift Beast is dark green, the color of swampland."

Martha looked at her nana and down at the tassels on the rug on the floor. It transported her back in time, to when she lay scribbling in her notepad. Words began to pop into her head and she joined in with the story. "It's so he's camouflaged against the seaweed on the sand. Each morning, before any-one wakes, he gobbles it up for his breakfast. People think he's scary but really he's shy..."

Zelda nodded. "Some say he comes from Romania, Count Dracula country. He came over on a boat, an exotic pet for a wealthy aristocrat. But the dragon set fire to his mansion. Somehow he escaped and found his way down to the sands..."

"He'd never seen the sea before," Martha said. "Or sand. He loved the quietness of the cave. If you ever hear a roar in there, sometimes it's the tide coming in, but often it's the dragon testing out his lungs. He likes to paddle in the shallows and sometimes goes for a swim..."

Will gave a deep sigh. "Oh, sure. Dragons can't swim."

"The Loch Ness Monster swims. He's not a dragon, though he's some kind of distant relative." Martha shuffled back by a few inches, moving her head to examine her work. "I think this fellow is finished."

Will and Rose smiled, proud at what they'd accomplished, yet Zelda wore a look of contemplation. She kept hold of her paintbrush.

"Are you okay?" Martha asked.

Zelda stared at the dragon and then at her. "You've done it," she said.

"Yes. We all have. He looks great, doesn't he? You'd never know he was damaged before."

"No. I mean that *you've* done it. You told a story. You remembered how to do it."

Martha swallowed as a warm feeling began to creep over her, just like the one she sought by doing things for other people. It was as if she'd just stepped out of an air-conditioned room, and she savored it for a while.

"Yes, I did, didn't I?" She nodded. "Maybe we should write the story down."

29

Books

The next morning, the four of them took the bus over to Maltsborough. They sat on the back seat together and chatted for the entire journey. Zelda had decided to leave her wheelchair at Martha's house. "It gets in the way and I want to move freely," she said, making her hand into a snake. "I want to see the amusement arcades."

As they neared the town, Rose nudged Will in his side. "You ask her," she said.

"No." He pushed back. "You do it."

"What is it?" Martha asked. "What do you want?"

"Rose wants to go to the bookshop," Will said with a smirk.

"It's you who wants to go," Rose retaliated.

"Is this the bookshop you refused to visit with me?" Martha frowned. "When you preferred a slice of chocolate fudge cake instead?"

"It didn't taste as good as I remembered," Will said.

"Too rich and sticky," his sister agreed. "I want a new book to read, for school. And Mum says Will has got to spend less time on his phone."

Martha thought of how she hadn't seen Owen since the

dinner party. He hadn't been in touch, now the author of the little battered book had been revealed.

"I'd like to see Owen again," Zelda said, as if reading Martha's mind. She cast a sly glance at her granddaughter. "He's very knowledgeable about books. And he's a very attractive man."

Will grinned. He clutched his stomach and made a sound like he was going to be sick.

Martha felt her cheeks begin to heat up. "It's Sunday." She bristled. "I'm sure that Chamberlain's will be closed today."

"We should take a look, anyway. Just in case," Zelda said.

Martha tried to insist there was no point, but she found herself outnumbered, three to one.

Rose and Will walked a few meters apart and Martha crooked her elbow for Zelda to use as a crutch.

As they turned around the corner from the lifeboat station, Martha found that her pulse quickened when she spotted a figure standing outside the bookstore. As they drew closer she saw it was Owen.

He wore his suit with a T-shirt and red slippers, and no socks. Standing on one leg, he held a coffee cup in one hand and a book in the other. He sipped as he read.

"See," Zelda said smugly when she noticed him. "It was worth checking."

"He's having his breakfast, not working. The shop will be closed, and we're going to disturb him," Martha said. But her nana had already raised her hand and waved.

"Owen. Owen," she called out. "It's so lovely to see you."

Owen lowered his book. He set his coffee cup down on the windowsill where, Martha was sure, he'd forget and leave it. However, she quite liked that. There was an easiness about him, a comfortable lackadaisical air.

"Ezmerelda." He grinned. "How wonderful to see you again."

"Martha is here, too. And she's not drunk," Zelda said.

"That's…um, good to know."

"Yes." Martha didn't know what to say, so she shrugged and said, "Totally sober today."

She was glad that she'd made an effort with her appearance again. She wore a Breton striped T-shirt with embroidered red roses on the front, and a slick of mascara and lipstick. Instead of her lace-up shoes, she wore a pair of ankle boots that she'd found, unworn, in the back of her mum's wardrobe.

"Is the shop open?" Rose lifted her chin. She peered into the dark space behind Owen.

"Not usually on Sundays, but you're welcome to browse," he said. He opened the door for her. "The light switch is next to the counter."

Before Martha could say anything, Will and Rose shot inside.

Owen gave a surprised shrug. "It's great to see they're so interested in books."

"We won't keep you for long." Martha smiled apologetically.

"We wrote a story together, last night," Zelda said proudly. "It's about a dragon. I want to read it out loud to an audience."

"Not today, though." Martha cast her a stare. "I thought we were going to the arcades."

"We can do both. Do you want to join us?" Zelda asked Owen. "I read to anyone I can get to listen."

"That sounds, um, intriguing. I'd love to tag along."

Zelda let go of Martha's elbow. She patted the top of Owen's arm and headed into the shop, too.

Martha found herself alone with him on the pavement. "Are you sure we're not disturbing you?"

"No. My Sundays are pretty uneventful these days. Greg usually vanishes on a Friday night and I see him again on Monday morning," Owen said. "It's good to see Zelda again. She's quite a character. Reminds me of one of my ex-mothers-in-law."

Martha scratched her neck. "How many wives have you actually had?"

"Not that many...um, three."

"Three failed marriages are rather a lot," Martha observed out loud, then wished she hadn't.

"I don't think they failed...they were reasonably happy ones. Why does something have to last forever to be classed as successful? Surely it's okay to give things a try."

Martha studied him as he leaned against the door frame. Joe had been young and ambitious, whereas Owen was maturing and steady. He came with an interesting history but, then again, so did she.

She thought about his words and wondered if she could manage to see Joe in this way, too. That they'd shared five wonderful years together, and that she should be thankful. Even if they had married, it didn't guarantee them a happy ending.

"Do you mind if I watch Zelda's reading? Or is it a family thing?" Owen asked.

Martha glanced at him and thought that, actually, she would like him to join them. "It's probably the more the merrier, in Zelda's eyes. I think she'd be delighted if you came along."

And actually, she knew that she'd be rather pleased, too.

After they browsed the bookshop for half an hour, Will and Rose selected a few books each and Zelda insisted on paying. "I'll buy them. My treat," she said. "No arguing."

"I have business over in Sandshift next week," Owen said.

"I could drop the books off at the library for you, so you don't have to carry them around today. We could grab a coffee afterwards, Martha?"

He asked her so casually that no alarm bells rang in her head. Her father didn't scold her, and she didn't break out in a hot sweat thinking how to turn down a slice of cake. She also didn't want to lug a stack of books around Maltsborough.

"That would be lovely," she said, finding no problem at all with accepting his invitation.

People bustled along the promenade. Kids sat in a row along the seawall, their legs swinging. They studiously tied scraps of bacon to string, to lower into the sea and catch crabs. A multitude of bright plastic buckets lay in wait as holding bays for the crustaceans.

Couples strolled arm-in-arm, wrapped up in their anoraks and boots. Dogs scampered along, stopping to sniff at the exciting things dropped on the pavement—blobs of ice cream, scraps of cone and chips.

Zelda pulled up the collar of her woolen coat against the wind.

"It's chilly here," Martha said. "Let's go to the arcades first."

"I want to read this now." Zelda took the piece of paper from her handbag. She watched as a stream of people walked by, choosing her moment.

"That story is ours," Martha said. "When I wrote it down last night, I didn't mean for it to be shared."

"I want to read something new," Zelda said. "The Read and Run at the football ground was the final one from *Blue Skies and Stormy Seas*. I've given my last spare copy away. Mission accomplished."

Martha pursed her lips, knowing there was no point in arguing. She also noticed how her nana's sore throat had miraculously vanished.

There was a flea market held in the town each Sunday, and people flocked to it. Martha spotted Nora in a ruby-red velour tracksuit. She was holding hands with a tall handsome man who wore indigo jeans and a black shirt.

Zelda coughed and looked around her, waiting for the optimum number of people to pass by. Martha stood with the kids and Owen.

When a surge came towards them, Zelda spoke aloud. "This is a story that my family created together. It's about a dragon who lives in Sandshift. I think you'll enjoy it."

People stared and walked past. Martha saw raised eyebrows, rolled eyes and smirks, yet Zelda carried on reading.

A man carrying a Chihuahua stopped to listen. Two elderly women who wore matching plastic rain hoods took a seat on a nearby bench. A boy trundling past on a small bike tugged on his father's sleeve and they paused, too. Others joined them, forming a loose circle around Zelda.

Zelda told the story. She clawed her hands and spread her fingers. She brought the story to life with her actions and words.

When she finished, she took a small bow. A round of applause started up, and her eyes shone as a few people dropped coins on the floor in front of her.

"Thank you," she said. "Thank you all very much." She glanced down at the paper in her hands. There was nothing to leave behind this time. She looked up at Martha, her eyes and hands empty.

"It's okay. You've done it," Martha assured her. "We have new stories now."

Zelda's hands shook as she folded up the paper.

"You were brilliant." Rose bent down and bumped the top of Zelda's arm with her own.

"Pretty damn good," Will admitted.

Zelda found a smile. "Yes. I was, wasn't I?" She put the story in her pocket.

"Well done, Zelda." Owen said. "Perhaps you'd like to do a reading at Chamberlain's sometime?"

Zelda broke into a gap-toothed grin. "That sounds ah-mazing."

"Great," Owen said. "Well, I'll head back to the shop now. Thanks for inviting me, and I'll see you for that coffee soon, Martha."

Martha smiled. "I'm paying this time, though."

"Okay. I won't argue."

Zelda staggered a little to the side, then caught her balance. "I enjoyed that, but I need a bloody sit-down before the arcades."

Martha caught her arm. "Come on, then. You've done far too much this weekend and I don't want to be in trouble with Gina. Maybe we'll give the arcades a miss." She led her nana to a bench in a bus shelter.

"Perhaps you're right." Zelda sighed.

Martha's mouth dropped open. "You actually agreed with me for once."

"I know. I'm not all bad." Zelda winked.

Martha watched as the flow of people on the promenade resumed. Nora spotted her and waved. The boy with the bike rode it away.

But one person stood still, watching. Her blond hair danced in the breeze above the collar of her cream mohair jacket. Her eyes were pink-rimmed but set hard.

Zelda tugged on Martha's sleeve. "That woman is really staring at us. Do you know who she is?"

"Oh no," Will said with a groan. "It's Mum."

30

Father

Lilian marched toward Martha, her coat flapping open. She clutched her handbag under her arm and her lips were puckered.

Martha tried to find a smile but could see from Lilian's set jaw that she wasn't going to win one in return. Her feelings of positivity and happiness ebbed away.

"Hi, Mum," Rose said quietly.

Lilian came to a halt. She stared at Zelda before focusing her attention on Martha. "What's going on?" she asked Will and Rose. "You were surrounded by people on the promenade."

Martha inched forward. "We came over here for a day out." She glanced at Zelda and silently urged her to stay put.

"Zelda wanted to read a story to everyone. That's all." Rose gave a small shrug.

Lilian's nostrils flared. She glared at Martha. *"Zelda?"*

"I couldn't change my arrangements." Martha stepped forward. "You wanted to talk to Paul, and I wanted to see Nana. I told Will and Rose she's a family friend. Nothing else."

Lilian balled her hands into fists. "I warned you," she said.

"You should have left that stupid old book alone. I said I didn't want the kids to meet her."

Martha's stomach turned over with guilt. "I'm sorry, but Zelda told me the story behind the book."

"About why she left?"

"No. She'll tell me in her own time, though."

"I don't think so. She's hidden it for so long."

People began to slow down around them, listening in. A middle-aged couple, who wore matching red anoraks and hiking boots, pretended to look at something on a phone, while their eyes were really trained on Lilian and Martha.

Martha bit inside her mouth. "You know something, don't you?" she said.

Lilian looked away. "It's up to her to tell you, not me."

"But how can she, when you won't meet her? Let's both speak to her now."

Lilian glared over at Zelda. "That's *her*, isn't it?"

Martha gave a small nod.

Will sidled up. "You okay, Mum?"

"Fine," she said sharply. "You and Rose, get your things, now. I'm taking you home."

"Our bags are still at Auntie Martha's house..."

"What's wrong, Mum?" Rose asked.

"*This* is what's wrong." Lilian pointed at Will and then Rose. "I expected Martha to look after you both, not bring you here with your crazy great-grandmother."

Will's and Rose's eyes widened and slid over toward Zelda. She sat in the bus shelter, twirling her thumbs.

"Zelda is our...*what*?" Will said.

"Why didn't you tell us, Auntie Martha?" Rose asked.

Martha opened her mouth to speak but Lilian got there first. "I told you I didn't want her near them."

"Why not?" Will asked. "She's good fun. She made Auntie

Martha read in the middle of the football pitch. We painted a dragon's head, and Zelda read for everyone on the promenade."

Lilian's eyes hardened. "Thank you *very* much, Martha, for defying me."

"I didn't mean to. I couldn't think of another way. I'm really sorry—"

Her sister turned away. "Wait for me outside Chichetti's," she ordered Will and Rose over her shoulder. "I'll get the car."

The kids trudged away, each casting Martha a rueful smile.

"Please come and meet her, Lilian. There's so much for us to talk about," Martha pleaded. "We both thought she was dead."

"It might be better if she was."

Martha felt anger flare in her chest. She took hold of her sister's arm. "How can you say that? Mum and Dad are gone, but she's still here. She's the only relative we have left. She tried to come back into our lives, Lilian, but Mum and Dad wouldn't let her."

Lilian spun back. "You have *no* idea the amount of trouble that woman caused. It was better she left, no matter how it happened."

"We loved her. Mum loved her. I don't know why our parents lied to us. They told us she was dead, but it wasn't *her* fault. Dad probably caused all this..."

"Don't ever speak about him like that," Lilian hissed.

"He ruled our lives. You managed to escape. We can't blame Nana for doing the same."

"Dad might have been set in his ways, but he always did his best for us."

"Everything had to be his way. I know, Lilian. I looked after him for years, on my own."

"That's not *my* fault."

"Yes, but you could have helped more." Martha was entering a conversation that she didn't want to have. Words of frustration she'd held inside for years were beginning to boil and spill out. "You met Paul, but I gave up Joe, to be there for them. I gave up my own chance of happiness. I lost my identity and Zelda has helped me to find it again."

"You have no right, speaking like that."

Martha kept her arms ramrod straight by her sides. "I have every right. I'm the one who cooked and cleaned for Mum and Dad. I made their breakfast every morning and put them to bed every night."

Lilian's cheeks glowed scarlet. "You think you're a saint, Martha. A real do-gooder. Well, there's one thing you should know, before you try and write a happy story with Zelda as your heroine."

Martha jutted her chin. "Go on then. What is it?"

The two women stood with their faces close together, almost nose to nose. Martha could feel her sister's breath, hot on her cheeks.

Lilian glanced quickly at Zelda, then away again. "I—"

"Go on," Martha said. "Tell me, Lilian. Then I need to make sure that our grandmother is okay. I'll take her back to the house where I cared for our parents, for fifteen years—"

"Oh, stop with the dramatics, Martha." Lilian's top lip curled. "Thomas Storm wasn't even your real bloody father."

Martha froze. Everything seemed to stop around her. Sounds and people were wiped away. "What?" She frowned. "*What* did you say?"

"You heard me." Lilian held her coat tight to her neck and couldn't meet Martha's eyes. "Thomas Storm wasn't your real dad."

31

Party

Betty, 1982

Betty set the table for her and Thomas's anniversary party
using an old tea service that once belonged to Eleanor. The
saucers were adorned with fussy pink flowers and the cup handles were too small. They weren't to Betty's taste. However,
Thomas was proud of the set. It had been a wedding present
from his parents.

"They've been happily married for over fifty years," he announced proudly, as he watched Betty straighten a cup. "Let's
hope we make it to a half century, too."

Betty found a small smile.

Even though her own mother was coming to the party, she
would be glad when the evening was over.

Thomas had brought home an anniversary cake. It had
fuchsia-pink icing and was studded with white flowers. If
Zelda had bought it, he would have declared it *tacky*. However, because he'd selected it, he said it was *exquisite*. "Don't

scrimp," he said when he gave her a roll of ten-pound notes to buy food.

When Betty handled the money, she felt quite giddy at having so much to spend, for once. She bought the most expensive cheddar from the grocer's shop and salmon from the fishmongers.

Now she placed lettuce, tomatoes and cucumber in a bowl and sprinkled them with cress. She made sausages and pineapple on sticks, and homemade sausage rolls. When Thomas said his mother preferred the tomatoes cut into eight rather than four pieces, Betty fished them back out of the salad bowl and did as he asked.

After she finished, Thomas surveyed the table. "It looks wonderful," he said, kissing her on the forehead. "Well done. I think my parents will see now that the decision I made to marry you was the right one."

Betty cleared her throat. "Why? Did they ever think otherwise?"

Thomas presented one of his long silences. "Let's not talk about that now."

Snatching up her action list, Betty gave her tasks a green tick. "Can you help me out with the desserts? I've got an apple pie to make, and a rhubarb crumble."

Thomas hesitated. Wincing, he reached up and massaged his temples with his fingertips. "Ouch."

"Are you okay?"

"I've got a migraine. A real humdinger. Today of all days."

Betty wrinkled her nose sympathetically. "Martha's not feeling well, either. She's all shivery."

"Where is she?"

"In bed, in her pajamas."

"I'll tell her to get up and dressed. Mum and Dad will expect to see her."

"Hmm, okay, but she doesn't look well at all."

"She'll be fine when I've spoken to her." Thomas slipped his arm around Betty's waist. "It will be a lovely evening, won't it? My family, and Anthony…"

"And don't forget that Mum is coming, too…"

A shadow seemed to fall across Thomas's face. "Oh yes," he said. "How on earth could I forget that?"

Thomas tried to persuade Martha to come downstairs, but her forehead was hot and sticky. She had a fever and had been sick in the bathroom. Thomas used half an air freshener as he huffed and puffed about the smell.

"Perhaps I should take her to the doctor," Betty mused, looking up at the ceiling.

"She'll be fine," Thomas said. "Everyone will be here within an hour. You don't have time."

"I'll have to keep a close eye on her."

"Don't forget that you need to look after our guests, too."

Thomas's family arrived together, in a taxi from their hotel. Betty stood ready, by the door. She smiled and kissed cheeks, she cooed at brooches and dresses and hung up coats. Thomas paced the dining room with his hands behind his back. He dealt out handshakes to everyone, and his mother got a kiss to her cheek. He insisted that everyone admire a new blue dress he'd bought for Lilian.

"And where's our Martha?" Dylan looked around.

"Oh, she's got a bug." Thomas shrugged. "I don't want her passing it on to anyone."

Betty was relieved when her mother turned up on time. Zelda brought a good bottle of white wine and a classy box of chocolates. "Eleanor," she announced when she spotted Thomas's mother. "How delightful to see you again."

Anthony was the last to arrive, fifteen minutes late. "A busy day at the office," he said as he handed his coat to Betty. He was balding with a horseshoe of black hair. He wore round black-rimmed glasses on the end of his nose. "It's getting too much for me and I need to think about my retirement soon. Succession planning is a must."

Thomas smiled to himself as he pulled out the chair for his boss.

"This all looks very delightful, Betty. Very, very nice," Anthony said. Fixing his eyes on Zelda, his lips twitched into a smile. "And how wonderful you could make it, too, Ezmerelda. It's such a pleasure to see you again."

From across the table, Zelda smiled sweetly. "For me, too, Anthony," she said. "You haven't changed a bit."

Everyone filled their plates with food except for Eleanor, who took only the smallest amount of salmon. Anthony dug into the sandwiches, piling them into a pyramid on his plate. Betty limited herself to two small sausage rolls and a few crisps.

Before she started to eat, she allowed herself an inward sigh of relief. Her mother was behaving charmingly this evening. She hadn't sniped at Thomas, or rolled her eyes once, though she had already moved on to her second glass of wine.

And Thomas was being gracious, too, though Betty could tell he was still suffering from his migraine. His face was pallid and lips pursed. Occasionally, he closed his eyes and pressed a hand to his forehead.

The nine of them made conversation together about the weather and Lilian's schoolwork. Thomas and Dylan discussed accountancy. Trevor's fiancée, Teresa, was a small, dithery woman who Betty felt instantly protective of, but who she couldn't manage to talk to because of the seating arrangements. She tried to spark a random conversation about the engagement but no one else joined in. Lilian enjoyed the attention of the group. She played with her blond hair and giggled.

Anthony bit into a sandwich, a piece of grated cheese sticking to his top lip. He eyed Zelda. "It's lovely we're celebrating sixteen years of wedded bliss, for Thomas and Betty. Sadly, me and my wife have parted ways. It's not a pleasurable situation. Are you single, too, Ezmerelda?"

Zelda gulped a third glass of wine. "I think I need the toilet," she announced loudly and stood up. "I'll call in and see Martha."

As she left the room, Betty saw her shoot out a hand and pick up a half-full bottle of wine.

For the next twenty minutes, Betty's nerves prickled. She laughed, she smiled and she helped to serve food, but all the time she wondered where her mother had got to.

Thomas caught her eye, tapped his watch and pointed upward.

Betty stood up and smoothed down her dress. "I'll just be a moment. I'll see where Mum is."

She found Zelda and Martha sitting on the bedroom floor, reading a book together. Martha rested her cheek sleepily against Zelda's shoulder. The bottle of wine, now empty, lay on the carpet. "Tell me that you haven't given Martha any of that?" Betty demanded.

Zelda batted her hand. "Of course not. It's too good for children."

Betty clenched her teeth. "Come on downstairs, Mum. You've been gone for a long time."

"I think I'll stay here." Zelda shuddered. "Apologies, Betty, but you married into a very boring family."

Betty watched Martha trying not to laugh. *"Mum,"* she warned.

"It's okay." Zelda waved her hand. She got to her feet,

stumbling a little. "I'll come back down. I'll be polite and schmooze Anthony. I'll behave."

"Thank you."

Back at the table, Betty's spine felt stiff. As she promised, her mother smiled. She stroked Anthony's arm and engaged Eleanor in a conversation about diamond jewelry. Betty moved a bottle of wine away from her, but Zelda pulled it back again.

When everyone had finished eating, Betty took up a long sharp knife and, using the tip of her forefinger as a guide, poked the tip of the blade into the center of the cake. She was just about to plunge it in when the doorbell rang. Her hand jerked, the knife slipped and she nicked her skin. "Ouch." A bobble of blood appeared and a drop fell on top of the cake.

Thomas leaped up. He wiped it with a napkin, leaving a red smear on the icing sugar. "Leave the door alone," he ordered. "Carry on cutting the cake."

Betty wrapped a napkin around her bloody finger. She carefully pushed the knife down and along, completing the first slice.

The doorbell sounded again.

This time, Zelda pushed her plate away. "It might be for me."

"You?" Thomas raised an eyebrow. "Why would anyone call here, for you?"

Zelda held his gaze. "I told George that I was coming for tea."

"Ah, George? Someone else from school, perhaps?" Anthony asked.

"No." Zelda batted a crumb from her dress. "My new lover. Please excuse me."

Thomas's mouth hung open. He scraped his chair away from the table. "Stay there, Zelda."

Betty felt the atmosphere in the room switch. She glanced

at Thomas and watched a bead of perspiration trickle down his forehead. She placed a hand on top of his, but he snatched it away. "Let's carry on with our tea, shall we?" he said.

The doorbell rang, a further three times in a row.

Zelda stood up. "I'll get it."

"No," Thomas boomed. He hit the table with the flat of his hand. "You won't."

Anthony's eyes shone wide. He fiddled with his watch. "Oh, is that really the time?" he murmured.

Eleanor gave a small beatific smile.

Betty hurriedly cut the cake into ten pieces. "I'll go and see who it is."

Before Thomas could object, she slipped out of the room. Winding the napkin tightly around her finger, she opened the door.

A young lady with long platinum-blond hair down to her waist stood on the pavement outside. "Hi," she said, with a small frown. "Is Ezmerelda here?"

Betty wasn't sure how to respond. Thomas would not be happy that her mother had arranged for a visitor to call during the tea. She opened her mouth but Zelda appeared in the hallway, behind her.

"You came," she said, her voice full of joy.

The woman nodded.

"This is my friend, Georgina," Zelda said to Betty. "I wanted you to meet her."

"You can call me George," the woman said and offered her hand. "Or Gina. I use both."

"George?" Betty repeated as the woman stepped into the hallway. She glared at her mother. "I thought that George was a…"

"You never asked." Zelda shrugged. "You've been too busy, running around after the Lord of the Manor."

"Now, that's not fair, Mum. I—" Betty stopped talking as she heard footsteps. Thomas appeared in the hallway with Anthony following close behind him.

"What's going on?" Thomas's eyes glinted.

"I asked Gina to call for me," Zelda said. "This tea *thing* has gone on longer than I expected."

Anthony edged towards the door with his back against the wall. "Well, this really has been a most lovely tea, Thomas. Betty, thank you very much."

"Stay," Thomas shot out his hand, placing it on Anthony's arm. "You've not had any cake yet."

"No, I, um, must go. It was lovely to see you again, Ezmerelda."

"You too, Anthony," Zelda said, her voice a little too singsong. She slipped her fingers into Gina's and they held hands. "Come on." She tugged her towards the dining room.

Betty watched the color drain from Thomas's face. His cheeks turned from red to white. The air was thunderstorm-heavy as Anthony muttered, "Goodnight now," and scurried away into the night.

"You've forgotten your piece of anniversary cake," Zelda called after him.

Thomas's eyes flashed. "Get her out, now."

Betty gave a short nod. Her knees shook as she followed her mum back into the dining room.

Zelda stood next to the table. She held on to Gina's hand, trying to swing it back and fro. Gina wore an embarrassed smile.

Dylan raised an eyebrow and Eleanor smirked. Trevor and his fiancée whispered to each other, and Lilian sat stiffly upright.

"This is my girlfriend, Gina," Zelda slurred. "Let's all welcome her to the family." She swept her finger around each person sitting at the table. "Well, of course, you're all Thomas's family, rather than Betty's. Not that we ever see any of you."

Betty stepped forward. "Mum. It's time to go."

"I've not had any cake yet."

"I've got your coat," Thomas said. He stepped forward and thrust it at her.

Zelda didn't move to take it, and it fell to the floor.

Betty surveyed the scene. Thomas's relations were sat in a line like a weird version of the Last Supper. "Perhaps you'd like to go upstairs, Lilian?" she said softly.

But her daughter remained rooted to the spot. Her eyes didn't move from her grandmother.

"Go home, Zelda." Thomas rubbed between his eyes.

"There's a couple of things I'd like to say first," Zelda slurred. She stared around the table before focusing on Elea-nor. "I've not been allowed in this house for eons, because of *your* son. He stops me from buying gifts for the girls. He keeps my daughter as a prisoner—"

"That's not right, Mum," Betty protested.

But Zelda nodded sagely. "Yes, it is. I can *see* things for what they are. For you. For Martha and Lilian. Thomas is only celebrating your anniversary to show off to his snobby family, and to get a promotion—"

"Mum," Betty said. "Stop it."

"Shhh," Zelda held a finger to her lips. "It's true."

Betty looked around blindly for her husband.

Thomas moved over and placed his hands on the top of Zel-da's shoulders. A foot taller than her, he physically dwarfed her. He walked forward and maneuvered her toward the hallway.

"You don't think she's good enough for him, but she is," Zelda shouted back to the group. "Just because she was preg-nant—"

"Zelda. Let's go," Gina urged her, following behind.

"Please, Mum," Betty begged. "Go home."

Thomas opened the front door. He stood stiffly beside it and pointed outside. "Out," he demanded.

Zelda glared at him. She took a step toward the door, bent her head, then rushed back into the dining room like a bull charging a matador. She snatched up her coat from the floor.

Betty and Thomas followed her.

Betty watched as Dylan and Eleanor each wrapped a protective arm around Lilian's shoulders.

"You think you're better than us," Zelda said. "But you're not. Look at you all, fawning over Lilian. Well, what about Martha? Not one of you has gone upstairs to see how she is—"

"Mum," Betty cried out. "Stop."

"Well, it's true," Zelda muttered as she wrestled on her coat. She pushed her hair back with her hand.

Eleanor stood up. "Really, Ezmerelda. Do listen to your daughter. You're making an awful show of yourself."

Zelda's eyes had fire in them. She raised herself as tall as she could. "Well," she said. "Well, *Mrs. La-di-da.* At least I'm Martha's *real* grandmother."

Everything seemed to fall into slow motion for Betty. She watched Lilian frown and look at her father. Eleanor stared blankly and Dylan touched her fingertips with his. Trevor's fiancée started to cry.

"Oh," Zelda said aloud in mock surprise. "None of you knew, did you? That your darling Thomas isn't Martha's daddy?"

Thomas swooped over. He wrapped his arms around Zelda and bundled her out of the room. The front door was still open and he pushed her outside. She raised her hand to push against it, but he forced it shut behind her. He held his hand against it.

"Let me back in," she shouted, hammering it with her fists.

"Zelda," Thomas said loudly over and over until she stopped

banging. He waited, then opened the door a little and pressed his eye to it. "I never, *ever* want to see you here again," he said slowly and firmly, his jaw clenching with anger. "You. Are. Dead to us."

He shut the door and quickly locked it behind him.

Betty stood helplessly, chewing her lip. She could hear her mum shouting in the street. She peeked through the glass in the door to see Gina pulling her away.

Thomas's hand shook as he raised it. Betty cowered as he forced it into a finger point. "I told you, Betty," he seethed, prodding the air.

"Thomas. I'm so sorry." She reached up and took hold of his jacket lapels. "She promised me—"

"You heard *what* she *said* to my family," he hissed.

"We can tell them it's not true. They saw she was drunk."

"*Our* daughter was there."

Betty noticed how he said it, as if Lilian was the only one. "Honestly, Thomas. We can sort this out. No one needs to know. They'll believe us, not her. We'll go in and explain..."

Thomas fixed her with an icy stare. "I'll do it," he said. "But I want you to understand, Betty, that this was the last straw. It can't go on."

"What can't?"

"*This*. Zelda is uncontrollable. We can't trust her. You're going to have to choose."

"Choose what?"

"It's me, or your mother."

Betty blinked up at him. "Don't say that."

"I've always been here for you. I've never let you down," Thomas said. He cupped her cheek. "I said I'd always take care of you and raise Martha as my own."

"Please. We don't need to do this, Thomas—"

"Either Zelda goes. Or, I go."

"No!"

Thomas paused for a while before he walked backwards, towards the dining room. He held Betty's gaze as he opened, stepped through and then pulled the door closed behind him.

Betty was left on her own, trembling in the hallway. Her head thumped so badly she thought it might split open. She headed, blindly, for the front door and reached out for the door handle. Inside the dining room, she could hear Thomas talking. His voice was light and cheerful, as if nothing had happened. Betty turned the key and held it, ready to open the door, to go outside and follow her mother.

But something inside stopped her and her breath came out in a gush.

She'd learned to deal with Thomas over the years, but her mother was a loose cannon. Why hadn't she told her that George, or Gina, or whatever her name was, was a woman? Had she invited her tonight, on purpose?

She was so tired of being in the middle, trying to calm a storm.

She also knew that when Thomas said something, he never backed down.

Struggling for breath, Betty clasped her chest. She locked the door again and stumbled upstairs. She paused outside her daughter's room for a while before stepping inside. Martha lay asleep in bed, surrounded by pieces of paper. It looked like she was lying on a bed of water lilies.

With shaking hands, Betty slowly gathered the pages together. She saw they were stories and she placed them neatly on the bedside table. When she kissed Martha, her forehead felt cooler and her breathing was slow and peaceful.

Betty rested the back of her hand against her daughter's cheek. "Don't worry," she whispered. "No one will ever know."

All she wanted was a quiet, secure life, for her family. All she wanted was for the turmoil to stop.

And at that moment, Betty made her choice.

32

Grandmother

Martha hailed a taxi, to take her and Zelda back to the house. She didn't want to talk in front of the driver, so they didn't speak for the entire journey, each looking out of opposite windows.

In Martha's head, Lilian's words tumbled around. They gathered momentum like a snowball rolling down a hill, growing bigger and bigger.

Could it be true, what she'd said?

When they reached the house, they entered in silence. Martha tugged off her coat and dumped it on top of the dining table. She felt as if her bone marrow had been replaced with ice, and she crossed and rubbed her arms.

Zelda walked over to the window. As she gazed out over the bay, she looked small and frail.

Martha joined her, standing close behind. Their breath fogged up the glass. "Lilian told me that Thomas wasn't my father," she said quietly.

Zelda gave a small shrug. "Oh. What a silly thing to say."

Martha stared at her. Her nana's cheeks were pale and drawn, but she didn't want to listen to any more half truths, or avoidance tactics. Stepping across, she blocked Zelda's view. "Tell me if Thomas Storm was my real father or not. I *need* to know."

Zelda exhaled and sat down heavily in the wooden chair. As she wrung her hands together in her lap, the lines around her eyes looked like cracked pottery. She wouldn't meet Martha's glare. "You were right," she said eventually. "About their marriage certificate. Betty was pregnant when she walked down the aisle."

"I know. I saw it in black and white. That's not what I asked."

"They were different times then, Martha. Unmarried mothers were frowned upon in society. Thomas was mature and handsome. He promised Betty that he'd take care of her. I thought she should take more time, not rush into a wedding. Let people gossip if they wanted to. But she wanted you to be born in wedlock."

"But was he my real dad?"

Zelda lowered her eyes. "I don't want to lie to you…"

"Then don't."

Zelda nodded slightly. "Betty was pregnant by someone else."

Martha ran her fingers through her hair, trying to comprehend this. "Did Dad know?"

"Yes. They met while she was pregnant. He said that he'd raise you as his own child. And things moved quickly. They set a wedding date, even though your other grandparents objected. They thought Betty got pregnant on purpose, to trap him. But your parents went ahead with the wedding and things were okay, for a while."

When Martha thought back, she could recall pockets of her father's kindness. Her first memory was of him scooping her in his arms and singing to her, on the beach. "Lilian?" she whispered.

"He loved you, but Lilian was his own flesh and blood. They had an easier relationship."

"I always felt I had to fit to his ways," Martha said. "I saw Mum changing to suit him, too."

"She wanted you all to be looked after."

Martha thought of her father's rules, and his ways, and how all the women in the family clambered to please him. All except Zelda. "And my real father," she said quietly. "Do you know who he was?"

Zelda nodded. She waited for a while until she spoke. "There was a young man your mum loved dearly. His name was Daniel McLean."

Martha closed her eyes and saw the names on the mermaid's plaque. "He died in the fishing accident."

Again, her nana bobbed her head. "Your mum was devastated. She'd only just found out she had a baby on the way when she lost him. Her grief for Daniel, and her worries for the baby, brought her to Thomas. He was solid and strong. He offered her the security she needed."

"But what about love?" Martha asked desperately.

"It's not always enough. Life's not a fairy story."

Martha opened her mouth to argue, even though she understood. Her love for Joe hadn't been enough for her to leave her parents.

"Your mother loved Thomas, in her own way, but not how she loved Daniel," Zelda added.

"But *you* never told me that Thomas wasn't my dad."

"That wasn't my place."

Martha furrowed her brow. She rubbed the lines with her fingers. "What really happened to make you leave?"

Zelda pressed a finger to her lips, taking a while to gather her thoughts. "Your mum and dad held an anniversary party."

"I remember I was too poorly to go. Dad's awful boss was coming, and my other grandparents. I stayed in bed…"

"Me and your dad had a huge row, and everything spiraled out of control. I drank too much and opened my big mouth. I told him he wasn't your real father, in front of his family. It just slipped out. He threw me out and told me I was dead to the family." She let her words hang in the air for a while. "He'd had enough.

"I thought it was an exaggeration at first, something he said in the heat of the moment. But then Betty called to see me. Thomas had given her an ultimatum, him or me. And she had to make a choice. So, she told me that…that…" Her voice cracked.

"That you were dead?"

"To Thomas, I was. He said it, that night. Then he reinforced it. He told me to go and not come back. It was a terrible thing I did, Martha…"

Martha held her hands to her face, clamping them over her eyes. She took a few deep breaths. "But you could have stood up to him, Zelda, ignored what he said. You could have fought back or let me know you were still alive. I believed him. I believed Mum."

"Things went too far…"

"You could have done *something*."

Zelda shook her head. "No."

"Yes. you could." Martha's words tumbled out. "You always encouraged Mum to stand up to him, but you didn't do it. You ran away."

Zelda tried to get out of her chair but couldn't make it. "Now, just wait a minute, young lady—"

"How did Lilian know?" Martha demanded.

"She saw and heard everything, though I expect your parents tried to cover it up. They probably told her that I was drunk or said things to be spiteful."

"But, still." Martha stumbled. She felt her back press against the window. She gripped the sill with her fingertips. "Everyone knew. Except me."

"I made a huge mistake. No matter what happened between us all, he loved you. Thomas *was* your father."

Martha hung her head. She took her time to speak. "Did you know that *I* met someone?" she asked quietly. "His name was Joe."

Zelda nodded. "Betty mentioned him. She got in touch, now and again. She gave me small updates."

"Behind Dad's back?"

"It was an agreement we had. I promised to stay away, not rock the boat by coming back. And she let me know that you and Lilian were okay."

Martha shook her head. "But Joe and I were going to have a future together. I gave it up to look after Mum and Dad. If I'd known my entire family was keeping a secret from me, things could have been so different."

"You stayed with them, because you're a caring person. You made that decision."

"I might have made an alternative one."

"Or, you might have made the same one…"

Martha let out a sob. She knew her nana was right. Even if she had known about Thomas, she would have stayed, to look after her mother. She'd have felt it was her duty. "Where did you go to, when you disappeared?" she asked desperately.

"I told you. I went to Finland with Gina."

"You're *together*, aren't you? You always have been?"

Zelda gave a tight smile. "Yes…for the longest time."

"I thought she was your carer."

"I never told you that."

Martha looked around her blindly, at this empty house full of family memories that she no longer recognized.

Her nana, who'd she'd built up in her head to be some kind of fairy godmother, was just a normal, old woman. Who had lied.

And she'd never even known her real dad.

She had never felt more sapped of energy. "How did my copy of *Blue Skies and Stormy Seas* even end up with Owen?" she asked, her body sagging.

Zelda swallowed. "It was just an error. Gina was clearing out some books. She put it in a box by mistake with some others, to give away."

Martha forced a laugh. "So, you didn't even try to contact me? We found each other again, because of a *mistake*?"

"It was only when I got back to England that I found out Thomas and Betty had died. I expected Betty still to be here. She wasn't old. I was terribly ill for months, after my tumor…"

Martha felt her head was about to burst. The room suddenly felt like a cage. The feelings she experienced with the reading group in the library surged over her again. Her brain pulsed and she couldn't see clearly. Her vision flooded with red.

I've got to get away from all this.

When her eyes settled on her coat, she snatched it back up, off the table.

"Where are you going?" Zelda asked.

"Away from you. You were my best friend and I trusted you."

"You can't go. Gina will be here in a few minutes."

"I don't care about bloody Gina. You're a liar, Nana. For all these years…"

"No. I just didn't tell you the truth."

"It's the bloody same thing," Martha yelled.

She marched toward the front door and flung it open. A gust of wind lifted her stripy hair and, pulling her coat around her, she began to run.

33

Boat

Not sure where she was fleeing to, or concerned that she'd left Zelda on her own, Martha automatically followed her morning route.

Her feet pounded along the street and down the slope to the beach. She headed past the mermaid statue, not able to bear looking at Daniel's name.

Her father's name.

She pelted across the sand towards the teardrop-shaped cave, where she and Joe enjoyed laughter and picnics. When she reached it, her breath came out in billows and her chest hurt. She slowed down to stare into the cavernous dark space. A tear ran down her cheek and she let it fall from her chin, onto her coat. The cave felt still and eerie, not the happy place where she and Zelda shared stories, or where Betty held Lilian's hand. She pictured a dragon lurking at the back, in the shadows.

Her head throbbed and she couldn't process her thoughts. When she heard someone shouting on the beach, she darted inside the cave, where everything grew instantly quieter. The walls provided a barrier to the sound of the ocean and the wind whistling around outside. A strand of seaweed flew past the cave entrance and a piece of driftwood tumbled, making markings on the sand like a sidewinder.

Staring around helplessly, Martha remembered back to the scorching hot day that she, Zelda, Betty and Lilian had escaped Thomas's attention for a short while.

"You lied to me, Zelda," she shouted, and her words echoed around the cave and back at her. She felt a hollowness inside like nothing she'd felt before, as if her innards had been scooped out. Her skin felt raw and paper-thin. "Everyone lied to me," she cried.

As a child, she'd always felt there was something wrong in the family. She'd sensed the thing in the air so thick it felt like glue, but that she couldn't see or fathom out. She hadn't understood the coolness in Thomas's eyes when he looked at her, or the tension between him and Betty, and with her nana. Or why he seemed to love Lilian more than her. But now she could.

Yet her dad had been happy to let her care for him, and to give up her own chance of getting married and having children. And Betty had watched it happen, too, and had even begged Martha to stay, in a moment of desperation. Thomas had banished Zelda, and the Storm family knew and accepted it.

Why did no one put up a fight?

She wondered how Lilian felt, knowing that Martha was looking after a man who wasn't her real father. Her sister had constructed her own family with Paul, Rose and Will, and not said a word.

But the worst betrayal, for Martha, came from Zelda.

She might have been declared dead by Thomas, but she left Sandshift knowing that Betty was indebted to her controlling husband. Her nana deserted the Storm family and left its secrets behind her.

Martha shivered. She wrapped her arms across her body and stood shaking on the sand.

A red setter dog ran past the entrance of the cave and paused to stare at her. "Billy," a voice shouted and Martha quickly stepped backwards, toward the rear of the cave. She stayed there, looking up at the long black slit in the rocks. She imagined a flash of turquoise as Zelda's skirt disappeared through it, and her hand playfully grabbing the air.

"Billy." The voice came again, closer now, and the dog wandered farther into the cave. It sniffed at the seaweed that lined part of the floor like a carpet. The dog owner's red anorak came into view.

Not wanting to be seen, Martha raised her foot and climbed the rocks leading up to the slit. They were slippery and wet to her touch. Even though she hadn't done this for over thirty years, her feet knew what to do and where to go.

"There you are, Billy. Good dog."

Martha slipped through the gap and into the hollow on the other side.

There was no underground lagoon here today, just a small pool of water. Martha listened out and heard the person and the dog moving away. She sank to the floor, not caring that the sand was wet. She cradled her head in her hands and tried to block out the thoughts that made her temples ache, about who was to blame for all this mess, hurt and confusion. Was it Zelda's fault for leaving? Or her father for declaring her dead to the family? Was it her mother for being weak-willed? Or even Lilian for not sharing with Martha that she knew something?

Perhaps it's ultimately my own fault, for not being brave enough to follow Joe, Martha thought. *I could have had a different life.*

A better one.

Leaning forward until her forehead touched the sand, Martha sat there, furled like a fern leaf, with her hands over her ears. She rubbed her fingertips into her hair as she let her tears flow. When she cried out loud, her sobs echoed inside the cave and it sounded like a dragon roaring.

Sometime later, Martha sat up straight, unsure if she'd fallen asleep or not. The cave had grown dark and she blinked, trying to adjust her eyes. He back was stiff and she felt something lap, wet, against her outer thigh. Raising her head, she watched a stream of water, snakelike on the floor of the cave, trickling toward her. Her eyes followed the silvery trail, along and upwards, to where it spilled down the rocks, a slim waterfall.

She got to her feet, not being able to feel them. After stamping away the numbness, she stepped over the water and made her way back toward the slit in the rocks. A sense of foreboding hummed inside her, as she grew closer and saw what was happening.

The tide was coming in.

She immediately reached up and grabbed onto the rocks. Struggling to find a foothold, she managed to wrench herself up and across to the edge of the slit. Straining her neck, she peered through to the other side.

And she gave a sharp intake of breath.

Instead of the familiar igloo-like room of the cave, empty with a sandy floor, it was now half-full of water. The sea sloshed around inside it.

Martha inched back. She tried not to think of the horrors of her recurring dream of being surrounded by the sea, but her heart beat so fast she thought she might faint.

Think, Martha, think.

She tried to estimate the depth of the water in the cave. If she was lucky, she could wade out. If she was unlucky, then she'd have to swim.

As the quicksilver waves crashed and glided away, her stomach churned with fear. She imagined the Sandshift Seven, their noses and mouths thick with salt water as they pawed at the water.

She spotted her and Joe's initials, white against the dark wall. He had stood on his tiptoes to scratch them there. The sea almost touched the bottom of the letters.

Martha knew that her only way out was to get into the water.

She jutted out her chin, ready for action, then hurriedly took off her shoes. Her coat felt heavy as she tugged it off, and she delved a hand into its pocket. When she pulled out her Wonder Woman notepad, the cartoon superhero grinned at her with a scarlet smirk. She reminded Martha of the life she'd chosen, to be of service to others.

Letting out a frustrated cry, she flung the notepad with all her might. Wonder Woman and her lasso spun through the air. The pad hung in the air for a moment before splashing into the sea.

Martha placed her coat and shoes high above her head, on a shelf in the rocks. Tears streamed down her face as she tentatively lowered her foot into the water. The sea slapped against her toes, then her calf and knee. She held on to the rocks, wincing at the coldness, before she let herself go.

She crashed into the water and felt the sea maul at her clothes.

She pointed her feet into tiptoes, to try to reach the bottom, but couldn't feel anything beneath her. The white surf surged and when Martha managed to swim her way out of the cave, she was met with a frightening sight. Miles of sea stretched in front of her.

She didn't see a wave coming at her, its grayness bubbling and rearing up. There was a roar, then a few moments of silence, as it broke then crashed over her head. It raked her hair with its icy fingers and pulled her under.

Martha resurfaced. She coughed, spluttered and shook her head. Disorientated, she tried to get her bearings. But another wave engulfed her, causing her to flounder in its midst. Sea salt stung her eyes and she watched as her notepad bobbed on the waves, a few meters away.

Retrieving it suddenly felt like the most important thing in her world. She had been okay when she had her tasks to focus on. She had a purpose, an anchor. And now that was gone. She'd tried to make changes to her life and they hadn't worked.

I just want my old life back.

She reached out for the notepad, but her effort felt feeble and the sea took the pad farther away. Martha watched as it bobbed and swirled into the distance, and she reluctantly let it go.

She now had to focus on trying to swim towards the mermaid statue. But the water had its own agenda. A riptide pulled her in the opposite direction, out towards the jut of rocks and the lighthouse.

A wave came at her with the force of a brick wall falling down, so she no longer knew which direction she was facing. The sea tried to suck her under and tears burst, fearfully, from her eyes.

She tried to call for help but each time she opened her mouth, the sea gushed down her throat. It expanded in her mouth like dough. She tried to wave, but her hand splashed weakly against the tide.

Beginning to lose her fight and strength, Martha closed her eyes. Zelda appeared in her head, with her gappy smile and kind eyes. She half sobbed and half retched at this image of her nana.

She'd expected Zelda to save her from life. To be her fairy godmother again. And now she had no one.

She imagined the sailors from the *Pegasus* below her, on the sea bed, staring up at her kicking feet. Their blue hands might reach up and pull her toward them. Daniel could be down there, waiting for her.

The thought took hold and stuck in her brain.

Would it be so bad, to join him under the waves?

Perhaps it's best to stop fighting.

Would anyone even care?

Martha let her kicks dwindle, allowing herself to be at the mercy of the sea. She no longer tried to swim.

She felt herself sink. The water covered her ears then the top of her head, welcoming her to its darkness.

It was calmer under the surface, her ears plugged. Martha's skirt floated up around her body like large petals on a flower, closing when daylight ends. A strange feeling of peace engulfed her and she readied herself for her feet to touch the bottom. She opened her eyes and looked up, to say goodbye to the sky.

A dark shape on the surface moved over her, like a shark, obscuring her view. She saw a shadow moving down, reaching for her. Something fastened tight around her wrist.

She tried to wriggle, to remove it, but it remained firm.

The something pulled at her arm with such force that Martha yelped and water flooded her mouth again. She gagged and felt her body tug upwards, until the top of her head broke the surface. Yellow light blared in her eyes as a beam from the lighthouse swept over her. She tried to shake the thing from her wrist but it tightened even further.

Arms crushed around her back and she didn't fight them. Her cheeks scraped against wood, and then her chest and stomach, as she was lifted out of the sea. She saw a person, a beard and woolen hat in silhouette. Moonlight reflected in a set of determined eyes.

Then Martha felt her body and the back of her head hit against the deck of a boat.

And the last thing she saw was the moon in the navy sky, shining like a silver bottle top. Like a giant's waistcoat button.

34

Lighthouse

When Martha next opened her eyes, she saw black-and-white checkered linoleum in close-up. She was surrounded by pale-blue kitchen units and her forehead was pressed against a table leg. She heard a door slam and saw boots and a man standing over her. His coat almost reached his ankles.

Siegfried.

She watched as he wiped his mouth with the back of his hand.

Martha tried to move her limbs, but her clothes were wet and heavy, pinning her down. A large puddle of water encircled her and she instinctively tried to mop it up using her hands. "Sorry," she spluttered. "I'm making a mess of your floor."

She felt a weight fall on top of her legs and saw two folded gray towels. She reached down with one hand and pulled them towards her. Clutching them under her chin, she eased herself onto her knees. She was so sapped of strength she had to use the back of a chair to help her, to get to her feet.

She was dripping from everywhere, her nose, her finger-tips, and water trickled down the back of her neck. Her throat crackled with salt water. With her body jerking uncontrollably from the cold, she weakly shook open a towel and wrapped it around her like a cloak. She used the other towel to wipe her face. "How long was I there for?"

"Not sure." Siegfried was soaking wet, too. His clothes clung to him like a shroud. "Hospital?" he asked.

She shook her head, not wanting to face anyone. She was shivery and wet, and wanted to be alone. "I think I'll be okay," she spluttered.

"Hmm." He stared at her for what seemed like a long time. "Wait here." He trudged towards a room at the back of the kitchen.

Martha took this time to make a hood out of her second towel. As she rubbed her hair, she could feel that her glittery slide was missing.

When Siegfried reappeared, he was wearing fresh clothes, gray tracksuit bottoms, a hooded top and a dry woolen hat. He pointed towards a spiral staircase in the middle of the room and crooked his finger.

Martha's legs shook as she walked slowly towards the stairs, concentrating on placing one foot in front of the other. She held out her hands for balance. When she looked upwards, the staircase structure looked like the cross-section of a nautilus shell.

Her feet splatted and squelched on the wooden treads as she followed Siegfried. He moved quickly upwards, but Martha clung to the handrail, afraid that her legs might give way. Her limbs felt concrete-heavy as she climbed.

When she felt sure they must be close to the top of the lighthouse, Siegfried stopped and opened a door.

Martha looked down, behind her, at the pools of water she'd left behind on each step. "I need to dry your stairs."

He didn't say anything and pointed into a room.

She stepped inside and saw a single bed. A small lamp shone on a bedside table.

"Rest." Siegfried pulled the door closed behind him. She heard him head back downstairs, leaving her alone.

Martha stood for a while, her body still swaying from the movement of the sea. Unsteadily, she walked over to a large curved window and looked out at the dark sky. Below, the sea was beetle-black and strangely calm. It was wide and free and didn't look deadly at all. She picked at her crusty eyelashes with her thumb and forefinger. Her first instinct was that she couldn't stay here. She had to get back home.

But then she questioned, *what for?*

To return to an empty house?

To face Lilian's and Zelda's lies?

And she couldn't leave, dressed like this. The tide was in, too, cutting the lighthouse off from the mainland.

She listened as Siegfried's footsteps faded out of earshot.

Spotting that she was dripping onto the floorboards, Martha sidestepped onto a rug. Across the room, she saw an en-suite bathroom and made a dash for it. When she switched on the light inside, it hurt her eyes. She turned it back off and got undressed in the dark. Her wet clothes made a sucking sound as she peeled them off.

After folding them loosely, she dropped them into the bottom of the shower cubicle. Then, on her hands and knees, she crawled back into the bedroom, using a towel to dry the trail of water she'd left behind.

On the bed, she found a folded white toweling dressing gown and pulled it on. The fabric was fluffy against her water-wrinkled skin and she gave a small groan of relief. Wondering when Siegfried last hosted anyone to stay, she towel-dried her hair and sat down. The bed rocked under her weight, momentarily reminding her of the shift of the waves. She fought against the tears that welled inside her. Her body began to quake, as if the sea was churning in her belly.

She let her body fall, resting her cheek on the pillow and relishing its softness. She closed her eyes and imagined she was a child again, with Zelda's fingers walking through her hair. Reaching up, she made to brush them away. She didn't want them there, not now. But the feeling came again, as if her nana was in the same room, looking over her.

Martha tucked her knees up and bit her lip. She tried not to sob into Siegfried's sheets, but she couldn't stop tears spilling from her eyes, for what might have been, the life she could have had. One filled with love.

Time slipped and shifted around her and when she raised her head, she had no idea what hour it was, but the sky outside was jet black. She rubbed her nose and dabbed her cheeks with her fingers. She closed her eyes and tried not to think of the sea surrounding her. Slowly, she fell into a deep sleep.

When she opened her eyes again, she frowned as she took in her view. The curtains were open and the sky was a powder blue outside. Everything was lighter and brighter. The room was circular and painted white with naive gray swoops to represent seagulls.

On top of a white wooden chair by the window lay a pile of clothes, neatly folded into large squares. There was a pair of glittery sandals on top. Some items were her own, and there were others, too.

As she blinked against the hazy sunlight, there was a knock on the door. It made her jump and she pulled her covers up to her chin. "Hello," she called out.

The door opened and the toes of Siegfried's boots, and then his hat, appeared.

He didn't look at her as he walked over and placed a tray

down on top of a small low table, next to her bed. There
was a large white bowl with a lid and she could smell tomato
soup. Raising herself a little she saw a cube of butter and thick
slices of bread on a saucer. Steam spiraled from a huge mug
of golden tea.

Martha suddenly found herself ravenously hungry and her
stomach growled.

"Eat," Siegfried said.

Martha inched her way onto her elbows before she sat up.
Every bit of her body felt like it had been through a mangle.
"How long was I asleep for?"

"Thirty-six."

"Hours?" Martha frowned. "No. That can't be right."

Siegfried gave a small shrug. He moved back to the door
and closed it behind him. She heard him move away.

"Thirty-six hours?" Martha whispered as she positioned the
tray on her lap. She took the lid off the bowl and the steam
from the soup warmed her face.

She savored it for a while, then plunged in her spoon. The
tomatoes tasted tangy and sweet. She tore the bread and the
thick butter tasted divine. The warm tea soothed her tight
throat.

You were lucky, she told herself. *You might have drowned. Then
you'd never have tried Siegfried's soup.* She gave a small laugh at
such a random thought, and she liked the sound it made.

She ate slowly, savoring every mouthful, and when she'd
finished, she placed the tray back on the bedside table. She
got out of bed and her legs wavered as she walked over to the
window. The sea was a shimmering blanket of petrol blue and
diamonds seemed to shine on its surface. It was beautiful. She
searched through the pile of clothes on the chair, recognizing
they were ones Suki wore.

Too tired to think how they got there, she returned to the

bed. She sank back into it slowly, wondering what to do now she was awake. She tried to think back, to Zelda and the Storm family revelations, but her brain wouldn't let her. It shifted its focus away, making her thoughts flit around.

Running her hand through her hair, she found it was encrusted with salt. The skin on her cheeks was tight. More than anything she wanted to take a hot bath, to wash away all the traces of the sea.

She sat for a few moments, this longing overtaking her until she couldn't think of anything else.

Standing up, she fastened her robe firmly around her waist and left the room. She clung onto the bannister and made her way down the staircase to the next level down. It was a sitting room with a log-burning stove and comfortable-looking brown leather sofas. It had old black-and-white photos of ships on the walls and a big black frame with a display of knots in it.

On the next floor down from that, she found a bright, white bathroom. It had terra-cotta floor tiles and a towel warmer that looked like a silver ladder.

A strange clattering noise sounded from the bottom of the next flight of stairs down, and she could hear muffled music from a radio.

"I'm taking a bath," she shouted out, cocking her head to listen for a reply.

When she didn't hear a voice, she assumed that Siegfried had heard her and she locked the bathroom door.

Running the water, she poured in a generous amount of blue bubble bath and swished her hand through the froth. She folded her robe and left it on the floor. Then she lowered herself into the hot water. As she picked up a bar of soap, the scent of roses and vanilla reminded her of Zelda and she felt a familiar wobble of her bottom lip.

Then she bit it away.

She wasn't going to spend time thinking about her family. For the first time in her life, she was going to think about herself.

She washed her feet, and legs, and under her arms. When she slipped her head under the water, the hotness soothed her scalp. She couldn't find any shampoo, so she used the bubble bath and her hair squeaked as she rinsed it through.

She lay there, her ears submerged, until the water cooled around her. Goose bumps formed on her legs and shoulders. And she listened to the strange clack, clack, clack from the room below.

35

Typewriter

Back in the bedroom, Martha wrapped her hair in a towel and got dressed in a purple cotton dress she remembered Suki wearing when she first started her job. It was a maternity one, a perfect roomy fit. She draped the white toweling dressing gown around her shoulders and made her way, barefoot, down to the kitchen.

Siegfried sat at his kitchen table. He wore glasses and his gray woolen hat was pulled down low over his eyebrows. His face was almost obscured by an old black typewriter. His fingers danced across the keys, which rose and fell with a clack. There was a pile of paper next to him, all typed up.

Martha watched, hypnotized, as the typewriter barrel traveled to the left, pinged, and then Siegfried swiped it back again.

"You're a writer?" she asked.

He didn't look up.

Martha glanced around the room. Books and photos in frames lined rows of shelves, constructed to fit into the circular space. There was a wine rack carved from driftwood, and a large ship in a bottle on a sideboard. She reached out and picked it up, examining the models of tiny sailors on board, and the white froth on the tips of the blue waves.

There was a photograph of Siegfried standing alongside author Lucinda Lovell. She smiled at the camera, while he stood stiffly by her side. The words *Siegfried and Angela* were written under it.

"Isn't that Lucinda Lovell?" Martha asked.

"Hmm," he grunted. "My sister."

"Oh," Martha frowned as she tried to work this out. "So, Angela is your sister but she uses the pen name Lucinda?"

Siegfried didn't reply.

Martha set the ship in a bottle back on the sideboard. "What are you writing about?"

Siegfried reached out and straightened his pile of paper. He picked up a paperclip, stared at it and placed it down again. He tucked his chin into his chest and then raised his eyes at her for the briefest moment. "What's wrong?" he asked.

"Me?" Martha's voice wobbled.

"Yes."

His small words of concern made her feel like she was melting. She would have liked to have heard them so many times, over the years. Just someone asking if she was okay.

She sat down heavily on the bottom stair, her bare toes pointing together. She thought of Siegfried's strong arms hoisting her from the sea and decided that he deserved an explanation.

She told him about caring for her parents for years and what she'd given up to do that. She spoke of *Blue Skies and Stormy Seas*, reminding him that he'd admired the blackbird illustration. "The book led me to my nana, Zelda, after I thought she was dead. But I also learned that Thomas Storm wasn't my real father, and my sister knew that. I just feel that everyone in my family lied to me…" Her body shrank as she talked.

Siegfried didn't speak for a while. He stared at his typewriter and shrugged with one shoulder. "It doesn't mean they didn't love you."

They were the most words she'd ever heard him say and, as she considered them, emotion rose in her chest. "I suppose not."

He nodded once.

Martha rearranged her dressing gown. "I thought of the *Pegasus*, when I was in the sea. Thank you so much for saving me."

Siegfried sat motionless, his face a blank. He cleared his throat before he stood up. Walking over to a bookshelf, he picked up a photograph and handed it to her.

Eight fishermen stood in a line in front of their boat, the *Pegasus*. The handwritten date on the bottom of the photo said 1964.

"The year before the accident," Martha whispered. She peered more closely at the faces of the young men and her eyes alighted on one stood on the far right. He had a mop of dark hair and piercing eyes. His hat was pulled down too far onto his forehead. "You?" she asked.

Siegfried nodded. He took the photograph from her and pointed at the man standing next to him. "Daniel," he said.

Martha blinked hard as she found herself looking at her father. He had unruly hair and a too-large smile. He was stocky and young. Far too young. A tear rolled down her cheek and she suddenly felt a pointless urge to make him proud.

When she looked at Siegfried, he flicked his eyes away. They were glassy, too. "You knew about him, didn't you?" Martha said. "That he and my mum were together? Did you know about me, too?"

He nodded once. "I tried to save him..." He shook his head and pinched the bridge of his nose. "I couldn't."

Martha tried to take in the magnitude of his words. She touched his arm gently. "The storm was so strong it swallowed a boat and its crew. You couldn't have done anything. I know the power of the sea and you saved me from it," she said.

She thought of how Siegfried followed her out of the library, after her outburst. She pictured the shopping trolley appearing outside her house with her hair slide inside it. The other touches of kindness that he'd shown her over the years were too small at the time for her to notice. They weren't the big hits of gratitude and appreciation that she sought from others. They didn't give her a warm glow.

But now they did.

Siegfried set the photograph back on the shelf.

Martha pulled her robe around her shoulders, suddenly feeling cold. "I used to tell stories when I was younger. It helped me to deal with things. Is that why you write, too?"

She waited for his reply, though it didn't come.

Feeling that their conversation was over, she took a step back up the staircase. A wave of exhaustion surged over her and she grabbed hold of the handrail. "I'll get my things and leave you in peace."

Siegfried glanced at her. He shook his head. "Stay."

"I'll be needed at the library, and Suki's baby is due soon. I left Zelda alone and I want to know that she's okay. I've not completed my application form yet, for the librarian job…"

With each thing Martha listed, she felt herself diminishing, like a sandcastle washed away by the sea. She pictured the tasks in her head, listed in a column with glaring red dots next to them.

Siegfried waited until she ran out of steam. "Stay," he repeated.

He opened a drawer, then removed a flat cardboard box. It was brown and worn. He walked over and handed it to her.

Martha frowned. "What is it?"

"Daniel," he said.

For the rest of the day, Martha lay in bed in her small room in the lighthouse. Or she sat in the armchair, her face warm as she soaked up the sun rays through the window.

She leafed through the few pages in the box. It contained a couple of poems, an essay on the sea and a birthday card for Siegfried. They were things that someone else might have thrown away. Unless a terrible event had increased their significance.

They were all written by Daniel. His words were simple yet strong. They were emotional and expressive.

Perhaps I took after him all along, Martha told herself. And she clung to this thought.

A feeling of calm began to fall upon her and here, alone at the top of the lighthouse with Daniel's words, she was able to view everything more clearly. She took the time to think about her family and what they meant to her. They hadn't been perfect, but what family was?

She could appreciate what her mother went through, the choices she made, that she thought were for the best. Betty had wanted a strong, secure household for her family, after losing a true love, but it came at a price. She had to juggle a difficult relationship between her husband and mother.

Martha imagined Zelda being forced to leave her home and family behind, to start afresh someplace new, because she hadn't been able to adapt her behavior to suit her son-in-law. She must have been so hurt and bewildered, even if she had Gina's unending support.

Martha tried to see things from her dad's perspective, too. A man who had fallen in love with a woman who was already pregnant with another man's child. Someone she had loved and lost. Thomas made a promise to raise the baby, without his own family knowing he wasn't the father. He only knew one way to do things, and that was his own.

And Lilian had known that she and Martha had different fathers and kept this secret for decades. Perhaps it had eaten away inside her and shaped her life, too.

And finally, Martha turned her attention onto herself.

She was the same person as before. But after the last week or so, what she'd done and what she had learned, about others and herself, meant that her skeleton felt it was reinforced with steel. The past was in the past, and she had to accept it and lay it to rest, so she could look to the future.

She was no longer angry at Zelda, just terribly sad about the happenings that touched decades of her, Lilian's, Zelda's and Betty's lives. She could spend hours and days allowing them to mill in her mind, or she could strive to put them behind her.

I have to find the strength to move on.

Because there's no alternative.

She decided that she wasn't going to focus on always trying to please others. She felt determined to take the time to get to know, and love, herself. And she hoped that the warm glow of appreciation she always looked for might actually come from within.

I want to be glorious again.

Siegfried brought Martha's supper for her, a glass of milk and hot buttered toast. Two other things also lay on the tray—an envelope and a small sheet of paper. On the paper were a few lines, written neatly in blue pen.

Suki is okay. She's given Ben his culmination (ultimatum?)

Zelda says she's truly sorry

Lilian sends her love

Job application deadline—tomorrow
Owen wants to take you for coffee

"How do you know all this?" she called after him, but he moved quickly away.

Martha opened the envelope and found her job application form inside. It had a yellow sticky note attached, with Suki's handwriting on it. "Go for it," it said.

And so she did.

In addition to the questions, Martha thought about the big box full of fancy dress costumes in her shed, and how an *Alice in Wonderland* outfit wouldn't be too difficult to put together. She wrote up her idea for a literature festival, where everyone dressed up as their favorite fictional character. She put forward an idea for intergenerational reading groups, where children came together with older people, to share a love of books. She suggested promoting and expanding the reading group further. She stated that the library needed more support from head office.

With Daniel's words surrounding her, Martha poured out her heart, about what the library and its people meant to her. The library was there when she needed it, and she wanted to devote her time giving something back.

She told her own story.

She woke early the next morning, at 5:31 a.m. Siegfried was already seated in front of his typewriter.

Martha washed the dishes while he clack-clacked away. They had found a strange easy rhythm of being in the same space together.

She placed her completed application form in front of him, knowing that she wasn't quite ready to leave yet.

He nodded once, then opened and read it.

Martha looked out of the window. The tide was going out and her stomach was tight at the thought of leaving the calm white space that had been her haven.

Siegfried handed the form back to her. "Top marks," he said.

He resumed his tapping away and Martha didn't ask what he was writing. He was focused and, in his own way, seemed content.

She wanted to tell him that he'd helped to restore her faith in people and that her time in the lighthouse had helped to quiet her mind and allow for her heart to heal. But she thought that he probably knew.

At just after 7:00 a.m., she unlocked the lighthouse door. Siegfried stood beside her, his hands stuffed into the pockets of his long coat.

"Thank you," she told him. She sought out a spot on his cheek, above his beard and below his hat, and planted a quick kiss.

He gave a jerky nod and held the door open. He placed his hand inside his coat and handed her a blue envelope. It had "To Whoever It May Concern" written on it.

Knowing he'd be embarrassed if she asked what it was, Martha placed it neatly in the large patch pocket of the purple dress. Her toes were bare in the glittery sandals. She picked up Daniel's cardboard box and held it close to her chest. She welcomed the sea breeze that whipped her hair and speckled her face with salt water. Inhaling, she held the air in her lungs for a moment before stepping onto the uneven rocks. "If I can ever do anything for you, just let me know," she said.

Siegfried stood still, his coat whipping in the wind. "One thing," he called back to her after a few seconds.

"What?"

He tugged his hat down farther so she could no longer see his eyes. "Stop Branda picking bloody Scandi thrillers," he said.

36

Sisters

The beach was quiet, except for a few people walking their dogs. Something orange bobbed in the gray sea and Martha craned her neck to see what it was. A swimming cap? *Don't they know about the riptide?* Then she saw it was a football. A black Labrador splashed into the sea, then swam out to retrieve it.

Sighing with relief, she looked up and saw her house at the edge of the cliff. The fence was wonky and she pictured five figures in the garden, a mum, dad, grandma and two girls. In her imagination, they waved down at her. She briefly raised her fingers in return, but they were gone as quickly as they appeared to her.

She walked across the sands and stopped in front of the teardrop-shaped cave. It was empty, dark and calm now. The sea had left behind a wet tide mark inside. It reached above her and Joe's initials, so the white of the letters had darkened.

Martha placed Daniel's box gently on the sand and stepped into the cave. She climbed up onto the rocks, towards the slit, to retrieve her coat and shoes. She was relieved to find they were dry, untouched by the sea. Slipping them on, she climbed back down while carrying the glittery sandals.

She walked over to the wall and stared up at the initials. She pictured Joe reaching up to write them. His hair was thick and dark, and his shoulders strong. She had locked him in her mind so that he was forever young, and that they were forever in love. She could see now that he was a figure of fantasy, representing her past happiness.

She now knew this responsibility was all hers.

She could take up Suki's offer to seek Joe out, to find out where he was in his life. Or she could let him remain as a lovely memory.

She pictured Siegfried's note on the side of her supper tray, and his updates. *"Owen wants to take you for coffee."*

It was definitely her turn to organize and pay this time. She broke into a warm smile at the thought of his lapel badges and his red slippers. He probably didn't dance in the sea at dusk, whatever the weather, but did she want that any longer?

She wriggled her toes and imagined her nails painted petal-pink, as she used to do for Joe. She'd never had a steady hand and hated the smell of the polish. After almost drowning, she didn't ever want her feet to get wet, by the sea, again.

She smiled up at the initials and briefly stretched up to press a fingertip against them. "Goodbye, Joe," she murmured.

She made sure that her door keys were safe in her coat pocket and she picked up Daniel's box. Leaving the cave, she headed towards the mermaid statue.

As usual, she stopped to read the plaque, and this time she let her eyes linger on the name Daniel McLean. Expelling her breath, she traced her fingers over the raised letters.

"You knew about me, and now I know about you, too," she whispered. "I'm sorry that we'll never meet. But reading your words has helped me, more than you'll ever know. I'll keep an eye on Siegfried for you."

And although there was no one else around other than a few dog-walkers, and the voice she heard was more likely to be the whisper of the wind, she thought she heard someone say, "Martha."

When she got home, she found that her front door was locked. The only person who had a spare key was Lilian, and she wondered if Siegfried had arranged for her to secure the house.

She opened the door, walked in and stood in the dining room. The cuckoo clock ticked and in five minutes' time he would pop out his head and call eight times. But Martha didn't want to hear him ever again, counting her time away.

Reaching up, she took the clock down from the wall. She took the batteries out and put them in her pocket. The ticking stopped. Perhaps she would buy a new clock, a big chrome thing with a modern white face. She could venture into the scary world of home decoration shops.

She strolled around her dining room and the house seemed quiet without the loud ticking sound. Making herself a strong cup of tea, she sat in the wooden chair and looked out at the bay and the lighthouse. She pictured Siegfried and Daniel together, as young men, laughing with their crew as they pushed the *Pegasus* out to sea. She saw them clambering aboard as the waves slapped the sides of the vessel.

She reached into her pocket and took out the envelope Siegfried had given her. It was unsealed, and the address on the front could be for anyone. So she opened it.

To whom it may concern
I, bestselling author Lucinda Lovell, am pleased to give a ref-

erence for Martha Storm. I can vouch that she is a committed worker, a good person and brings enthusiasm and knowledge to her role. I can think of no better person to attain a full-time position at the library. She breathes life into it.

If you wish to contact me for more information, please do so in writing, c/o Siegfried Frost, Sandshift Lighthouse, Sandshift Bay.

Martha's body flooded with warmth. Her chest radiated with heat at Siegfried's glorious gesture. "Thank you," she said aloud.

She'd probably never know for certain if Lucinda Lovell was the pen name for Siegfried's sister, Angela. Or if Angela was the face for Siegfried's words.

All she knew was that her father's friend had been there for her again. And they'd be there for each other, from now on.

She placed the reference in the same envelope as her job application and set it down on her dining table.

Martha had just finished her drink when she heard her front door open.

The floorboards in the hallway creaked and she sat up to attention. She gripped her cup and waited for the person to enter.

Lilian's blond hair was mussy and her eyes dark underneath. She wore a cream sheepskin coat with the collar turned up. "So, you're back, then?" she asked. Her eyes flitted around the room as she took a seat on the sofa. "Your friend at the library, with the floaty clothes and strange hair, said you've been staying in the lighthouse."

Martha nodded. "With Siegfried Frost. I needed some time out, to think things through."

Lilian pursed her lips, then nodded her head. "I totally get it. I need time, too, because of Paul..."

"How are things?"

She gave a small shrug. "Rocky, but I'm trying my best. It'll be a shame if we can't sort things out. We're well suited, I think." She gave a short laugh. "Not like Mum and Dad."

Their eyes met.

"Would you like a coffee?" Martha asked.

She half expected her sister to say that she had to dash, but Lilian nodded. "I'd love one. A cappuccino, extra frothy, if you have it?"

"It's kind of just normal coffee."

"Well, that's fine, too."

Martha made their drinks and carried them back into the dining room.

Lilian wrapped both hands around her cup and glanced around. "The house looks really different. You've cleared out loads of stuff."

"I've moved some into the shed, too. The house was a mess."

"Oh, it wasn't that bad," Lilian started, but then they both laughed at how unconvincing she sounded.

"I let things get out of control," Martha said firmly. "I need to look after myself, rather than other people."

"Good for you. And I'll help with the rest of Mum and Dad's things," Lilian said. "We can look through them together."

"It's fine. I'll—"

However, Lilian raised her hand. "I'd like to do it." She reached down and fingered the fringes on the rug on the floor. "I've not seen this old thing for ages. You used to lie on it and write your stories. I was always really jealous of your imagination. I could never think of anything so creative."

Martha raised an eyebrow. "I thought you hated fairy stories. You refused to believe that Cinderella's carriage was made from a pumpkin."

"I did, didn't I?" Lilian shook her head. "I preferred the facts in the encyclopedias. Maybe it's because I knew Dad liked us to read them. Both of us loved the funfair, though, didn't we? We went crazy for candy floss. Do you remember when Nana bought that toffee apple and it pulled her tooth out?"

"Yes. It was stuck in the sticky red sugar."

"That was gross."

"She still has the gap." Martha pressed a finger against her own teeth.

"Really?" Lilian smiled, but then it faded away. "It's difficult to imagine what she's like as an old lady. She was always so glamorous and used to buy us the best presents, pink plastic stuff that Dad hated."

"She's not changed a bit."

"No?"

Martha thought how her sister's tone sounded hopeful. "You should meet her."

"Hmm." Lilian took a sip of her coffee and gave a small nod. She cleared her throat and her eyes glistened. "I said things that I shouldn't have to you. I'm so sorry, Martha..."

"Zelda told me that you were there, the night of the party."

Lilian nodded and set her cup down. "I was stuck with all the adults because you were feeling poorly. Something was brewing all night between Nana and Dad. They'd both had a drink, and things reached boiling point. Nana announced that you weren't Dad's daughter to everyone. It was so awful. And then—"

"Dad told us that Zelda died," Martha said.

"I've always questioned fairy stories, but somehow I didn't query that. Why would he lie about such a thing?"

Martha imagined her sister at the party, wide-eyed, inno-
cent and scared. She leaned in towards her. "You were only
eleven years old. We shouldn't blame ourselves for any of this.
We were only children. But when did you find out for sure
that Zelda didn't die in 1982?"

Lilian sniffed. She ran a hand around the back of her neck.
"I saw Nana again, three years later. She came to the house.
I was in my room but I heard her. I knew her voice and sat
frozen on the bed. She tried to give Mum a book, but Dad
wouldn't let her... I knew then that he'd lied to us."

"Did you say anything to him?"

Lilian shook her head. "Mum begged Nana to go. She
said that things were settled, and it was all too late for her to
come back."

Martha reached out and lightly touched her sister's arm.
"You've carried a huge weight, for all these years..."

Lilian nodded. "I tried to shut it all away in my head. I
never told anyone what happened. But then you found that
old fairy tale book, with that date in it. I warned you to leave
it alone. I was worried what you might uncover, what should
be left buried..."

"But then I wouldn't have found Zelda again."

The two sisters reached out and clumsily found each other's
hands. They entwined fingers for the briefest moment before
letting go again.

"Do you know who my real father was?" Martha asked.

"As far as I'm concerned, it was Thomas," Lilian said
fiercely. "And we're sisters, whatever happened. I need to tell
Paul what I saw and overheard that night, too. Then he might
understand what I've lived with, and why I bottle things up
so much. I'm going to ask him to stay. I owe Will and Rose
a break, too. They're great kids."

"They can stay here anytime, now there's room."

"Thank you." Lilian paused for a few seconds. She met Martha's gaze. "And I've decided I'd like to see Zelda again. She's family, no matter what happened."

"We should do it soon. Things don't sound good for her—" Martha halted her words, finding them too difficult to find. She cleared her throat. "One of her dying wishes was to read to a big crowd, at the football ground."

"She wanted to do *that*?"

"Yes, and to see one more Christmas. Though it seems unlikely."

"That sounds like our nana, thinking about Christmas at the beginning of March," Lilian said. She stood up and picked up her bag. "Please think about the best way for me to meet her. I'm going to the library now, to pick up my Philippa Gregory. It's finally arrived in stock. Do you want to join me?"

The thought of going to the library with her sister appealed, but Martha shook her head. "I'd like to take a little time for myself here first. Will you give something to Suki for me, though? It's really important." She passed her completed application form and reference to her sister.

"I'll do it now."

Martha waved Lilian off and went back inside the house. She found an empty cardboard box and placed the cuckoo clock inside it. She folded down the flaps and felt a strong urge to pull her family back together again.

And she had the perfect idea for how to do it.

37

Christmas Tree

Two days later

Martha found a new notepad among a selection Betty stored in a kitchen cupboard. She made a new task list and it featured things she wanted to do, that were important to her, rather than things other people wanted.

It was the start of a new plan of action, to reunite her family.

There were deep conversations to be had and history to unravel but, for today at least, she wanted it to be a celebration.

Her nana said her dying wish was to see another Christmas and Martha wanted to make sure it happened.

Her dining room now twinkled with fairy lights, and she'd set up a large Christmas tree next to the Chinese dragon's head. She'd bought the supermarket's finest sherry and napkins edged with gold. Thirty-six small mince pies sat baking in the oven, and the air smelled of spices and warm orange peel. Holding her hand to her forehead as a visor, she peered at them through the glass door. The lids were turning a golden brown, and the turkey was cooking nicely in the bottom oven.

Will and Rose were setting the dining table with gold

candlesticks and place mats. Will wore a sweater featuring a reindeer with a light-up red nose. He had created a list of carols to play on his phone. Rose added the final touches to a center table display she'd made using a few shiny baubles and cotton wool for snow.

Lilian pushed her way into the room, her arms full of brightly wrapped presents. She bent down and arranged them under the tree. "Paul can't join us, because of work," she said. "But he sends his love."

"Is everything okay between you?" Martha asked.

Her sister gave a small smile. "Only time will tell. I talked to him about what happened in our family, and how it affected me. I tried to tell him what he means to me. I'm not good at that kind of thing, so I hope it works."

"Is one of those presents mine, Mum?" Will sidled up to her. He rested his cheek on her shoulder. "What's Santa brought me?"

"You'll have to wait and see." Lilian pecked him on his cheek.

"What time will Nana be here?" Rose asked as she helped Martha to slide the mince pies onto a cooling tray when they came out of the oven.

"Soon. It sounds strange to hear you call her that. Nana is my and Lilian's name for her."

"Well, Great-Nana sounds a bit weird."

Martha agreed that it did.

An hour later the doorbell rang. Martha, Lilian, Will and Rose stood to attention in the kitchen. The food was all almost ready to serve. "Shhh," Martha said. "Our guests are here. Everyone stay quiet." She hurried to the door and opened it.

Owen stood outside, alongside Gina and Zelda. "I've picked these ladies up, so they can both enjoy a few sherries," he said.

"Thank you." Martha smiled at him.

"My pleasure." He entered the hallway and gave her a kiss on both cheeks. When she inhaled, his jacket smelled of ink and amber.

As she pulled away she spotted a blue mark on his face. "You have a smudge on your cheek," she said.

"Oh. I don't have a mirror. Just get it for me, will you?"

Martha took a tissue from her pocket. She dabbed at his cheek and rubbed it away. When she finished he briefly placed his hand on the back of hers. "Thanks." He smiled.

She nodded in reply, her own cheeks flushing.

Gina helped Zelda inside the house. She wasn't using her wheelchair today.

"Something smells good." Zelda sniffed as she took off her coat and handed it to Martha. She smiled but her eyes were pink and puffy, and her cheeks were drawn.

Martha wondered if she had been replaying things through her mind, too, over the last few days. "Thank you," she said.

"If it wasn't March, I'd swear it was Christmas dinner."

Martha smiled. She placed Zelda's and Gina's coats in the pantry. Placing her hand on the dining room door handle, she rested it there. "You said you wanted to see another Christmas."

Zelda swallowed hard. She gave the slightest nod of her head. "I'm not a betting woman, but I'd say it's unlikely."

"Well." Martha took a deep breath. "We decided to bring it forward."

Zelda blinked. She frowned and looked at Gina.

Gina nodded in reply.

Martha had spoken to her on the phone the day before to confide and discuss her plan, and Gina had been an essential part of bringing it to life.

"*We* decided?" Zelda questioned.

"Lilian is here. And Will and Rose. We'd like to spend a special day with you."

A tear rolled down Zelda's face. She wiped at it but her cheek still glistened. "Really?" she said, her eyes shining. "After everything that's happened?"

Martha reached out and took hold of her hand.

"I thought you might have asked me here to tell me you never want to see me again." She hung her head.

"That would never happen."

Zelda let out a silent sob. Her forehead crumpled. "This is all I ever wanted, to be welcomed back home. To be here with you, again."

"I want it, too. We all do."

Zelda didn't move. "I'm so sorry, Martha," she said solemnly. "For everything. I made a mess of things but I never meant to hurt you, or Betty or Lilian. I've tortured myself for years. I could have seen the two of you grow up. I could have been part of your lives...and Betty's. My own darling daughter... I lost her..." She broke down and buried her head under Gina's chin.

Martha placed a hand on her shoulder and gently caressed it. She passed her an aloe vera–enriched tissue and tried not to cry, too. "That's all in the past now," she soothed. "We can spend what time we have together, wishing we'd done things differently. Or we can use it wisely."

Zelda nodded. She wiped her eyes, sniffed and stood a little taller. She touched the ends of Martha's hair. "Time is so precious."

Martha choked back a tear. She jutted out her chin. "Yes, it is. So let's try and make it glorious." She took a deep breath to compose herself and let it go again. "Now, we're all going to have a family dinner together. We're not going to discuss the past. There will be no secrets and no tension and we're all going to have a good time."

"But I—" Zelda started.

"No *ifs* and no *buts*." Martha wrapped her arms around her and held her tight. She relished the warmth of her nana's soft cheek against her own. "It's Christmas, Nana. Everything is forgotten and forgiven on Christmas Day. Other things will wait. Now, let's go and open the presents under the tree, before I serve dinner…"

Zelda sat in the wooden chair and Gina stood by her side. Will and Rose lay on their stomachs on the rug. Martha and Lilian sat on the leather sofa and Owen appointed himself the hander-outer of presents. He read each person's name in turn and they opened their gift. Each one was a book.

Lilian and Martha had chosen them together, the day before, from Chamberlain's, and Lilian wrapped them in silver paper with bows and tags.

Will said, "Cool. Thanks," when he unwrapped *The Maze Runner* trilogy.

Rose stroked the cover of *How to Train Your Dragon* lovingly. "I've always wanted to read this," she said.

Martha had bought Lilian *The Little Dictionary of Fashion* by Christian Dior (when she wasn't looking) and, for Gina, a book on Scandinavian architecture.

Owen presented Martha with a limited-edition copy of *Alice in Wonderland.*

For Owen, Martha had asked Gina to call in and see Rita at Monkey Puzzle Books, to pick up a copy of *The Little Paris Bookshop.*

Zelda adored her copy of *Good Night Stories for Rebel Girls.*

They ate dinner together sitting around the dining table. As Martha passed the bowl of carrots to Lilian, an image popped into her head of the table piled high with books, and Horatio's potted plants and fish. For the last five years, she had sat down alone to eat, but now she had her family, as well as Gina and Owen. She looked down at her plate and smiled at the sight of the delicious turkey, vegetables and gravy, rather than cheese on toast.

Owen touched her sleeve. "Are you okay?" he asked.

Martha glanced at her sister and nana talking to each other, at her gorgeous niece and nephew who were chatting about their books. She smiled at the white-haired lady who had supported Zelda for so many years, and finally back at Owen, the kind man who helped to kick-start her future by leaving a small book for her at the library.

"Things are good," she said. "How can I thank you enough for all you've done?"

He broke into a smile. "You did most of it. And I've told you before. Coffee and cake are always welcome."

Zelda made everyone laugh with her stories about life with Gina in North Carolina, and Lilian boasted about her designer garden. Owen recounted stories about the eclectic range of people who visited his bookstore, and Martha loved the buzz of the conversation around her. The air was full of fun and laughter, and she couldn't feel anything sticky and invisible at all.

At the end of the meal they pulled Christmas crackers and wore paper crowns. They shared corny jokes before Will and Rose slipped away upstairs with their books.

"You always used to tell one of your stories at the end of our Christmas meal, Martha," Zelda said as she finished eating her third mince pie. "Have you got one for us now?"

Martha shook her head. "I don't have a new one, but I *am* going to start writing again. Words are beginning to come back to me."

"I've done my last ever Read and Run," Zelda said. "So I'll let someone else tell a story today."

Lilian cleared her throat. She glanced around the table. "Um, I have one to share," she said.

Martha frowned at her. "You do?"

Her sister nodded. "I never believed in fairy stories, all that stuff about crystal carriages and handsome princes, but for some reason I kept this..." She picked up her bag from the floor and took out a piece of paper. She slowly unfolded it. "It's one of Mum's stories that I kept. It didn't mean that much to me at the time. But now it does."

She gave a small cough, then read it aloud.

The Nightingale and the Woodcutter
by Betty Storm

Once, a woodcutter lived in a small hut in the forest. He was a kind man who enjoyed his simple life. However, sometimes he found himself to be very lonely. Each day he would set off with his ax and chop wood. He sold some of the logs and kept others, to light his fire each night. He sat by the fireside and wished he had a companion.

One day, when he was in the forest, he spotted a nightingale in a tree. She had the most beautiful voice and it felt as if she was singing just for him, so he didn't feel alone.

She was there the next day, and the next, and when he saw her his heart was filled with joy.

He started to bring her bits of bread, which she ate gratefully. She seemed to welcome his attention. Though when the woodcutter returned to his hut at night, the feelings of loneliness engulfed him again.

One day he held out a piece of bread for the nightingale

and she swept down and hopped onto his finger. "I'll take you back to my hut, little bird," he said. "Then I can keep you, feed you and look after you forever. You can sing for me and neither of us will be lonely again."

He made a cage out of twigs, placed her inside and fastened the door so she couldn't fly away. He gave her seed, bread and water. He made up a fire to warm them both and smiled at his new friend.

At first the nightingale seemed happy, because she sang to him each morning and at night. Even though he missed her song during the day at work, the woodcutter knew she was at home waiting for him.

But with each day that passed, her song began to grow quieter. She stopped hopping around to greet him. He moved her cage to the window so she could see the forest, and he brought wild berries for her to eat. "Please sing for me, little bird," he whispered through the cage. The nightingale cocked her head to one side and sang, but her voice was so small he could hardly hear it.

He tried taking her out of the cage and set her on the windowsill. She gave a small chirp, but her happy cheep was now a small croak.

The woodcutter was very sad. "I'm so sorry, little bird," he said. "I didn't mean you any harm. I was trying to look after you. I'll take you back to your home in the forest."

When they stood back among the trees, the nightingale had forgotten how to fly. She didn't know how to find her own food any longer. She hopped around and was lost.

The woodcutter took her back to his hut, where they stayed together for the rest of their days. The little bird did her best to sing, to please him. She greeted him with a small song when he came home, but he could tell that her heart wasn't in it. And the woodcutter was forever full of regret, because he had taken a beautiful thing and tried to turn it into something else.

38

Crocodile

Entering the library, the day after the Christmas dinner, Martha closed her eyes and breathed in the aroma of the books, the old radiators and the fraying carpets. She patted the yellowy-white computer and straightened a few books on the shelves. It felt like she was home.

She spotted a chocolate wrapper left on the science shelf and she threw it in the bin. The return shelves needed emptying and there was a Polaroid photo pinned to the noticeboard, of a man dressed as a large brown ferret. She heard movement in the kitchen and Suki wandered out.

"Martha." She sped forward and flung out her arms. Her bump got in the way as she threw a hug. "You're back where you belong."

"Yes. Have you been looking after yourself? Should you really be in work so early? Sit down and leave the returned books to me. Thank you for passing some clothes to Siegfried, for me to wear."

Suki pulled away. "I'm fine. I wasn't sure when you'd be back, so I moved the reading group session to an earlier date. I'm having a crustacean section next week."

"A cesarean? Oh, Suki. I didn't know. I'm so sorry I wasn't around…"

"I only found out the day before last. The baby is lying in a beach position."

"Do you mean breach?"

"Yes. That's it. It's the safest way to deliver, for both of us. So, I want to ask for your help with something."

Martha expected her to run through a list of tasks, all to do with administration of the library, but instead Suki took a deep breath. "Will you come to the hospital with me?" she asked. "After my culmination, Ben has made his mind up and he isn't coming back. My mum is in Marbella-ella, and I could really do with a friend right now."

Martha glowed inside when she heard that word. Perhaps there wasn't a particular time, or happening, that made an acquaintance become a friend. Maybe it was just an organic thing, not to be studied or planned. "I'd love to help out," she said. "Have you thought about your hospital bag, and what to pack? I believe that you won't be able to lift anything afterwards for at least six weeks. You should stock up your kitchen cupboards with tinned food."

Suki sighed with relief. "I knew you'd be good at this. I've told Clive that he'll have to appoint someone here, sooner rather than later. Your sister gave me your job application and I passed it to him."

"I thought about my Cumulus Vitae when I wrote it," Martha teased.

"Do you mean your Curriculum Vitae?"

"Something like that."

Branda was the first person to arrive for the reading group. "Martha," she exclaimed. "You're back. I've bought you a new book." She reached into her large purple handbag and took out a hardback with a black cover and big orange capital letters. "It's very noir," she said. "I totally recommend it for our next read."

Nora reached under her seat. "I've brought you chocolates, to say thanks for doing my laundry," she said sheepishly. "My new boyfriend fixed my washing machine."

Siegfried was the next to arrive. He gave Martha the briefest glance, then rolled his eyes when he saw Branda's book.

"I'm not sure what we're supposed to be discussing," Horatio said. "I've brought the book about the inmate and the goldfish."

Martha waited patiently for them to settle down, to take things from bags and to remove their coats. She found their chatter warm and animated, rather than stressful.

Clive arrived and sauntered into the library. "Martha," he said with surprise in his voice. "It's, um, good to see you back."

"It's nice to be back. I trust you received my job application and reference?"

"Yes. Um, it was very interesting. It's gone to the panel for consideration."

"Panel?"

"It's a new appointment system," Suki said. "A panel of people read all the applications, to ensure they're all considered fairly. It's good for diversity, isn't it, Clive?"

Clive's cheeks reddened. "Um, yes."

"Well, I thought you might like to take this session, Clive," Martha said. "Suki is having her baby next week, so someone needs to look after the reading group."

Clive's eyebrows sprang upwards. "Me? Can't you—" he started.

Martha held up her hand. "I'm sorry but I have a reader to attend to." She raised herself on the balls of her feet as the library doors opened. She watched as her nana came inside.

Clive looked over at Zelda, who wasn't wearing her headscarf. His Adam's apple dipped when he looked at her hairless head. "Well, I suppose I could, um…"

"There are packets of biscuits in the cupboard," Martha told him. "But the group do appreciate homemade ones. Suki can give you copies of my book-rating spreadsheet, so you can facilitate the discussion. You'll need to select the next book for everyone to read. Don't pick a thriller, though. We've had our fill of those."

Branda cast her a pleading look but Martha had already moved away.

She and Zelda found a quiet corner in the library. It was where they used to sit together when Martha was a teenager, when they wedged together to read a book.

They took a similar position now, rather older but still the same people underneath. Time and life events might have battered them but Martha felt strong. She knew what she wanted, and it didn't need green ticks, or amber stars, to tell her it was good enough.

Zelda's forehead wrinkled as she looked around at the books. "The library hasn't changed much. It's still ah-mazing." She brushed under her eye with a finger.

"So why are you upset, then?" Martha stuck out her chin. She reached in her pocket and handed her a tissue. "Aloe vera." She nodded.

"Because I get scared sometimes. I'm here with you now, and we've had Christmas together and it was glorious, but I don't know how and when things…will end…"

Martha took her hand. "I thought you were the woman who battled a crocodile and won."

Zelda gave a small laugh. She reached up and touched the back of her head. "I have the scar to prove it."

"And are you one of those people who reads a book and tries to guess the ending?"

"No. I hate that. I like a nice surprise. I don't want to know what comes next until it happens. I take each page and chapter as they come." Zelda smiled as she realized what she had just said.

"Shall we choose something to read together?" Martha asked.

Zelda nodded. "Remember how we used to crawl on the floor to look at the bookshelves?" She pressed her hand against a shelf and slowly lowered herself down to the floor.

"Are you sure you can get down there? Let me help you. You could really use a cushion. You might hurt your knees," Martha said.

Zelda gave a pronounced sigh. "If I can fight a crocodile, I can get down on the bloody carpet."

Martha grinned and knelt down beside her.

Then, together, they slowly walked their fingers across the spines of the books.

★ ★ ★ ★ ★

Acknowledgments

As always, I'd like to thank my mum, dad, Mark and Oliver for their unending support.

I have a fantastic team around me at my literary agency, Darley Anderson, including my superagent, Clare Wallace; Mary Darby; Emma Winter; Tanera Simons; Kristina Egan; Sheila David; Darley himself and Rosanna Bellingham.

To all at Park Row in the US, especially my brilliant editors Erika Imranyi and Natalie Hallak, publicity ace Emer Flounders and the rest of the team. In the UK, I'd like to thank my fab editor Sally Williamson, and everyone at Harlequin.

Thanks to my lovely circle of author friends who provide meet ups and online support, including B. A. Paris, Pam Jenoff, Mary Kubica, Antoine Laurain, Ben Ludwig, Keziah Frost and Kim Slater.

My huge thanks go to the libraries I visited in the UK as part of Read Regional 2017. Everyone I met was friendly, knowledgeable and happy to share their experiences and expertise. (And, just in case you're wondering, the man in the ferret costume and bacon rasher bookmark are true stories!)

Thanks also to Suzanne Hudson at Oldham Library, and Danny Middleton at Manchester Central Library for their support.

I've met lots of fantastically supportive independent booksellers on my writing journey. They are too numerous to name here, but my special thanks go to Pamela Klinger-Horn, Mary O'Malley and Jordan Arias. Also, many thanks to readers, bloggers and reviewers everywhere, and to Waterstones Oldham.

For more information, and writing tips, please visit www. phaedra-patrick.com. I'm happiest on Instagram, but you can also find me on Facebook and Twitter, too.

Questions for Discussion

1. Books and libraries are vitally important to Martha's childhood and her present. What do they mean to you? What were some of your favorite books growing up, and what do you like to read now?

2. Martha struggles to say no to other people and stand up for herself. Do you also find it difficult to say no? Why is this the case? Would you like to change?

3. Do you think that Zelda and Thomas go out of their way to aggravate each other, or do some people just clash more than others? How could they have handled their relationship better?

4. Should Martha have followed her fiancé, Joe, to America, or was it right for her to stay with her parents? If she had followed him, do you think their relationship would have worked in the long run? Have you ever made a sacrifice for someone you love?

5. Betty had to make a terrible decision: choose between her mother and husband. What toll would this have taken on

her in the years that followed? What might have happened if she'd made the opposite decision to stand by Zelda instead of Thomas?

6. Martha finds escape in writing fairy tales, and Zelda finds her way back into her life through a book filled with fairy tales. Which of Martha's fairy tales was your favorite? Why do you think the author chose to include those fairy tales throughout the book? Are there any classic fairy tales that you love, and if so, which ones?

7. Betty believed that she owed Thomas a debt of gratitude because he married her while she was pregnant with someone else's baby. Would she still feel the same way if this happened today, rather than in the '60s? How have times and societal attitudes changed?

8. As sisters, Martha and Lilian are very different people. If you have a sibling or siblings, how do you differ from them? Do you get along? Does the responsibility of caring for older relatives usually fall on the shoulders of one sibling more than others? Has this happened in your family?

9. How would you describe Thomas's relationship with his wife, Betty—overbearing, overcaring, protective or controlling? Do you think that Betty and Thomas really loved each other? Do you see Betty as a weak person for allowing Thomas to control the household, or is she strong for holding her family together? Or both?

10. Where do you see Martha in two years' time? Do you think she'll get the job at the library? Do you think her relationship with Owen will develop further? What do you think she has most learned about herself?

Read on for a sneak peek at Phaedra Patrick's
next perfectly charming novel,
The Secrets of Love Story Bridge.

The Lilac Envelope

The night before

As he did often over the past three years, Mitchell Fisher wrote a letter he would never send.

He sat up in bed at midnight and kicked off his sheets. Even though all the internal doors in his apartment were open, the sticky July heat still felt like a shroud clinging to his body. His nine-year-old daughter, Poppy, thrashed restlessly in her sleep in the bedroom opposite.

Mitchell turned on his bedside lamp, squinting against the yellow light, and took out a pad of Basildon Bond notepaper from underneath his bed. He always used a fountain pen to write—old-fashioned he supposed, but he was a man who valued things that were well constructed and long lasting.

Mitchell tapped the pen against his bottom lip. He knew what he wanted to say, but by the time his words of sorrow and regret traveled from his brain to his fingertips, they were only fragments of what he longed to express.

As he started to write, the sound of the metal nib scratching against paper helped him block out the city street noise that hummed below his apartment.

Dearest Anita,
Another letter from me. Everything here is fine, ticking along.
Poppy is doing well. The school holidays start soon and I thought
she'd be more excited. It's probably because you're not here to
enjoy them with us.

I've taken two weeks off work to spend with her, and have
a full itinerary planned for us—badminton, tennis, library vis-
its, cooking, walking, the park, swimming, museums, a tour
of the city bridges and more. It will keep us busy. Keep our
minds off you.

You'll be amazed how much she's grown, must be almost
your height by now. I tell her how proud I am of her, but it al-
ways meant more coming from you.

Mitchell paused, resting his hand against the pad of paper.
He *had* to tell her how he felt.

Every time I look at our daughter, I think of you. I wish I
could hold you again, and tell you I'm truly sorry.

Yours, always,
Mitchell x

He read his words, always dissatisfied with them, never
able to convey the magnitude of guilt he felt. After folding
the piece of paper once, he sealed it into a crisp, cream envelope, then squeezed it into the almost-full drawer of his
nightstand among all the other letters he'd written. His eyes
fell upon the slim lilac envelope he kept on top, the one addressed to him from Anita that he'd not yet been able to bring
himself to open.

Taking it out, he held it under his nose and inhaled. There
was still a slight scent of her violet soap on the paper. His fin-

ger followed the angle of the gummed flap and then stopped. He closed his eyes and willed himself to open the letter, but his hands began to shake.

Once more, he placed it back into his drawer.

Mitchell lay down and hugged himself, imagining Anita's arms were wrapped around him. When he closed his eyes, the words from all the letters weighed down upon him like a bulldozer. As he turned and tried to sleep, he pulled the pillow over his head to force them away.

1

A Locked Heart

The lovers who attached their padlocks to the bridges of Upchester might see it as a fun or romantic gesture, but to Mitchell, it was an act of vandalism.

It was the hottest year on record in the city and the morning sun was already beating down on the back of his neck. His biceps flexed as he methodically opened and squeezed his bolt cutters shut, shearing the padlocks off the cast-iron filigree panels of the old Victorian bridge, one by one.

Since local boy band Word Up filmed the video for their international smash hit "Lock Me Up with Your Love" on this bridge, thousands of people were flocking to the small city in the North West of England. To demonstrate their love for the band and each other, they brought locks engraved with initials, names or messages and attached them to the city's five bridges.

Large red-and-white signs that read NO PADLOCKS studded the pavement. But as far as Mitchell could see, the locks still hung on the railings like bees swarming across frames of honeycomb. The constant reminder of other people's love made him feel like he was fighting for breath. As he cut off the locks, he wanted to yell, "Why can't you just keep your feelings to yourselves?"

After several hours of hard work, Mitchell's trail of broken locks glinted on the pavement like a metal snake. He stopped for a moment and narrowed his eyes as a young couple strolled toward him. The woman glided in a floaty white dress and tan cowboy boots. The man wore shorts and had the physique of an American football player. With his experience of carrying out maintenance across the city's public areas, Mitchell instinctively knew they were up to something.

After breaking away from his girlfriend, the man walked to the side of the bridge while nonchalantly pulling out a large silver padlock from his pocket.

Mitchell tightened his grip on his cutters. He was once so easy and in love with Anita, but rules were rules. "Excuse me," he called out. "You can't hang that lock."

The man frowned and crossed his bulging arms. "Oh yeah? And who's going to stop me?"

Mitchell had the sinewy physique of a sprinter. He was angular all over with dark hair and eyes and a handsome dorsal hump on his nose. "I am," he said and put his cutters down on the pavement. He held out his hand for the lock. "It's my job to clear the bridges. You could get a fine."

Anger flashed across the blond man's face and he batted Mitchell's hand away, swiping off his work glove. Mitchell watched as it tumbled down into the river below. Sometimes the water flowed prettily, but today it gushed and gurgled, a bruise-gray hue. A young man had drowned here in a strong current last summer.

The man's girlfriend wrapped her arms around her boyfriend's waist and tugged him away. "Come on. Leave him alone." She cast Mitchell an apologetic smile. "Sorry, but we're *so* in love. It took us two hours and three buses to get here.

We'll be working miles away from each other soon. *Please* let us do this."

The man looked into her eyes and softened. "Yeah, um, sorry, mate," he said sheepishly. "The heat got the better of me. All we want to do is fasten our lock."

Mitchell gestured at the sign again. "Just think about what you're doing, guys," he said with a weary sigh. "Padlocks are cheap chunks of metal and they're weighing down the bridges. Can't you get a nice ring or tattoo instead? Or write letters to each other? There are better ways to say I lov—well, you know."

The man and the woman shared an incredulous look.

"Whatever." The man glowered and shoved his padlock back into his pocket. "We'll go to another bridge instead."

"I work on those too..."

The couple laughed at him and sauntered away.

Mitchell rubbed his nose. He knew his job wasn't a glamorous one. It wasn't the one in architecture he'd studied hard and trained for. However, it meant he could pay the rent on his apartment and buy Poppy hot lunch at school each day. Whatever daily hassle he put up with, he needed the work.

His workmate Barry had watched the incident from the other side of the road. Sweat circled under his arms and his forehead shone like a mirror as he crossed over. "The padlocks keep multiplying," he groaned.

"We need to keep on going."

"But it's too damn hot." Barry undid a button on his polo shirt, showing off unruly chest curls that matched the ones on his head. "It's a violation of our human rights, and no one can tell if we cut off twenty or two hundred."

Mitchell held his hand up against the glare of the sun. "We can tell, and Russ wants the bridges cleared in time for the city centenary celebrations."

Barry rolled his eyes. "There's only three weeks to go until then. Our boss should come down here and get his hands dirty, too. At least join me for a pint after work."

Mitchell's mouth felt parched, and he suddenly longed for an ice-cold beer. A vision of peeling off his polo shirt and socks and relaxing in a beer garden appeared like a dreamy mirage in his head.

But he had to pick Poppy up from the after-school club to take her for a guitar lesson, an additional one to her music class in school. Her headteacher, Miss Heathcliff, was a stickler for the school closing promptly at 5:30 p.m., and it was a rush to get there on time. He lowered his eyes and said, "I'd love to, but I have to dash off later."

Then he selected his next padlock to attack.

Toward the end of their working day, Barry sidled up to Mitchell and wiped his brow. He crouched and packed up his toolbox before staring at his mobile phone. "Brilliant, a lady I've been messaging can meet me for a drink."

Since Barry had lost three stone at Weight Whittlers, he'd discovered the enticing world of dating apps and was now like a dog let off its leash. Mitchell had long since given up advising him quality was better than quantity when it came to women.

"You have *another* date?" he asked. "And we're not supposed to finish work for another five minutes."

Barry smiled proudly. "Five minutes doesn't matter, and going out beats sitting on my own all night. Tonight's lucky lady is Mandy." He side-glanced at his friend. "Maybe you should get back out into the wild, too. Start to live a little."

Mitchell shuddered. "I'm fine as I am, thanks, just me and Poppy."

If he ever thought about going out with someone new, his head spun: getting dressed up, meeting someone in a bar, making light conversation, laughing politely at their jokes, debating who was going to pay for the drinks, going through that excruciating moment when you might offer to see them again, moving in for a kiss or not. And that was on top of the baby-sitting logistics, because his few family members lived miles away. Before he even went on a first date, he could already picture first arguments, awkward silences and accusations at him for being emotionally frozen. And the line, "I'm a single dad to a nine-year-old girl," wasn't an ideal conversation starter. He looked at his watch. "You go enjoy yourself," he said. "Have a pint for me."

"Will do," Barry shouted over his shoulder as he walked away.

Mitchell stared at his own trail of padlocks and at Barry's petite pile on the other side of the bridge. A couple of lads from the Maintenance Team pulled up and began to shovel up the scrap metal. Mitchell gave them a wave and rushed off along the street that followed the edge of the river.

As he hurried, he didn't notice the clustered rows of black-and-white Tudor shops, or the intricate carvings on the twin towers of Upchester cathedral, the tallest building that loomed over the medieval, walled city. He didn't stop to admire the glistening River Twine that gushed fiercely a few meters lower besides him, or the architecture of the five bridges that spanned it. He had given his own nickname to each of them.

The Slab was a drab concrete construction on the far side of the city. Built in the 1970s to ease traffic flow, it was more useful than attractive and, in Mitchell's opinion, spoiled the aesthetics of its surroundings.

Vicky was the next one along, the Victorian bridge he and Barry had been working on that day. It had handsome stone arches and ornate panels depicting flowers and leaves. It connected the cathedral on one side of the river to the library on the other.

When he reached the third bridge along, his palms itched as he spotted dozens of fresh padlocks hanging there. This was the oldest bridge in the city, with parts of it dating back to the fourteenth century. Mitchell christened it Archie, because it had three pale stone arches.

The newest bridge had been commissioned to celebrate the centenary of Upchester's city status. Due to open soon, Mitchell named it the Yacht. It was supermodern, all sleek white railings and thin white struts that looked like the laces of a lady's corset, securing two tall white masts to the road.

He called his favorite bridge Redford, because of its red bricks. It was a sturdy construction, erected one hundred and fifty years ago. It might look dull and traditional, but it did its job.

As he crossed over Redford, the people he passed came at him in twos, like animals boarding Noah's Ark. They laughed and kissed with abandon, and Mitchell picked up his pace, finding it painful to witness.

He still saw Anita sometimes, catching glimpses from the corner of his eye of her copper-brown curls in a crowd or a flash of her favorite tomato-red coat. Every time he felt as if someone had stabbed his heart. His breath would catch, and he'd crane his neck to look for her, desperate to see her one more time.

As he strode on, Mitchell noticed a woman standing in the middle of the bridge's pavement. Her dress was vibrant, a daffodil yellow. Everyone else was heading across the bridge, but she was stationary, absolutely still, so people had to part and move around her. As Mitchell drew closer, he noticed her nose had a bump on the bridge that made him feel an immediate kinship with her. Her walnut curls reminded him of Anita's hairstyle.

Her warm, familiar smile seemed to say, *Oh, fancy seeing you here.* But he was certain he'd never seen her before. He couldn't help staring at her, as if catching sight of his own reflection in a shop mirror and doing a double take.

As they caught each other's eyes, a wash of color circled his neck, but he found it difficult to look away.

You're still in love with Anita, remember?

Mitchell's eyes fell upon the sweep of her collarbone and her shoulders, before stopping on the shiny thing in her hand. It was large, heart-shaped and glinted intermittently gold and then white in the late afternoon sunlight.

A padlock.

He gritted his teeth as the woman stepped toward the railing and stooped to secure her lock. After straightening back up, she tossed its key into the river and peered down at the water. She brushed her hair back with her hand then patted her ear. Her forehead furrowed and she spun around on the spot, searching on the pavement. She then looked over the railing at the narrow ledge on the other side.

Mitchell wondered what she'd lost, but told himself he didn't have time to help her to find it anyway.

His view of her was obstructed by a young man carrying a large shiny shovel on his shoulder and a few other passersby. When he saw the woman again she was leaning over the railing on her tiptoes, reaching for something on the other side. Her fingers padded around and she raised a leg off the ground, pointing her foot to balance herself as if performing a ballet move.

A feeling of worry reared up inside him at her precarious position. "Hey, be careful," he called out.

His view was interrupted again by a large group of students traipsing along. When they had passed, Mitchell stared at the spot where the woman had stood. Except she was no longer there.

He saw a flash of her yellow dress through the railings, vivid in the rushing river below.

"*Damn*," he said out loud.

And in that split second, all thoughts of Poppy flew from his mind. He dropped his toolbox to the ground, ran and swung his legs over the railing with ease.

When the base of his back caught against the ledge on the other side, he knew a jolt of pain should accompany it, but Mitchell didn't feel anything as he crashed down into the violent water.